1 of 26

Part I

by

ZWT Jameson

Printed in the United States of America
North American and Worldwide Distribution

First trade edition 2022

ISBN 978-1-954804-44-9

1

Paris.2323.

Paris was silent. Eerily silent. Cities seldom feel like cities when they are deserted. They tend to feel like unwanted relics of the past, photo opportunities for extreme tourists, and magazine features depicting a bygone era of industry and progression. Whether this was an involuntary consequence of a fleeing population or the inevitable conclusion of conflict, the result was always the same, an ominous emptiness.

"Control: this is Commander Martin Johansen, we're on approach to Paris Central Sector 2.0 for a routine soil inspection. Can you advise on the scanning data we've just transmitted to you and confirm if you can give us clearance to land?"

"Commander Johansen: this is Control, we've analyzed the data and are satisfied there is minimal risk. Landing clearance is approved. Proceed with caution, risk is only minimal at this stage, keep all channels of communication open and ensure that your weapons mode is set to kill. We don't want any accidents while you're out there."

"Control: this is Commander Johansen, received and acknowledged."

The shuttle appeared in the distance, the sun bouncing off its streamlined metallic shape as it glided effortlessly at about two hundred meters above the surface towards the city. On the horizon lay what was left of the Parisian skyline: a broken city full of memories from a previous life. The shuttle punctured the quiet stillness of the air with a stealth-like hum as it approached what was left of the Trocadero and the Eiffel Tower; two of the city's most recognisable structures.

The Eiffel Tower was snapped in two above the second viewing deck, the top half was pointing downwards and lent against the bottom half that stood resolute. The uppermost observatory deck was partially buried into the ground. At the point of the break, the wrought-iron construction exhibited signs of an explosion. The charred brittle metal appeared to have snapped like a toothpick in the aftermath of that catastrophic event. It was another vivid reminder of what went before. Its tall structure now caved into submission from the relentless abuse it failed to withstand.

      Martin monitored the flight controls while the automatic pilot guided the shuttle into the city on a preset route that was vetted for safety. James sat next to him, observing the ground below. They came to conduct tests on the soil, to see if the land could be salvaged for farming. Both were scientists. Martin's specialism was primarily in the field of radiation and its impact on environments. He'd also trained as a pilot, however, that was primarily out of necessity. James specialised in botany but had a working knowledge of biology. Their paths crossed on several occasions in their quest to source new land safe for farming. Both men had undergone basic combat training and were sufficiently skilled to take care of themselves. They were part of a project named the New Beginning. A project that began in New London, a city full of life, optimism, ideas, and youth. However, hanging over this newfound optimism was a desperate need to secure ever-increasing areas of land to help sustain the city's growing population.

      A sinister, hushed atmosphere replaced the hustle and bustle of the Parisian streets. The lack of human life had left the damaged and abandoned buildings looking pointless; purpose and personality giving into slimy-green obsolescence.

      The streets were littered with abandoned vehicles and some of the large advertising boards were still intact. "Paris: the European city of Culture in 2092," one board declared. Another offered energy-saving tips for homeowners. Both were now covered in graffiti from an angry and dissenting population. The tarmac was cracked and overgrown with weeds, walls were covered in multilingual graffiti, and shop windows were smashed. As society collapsed around them people took to looting for life's essentials in a desperate attempt to survive. But the shelves now lay empty.

"I don't like this one bit," James remarked as Martin concentrated on locating a suitable area to land the shuttle near to the Eiffel Tower.

"Calm down man, what the hell do you think is going to happen? The area has been declared clear, they've been scanning the place for months and found no sign of human or animal life." Martin was confident about this fact.

"They said that about Madrid and look what we bumped into."

"Madrid was a one-off, they were living underground, they were well organised and they were dealt with, as you well know."

"Yes, dealt with, of course … I forgot that part."

"Well, they were," Martin snapped back.

"What makes you think there won't be people like that here? Paris had a huge Metro system you know. Just check out the intel on the catacombs. They were full of people living underground."

"Dead people, you mean?"

"Yes, some were dead but not all of them …" James frowned.

"Paris has been deserted for at least fifty years. There's no way that anyone could survive here. Look at this place!" Martin pointed to the screens monitoring their approach. The ground looked scorched in places and the sun was relentlessly beating down upon it. "What would they eat?"

"What about those plants?" James pointed to one of the screens.

"Oh, come on…surely nothing dangerous to us could survive on that…"

"Just remember that I'm the botanist here, and I'm telling you that's a meal for something," James said and glared at Martin.

James then looked across at one of the screens and thought he noticed evidence of life on the ground. He tapped the screen and froze the frame to show Martin who peered across at the screen at what looked like animal footprints imprinted into the ground.

"You can't be sure that they're footprints. Anything could have made those marks. And even if they were, whatever made them is probably long gone by now."

"Let's hope your assumption is correct," James replied whilst tapping the screen.

"Call it a hunch. I've seen many things over the years to suggest evidence of life and nothing was ever conclusive after we examined it; let's just say I'm not convinced until we land and get a closer look."

"Well, you can get closer if you like, I'll just observe it from the screens."

"You know the drill; we both have to carry out this mission."

James sighed and folded his arms.

Martin decided it was safe to land, he took control of the shuttle and circled a small area near the Eiffel Tower. Dust kicked up as the engines stabilised the craft.

They were close to the River Seine, which was once the lifeblood of Paris. Now, however, it was reduced to a stream that meandered its way through the riverbed which was crammed with maritime debris. The rotting carcasses of ships abandoned decades ago lay on their sides, propellers bent out of shape and crumbling into rust. Bridges had long since collapsed into the dusty riverbed. The shapes of disfigured road signs still present on some of them; one makeshift sign directing traffic towards a safe zone.

The air was still. The searing heat created a haze that rippled along the cracked tarmac where it was still largely intact.

"May all your hunches be correct," James said and then stood up and looked down at Martin who sat at the controls.

James and Martin suited up so they could leave the safety of the shuttle behind them. As the door of the shuttle cracked opened shards of light pierced the interior forcing both of them to shield their eyes with their gloved hands. Martin squint as he stepped out into the sun and looked around to locate a suitable place to carry out the tests on the earth.

James stood and gazed in amazement at what was left of the Eiffel Tower. Even broken, the Tower had lost none of its power; the legs were now covered in weeds and rusting. Martin noticed that they were also riddled with bullet holes.

"How can they possibly think this place is suitable for growing crops? There's no water…" James laughed at the idea as he followed Martin to the small patch of land he wanted to examine.

"Water isn't the issue. We can get that transported into the area. It's the soil we need. If this area is suitable then it will be invaluable as we can control it, you see?" Martin pointed to the surrounding area, "These buildings will help shield the soil from the harshest winds which in turn will help preserve the crops. Every controllable scrap of land we can salvage for farming is priceless."

"You don't need to lecture me. I know about the battle for land, I understand the issues we're facing."

"Then you also know that the battle for land is crucial to all our futures and a priority for us."

"Yes, but why here?" James shrugged his shoulders.

"This area was hit by a so-called dirty bomb about 200 years ago. Silly bastards didn't think of the repercussions," Martin said, crouching down and poking the ground with a thin metallic probe, "but hopefully this area could be viable now."

"I don't think we'll find anything viable here," James shook his head as he looked around at the immediate area. The Eiffel Tower cast a huge shadow across the ground.

Martin looked on a small screen on the arm of his suit as he started to analyse the data that the probe was collating. Trace elements of radiation were still in evidence; there were tiny traces of fallout from the dirty bomb still in the soil.

"It's not going to work; this place is still affected by radiation. The reports I read stated it was a small bomb, unsophisticated, and had little effect; but, clearly, that is not the case. Look, I know you're the expert but I don't think anything of use to us will grow here," Martin declared. He dug around the area he just analysed with a small spade. He needed a sample of soil to take back to the lab for further tests just to be sure.

"What about that?" James looked at the collection of small plants growing near the Eiffel Tower that they had seen on the scan in the shuttle.

"Get a sample, we need to find out what it is and how it can survive in this ground."

James pulled out a small clear bottle from a pocket in his suit and walked over to the plants. He took out a pair of pliers from another pocket and cut off a sample from one of the plants, placed it in the bottle, and closed the lid.

"How could this happen here?" James mumbled to himself in disbelief. Even after all these years, man's ability for destruction still had the power to shock him. Martin looked across for a moment to see what James was talking about but decided it wasn't important enough to discuss and continued digging.

Martin's small spade hit something hard in the ground. He continued to jab at whatever it was and eventually managed to loosen it enough to pull it out of the ground. He rubbed the small rock against his suit to clean it up and then held it up to the sunlight. The rock was clear and the sunlight caught it, shining a beam of light across the ground.

James looked across to see what was causing the light but Martin had now placed the rock into the small clear cube to analyse it. The results on one side of the object confirmed that the rock was a diamond.

"It's a diamond," Martin shouted across to James.

"What the hell is a diamond doing here?" James quizzed the find and looked across at the bullet holes on the tower. *Was there a connection?* He wondered.

"I don't know but look on the bright side, we could be very rich." Martin chuckled, holding up the diamond to the sunlight.

"Maybe, but who the hell buys this stuff now?" James failed to see the funny side.

"Who cares, it's a diamond. There will be someone out there who wants it." Martin tucked it into a pocket on his suit.

"It doesn't work like that as you know. It needs to go back for analysis and tests and then we need to come up with a rational reason as to why it was found here," James said, walking towards Martin.

"Did anyone tell you that you have a real way of spoiling someone's fun?" Martin snapped.

"And?"

They returned to the shuttle and departed into the horizon.

Paris was deserted once again.

2

Manchester.Present-Day.

Steve Garner slumped into his couch. His ground-floor apartment in Manchester was modern, if slightly soulless, and a place he could finally call home. Perhaps he was a little young for a mid-life crisis but the lethal combination of a divorce, alcohol abuse, and an increasingly dull job led him to question what was next. His thirties had not been a good decade for him.

Cartons of Chinese food lay abandoned on the low coffee table in front of him. A fine bottle of single malt whiskey was open and half-empty, the accompanying glass was also half empty. Records covered the floor and the television was on in the background, although it was silent. Steve staggered the short distance across to the record player and replaced the shiny black disc on the turntable with Hot Buttered Soul by Isaac Hayes, the record soon punctuated the silence. He slumped back into the couch and continued drinking the night and the tedium away, this was now his new normal.

He picked up his phone off the coffee table and started sifting through old family pictures. As he swiped through them, he came across some pictures of his ex-wife, Janine, and their daughter, Tanya. He paused for a moment on one where they were on holiday in Tobago. It was a family holiday to visit Janine's parents, and he still craved that life. He then came across an old Polaroid picture he'd scanned into his phone of himself posing with his younger brother, Joshua, taken when they were both teenagers and dressed in their school uniforms. Those were happier times before Joshua got tangled up with the wrong crowd and got himself arrested. Joshua became trapped within the gang culture of Manchester and died in police custody after taking a lethal cocktail of drugs. Given his condition at the time of arrest Joshua never stood a chance in custody, and the medical staff couldn't save him. Steve let out a long sigh, thinking how things could have been so different for Joshua. His death had sewn a deep-rooted distrust of authority into Steve's life. Apart from a couple of minor cautions for possession of cannabis in his teenage years, Steve had managed to avoid any contact with the police. That was how he liked it.

Steve dragged his thoughts back into the room, he took a sip of his whiskey. The voice of Isaac Hayes filled the room, the music was both sad and yet uplifting, it was the perfect complement to the long and lonely night.

Some show about paranormal investigators uncovering the truth behind various video clips played out on the television; Steve had a cursory interest in it, nothing too serious though, he had the TV on mute, he could get all he needed from the show simply by looking at the pictures.

Steve peered up at the clock on the wall, it was nearly 3:00AM. He abandoned the glass on the table, the near-empty bottle of whiskey was next to it and he removed the needle from the record. He was too drunk to place the record back in the sleeve.

Steve got a glass of water from the kitchen and tentatively started to walk towards the bedroom. He momentarily glanced back down the hallway at the TV which cast a creepy moving shadow across the lounge; the light and shade from the show emanated across the carpet. Steve made it into the bedroom, placed the glass of water on the bedside table but then wandered back into the lounge to turn off the TV. His knee collided with the arm of the couch, he cursed in agony as he hobbled back to the bedroom and slumped into his unmade bed.

Sleep was no longer a perfect bed partner for him. He spent more time tossing and turning than sleeping. His mind was full of *what if* scenarios: What if he had been a better husband? What if he had a better job? What if he was a better father? Finally, his red eyes could not take the strain that his brain was putting them through; he started to drift deeper into his own world.

What seemed like hours later, Steve sat bolt upright on the bed, he screamed and reached out to grab something or someone, anything. His brow was covered with sweat and he was shivering all over. He quickly looked left and then right to gain a sense of where he was. He didn't know what it was or where he was but his instinct was to protect his dead brother. He started to feel a burning sensation emanating from the skin on his arms, he rubbed one of them furiously with his hand. The sheets were drenched with his sweat and sticking to his body, the room spun around him and his throat was bone dry. The sensation receded as he regained a sense of where he was; he took a deep breath and glanced at the alarm clock. He had been asleep for about twenty minutes. What had just happened in that dream? Steve was frightened, these sensations were too real for him and that was unsettling. Gone was the chance to cling onto someone, a security blanket to help ease the fear. He was alone.

He lay back down on the bed. He knew he needed to try and get at least a few hours of sleep before getting up for work. He gradually succumbed to the darkness.

"Police! Open up! This is Detective Roger Silverton and I have a warrant to search your property."

The shouting was followed by a loud bang on the door as Silverton bellowed his instruction; and then repeated it, only this time louder.

Steve woke abruptly and jumped out of bed. The banging was getting louder and the voice grew impatient. He quickly threw on some trousers, a shirt and stepped into some shoes. He had no idea why the police would be knocking at his door at this time of the morning. He walked down the short hallway to the front door muttering to himself about this latest intrusion into his sleep. He peered through the viewer and saw two uniformed police officers, accompanied by a plainclothes officer.

They knocked again, repeating their instruction. Silverton peered through the viewer, eyeballing Steve. This spooked Steve so he pulled away into the hallway.

"We know you're there. It will be easier for us all if you just opened the door and let us in," Silverton shouted.

Steve panicked, he thought of his brother, the picture of them both in their school uniforms flashed through his mind. What did the police want with him?

"What do you want?" Steve yelled.

"I told you, we have a warrant to search your property," Silverton replied.

"Search it for what?" Steve yelled back, rubbing his tired eyes.

"Just open the door and let me explain," Silverton shouted.

"How do I know you are the police?"

"Look through the viewer and I'll show you my ID," Silverton persisted.

"Who issued the warrant?" Steve asked.

Silence.

Steve peered through the viewer to see Silverton shrugging his shoulders to the accompanying uniformed officers. "Who issued the warrant?" he repeated but no one replied.

Steve was tired but the adrenalin coursed through his veins. He didn't know what to do but instinct gripped him. He knew something was wrong, he just didn't know what it was. He had to find somewhere safe where he could call someone, anyone, and find out what the hell was going on; that was the plan he thought, and a good one. He ran towards the large balcony window in the lounge. He opened the window and leapt down onto the damp grass below, then ran as fast as he could.

He paused to gather himself and spotted a car in the distance. The taxi sign was illuminated on the roof of the car, the lights were on and there was exhaust smoke rising into the air.

Steve glanced back towards the balcony window to see the two uniformed officers jumping over the balcony and running towards him.

Silverton waved them on from the balcony. "Don't lose him whatever you do," he shouted.

Steve watched on as the officers started sprinting after him, he took a deep breath and staggered the final agonising steps towards the taxi. He yanked the door open, jumped into the back, gasping for air as he locked the door. Steve slumped into the back seat of the car, looking out of the window, his nerves were frayed by what had just happened.

"Where to, sir?" the driver inquired.

"Anywhere but here and make it fast," Steve ducked down in the seat to remain out of view.

"I know just the place," the driver replied.

Steve was in no mood to argue, his priority was only to get away from the officers.

The driver hit the gas and took the road leading towards the M6. The streets were slowly coming to life with the early morning routine of delivery drivers rushing to their destinations, lights flickering into life in the offices and shops, and the local tramps awaking from their improvised shelters. The sun was trying to make an appearance through the dullness of an early autumnal

morning but the clouds were doing their best to keep it
at bay, and they succeeded.

Steve's cab was making steady progress through
the city and he was now brave enough to sit up and
observe where they were going. The car had a stale,
smoke-riddled smell to it, transporting Steve's memory
back to the taxis he'd hired in the 1990's. The roof
lining was tanned from the onslaught of nicotine and the
seats were sagging; this was a well-worn taxi. He wasn't
complaining, however, but he was perplexed. Something
wasn't adding up for him.

"I can't believe I found a cab at this time of the
morning," Steve said.

"Who said I was a cab driver? The name is Roy
now sit back and relax, Steve…and enjoy the ride, my
friend."

Steve was too exhausted to argue, and probably
still a bit drunk.

3

All three lanes of the M6 heading towards Birmingham were filled with traffic. Steve slumped on the back seat, half asleep, although his mind was doing overtime about his predicament. Roy managed to manoeuvre the car in between two lorries which would obscure any view from behind for the time being.

Steve glanced back through the traffic, he thought he could make out the police car but wasn't sure.

"How do you know my name?" Steve said.

"We know everything, Steve – everything," Roy said and smiled.

Steve couldn't work out whether he should be afraid and try to escape or sit tight and see how this unfolded. It wasn't a normal situation for a company accountant to find himself in, but then recent events had shown his life to be anything but normal.

They were approaching Birmingham, but the traffic was slowing as morning rush hour started to take hold. A child in the back of the car next to them looked across at him and pulled a face. The sound of the wipers scraping across the windscreen punctuated an uneasy silence.

The rush hour traffic was bumper to bumper as they crawled towards Junction 12. The sky was relentlessly dull and the clouds refused to clear, and the damp drizzle persisted.

Roy reached into his jacket pocket and placed a small cube-shaped device onto the dashboard, it sprang into life displaying some sort of information onto one of the sides. Steve stared at it, recognising it, but he didn't want to question Roy about its origins.

Roy's car approached junction eleven. The traffic gradually snaked its way down the motorway, picking up speed, the procession of blurred red lights visible through the rain-covered windscreen.

"Where are we going and how do you know my name?" Steve wanted answers now. To hell with caution.

"It's probably simpler to say that my focus is to get you to London as quickly and as safely as possible."

"Why London? And wouldn't it be quicker to fly?"

"Quicker yes, but it's too risky. Too much information is needed and it makes you easier to track."

"Who the hell would want to track me?"

"Like I said, I need to get you to London and it's simpler to hold these questions for another time."

They approached the bridge at junction eleven travelling between a lorry on the inside lane and a car in the outer one. The boy who had earlier pulled a face at Steve was now playing on his phone; he briefly looked up at Steve but the phone seemed to be his priority.

Roy glanced across to the grass verge, his pulse quickened, his instincts told him something was wrong. The wipers slowly cleared the windscreen to reveal two people struggling for cover under the bridge at the junction.

"Hold on," Roy muttered. He hit the brakes as they approached the bridge, but it was too late. Far too late. The damp conditions made it impossible to stop in time. Rows of traffic behind them reacted to the sudden braking and started to brake in an attempt to avoid colliding with the vehicles immediately in front. The concertina effect rippled back through row upon row of traffic as the sound of skidding vehicles followed, and the impact of metal hitting metal filled the air.

One of the men under the bridge pointed a taser-like device across the carriageway and pulled the trigger.

19

A piercingly bright light blasted out of it. Steve heard a crack and shielded his eyes from the wall of light as it moved up the bonnet of the car and progressed into the cabin. The light immediately disseminated into the air after Roy's car had passed through it.

Roy wrapped his hands around the steering wheel and tried to regain control of the car, but it was losing power and began to freewheel under the bridge. He lost control of the car as the power steering died. Steve tried to shout out but his vocal cords felt frozen tight, suffocating his voice.

In the car beside them, the boy sat with his mouth wide open as all three vehicles crossed under the bridge and through the wall of light at the same time. The vehicles behind them ground to an agonisingly slow halt on the rain-soaked carriageway.

Steve clutched the edge of the back seat. Roy appeared to glow such was the intensity of the light. The noise of metal grinding on metal filled the cabin and Steve started to feel a spinning sensation.

The spinning sensation became faster and faster, disorientating Steve into a blur of light, colour, and sound. His stomach tensed as motion sickness kicked in. He could just about make out Roy dissolving into the wall of light in front of his eyes. The stress on Steve's body was becoming unbearable. He didn't know what to do, or what he could do.

Then nothing.

Silverton could see the flash of light hundreds of yards ahead of them. He jumped out of the car and tried to get a better view of the scene ahead of him.

People ahead of Silverton got out of their cars to try to capture a view of what had just happened. Some reached for their phones in an attempt to record whatever had just happened and the aftermath that followed. Others were ringing the emergency services.

"Get out of the way!" Silverton shouted and waved his arms in a desperate attempt to clear his view. "Get out of the way!" he repeated the instruction but to no avail.

The northbound carriageway was slowing down as people tried to get a glimpse of the crash scene. Those vehicles passing in the fast lane were now moving the slowest, trying to get the best view of what happened.

"Something major has happened down there, buckle up guys we're taking a look," and with that Silverton hit the siren. The effect of the siren was immediate, people got back into their cars and manoeuvred out of the way to create just enough space for Silverton's car to squeeze by on the hard shoulder. Silverton stamped on the accelerator and drove towards the bridge.

Silverton tentatively approached the bridge, as he closed in on the crash scene. He could see some people had remained in their cars, looking visibly shaken. The sight of the motorway littered with slow-moving people approaching the carnage in the drizzle had an apocalyptic feel to it. Witnesses were encroaching around the front three vehicles with phones in hand, making calls to emergency services and taking footage of the crash scene.

***

As Silverton drove closer to the crash scene, he could just about make out the three vehicles randomly positioned on the other side of the bridge that had crossed through the light. The carriageway was completely blocked, the M6 was empty beyond the vehicles, nothing could pass. He parked at the bottom of the slip road near the bridge. The two uniformed officers jumped out of the car and went to the boot to get out some police cordon tape.

"Secure the area, nobody gets near those vehicles. I'll call it in to ensure that emergency services are on the way." Silverton instructed the officers and then called in the accident to the control room. The two officers quickly set up a basic cordon cutting across the carriageway in an attempt to prevent people from getting through to the crash scene.

"We need immediate emergency services support here. I suspect we have some serious injuries…" Silverton continued the conversation.

Finishing the call, Silverton noticed the small gathering of witnesses on the other side of the police cordon.

"Oi! Get away from there!" one of the officers shouted, waving them back to the other side of the cordon.

Silverton looked on, incandescent with anger as he watched the witnesses lift the cordon tape and stand on the other side.

"There's no one in those cars!" one of the witnesses shouted towards Silverton.

"Am I making myself clear enough? I don't want anybody inside the cordon!" Silverton replied.

"But…" one of the witnesses tried to speak.

"You saw nothing, do you understand me? Nothing!" Silverton looked at them, "And you! Stop filming! Now!" he shouted.

"What's the problem?" the witness replied.

"This is a crash scene, not a fucking movie set!" Silverton yelled at them.

4

Junction 11. M6.
The year 2618.

The darkness gathered into a small area on the ground. Any sign of life scattered as the wind picked up and a loud bang followed. The darkness dissolved and was replaced by bright sunlight. Steve stood there in the middle of it all, shivering. "What just happened?"

He collapsed to his knees and started to throw up. The sick splattered from his mouth onto the ground and mixed into the dust. He looked up to the sun, squinting as his eyes tried to adjust to the light.

The sun beat down on his head as he tried to focus on what he saw before him. He could see for miles into the distance. Narrowing his eyes, he tried to focus on something, anything, but all he saw was a vast nothingness of land littered with the vague outline of an old motorway. Burnt out vehicles, road signs overgrown with plants, and bridges that had collapsed into what was the motorway now dominated his view. It was silent, there was little or no sign of life apart from the overgrown foliage that clung onto the abandoned vehicles.

He staggered to his feet and tried to take a few steps but was overcome with dizziness. Roy ran over to help him back up to his feet.

"What the hell is this?" Steve reached out and grabbed Roy's arm to steady himself.

Roy steadied him and gradually Steve started to regain control over his limbs. Another man sat on his haunches, looking at the ground and cursing about how he was going to be late, although Steve had no idea for what.

Steve thought he heard a kid shouting but couldn't be sure.

"Kallyuke will be furious with me," Roy mumbled to himself.

"Who?" Steve managed to utter a word.

"Don't worry about it. That's my problem."

Two other adults gathered themselves as they got to their feet – the parents of Kieran, the boy in the back of the car on the M6.

Roy pulled Steve to one side. "We've got a problem."

"A minute ago, you said it was your problem. Why is it now *our* problem?"

"That was before I saw these people. Before it was simply a case of us getting knocked off our trail, now we have things to, shall I say, tidy up."

"Where are we, Roy? What the hell just happened? And where's the car? In fact, where are any of the cars? And the bridge? And while we're at it, where the hell is the road?"

"You're standing on it."

"What do you mean?"

"This *is* the M6."

"Excuse me?!"

"This is it!" Roy gestured to the ground.

"How do you explain—"

"This is the same place, it's just not the same time."

"The timeline…" Steve's voice cracked with fear.

"How do you know about that?"

24

***

Santa Monica.
A few months earlier.

Steve sat in a busy restaurant called the Galley in Santa Monica. Sat opposite him was Charley Sandford, They sat at a table against one of the walls, a bottle of wine was open and glasses had been poured.

"You know what I love about this particular time?" Charley was suave and sophisticated in his manner.

The waitress returned to the table with some plates of food, fish of the day for Steve and Charley opted for the lobster.

"No, but somehow I have a feeling you're going to tell me," Steve rolled his eyes and reached for his wine

"The food Steve, the food. When I come from…"

"What do you mean *when*? Don't you mean *where*?" Steve felt compelled to interrupt

"No, I meant *when*… but thanks for pointing that out, it shows you're actually paying attention. So many people fail to do that… and that annoys me… no, you see the food is bland. Here there are ingredients and flavours that, frankly, we can only dream of. Make the most of it Steve, and trust me when I say that, this will all be lost in time and take decades, maybe even centuries to rediscover. Of course, with our help that may be quicker."

"Are you quite finished?"

"Oh no, I only just got started and we have a lot to get through," Charley greeted his main course with glee and tucked into it with a messy enthusiasm. Steve was more reserved as he set out to tackle the giant fish that now adorned the plate in front of him.

"Why here? Why now?" Steve felt like he should at least find out why on earth he ended up in Santa Monica, if only for the sake of his dwindling sanity.

"You read the e-mails, Steve, that's why you came."

"When someone writes an e-mail like that you tend not to ignore it."

"I had to get your attention," Charley replied.

"And I guess it worked."

"I appealed to your sense of adventure. You see you wanted this, deep down, you secretly wanted this," Charley dabbed his lips with a crisp white napkin.

"Is everything okay with your meals?" the waitress sneaked in her platitude before Charley could respond.

Both of them looked up to acknowledge her and smile to confirm that their food was fine. Steve watched as she retreated to the bar and started talking with the barman. Steve noticed how the barman nodded slowly as he cleaned a glass and then looked across at the table.

"You see all this?" Charley gestured to their surroundings with his fork

"What of it? There are thousands of restaurants in this region."

"Well, probably not for long…you see, everything here now will cease to exist in the coming decades, destroyed and lost forever, and they sent me… how can I put this," Charley chewed nonchalantly on a mouthful of lobster he pulled from one of the claws, "to tell you that unless we stop certain things happening that this destruction may happen even quicker… and we don't want that do we?" Charley wiped his mouth with his napkin.

"Certain things? Are you for real? I mean can you be slightly more specific?" Steve questioned

Charley, the fish was good Steve thought to himself, he held up a fork of it to the light.

"Specific yes. And it is very real, and you are as well. Enjoy this time Steve. You see everything that has led you to this point has, almost, been to a design. Your destiny was always to be sat there in front of me," Charley vigorously pointed to Steve's chair, "How you got here, well, that's different than how we wanted it to happen. But from now on, you are part of something far bigger than you or I can imagine," Charley needed no reassurance to say what he said, his confidence was evident enough to Steve.

"No, sorry, just no! I'm sorry I'm calling bullshit, this must be some kind of elaborate prank. Am I on camera? Please? Is someone going to jump out from behind a plant and say *gotcha!* I mean, this just doesn't happen like this mate. You got the wrong guy. Now, enjoy your meal and I'll be seeing you around…although probably not," Steve went to stand up but Charley firmly grabbed his arm and implored that he sit down and finished his meal.

A couple of other diners looked across at Steve as if to offer support, Charley stared them out and Steve returned to his seat.

"Why the hurry? After all, I hear the dessert here is wonderful," Charley mocked Steve.

"If you don't mind, I'd settle for a serving of sanity at the moment, with a side order of reality," Steve replied.

"I'm trying to be easy on you Steve, keep it simple. Do you honestly think I wanted to do this?" Charley stared at Steve, "I have better things I could be doing with my time."

"Like what exactly?" Steve asked.

"Have you seen the beaches?" Charley wore a mischievous smile on his face.

"I don't know what to think, but this isn't happening, I wasted my money coming here and I can accept that. What I can't accept is—"

"Is what? That this reality is not *your* reality?" Charley shrugged his shoulders dismissively.

"Not my reality?" Steve quickly drank some more wine.

"Steady my friend, enjoy it. Don't guzzle it." Charley grabbed Steve's arm to lower the glass back onto the table.

"This isn't happening," Steve said.

"Oh, it is, it's happening all around us. You are sitting here now and we *are* talking believe me."

"Then give me something tangible that I can believe instead of this dance we appear to be doing. I'm an accountant, someone who deals in fact and figures, not fantasy." Steve took another gulp of wine.

"You want the truth?" Charley placed his hands on the table.

"I'm all ears." Steve mirrored Charley and placed his hands on the table.

"Okay, here it goes. We opened a line in time so we could travel to collect key compounds to create a vaccine to protect our people against a highly virulent strain of virus that is decimating the population of the future. We needed to source compounds that are not readily available in our time anymore. This time represented the perfect chance for us to obtain what we needed. There, I've said it."

"And you expect me to believe that explanation? Even if this was true I'm no doctor but what about antibiotics?"

"In the future antibiotics don't work anymore. The virus became immune to their effects and spread like wildfire. This was a direct consequence of living in contained environments that were sterile but deemed safe places. The human immune system that had built up

over millions of years of living around tiny microbes
became undermined in its effectiveness, it went to sleep.
They couldn't have known this would be the result. The
plan was to create more of the compounds we needed
synthetically but we needed a blueprint sample to
achieve this."

"What about the risk of a paradox? How have
you managed to avoid that? I take it you've heard of
these things?"

"You catch on quickly."

"Call it too many late nights in front of the TV."

"The plan was for a very quick mission, you
know, in and out before anyone knew about it. Thereby,
minimising the risk of any issues. However, things
didn't quite go to plan."

"I suspect that wasn't in the script, was it?"
Steve chuckled.

"It's not a script Steve, this is reality. Whether
you care to believe it or not is up to you but trust me
when I say, this is real." Charley looked straight into
Steve's eyes.

"Okay, so taking this on face value, what next?"
Steve looked down at the table.

"You're not surprised?"

"Surprised isn't the word that springs to mind.
However, I'm here and I knew something mad like this
would be behind your e-mails. I mean, why not throw in
the whole time travel thing and make it totally crazy.
We're quite enlightened in this time you know. You read
about these things all the time and watch them on the
telly. Ronald Mallett for example. He always said it was
possible. I guess if you think about it, here you are,
proving him right." Steve stared back at Charley.

"And you believed him?"

"Let's just say it's very difficult to disprove his
theories, so yes, I believe it's possible. And yes, I had a
passing interest in what he had to say. More than a

29

passing interest in fact. Apparently." Steve picked up his glass of wine.

"You're taking this remarkably well."

"You know what? I think I'm past the point of arguing with you, maybe the wine is numbing my senses and besides I came here for answers, whether I choose to believe them or not is another thing. But that doesn't answer the one big question; why me?"

"I'll come to that soon. You see in our time there are wars, not on the grand scale you may think, more tribal. But over the years these wars have ravaged the planet and the natural resources available to us. One of these so-called tribes was headed up by a group of scientists who went rogue after assisting in the development of the technology to create a device to open the timeline. They saw an opportunity to exploit the timeline we opened and used it to hatch their own plan, a plan to travel back to this time, locate and send forward the resources they needed, resources no longer available in our time. We call them Traders."

"This gets better by the minute. What are they doing with these resources?"

"We're not sure but we are sure they have Traders operating in this time."

"Let's just pretend for a minute that I believe you; I'll repeat the question, what has any of this to do with me?"

"Sleeper agents. We needed sleeper agents. You're part of a special covert operation that is so deep fake that you couldn't even know about it, that is until now."

Steve took a deep breath and placed the glass back on the table, "Okay, you have my attention now."

"Finally. You see the plan was created to bring back babies from our time and supplant them into the near past with adoptive families to ensure they were of the correct age to be activated now. We opened a timeline, the perfect timeline, one that couldn't cause a paradox because you didn't exist beforehand so you couldn't impact on this time or the future." Charley took a sip of his wine.

"You're telling me I'm from the future. Am I correct so far?"

"Yes, and this is part of the activation process. To be precise, you were born in the late twenty-fifth century and then planted into this time so that you were of the optimum age to carry out our plans."

"Wow, I guess at least I won't hit fifty for a few hundred years!" Steve laughed out loud.

"You may laugh but we looked at the Russian program called *Illegals* and decided this was the best course of action to ensure you remained undetected while we worked out the details."

"Illegals?"

"Yes. The Russians set up sleeper agents all the time, but not with babies, as they can't travel through time. For example, go have a look at the Maria Butani case. We chose this route because we thought it would be easier to mold you into what is needed at the point of activation."

"And what exactly is that? I mean I'm hardly spy material. I'm an accountant." Steve raised his eyebrows and opened his hands on the table.

"Most spies are fairly normal people. They're the ones that do a regular job, live regular lives, and are completely off the radar; that's how the Russians do it. That's what we needed, boots on the ground, people strategically placed in this time to try and disrupt their operations. Everything they do is disguised behind the thin veneer of normality."

"With all your so-called technology, there must have been another solution." Steve shrugged his shoulders, "And what about you? Where do you come into all of this?"

31

"I guess you'd call me a messenger. And whilst we did consider other options, this plan afforded us the most amount of cover and was the most resilient to detection."

Charley reached into his jacket pocket and pulled out a small cube-shaped device and placed it on the table. He pressed the top and suddenly small screens sprang into life and started to show information and images.

"What's that?" Steve pointed to the device.

"CCS, the computer command system. Or as we call it, the *all-seeing eye.* This baby may just save your life one day," Charley said and winked at the little cube.

"Earlier you used the word *babies,* as in plural... Are there more of us?" Steve asked.

"You'll find out soon enough." Charley sat back in his chair and clasped his hands together.

Steve reached across to pick up the device but Charley pushed his hand away.

"Don't. Power like that needs to be understood before you try to use it."

"What does it do?"

"It's a data accumulator. It collates information about potential Trader activity from all over this world. It feeds off your satellite systems as well, we just filter what we need into concise packets of information. Whether that be financial information, geotagging information on images...it can track anything you like. If it's digital we can get it. But in the wrong hands, this little device is a powerful way to get into the world's electronic infrastructure without the need to hack."

"Why would you need financial information?" Steve drank more from his wine glass.

"We reckon that someone has infiltrated one of the big commodities brokers in London and they are using the confidential information about certain mining companies to locate resources suitable for extraction."

"There are so many unanswered questions buzzing around my head." Steve shook his head slowly and looked up to the ceiling of the restaurant.

"The answers will come. Just not all here. The future was always going to start here and now for you and…" Charley's voice grew faint.

***

"I struggled to believe him," Steve said, "in fact, I all but ridiculed him at one point. Well, I guess he'll be smiling now." Steve shuffled his feet on the ground kicking up dust. "I'm still not saying I believe him."

"Don't question your own eyes, Steve."

"But where are we now? Or should I ask *when*?"

"This is the year 2618, we've been blasted along the timeline by illegal Traders who are trying to disrupt our mission – your mission. I messed up doing the most basic thing." Roy looked to the ground and bit his lower lip.

"Right, my name is Richard Thomas and I demand to know who's in charge here and when do we get back?" Richard, one of the boy's parents strode over and interrupted the conversation between Steve and Roy.

"You can't go back," Roy said.

"What do you mean?" Richard folded his arms and glared at Roy.

"What I said. You've seen and experienced too much."

"Too much of what? I don't know who you think you are, mister, but in Manchester, I'm a big thing, you know. People in power know me and do business with me. They'll be wondering where the hell I am."

"You mean you'll be missed?" Roy enquired gently.

"Dad, there's no signal. Can we go now?" Kieran shouted then bent down and picked something up from the ground. It looked like a rusty piece of metal piping.

"In a minute, Kieran. Daddy has some business to attend to."

"Tell your son to put down that weapon before he hurts himself," Roy said softly, so as not to alarm anyone.

"What weapon?"

"That weapon." As Roy uttered the words the weapon fired a blast out of the barrel into the ground, dust flew into the air as the round dispersed.

Kieran jumped back, startled by the noise, and threw the weapon down. Tamsin, Kieran's mother, ran over to him and grabbed his hand.

"Come with me young man, and don't touch anything else!"

"Convinced now?" Roy turned to Richard.

"Of what? Convinced by a toy gun?"

"It's crude, and probably long past its best, but it wasn't a toy."

"Rubbish."

Roy sighed. "You're stuck here."

"Stuck where?"

"The year is 2618 and as I've said, you are staying here. Don't worry. You'll be given all the support you need to assimilate, but for now please be quiet. I need to concentrate."

Richard took a long slow look around. "You're not making sense."

"Nothing will make sense for a while, trust me on that."

"What was that light?" Tamsin asked.

"The light was a cut in the timeline."

"I see. So, how much money do you want? I've read about how you people operate, kidnapping rich people to maintain your lifestyle, fucking leeches." Richard stamped his feet on the ground.

"Who mentioned money?"

"Hold on!" Steve threw his hands in the air and tried to broker the peace, "it's the same for that man over there as well, none of you can go back."

"And what about you?" Richard asked.

"I'm…I'm the one they wanted."

"Who wanted?" Tamsin asked.

"The people that sent us here," Steve pointed to the ground.

"So, it's *your* fault we're here?" Richard stepped closer to Steve and looked him up and down.

"Partially, but it's more my fault for allowing us to get caught in their trap," Roy chipped in.

"Let's say I'm willing to accept we're somewhere else, why can't *we* go back? We won't say anything, I can promise you that. They were after him, not us," Richard said while pointing at Steve.

"Because when the police interview you on your miraculous disappearance and reappearance and you are forced to tell them what happened you will be considered crazy." Roy made a twirling gesture with his finger pointing to his temple. "The CCTV evidence from the motorway cameras will probably disappear, as these things tend to. After that, all the authorities will want to do is cover this up, and you and your family and that man over there will be consigned to history. They will make up any story they please to ensure the truth never escapes, and you will never taste freedom again. You will be made a laughing-stock, and probably sent to a secure unit for the insane for your safety, according to official reports. How does that sound?"

"A bit melodramatic actually," Richard said and licked his drying lips.

The lorry driver stepped into the conversation. "I'm Stan, now I've heard what you're all saying but I still don't get one thing, *where* are we?"

"In exactly the same place that we were before, just a few hundred years in the future," Roy replied.

"If that's the case, then where the hell has everyone gone?"

"Gone."

"But where?" Stan said. "I've heard about these things, you know, on the late-night radio shows whilst on the road and all that shit. Government cover-ups, aliens, and all that crap, but where has everyone gone?"

"They're dead. Many millions died hundreds of years ago. I'm not qualified to give you all the answers you seek and for now, the best thing you can do is wait until we work out how to deal with this situation."

"Looks like something is on the way over." Steve pointed to a shiny metallic oblong object skimming the surface of the ground.

Silence descended as Kieran continued to take pictures.

"Kieran will you please calm down," Tamsin pleaded with her son.

Within moments the shuttle arrived and the door opened. A tall distinguished-looking man, in his sixties, stepped out. He was dressed in a black suit, nothing out of the ordinary.

The man approached Roy. "You messed up – big time."

"I know." Roy looked annoyed with himself.

"Silverton will help you cleanse the situation. He is there for a reason, as you well know."

"Silverton? That's the cop who chased me out of my apartment," Steve said.

"Yes, his methods are a little, shall we say, unorthodox, but he means well."

"Unorthodox? Next time he could do with telling me he's there to help," Steve said, looking annoyed.

"That is why we had Roy stationed near your apartment, we had no idea how you'd react, what with what happened to your brother in police custody. Silverton thought his methods were best, but, clearly, they weren't, were they? Sandford had tried his best in Santa Monica, but none of us was sure about how you'd react when you were activated."

"Activated?" Steve repeated.

"Yes, that is what Charley Sandford was attempting to do in Santa Monica."

"Charley Sandford? Well, how did I know his name would come up sooner or later in the conversation," Steve briefly closed his eyes.

The man held out his hand. "My name is Kallyuke, I am the reason you are in this situation. You undoubtedly have many questions, but now is not the time. We have far more pressing things to deal with, like getting you to London," he paused and glanced at Roy, "and securing the crash scene."

"There was a bright light. It came from nowhere, blinded us. There was no time to do anything." Roy's voice quivered as he spoke.

"I understand, and I have no explanation for this at the moment. Although we have our suspicions, we have more pressing issues to deal with. We still have a crash scene to cleanse."

"What's happening with that?" Roy asked.

"Silverton is dealing with it now. He will put the usual false flags in place to ensure our tracks are covered."

"Is that necessary?" Roy looked at Kallyuke.

"You had one job to do – get Steve to London safely. And look at what we have now. More issues to deal with. I can't keep covering this up. You know what these people are?" Kallyuke pointed towards them.

"I don't know…" Roy muttered.

"Liabilities. But I don't entirely blame you. We never thought they would make a move like this in such a public place. We even planned for traffic and all other variables, we thought it would be safer to use the road network. Silverton is very meticulous, so the fact this happened proves to me they are getting bolder, more confident, and we need to be wary."

"It would be nice to be in on these plans in the future."

"You can't know everything, Roy. I'm afraid it doesn't work that way and you know that." Kallyuke dismissed Roy's request.

"So, the *liabilities*...what happens to them?" Roy asked.

"They are loose ends that need tidying up. Gaps in the timeline, and you know what? We have to vet every single one of them to ensure that none of them is significant to their time. For now, we've been lucky, the assortment of people we've had to assimilate are nobodies, they had no consequence on the timeline. But one day we may not be so lucky."

"Then what?" Roy asked.

"I don't want to think about that outcome," Kallyuke replied.

"One thing I don't understand...why here? And why now? I mean what purpose does this serve?" Roy frowned.

"It's a message, a way of showing they mean business." Kallyuke looked around at the mess of rusting cars, preoccupied with the issues he now faced.

"The unit they used, it's powerful, I never knew that was possible, I mean, to cut a line in time like that across an entire carriageway...well...let's just say that takes a lot of energy."

"Maybe they're developing the tech, making use of what they took back and then adapting it there. If that's the case, we need to get our hands on one of those units, find out what they're using and try to understand how we can track it to avoid any more incidents. An energy source of that magnitude will be easy to track, we just need to identify the pattern so CCS can track it." Kallyuke clicked his fingers.

Roy looked back at Kallyuke, "If you're right then we need to act fast."

Kallyuke and Roy returned to the small gathering. "Now, for you, my friends, this is the beginning of a new journey. You may not appreciate it yet, but you have been given a chance that no one could ever dream of, a chance to glimpse the future and start new lives here," Kallyuke said.

"What if we don't want new lives here? What if we were perfectly happy where we were?" Richard asked. "And anyway, what gives you the right to boss us around?"

"Happy? My friend, in the next few years there will be people from your time positively begging to be in your position, just remember that. You will be safe here, you will be looked after, and you will be given support in your transition to our time. And most importantly, you will have a future to look forward to."

"What does that mean exactly? What do you mean *have a future*?" Richard threw his hands in the air.

"You'll find out, all in good time." Kallyuke stood motionless.

"This is great, Dad, wait until I tell my friends!" Kieran still tried to get a signal on his phone by holding it up in the air.

"I'm afraid that won't be possible. You see that kind of ancient technology won't work here," Kallyuke looked at Kieran's phone.

Kieran stopped holding his phone in the air and stared at it in the palm of his hand.

"Just what exactly did you mean when you referred to us having a future?" Richard squint in the bright sunlight.

"I can't tell you at the moment," Kallyuke replied.

"You're full of shit!" Richard fired back.

"Really? This machine I traveled in…recognise it?" Kallyuke pointed at the shuttle.

"That doesn't mean anything, the military have technology that is so advanced that it can--"

"Float? And now they can remove an entire highway from the face of the earth?" Kallyuke pointed to the ground, "You can continue. Don't let me stop you but I can assure you that none of what you see here is an illusion or a trick, it is as it is, and you are here and will stay here."

"We're prisoners?" Richard eyeballed Kallyuke.

"If that is what you want to call yourselves, then I cannot change your mind, but rest assured you will not be treated like a prisoner, you are our guests." Kallyuke stared back at Richard.

"We have to go," Roy said to Kallyuke.

"Clearly, these people not only have intel on your movements but on where to strike next. We need to stop them, *you* need to stop them, get to London and we can work from there," Kallyuke took a deep breath.

"Maybe there's a mole?" Roy asked.

"Possibly, but I'd like to think not. We can't keep covering up these incidents, someone will find out and blow our cover, cover that has taken us years to establish," Kallyuke said.

And with that Roy beckoned Steve to follow him; they walked a few hundred yards up the track that was once the M6 into the hazy sunshine.

***

The shuttle doors closed with a thud and then the shuttle slowly rose five feet off the ground and started on its journey. Steve looked back and noticed the boy's face was pressed up against the window looking out at them. This time the boy slowly waved at Steve.

Steve slowly waved back as the shuttle flew off into the horizon.

Roy pulled another device out of his jacket, a small silver disc, he pressed down on the display, the device lit up and started displaying numbers. The numbers were descending slowly.

"If we need to get to London why don't we just set the location on that thing and travel to London? I mean why all the drama and risks? Or doesn't it work like that?" Steve asked.

"What?" Roy looked at him with disdain.

"Can't we go to London with whatever that gadget is?"

"It's called a phasing unit."

"Can that phasing thing send us to London?"

"Exactly what do you think this is? This is reality, not fiction and what you are suggesting can't be done, at least not yet. Plus, we have some unfinished business at the crash scene."

"How does it work? If I'm meant to know about this stuff I should know everything. And I mean everything."

"Okay, you asked. This miracle device creates a doorway through time, it allows us to travel across the…"

"Timeline?"

"Exactly." Roy glanced at the silver disc in his hand, "But you have to be sure that you are in the correct location otherwise things can go horribly wrong. As well as traveling across time, it also verifies that the arrival location is safe and free from unexpected foreign objects."

41

"Such as?" Steve looked at Roy.

"Such as a wall that isn't at the current location for example. If it detects anything that could jeopardise the journey it simply aborts."

"What unfinished business?"

"You have a knack for asking too many questions at the wrong time. And while you're at it, let's just move away from here." Roy grabbed Steve by the arm and directed him onto the dusty dunes away from the track. "We need to be away from the road when we arrive back. I don't want any more unwanted attention. I reckon I just burnt a life with Kallyuke if you know what I mean?"

Roy pointed the phasing unit towards the ground, they were immediately enveloped by a bright light and disappeared into total darkness.

5

Santa Monica.
A Few Months Ago.

Charley sat at a desk at one end of the portacabin and beckoned Steve over. He typed something on the laptop keyboard and turned the screen around to show Steve.

"You see this?" Charley pointed to a map of the world with flashing markers at various locations, one of them signposted a city in China called Baise in the southeastern Chinese region of Guangxi. "This is where we have confirmed activity."

Charley clicked on the flashing marker above the province, the scene of 19 major sinkholes. Headlines popped up on the screen from various news sites around the world. One story carried a quote from Senior engineer Zhang Yuanhai who told reporters: *"It is the largest sinkhole cluster south of the Tropic of Cancer which also has the largest number."*

"What do you think this proves?" Steve asked.

"This proves that these extractions are happening. Mainly small time and mainly in remote locations so they don't arouse any suspicions, it's as if they're testing out a theory, but each one of these impacts on the timeline of this planet. The bolder they get, the worse it will get for the future. And they *are* getting bolder, we can see a pattern forming. Steve, we've been monitoring this for years, in some instances, lives are being lost. Would you look at the proof!" Charley pointed aggressively at the headlines on his screen.

"Okay, just for a moment, let's assume there's an element of truth to these headlines. My next question is who is carrying out these so-called extractions?"

"Traders, of course. Aren't you listening to me?" Charley raised his voice.

"I do listen, but all we've done since we met is go around in circles. You have made lots of big statements but given me very little in the way of detail. I'm a details man, Charley. I work with figures, and figures don't need to be dressed up in hyperbole to do their job. They function as they should and don't require huge explanations. Figures don't need fancy software to convince me of their existence either."

"You want details, they're right there on the screen. You just need to accept what your eyes are showing you."

"More big statements but with little in the way of evidence to support them, do you see my point? And as for your information, anyone can fake a headline. It's a very twenty-first-century thing now. Why bring me here, Charley? I mean, really...*why* bring me here?"

"Planet Earth is dying. And a lot quicker than we thought it would. These extractions are only serving to speed up the process and push us closer to the brink."

"The brink of what exactly? Extinction?" Steve folded his arms, pursed his lips, and looked around the scruffy office.

There was a stale smell in the air and the coffee machine had definitely seen better days. A few filing trays were scattered around the place, a pile of newspapers was stacked neatly against one wall and a large metal chest of drawers dominated another wall.

"We need to stop these people and fast!" Charley reiterated his point by pointing at the screen, "Read the reports!"

Steve sat back in the rickety wooden chair and looked at the headlines on the screen.

"You don't belong here. You know that don't you?" Charley leaned forward to eyeball Steve.

"Don't belong where?"

"Here!" Charley pointed to the ground.

"Of course, I do. I have a wife..."

"Ex-wife."

"And a daughter. People I love and care for. Friends."

"That may be the case, but you were marked for duty at the time of your birth and your placement into this time, having family members does not mean you can abdicate your responsibility to our needs."

"Who's abdicating what responsibility? What are you going on about?" Steve stood up and paced around. "If this is so damn important why not send back some hitmen from the future to deal with it? I mean you can do that, can't you? You guys are from the future, you can do anything, can't you?"

"They wouldn't stand a chance. Their identities would be compromised before they even arrived."

"Compromised by what?"

"There are security issues, even in the future, and before you say it, these issues lead us to believe some key identities have been leaked into the wrong hands."

"Leaked?"

"Most probably by a mole or a data breach." Charley shook his head when he revealed this revelation.

"You cooked up this plan instead? Tell me this, if I was, as you say, supplanted at birth into this time, where was I supplanted from? And why wasn't I traced? Because surely, I had no parents when I arrived, isn't that true?"

"You went to an orphanage, like all of them. Questions were kept to a minimum."

"You thought of everything, didn't you?" Steve looked down to the floor and shook his head. Steve knew some of his background matched up to this explanation.

"Supplanting you into this timeline and then activating you as and when we saw fit was the perfect alternative. Steve, to us, you are the perfect agent and an important asset to our operations. No one knows who you really are, not even *you*."

"If I'm so perfect, how come I don't know a thing about this?"

"We needed to get you into the right mental state, which means coping with what is happening around you."

"Well don't make it a career choice because so far you've been lousy at it…"

"Whilst we couldn't influence how you grew up and what decisions you made in life everything was ultimately building to this point, Steve. Who you are, and what you are, start from here onward. Everything that went before has no relevance to your future. I know you think I'm a madman and that you've blown a lot of money, but trust me, this won't go away and the more you fight it the worse it will get; this will eat you up unless you embrace it."

"Embrace what? Give me a clue here, help me out a little. You can show me all the screens you like but I don't see anything fundamentally different or futuristic about anything you've said so far." Steve sat back down again. "This shit happens all the time, and smuggling is not a new concept. Do you see what my problem is with all of this?"

"We're not so different in the future, in fact, there was a time when the lights went out on planet Earth and we probably took a few steps backward in our evolution."

"Riddles, Charley, riddles!" Steve stretched out his arms in frustration.

"It will all make sense one day, I promise."
Charley nodded in approval of his own statement

"I hope so, Charley… for the sake of my sanity I
hope so because, right now, I feel like I'm at a bursting
point."

"Get back to Manchester and prepare yourself
because you are caught up in something that is far bigger
than you can ever imagine."

"Or believe."

"That's your choice, Steve, but don't say I
didn't warn you."

6

London.2618.

Kallyuke cast a solitary shadow across the floor as he stood in a large, oppressively grey room. One wall was completely covered by huge screens projecting light into every corner of the room. His thin frame and greying hair were the only clues to his age as he still retained the boisterous attitude and energy levels of someone half his years. Kallyuke was captivated by what he saw.

A group of rogue scientists had taken hostages in a small region near the west coast of America. Their demands and motives were unclear but official channels suggested it was another attack aimed at destabilising the fragile period of peace Kallyuke had successfully overseen in recent years.

The room was imposing. There were no windows and it relied heavily on the dim light to offset the glare from the screens. In the middle stood a large oval table surrounded by several tall-backed chairs. Kallyuke stood in front of the table and used his index finger, which contained a tiny electronic sensor implant, to point to and control the screens.

One news channel from the 21st century was finding it difficult to cope with the number of breaking stories coming in from all over the world. The transmission was being piped in via a network of CCS devices that were planted in strategic positions across Earth of the past. Once collated, the information was bounced off the existing satellite systems via the CCS devices planted on them. The information was then compacted into digital packages and channeled through

time into Kallyuke's control room. A particular set of
headlines that caught Kallyuke's attention focused on a
peaceful protest in Paris, over a new carbon rationing
scheme, that was threatening to turn violent. In
Venezuela, civil unrest continued as the country ground
to a halt through years of economic profligacy. In parts
of Africa, there was famine and civil unrest as people
did their best to survive another drought. In Europe,
there was political uncertainty as election after election
appeared to be a breeding ground for rioting as Populism
took hold.

After Kallyuke was unmoved by the chaos. It was the
natural order of things to come and they were prepared
for the fallout; they had a plan. The combination of
political unrest alongside the added dimension of Trader
activity against the backdrop, and the ever-growing
pressures on the planet's dwindling resources created a
perfect storm. But Kallyuke knew they were unable to
change these events outside of the scope of their
mission; to do so could create a paradox and impact on
their future.

Sayssac walked into the room holding a
steaming mug, "I thought you could do with this." He
handed a coffee to Kallyuke.

Sayssac was an older, frailer man who had
known Kallyuke for years. Initially, they were political
adversaries, but their rivalry dissipated when it became
obvious that solidarity and a pooling of knowledge were
required to reboot society. London was held as *the*
modern success story. Proof that you could rebuild from
the ashes and that society, when given a purpose, was
inherently good and could start again. Kallyuke was the
master of that reboot and wanted the world to know
about it.

From London came optimism and soon other
cities would follow, Los Angeles, New York,
Manchester, Rio, Beijing, and Delhi all prospered as

Kallyuke's blueprint to create a brave, new society was soon replicated around the world by the various leaders. This brave new world was set against the backdrop of centuries of conflict that had decimated large parts of the planet. Kallyuke held firm, his control over his brave new world had been instrumental in revitalising the planet and ensuring that peace was maintained.

Kallyuke wanted to maintain this status quo, and the only way to achieve it was to grow the power base he held in London so that no rival would question their strategy; to him, whatever the cost, it was worth it to preserve their way of life.

One of the screens displayed a small news story about the crash on the M6 near Birmingham, followed by another screen displaying footage captured by some of the witnesses.

"This is not good." Kallyuke looked at Sayssac as the story began to gain coverage from various smaller online news sites.

"What did you expect? You knew the risks," Sayssac replied.

"This isn't about risks – this is about them playing God."

Some of the footage came from the bridge. Kallyuke pointed at the screen. "Pause." The screen displayed a grainy shot from one of the witnesses" cameras.

"What have you seen?" Sayssac enquired.

"Look at this." Kallyuke pointed to two people captured at the edge of the frame as they walked up the slip road from Junction 11.

"And?"

"Where's their car? You wouldn't abandon your car on the road if it was damaged, and if they were close to the front of the crash how come they aren't injured?" Kallyuke circled them and increased the size of the image by stretching his thumb and index finger as far apart as possible.

"Perhaps they were being inquisitive?"

"No, I don't believe that. These are the people responsible for the crash, I'm sure of it. Let's wait to see what Silverton finds on the CCTV footage, but I bet they are part of this mess."

"If you're right, and I hope you're not, then they're growing reckless. To do this on a public highway – in daylight – is not what I expected." Sayssac shook his head.

"What concerns me is what they used. Roy told me all he saw was a bright light, something that cut into the timeline. To carry out that kind of attack and to move so many people takes a lot of energy. I don't recall us having that kind of tech. They must have adapted the technology with what they have at their disposal in that time…"

"It could open up many different issues for us," Sayssac replied.

"Which is something we have to be prepared for." Kallyuke didn't like surprises.

"And what of the new arrivals?" Sayssac asked.

"Luckily, no one of any significance."

"No long-term impact on the timeline then?" Sayssac replied.

"Not as far as we can tell but it is never a perfect science and that is the only positive."

"What about other family members? What about jobs?" Sayssac asked.

"With everything that will happen in the coming years, priorities will switch to survival and all else will eventually be forgotten." Kallyuke looked down to the ground.

"And Steve Garner?" Sayssac asked.

"I didn't say much to him. Charley met with him in Santa Monica. When he gets to London there will be more time for him to acclimatise to the task in hand."

"Why didn't you talk to him?"

"There are bigger issues to address and besides, I don't want to bombard him with information. It's better to leave it to the others, plus I need to focus on getting Silverton to cover up this mess."

"We can't keep using him to cover up these incidents…you are aware of that, aren't you?" Sayssac was concerned.

Kallyuke shrugged, "What options do I have?"

"Not many, but sooner or later…" Sayssac was like a broken record.

"Yes, I know, sooner or later something catastrophic may happen. Let's just hope we don't get to that point."

"Is Silverton. still trustworthy? I mean, will he crack if provoked? You place a lot of confidence in him." Sayssac was skeptical of Silverton.

"He's a loner."

"And for precisely that reason I think we should be careful about how much he knows, after all, he already has enough knowledge to blow our mission wide open."

"If I thought he would do that I wouldn't have initiated contact," Kallyuke shook his head.

"Then why don't you try and negotiate our way out of this mess?" Sayssac looked straight at Kallyuke.

"Negotiate what?" Kallyuke rebuffed the suggestion.

"A truce, something that is more substantive than the current impasse. We don't want to keep covering up these kinds of incidents. That is not what we are trying to achieve here."

"A truce is impossible, no one will talk with us, you know that."

"Close the timeline then, before it's too late."

"It may already be too late, and you seem to forget that thanks to these criminals," Kallyuke pointed to the screen reporting the hostage crisis on the west coast of America, "The technology to open another one is now readily available. We close one, they then open another. The only way is to bring them to their knees, make them see sense."

"Maybe they feel the same way about us."

"Maybe. But we're not the ones killing the planet," and with that Kallyuke switched the main screen to show a model of planet Earth. It showed the same information that Charley Sandford had in Santa Monica, only in more detail, with news headlines relevant to specific extractions. "Look at what they did in Chile, China, and South Africa. Everywhere they go we see the same issues, sinkholes, failed mining companies, and power outages. And for what?"

In China, days after an attempted extraction, news stories began to circulate of a huge sinkhole opening up and an entire village being swallowed up. The stories were quickly suppressed by the Chinese authorities and disappeared from view as they were keen to downplay the significance of the sinkhole, not least because they believed the mine that had caused it had been closed for decades. But the stories still made the conspiracy websites and circulated for months. Chinese authorities did their best to try and suppress the stories and close down the sites but were unsuccessful; Sayssac looked down in shame as the headlines kept coming. Hundreds of people died and an entire village was destroyed, but the mainstream media never covered it so the story soon disappeared.

"We have two sleeper agents activated now, and another twenty-four in place, but still dormant. I fear the worst if we activate them all at once. There will be no control and there will be more incidents like this recent one, and eventually, we will get caught," Sayssac sounded justifiably pessimistic after this most recent incident.

"I know my friend, I know. But doing nothing is not an option and trying to negotiate is not plausible until they decide they want to talk."

"But Earth is dying quicker with every move they make."

"Then it is up to us and these agents to thwart their next moves and send out a clear message that we will stop at nothing to halt this madness." Kallyuke bit his lower lip.

"And I thought the policy of M.A.D. had been consigned to history books," Sayssac said and then momentarily closed his eyes.

"Mutual Assured Destruction? No, we just had a slight change in the rules of engagement," Kallyuke pointed to the wall of screens showing various news articles from around the world, all of them were about death and destruction.

"Pull back then, let us see what they are trying to achieve and then make our move," Sayssac was trying to be the voice of reason.

"In the past twenty years I have taken this planet from the edge of destruction to the brink of a new age, and I will stop at nothing to ensure that these criminals are prevented from fucking it up and stopping our plans to begin afresh," Kallyuke said and pointed to the images of the rogue scientists now displayed on the news screens with captions of their apparent demands in exchange for the hostages they held.

7

Junction 11.M6.
Present-Day.

"I don't think I'll ever get used to this. I feel sick again."

"Steve, in case it hasn't dawned on you yet, you have no choice, this is your life now. You need to get used to it, and fast."

"And why the hell are we stuck in the bushes in the pouring rain? Not great planning was it?"

"We can't just reappear on the road out of nowhere. This was the nearest I could get us without being spotted."

"Well, thanks for nothing eh?"

"Shh…there are people over there, they may have heard a noise as we arrived."

"So what?"

"So what? I don't want them connecting the noise to our re-appearance."

"Do you enjoy what you do?"

"How do you mean?"

"I mean this, crouching behind these bushes in the soaking wet, trying to avoid detection, you know, do you enjoy this?" Steve gestured to their surroundings.

"If you mean this exact point in the here and now, then no I don't. But I have a duty to help and whilst enjoy isn't a word I'd choose; I would say that this happens to be part and parcel of this duty so I have to run with it."

"You don't talk like someone from the future."

"That's because I'm not, I'm from the present. I am one of those people sent to help you and the others. We're known as the Assimilated."

"How exactly did you get involved in this mess?"

"I was spotted."

"Spotted?"

"Let's just say I had more than a passing interest in UFOs and conspiracy theories and came into contact with people who asked for my help…and I said yes."

"And that's it? You became a time traveler? No training, just a phone call and you're off?"

"It was a bit more than that. We have to satisfy certain conditions."

"Conditions? Like what? The ability not to be sick?"

"Don't mock, it's unbecoming."

"There are more of you then?"

"Not many, but enough to establish what is needed in the present time."

"Don't you get itchy fingers and want to go off to other times? You know, the classic shoot Hitler scenario or go see the Roman Empire? Maybe even pay a visit to the land of dinosaurs? I mean you can do that with that gadget can't you?"

"No."

"No?" Steve frowned.

"Even if I wanted to, I couldn't, but I don't, so it's irrelevant and doesn't even enter my thinking."

"You have to admit, Roy, it's got to be tempting."

"What, and upset the entire timeline? As tempting as you think it might be, this is real, and to tamper with anything like that could—"

"I know, I know. *Have massive repercussions for the timeline.*"

"Don't mock it. Everything we do is monitored and if that device was programmed to move anywhere along the timeline that was unauthorised it would default back to 2618."

"Safeguards then? That's reassuring."

"Exactly."

"What's in it for you then? For doing all of this? I think I'm beginning to sound like your shrink."

"Nothing. But as I'm sure you're aware, for anyone interested in UFOs or the paranormal, this is by far the greatest thing you can have. Proof."

"I can see a logic to that."

"Right, Silverton is over there, we need to get into that crowd and try to get to him without being too obvious, do you think you can do that?"

"Well contrary to what you might think, I am very good at being subtle, so let's do this."

***

"Excuse me, are you the officer in charge?" The man in the brown rain mac approached Silverton as he waved people away from the bridge and directed the emergency services personnel working to clean up the crash scene.

Recovery trucks were stationed by the three vehicles at the front of the crash, a few men wearing bright green safety vests stood by them, scratching their heads while they looked into the cabins and then started examining the engine bays. It was still damp, the drizzle persisted.

"Who are you?" Silverton broke away from directing people to enquire.

"Birmingham Post. Can you tell me when the road is likely to open again?" The reporter held out a small Dictaphone.

"It's barely been a couple of hours. How are you already here? Tip-off from the control centre was it?"

Silverton shook his head, he waved away another officer, wanting to deal with this one alone.

"I got a call from a woman who witnessed the crash, and someone else sent me a video. Does this look familiar to you?" He held up his phone and played the footage captured by one of the witnesses.

"Publish this if you want but you'll get no cooperation from me, are we clear? As for your question, it'll open when I say it can, thank you. Now, please allow me to get on with the job in hand," Silverton hissed his reply.

"I take it this footage is accurate then," the reporter said, unperturbed by the threat. "What can you tell me about the circumstances leading up to this crash?"

A man in his early thirties approached and seemed to be trying to listen in on the conversation. Silverton broke away from his ongoing conversation with the reporter.

"Who the hell are you and what do *you* want?" Silverton threw his hands in the air.

"Mark Collins, freelance reporter…" he nervously stuttered.

"Where are you all coming from? And why *this* accident?"

"My brother was at the back of the traffic jam. He called me and told me to get my backside down here. He said something about a bright light? Is that correct?"

The other reporter looked annoyed.

"Yes, there was a light, but that's nothing new, or unusual, so what's the big deal?"

"I think the big *deal* is contained on this footage," the first reporter said, wrestling back the initiative from Mark Collins. "What happened to these vehicles?" The reporter paused the footage on one of the cars. It clearly showed the burnt-out engine bay and the empty cabin.

"As I said before, you have no authority to quote me. Now if you will excuse me, I have work to do. This meeting is over. Goodbye."

Silverton walked off to talk with the recovery truck drivers leaving Mark Collins and the reporter to talk amongst themselves.

***

The reporter held out his hand to Mark. "I'm Ian by the way, Ian Banks, Birmingham Post."

Mark shook Ian's hand briskly. "Mark Collins, freelance reporter, mainly Manchester, but I've been known to pop up at any location if the story is worthwhile."

"Like this one?"

"Well, yes, but what actually happened here?"

They retreated to the hard shoulder to talk.

"May I?" Mark held out his hand.

"Oh, of course. Here, be my guest." Ian passed the phone to Mark.

Mark studied the footage for a few minutes, pausing on the vehicles and the line on the tarmac.

"Whoever shot this video wasted no time in uploading it to YouTube." Mark held up his phone to show the screen. It displayed the clip under the banner *"M6 Paranormal Crash"* and had already been viewed hundreds of times.

"But they can do that and get away with it. I can't. I need something more substantive like witness statements, or quotes from the authorities and no one appears to be playing ball at the moment," Ian replied.

"I can publish a report. There will be no issues or editor to answer to either." Mark had a plan.

Ian stared at Mark. "How would you get away with it?"

"I'm freelance. I'll publish it on my blog and reference this clip on YouTube, as long as whoever posted this gets a mention I'm sure it won't be a problem. What do you think?" Mark was eager to get this written up and posted before anyone else did.

"I don't know. What if they trace it back to me? That cop looked serious. Incidentally, I've been covering road accidents here for years and I've never seen that guy before. Do you recognise him?"

"I'm from Manchester. I've no idea who he is." Mark again looked over to Silverton who was talking with the other two officers. Silverton paused for a moment and looked back through the carnage to Mark. Mark looked down at the tarmac, avoiding eye contact.

"I'll quote non-specific sources and ensure everything is kept suitably vague," Mark said.

"Won't that dilute the value of the report? I mean, someone could say you made it up."

"That's up to them. The most important thing is to document what we know. Hopefully, more witnesses will come forward. The allure of having their names in the press may just coax them into talking with me."

Mark had a final look at the crash scene, trying to make sense in his mind what Ian had told him. After that, he walked up the slip road, got into his car, and drove off.

8

At the top of the slip road, several police officers were asking drivers questions as they tried to piece together what had happened. It was a slow process and understandably, tempers flared. Some of the people just wanted to get on with their day; they'd had enough of the delays and couldn't believe it had taken two hours to get the cars off the carriageway.

Silverton was pacing in between the vehicles inside the cordon. He lit a cigarette, took a drag, and then looked at it as if searching for inspiration. He paused next to Roy's car, spotting something, and reached into the cabin to pick up the CCS device that was now lodged next to the gear lever.

The two officers were busying themselves by ordering the recovery truck drivers around and seemed to be desperately trying to avoid crossing paths with Silverton.

Roy slowly approached the police cordon tape and looked at the crash scene, barely believing that they got out alive.

"Is that our car?" Steve pointed at the vehicle being dragged unceremoniously onto the back of one of the recovery trucks.

"Yep," Roy responded.

"Where's the bloody engine? It's just ash." The empty engine bay could be seen as the vehicle tilted during its ascent onto the recovery truck.

"I don't know. That beam of light must have reacted with something in the engine bay."

The two vehicles were now on the recovery trucks and Silverton walked over to the driver of one of the trucks. He passed Silverton a piece of paper, "Take it here for forensic examination, they'll be expecting you," the driver said.

"Whatever you say, guvnor."

The driver pulled off.

Silverton walked over to the other truck. "Follow him, they'll be expecting you." The driver acknowledged him. He then walked over to the tow truck and scribbled down some notes on a piece of notepad paper and handed it to the driver. The driver nodded his head and climbed into the cab of the tow truck and drove off down the southbound carriageway in pursuit of the other recovery trucks.

Silverton approached the two officers. "Now we've cleared the vehicles, I want this burn line covered." He pointed to the line on the tarmac. "I don't want any evidence that it existed otherwise the press will have a field day."

"But those other people already have evidence," one of the officers said.

"Let me deal with that. You just concern yourselves with sorting out that burn," and with that Silverton walked back to the cordon, lighting another cigarette in the process.

"They'll be the death of you," Roy said as Silverton crouched under the tape.

"What?" Silverton looked around.

"Keep smoking like that and it'll be the death of you," Roy repeated his statement.

"Roy?" Silverton smirked as he looked back at Roy.

"Detective Roger Silverton."

"It's been a while, although I wish we were meeting under better circumstances." Silverton took another drag on his cigarette as he vigorously shook Roy's hand.

"We had no idea this would happen," Roy pointed to the cordon and the hard shoulder.

"How could you? I mean this was totally out of character, even by their standards."

"Try telling that to Kallyuke. He wasn't impressed."

"Well maybe not, but for now we need to get to London, so let's talk as we drive. I'll let the other officers know they have to make their own way back to Manchester, just give me a minute." Silverton ducked back under the cordon and gave the two officers the bad news; they shrugged their shoulders in understandable disappointment.

Silverton signaled at Roy and Steve to follow him to his car at the foot of the slip road. As they jumped in, Silverton put on the lights and siren to cut through the ever-growing queue of diverted cars. One of the officers held up the police cordon tape and Silverton drove slowly under the bridge and then sped off down the deserted M6.

Roy sat next to Silverton in the front. Silverton reached into his jacket pocket and tossed the CCS device he had recovered from the car into Roy's lap, "Try and be a bit more careful with stuff like this in future. Crashes I can cover up, this kind of tech is a bit harder to explain."

"Thank you, I had no idea where it was, everything happened in a blur." Roy put the device into his jacket pocket.

"How are you going to cover up this crash?" Steve asked, "I mean, this isn't your everyday kind of crash is it?"

"Car crashes happen all the time, the crash is the easy part. The people we lost, that's the tricky part." Silverton looked at Steve via the rearview mirror.

"If it's any consolation they are of no significance," Roy assured Silverton.

"That may be the case, but they'll be missed. People know them, and people will be wondering where they are. But I have a plan."

"What kind of a plan? I hope it's better than the one you implemented to help me, I mean, who wakes someone up at that hour of the morning?" Steve closed his eyes for a moment.

"You have no idea what this is about, do you? I would have thought the reality would have dawned on you by now," Silverton snapped.

"You two have to get over this, that was in the past..." as soon as Roy used that word he regretted it.

Steve frowned. "I don't know what is in the past at the moment, or the future. I barely know the present... so it seems."

"How are you going to explain what happened to those people?" Roy asked.

"The starting point is that we have no one from the vehicles to deal with, no one hanging around to contradict what story I manufacture. My officers will work with the emergency services to thoroughly cleanse the scene so they'll be little or no physical evidence. I think the next logical route could be to close down any potential questions that may arise by waving a diplomatic or national security risk flag along with a press embargo."

"Won't that attract more attention?" Steve asked.

"We won't put it out publicly, just on the quiet to any press inquiries we get. It usually works, after all as far as everyone is concerned this is just a car crash. Nothing more, nothing less. Very soon this will be yesterday's news and no one is interested in yesterday's papers. With no facts to embellish the story the press normally gets bored and moves on." Silverton nodded in agreement with himself.

"But this is also a crash with a strange bright light and witnesses," Steve said.

"That light could have been created by anything and as for the witnesses, all they have is some phone images of empty vehicles, hardly compelling evidence is it?"

"What could have caused the light?" Steve asked.

"There are many possible causes...someone let off a firework for example," Silverton replied.

"And won't this approach alert the conspiracy theorists?" Steve asked.

"For a while. But the lack of physical evidence combined with no one to interview from those vehicles will leave them lacking in facts, so, eventually, they'll get bored or create even more outlandish theories that will be dismissed by any sensible publication. It comes with the territory and is a risk I'm willing to take."

"But won't there be questions about the vehicles?" Roy asked.

"Those vehicles will never be seen again."

"How can you be so sure?" Steve asked.

"I can be sure because of where I've sent them."

"Where have they gone?" Steve persisted.

"A forensic testing site on the outskirts of London."

"Won't they suspect something is wrong when they're being examined?"

"Kallyuke didn't hire me for my good looks, my charm, or my wit."

"I did kind of guess that," Steve said.

"My network of contacts is what he wanted, access to people who can help smooth things along, make things... shall we say... disappear, and create explanations for things that need explaining, but in ways that we want them to be explained and controlled. We're not in the business of scaring away the press, we just want to mold them into our way of thinking." Silverton was careful in his choice of words.

"You mean lie," Steve was blunt.

"Lying is a strong word, I prefer to use the word…" Silverton took a dramatic pause and deep breath, "…manipulate. Yes, manipulate seems slightly more suitable. In any case, they will not be seen again and those awkward questions we need to avoid, will not arise. Without any tangible evidence, there is very little to suggest this was anything other than a routine crash."

Silence descended as they made swift progress towards London. Steve's mind drifted back to the boy in the car next to them, he wondered what had happened to him and his family, and if it had finally registered with Stan that his delivery would never be made.

"The future is starting now…" Steve muttered. He looked out of the window and mentally drifted into the scenery.

"What was that?" Roy asked.

"Oh, nothing, just something Charley said when we met." Steve continued to look out of the window at the passing scenery. His mind flicked back to the desolate dust-covered track of the future.

9

London.Present-Day.

Terence Armstrong sat at his leather-covered desk in his opulent office just off Park Lane in London. It was nearing the end of the day and Terence was feeling hungry, he pondered where he would dine that evening and surfed the net to find a suitable eatery amongst the fashionable West End haunts he frequented.

Terence considered himself fashionable in his dress sense and only bought suits from the finest tailors on Jermyn Street in central London. For him, this was part of the look and identity that he had to portray to gain the attention of his many contacts. It was part of the facade and was designed to do only one thing; help him gain their trust and eventually their most confidential business secrets.

His specialism was playing the markets and especially working in the futures market. He played with his Montblanc pen, shuffling it between his fingers, and then started scribbling notes down on a piece of paper. He then turned to type something into his laptop. The screen came to life with graphs and figures and then the word "buy" flashed up in red letters across the bottom.

Armstrong took a deck of cards out of one of the draws in his desk and started to shuffle them, occasionally pausing to look at whatever card was in his hand; this time it was the King of Diamonds; Armstrong smirked.

A knock on the door interrupted his concentration. "Come!" he shouted. Two men walked in – the same two men who had caused the chaos on the M6. Armstrong calmly placed the cards on the side of the desk, the King of Diamonds was face up on the top of the deck, he then looked up at the two men, gesturing them to take a seat.

Both men were dressed casually but looked uneasy as they walked towards the desk and took a seat in front of Armstrong.

"Where do we begin? Oh, I know, why the need for all the drama?" Armstrong inquired calmly but his face articulated his anger as he bit on the inside of his lower lip.

"It wasn't part of the plan, we thought—"

Armstrong stood up and smashed his fist onto the desk. "Thought? I doubt that. And you're absolutely correct. It wasn't part of the plan, in fact, it couldn't have been further from the fucking plan. I said I wanted to remove them and place them somewhere, away from us so we could concentrate on *our* plans. Plans that you are well aware of and you are also aware have taken a long time to implement. And now we have this to deal with." Armstrong sat down and pointed accusingly at the screen of his laptop.

"It won't happen again, I promise." Clint looked down toward the floor.

"I know it won't. Are either of you aware of the importance of this mission? Back home time is ticking away and we have a planet to escape from before it's too late," Armstrong sat down at the desk and leaned forward to stare at the pair of them in turn.

"Brutally aware. We're both completely on message and committed when it comes to the cause. We also know the risks that come with this," Matt volunteered.

"I understand that back in our time preparations to leave this planet are progressing well, therefore we need to keep pressing on with our work. I, for one, won't be sorry to leave a planet ravaged by years of sectarian violence and exclusion zones commandeered and ruled by Kallyuke. Our only hope of preserving our way of life is to escape, that will at least give us a chance of a future away from his tyranny." Armstrong clasped his hands together on the table.

"Amen to that," Clint replied.

"Now, as you know, they want to thwart this. Kallyuke is twisted by jealously and rage in equal parts, he cannot control us, but we keep presenting him with opportunities to foil our mission. That sleeper agent we tracked was activated by Charley Sandford. Do you know how much effort it took to gain the intel about his passage to London? How many people risked their lives to ensure you had a clear run at stopping him?"

"But we did what was asked. We went to the location as agreed and carried out the mission," Matt spoke softly.

"In truth you did. But you ignored the advice I gave that if that road was too busy then select another location for the extraction, somewhere quieter that wouldn't alert the authorities. We would have tracked the extraction location and made our move, wherever it happened."

"I guess we panicked. We saw an opportunity and went for it." Clint gingerly tapped the desk with his fingers.

"I know there was a comms blackout in place but you are experienced operatives, you know the drill, at times I need you to act on your own initiative. Clearly, I was asking for too much in this instance. We wanted to capture that sleeper agent to see what they knew but before we could make a move Kallyuke arrived at the scene."

"He must have been tipped off," Matt said.

"Obviously, which means they must have a failsafe in place, someone who is working alongside them who is under deep cover. Someone we've missed."

"But we can't be expected to equate for that, this was an unfortunate error but no one would have known about that." Clint reached across, picked up the card on top of the deck, and ran it through his fingers.

"What about the intel?" Matt asked.

"It's too early to say but at this time nothing obvious is showing itself. We have to be careful as our agents are vulnerable. Kallyuke has ways of tracking them down. I mean, some of their operatives are not as conscientious as others, take Sandford for example. He seems to spend most of his time in Santa Monica using the place as a personal playground. But that's good, he leaves a trail behind and we can exploit that. This other person, whoever they are, I'm not so sure. I suppose, at the very least, we've made them aware that we are onto them and can strike back. But that doesn't hide the fact that you were careless and far too public in your approach."

"It'll blow over soon," Matt nodded slowly.

"And how can you be so sure? Have you seen this?" Armstrong pointed to his laptop screen.

Headlines were beginning to surface online reporting the crash on the M6.

"They're calling it the *M6 Paranormal Crash,*" Armstrong said. "Can you imagine how much of an issue that could be if this spreads?"

"I don't see how they can call it that," Clint said, looking at the screen.

"You know that, and I know that, but they've got to call it something haven't they? Something that will attract maximum amounts of attention. There's a fucking video of the crash scene on YouTube. Fortunately for us, the imbecile that shot it must have been out of his head at the time because they haven't got a clue what they've filmed, but that doesn't matter. The fact is that there's footage placing your activity at the scene of this crash. The only thing they don't have is an image of you two idiots."

"We didn't expect it to go this way," Matt said, but Armstrong was having none of it.

"I'm sure you didn't but it has gone this way. And who the hell is Mark Collins?" Armstrong thumped the desk.

"Who?" Matt and Clint replied in unison.

"The journalistic genius who wrote this report. Who is he because I can't seem to find anything about him?"

"Never heard of him. Do you think he has something to do with them?" Matt asked.

"I doubt it." Armstrong spoke quieter, "Just be thankful that this half-arsed hack doesn't have a clue about what really happened, otherwise we'd be in serious trouble. This report is full of guesswork and hearsay. It is devoid of facts and with no sources to back him up. I think we got away with it. That doesn't mean you can pull a stunt like that again, though. Do I make myself clear?"

"Yes, very clear," Matt replied.

Armstrong walked over to the antique drinks cabinet to the side of his desk and poured himself a brandy. He returned to his chair, settled into it, reclining back as he took a sip of his drink. He then leaned forward and placed the large brandy glass onto the table. All without saying a word to Matt or Clint, who were sitting passively, watching his every move.

"What next?" Clint broke the silence.

"You will take the Eurostar to Paris tonight and check-in at the Hotel Richard on Rue Richard Lenoir," Armstrong said, tossing some documents on the table. "These are your tickets and ID documents. Lay low overnight. I don't want any further issues to clear up. You will receive instructions about where to meet with two colleagues of mine who will detail the extraction."

Armstrong pointed to the images of the two contacts they were to meet in Paris.

"Why Paris?" Matt was perplexed.

"The less you know now, the higher the chances of success. Your ultimate destination will be the Trocadero metro station, but once in Paris, all will be explained. We must keep things hidden until it is absolutely necessary to know. That way we avoid mistakes or information being leaked. When you arrive, head to the Voltaire Metro station and walk down to the hotel, no distractions do you understand me? Head straight to the hotel and await further instruction."

"But Paris is a city, hardly the place for—" Clint was cut short.

"I know Paris is a city. You have your instructions, this time they should be failsafe. Try not to prove me wrong."

Matt and Clint stood up, grabbed the documents from the desk, and walked out of the office, Armstrong took another sip of his brandy. They closed the large solid door behind them, paused for a moment in the foyer to check the documents, and left the building.

"What does he know that we don't?" Matt asked.

"I'm not sure and I'm not about to question him given his mood, but this time let's make sure we don't mess up," Clint replied.

They headed off into London's bustling centre.

10

London.Present-Day.

"How long before we arrive?" Steve asked.

"We're nearly there," Silverton replied.

Steve looked on as they meandered through London's labyrinthine streets in the early evening traffic. Silverton was an expert at avoiding traffic, he cut his teeth working the streets as a police constable for about ten years and then onto the Flying squad and various other undercover operations, so he knew the quickest way to virtually anywhere in the city at any time.

Silverton took a sharp right down a narrow street followed by a hard left turn onto a ramp that led into an underground car park. The underside of the car bottomed out once it got to the end of the ramp, Silverton then manoeuvred the car into a vacant space.

"We're here, so look sharp," Silverton said.

They exited the car in unison. The sound of the closing doors echoed around the damp, and dimly lit car park as they made their way to the exit door.

"This way." Silverton was like an excited school kid as he strode down the corridor and hit the call button for the lift. This was his kind of thing. The buzz was returning once again. The battered metallic doors opened and they got into the cramped, utilitarian box; Silverton chose the lower basement floor.

"Swanky location then?" Steve looked around at the tiny lift.

"It does what I need it to do, and more importantly, I'm left to get on with my work."

The short journey to their destination was completed. Once again the lift doors noisily slid open.

Steve and Roy followed Silverton who led them down another corridor. He stopped, pulled out a bunch of keys, and opened the door.

"Keys? That's a bit analogue for this day and age? I thought you guys would be carrying electronic entry cards."

"You watch too much TV. Sometimes analogue is good, and it can't be hacked." Silverton ushered them into his offices.

Silverton turned on the lights to reveal a small office simply arranged with a plain table with a laptop on it, a few chairs scattered around, and some filing cabinets. In one corner of the room stood a small table with a kettle, an array of chipped mugs, long-life milk, tea bags, and a jar of coffee. The walls were lined in whiteboards which were covered in annotated newspaper clippings. Silverton appeared obsessed with the paranormal, UFO sightings, and aliens. There were reports about Area 51, Bigfoot, the Bermuda Triangle, the Todmorden UFO sightings – and, in particular relevance to that case, the Alan Godfrey alien abduction and the disappearance of Zigmund Adamski.

Steve walked up to one of the whiteboards and read the headline declaring Godfrey giving an interview about his UFO encounter.

"He was a policeman," Silverton said.

"Does that make him a credible witness?" Steve asked.

"It makes him slightly more credible than many of the other cases I've studied."

"I'm not so sure," Steve said and turned around to face Silverton.

"You care to elaborate?" Silverton asked.

"Not really." Steve shook his head.

"You can't leave me hanging after you make a statement like that about the police."

"You want to know why I said that? Okay...I lost my brother while he was in police custody."

"I'm sorry to hear that but I didn't know you had a brother."

"You weren't to know. I was adopted into a family and he was the rock that helped me grow into the household. You know the type, going the extra mile to make me feel welcome as we grew up, never once questioning the fact that we weren't blood brothers. They were all there, the so-called credible witnesses trotted out at the hearing. Railroaded. The case was railroaded. I should have known. But as a black, teenage boy growing up in a world of hidden prejudices, when I look back at it, the outcome was probably inevitable, wasn't it?" Steve chewed on his lower lip.

"Not all policemen are credible, I get that. We're not perfect. Is that why you fled from your apartment when we came for you?" Silverton placed his hand on Steve's shoulder.

"Partly. And partly because I didn't want to place myself in that position, you know, the one my brother faced. I'm the kind the guy who would rather take their chances. I guess that's sort of counter-intuitive to being an accountant, eh?" Steve pulled back slightly allowing Silverton's arm to drop limply to his side.

"But understandable," Roy spoke.

"You have a thing for this kind of stuff then?" Steve eyeballed the headlines again.

"Call it an obsession, I guess, one that eventually led to a job," Silverton replied.

"What about the crackpots? The fakers?" Steve asked.

"The crackpots tend to surface when there's mass media exposure such as the incident over Jerusalem in 2011. That was fun. You should've seen the people that came out of the woodwork with that one. I got a call from someone pretending that he was the second coming around that time. Fucking crazy," Silverton said and laughed.

"What exactly do you do? Forgive me, but you appear out of nowhere and claim to be some sort of guardian angel and here we are, standing in a conspiracy freak's bat cave with little or no explanation." Steve continued to survey the headlines.

Silverton drifted over to the kettle and turned it on. "Tea? Or perhaps you'd prefer coffee?"

"Tea, with milk, one sugar, and an explanation." Steve wasn't letting this go.

"Same for me is fine." Roy was relaxed and seemed at home in the strange surroundings.

"You're looking at the offices of one of Britain's last remaining UFO experts. I work for the British Government's UFO investigation department. This is my research," Silverton gestured to the walls.

"Excuse me?" Steve shook his head, "I thought you guys were a myth from the Cold War era."

"No myths here. I'm deadly serious, but in these financially chastened times even the most important government departments cannot escape the clutches of budgetary reductions." Silverton closed his eyes for a moment.

"And where are your headquarters? Whitehall? GCHQ?"

"You're standing in them." Silverton beamed with pride.

"This place? You must be joking!" Steve laughed.

"Well, it beats a tent," Roy butted in.

"It probably does when you put it like that," Silverton said.

"Who is your boss?" Steve asked.

"I report directly to the Secretary of State for Defense and this office is no joke. This is what happens with budget cuts. I mean, why bother chasing stories about UFO encounters when most of them turn out to be faked for the YouTube and Instagram generation?" Silverton let out a long sigh. He placed the drinks carefully on the coasters and took a seat. Roy and Steve sat opposite him.

"This is it? Your entire department is contained in this office?" Steve asked.

"There are benefits."

"Such as?" Roy asked.

"They leave me alone to get on with things, and I have access to endless amounts of classified information. And of course, I can use my influence to ensure things get done in ways that avoid attention; *losing* vehicles, for example."

"False flags? And covering up mistakes?" Steve asked.

"Precisely. You catch on fast."

"And what about the government? What do they expect from you?" Steve folded his arms.

"Like all governments, protecting the flow of sensitive information into the public domain is a major strategy. Possible sightings that are deemed not in the public's interest tend to, shall we say, get sidestepped into non-threatening environments via official channels such as ours. That way we can handle the information, cleanse it, and repackage it in a way that is better suited for mainstream media and public consumption."

"You mean a cover-up?" Steve chuckled.

"Cover-up is a strong statement, but if you have to deal with an incident that could undermine the stability of a nation and its people then sometimes it is better to cleanse the incident to make it more palatable rather than deal with the impact afterwards."

"I thought you only dealt with UFO sightings?" Steve asked.

"Yes, mainly, but sometimes these stories, especially from the classified archives, can be used to take people away from the real story – stories other departments need to lose. You know, generate a human-interest story and keep the people happy, that kind of crap. But then, of course, there are the various unofficial channels."

"You mean unofficial leaks, like those from Assange or Snowden?" Roy asked. This was an area that held particular interest to Roy and Silverton knew it. "You realise that no government has declared any of the facts behind those leaks as false? They have, to use your word, *sidestepped* these leaks and chose to focus on going after the individuals. Don't you find that weird? I mean at least come out and deny this stuff if it's fake – *if* it's fake."

Silverton shrugged. "I'm just one man in an office doing my job. I tend not to stray far from the main subject matter."

"So, like Roy said, you operate in other areas?" Steve asked.

"Sometimes subject matter from other areas crosses into my sphere but I'm mainly talking about accidental UFO sightings, particularly of military and commercial aircraft. They always seem to attract the wrong attention. God knows, maybe these so-called little green men *are* spying on our technology." Silverton was getting carried away with himself, "The thing is, the monitoring technology these aircraft carry is so sophisticated that sightings are almost inevitable. And with passengers using their smartphones to capture images, well, you can imagine the number of incidents we have to trawl through. Most of them are completely explainable…"

"And those that aren't? What happens to them?" Steve asked.

"Well, that depends, sometimes it's good to see one make the mainstream press," Silverton sat back in his chair.

"Why? What makes a so-called sighting *suitable*?"

"Ones that take people's eye off the ball. Ones that divert them from the real story elsewhere. One that's safe to put into the public domain without causing mass hysteria," Silverton slowly nodded his head as he spoke.

"Let me guess, it was one such incident that brought you into contact with Kallyuke?" Steve floated the idea.

"Not exactly but close. Charley—"

"Sandford by any chance?" Steve had a hint of sarcasm in his voice.

"Yes. Persuasive, isn't he?" Silverton chuckled.

"I suppose he is," Steve said, thinking back to his first meeting with Sandford.

"We had to deal with a minor incident, a loose end that needed tidying up. He knew of my work."

"So, you cooked up a story to help him out?" Steve didn't have a hint of surprise in his voice.

"Well, yes, and to be honest it was almost like a test, you know, to see if I was up to the job."

"Don't you want to tell anyone about this? I mean, with your contacts in the press hasn't it once crossed your mind that you could sell this story for millions, retire somewhere sunny and kiss this shit hole goodbye," Roy asked.

"I wouldn't do it for the same reason that you wouldn't. Trust," Silverton replied.

"No wonder Kallyuke likes us." Roy smiled.

"And you can say what you like about our diversionary tactics but it's a tried and tested methodology that works." Silverton laughed.

"Let's just hope it is a methodology that we don't need to use too often," Steve said.

Steve looked on as Silverton logged in to the laptop on the table and turned the screen around so he and Roy could see it. He tapped away at the keyboard until the screen was full of different views of the same motorway. The grainy black and white images were captured on the same date and time as those taken by the traffic cameras placed along the road. They looped the same forty-five-second time period until each of the cameras whited out; Steve instantly recognised the location where the footage was captured.

"How did you get hold of this?" Steve asked.

"With great difficulty. I had to pull a few strings at the Highways Agency but as you now know, pulling strings is kind of a skill of mine," Silverton replied.

"Is this the only copy of the CCTV footage?" Steve pointed to the screen.

"Yes. We wiped the main drives at the monitoring centre and had this footage replaced with stock footage that matched the time of day and weather conditions and then overlaid the date and time information."

"You're very thorough at this covering up the game, aren't you?" Steve looked intently at the screen.

"We have to be. One tiny mistake, even a single incriminating frame, could unravel the whole operation and leave us answering a lot of unwelcome questions," Silverton said and then played the slowed-down footage of one of the cameras. "See this?" He pointed to the shadowy figures of the two men under the flyover.

Steve squint at the screen. "Just about."

"Watch this bit." Silverton slowed down the footage to a frame every few seconds. "This man here raises what looks like a weapon."

Steve stared at the screen. "What the hell is that?"

The shadowy figure fired a bolt of light across the carriageway. Silverton froze the frame and they all moved closer to the screen to study the beam of light.

"That's the source of the light," Steve said.

"And the light caused the line on the tarmac," Roy confirmed.

"I like to call it the *Time Travel Stinger*," Silverton said and then sat back in his chair and beamed a satisfied smile. "On account that this beam of light cuts across the tarmac, much like a stinger would with a line of nails to puncture tires, but that's where the similarities end."

"And, of course, it cut the line in time," Steve muttered while the advancing frames unraveled the mystery of what happened after they drove through the line.

"Precisely. This device opened a portal and sent you guys into the future, along with your guests. It was a reckless operation that was bound to attract public interest, we're lucky the subsequent crash didn't cause any fatalities."

"Do we know who those people are?" Steve asked.

"No, the images are too grainy, and they didn't stick around to watch the unfolding carnage. We think they made their escape via the slip road, and of course, once off the motorway there are very few cameras; whoever did this was well aware that CCTV cameras would be recording their actions. But in bad light, these cameras can only pick up so much, especially when you factor in the cover the bridge afforded them."

"They weren't that professional when you consider how risky it was. They could have easily been caught or even hurt during the crash," Roy commented.

"That may be the case and you may be right. They may have just been lucky, but of course, that is all in the past now and we have no further clue as to who these people were, apart from the evidence that points to Trader activity." Silverton reached over and closed the laptop.

"But why do this? And why me?" Steve asked.

"Probably to disrupt our plans, but this is a very public way to carry out that task, almost reckless. As for you my friend, you are one of the chosen few, the boots on the ground, here to disrupt their plans," Silverton said.

"Boots on the ground…Sandford said that," Steve replied.

"These people are agents of chaos, determined to pull the rug from underneath us all. They see no value in the future, they only see their plan to wreck our future. They won't see the consequences of their actions but Kallyuke hatched a plan to thwart them in their tracks and you are part of that plan. The perfect sleeper agent."

"Sandford also used that term, but what I don't understand is how an accountant can suddenly become some sort of James Bond agent."

"That's exactly what Kallyuke didn't want you to be. I'm not privy to every detail, as some of this is highly classified, but your normality is hugely in your favour. It makes you hard to track. You're not likely to wander into a swanky bar and order a Martini vodka are you?"

"You got me there!" Steve laughed. "But seriously, the evidence points to the fact that perhaps I'm not as hard to track as we may think."

"Maybe so. But Kallyuke needed people from the future here in the present who had little or no footprint from that time. It makes you harder to trace. Placing you here at birth and then activating you at the right time was the best way to achieve that goal."

"But that appears to have been a fallacy because as we now know they can track me."

"We think they can. Who knows what intel they had at their disposal to attempt that stunt on the M6. For all we know, it could have been luck. They may have been after myself or Roy."

"From what little I know at the moment I very much doubt it. You don't launch an operation like that and base it purely on luck," Steve folded his arms.

"But that doesn't change our mission. We have been entrusted to stop them from carrying out their plan, and collectively, with the support of Roy and myself, I hope we succeed, for the sake of all our futures. Kallyuke trusted my judgment enough to let me be a part of this mission and I am determined to repay that trust."

"But what if my cover is blown?"

"Only time will tell if that's the case," Silverton replied.

"You're not sure then, are you?" Steve tapped the table with his index finger.

"I don't know, but for now I need to wind down the crash investigation and ensure the files containing that footage never see the light of day," Silverton said.

"No wonder Kallyuke trusts you." Steve found himself agreeing with Roy's earlier comment.

"I was once told that when you understand how the mind of a conspiracy theorist works, you know, what makes them tick, then you can understand how to create a diversion that will enable you to smokescreen your way out of a tight situation and draw their attention away from the real story," Silverton said profoundly.

11

Paris.Present-Day.

Clint and Matt jumped off the packed Eurostar train at Gare du Nord in Paris. The station was a hive of activity, and the evening rush hour was starting to kick in.

"What was the nearest station to Rue Richard Lenoir?" Matt looked at the Metro map on the station wall.

People were bustling past them, in the background, a busker was playing on a guitar, in another area of the station a small group of people was huddled together, all wearing sleeping bags to keep warm as they held out paper cups to beg for money from the passing commuters, mostly without much luck. A woman in a dark uniform stood in the middle of the station holding out a collection tin for the Armee de Salut. The cafes and bars were doing brisk business as Parisians took advantage of the waiting time before their trains to grab some refreshment. The public announcement system played pre-recorded security messages, first in France and then English advising people to keep their belongings close by at all times. Street food vendors were selling a wide selection of easy-to-eat foods, their delicious aromas wafting their way through the station.

"Voltaire." Clint looked at the map. "The quicker we get this done, the quicker we get home. Don't know about you but I'm getting tired of this. I mean look at it?" Clint was tetchy.

"Look at what?" Matt looked around and shrugged his shoulders.

"It's just so damn backwards…trains? To think we questioned what happened in the next fifty years after this? You only need to look around to see we were doomed. This place is a disaster waiting to happen." Clint shook his head as he looked around. He pointed across to the huddle of people begging and the busker.

"We're not used to how they had to live, things we wouldn't even consider possible are taken for granted here," Matt said.

"Would you stay? Would you see out the rest of your days here? Live in this time?" Clint put Matt on the spot.

"I'm not sure. I don't think it is as clear-cut as you make out. There's so much we can learn and so much to enjoy here. Besides, it's not like we've done anything apart from following orders from the moment we arrived. We've not experienced what this period has to offer, have we?" Matt replied.

"Name me one thing you would enjoy more here and now."

"That's a fairly difficult one to answer but at this precise moment we have to get somewhere and we have a job to carry out, that's the priority." Matt wanted to push on.

"Maybe, but I doubt you'd be impressed even if you did spend time here, it's so damn basic. Look at how they live, what am I saying, *how* do they live like this?" Clint replied.

"Do you fancy sampling a bit of Parisian nightlife while we're here? I mean, if you want to see how these people live, what better way to find out than to do the tourist thing," Matt suggested.

"No, Armstrong will go nuts if we don't follow the plan and make a mess of things." Clint shook his head.

"We didn't mean to make a mess on the M6, we followed orders, anyway, do you always have to follow the rules?" Matt asked as they made their way to the platform.

"No, but I'm wary of the shit we caused back on the M6, our fault or not, so, you know what will happen if we step out of line…" Clint paused for a moment.

"You know what? You're probably correct. I think perhaps we leave these people to live their lives, just get the mission done and get the hell out of here," Matt said as he led the way to the correct platform to catch the Metro to Voltaire.

12

London.Present-Day.

Silverton took a sip from his mug and returned the cup very precisely onto the coaster. "I don't like stains and this table stains easily," he said by way of explanation. Roy and Steve looked to make sure their mugs were also correctly placed on the coasters.

"It wasn't meant to be like this, so I'm told," Silverton spoke again, this time in a softer tone.

"What do you mean?" Steve asked.

"The initial timeline was created by a team of scientists who were working under instruction from Kallyuke. But the motivation for it was forced upon him, he had no choice."

"You're talking about the virus aren't you?" Steve asked.

"Yes. Secure the source compounds to create a suitable vaccine or the human race could face extinction, those were the choices faced by Kallyuke. Not an easy decision is it? Especially given the risks of messing with the timeline," Silverton looked at the pair of them as he spoke.

"Charley discussed this with me in Santa Monica. He just blurted it out but he said so many things it was hard to take them all in. Will the virus really be this devastating?" Steve asked.

"Yes. It's a pandemic. It spread like wildfire, according to Kallyuke it has already killed millions and will continue to kill millions of people until the vaccine is developed," Silverton replied.

"That puts this whole thing into perspective, doesn't it?" Steve took a deep breath.

"It does." Silverton looked at the table, grabbed his mug, and took a sip of coffee before carefully returning the mug to the coaster.

"Was Charley right about coming back to this time to look for a cure? I mean you have to understand he said a lot and I've literally been dropped into this," Steve asked.

"Yes, Charley was right. Certain compounds are needed to create a vaccine that doesn't exist anymore in their time. This virus has been around for decades so the compounds they had available with the initial outbreak are no longer available. Plus, they didn't have the awareness of the virus nor the infrastructure to create the vaccine when it first broke so it spread without being checked. They had no choice but to come back to the here and now to find the missing compounds. This was the only failsafe option," Silverton paused and looked around at the various headlines. "What Kallyuke didn't realise was that by embarking on this mission the very thing that could save humanity could open the door to its eventual destruction."

"Why bother in the first place?" Roy asked.

"Because they had to. You don't simply give up on the human race, do you?" Silverton replied.

"And the vaccine was the only solution available to them," Steve muttered.

"Correct. There was an infection spreading through the planet, and fast. It only infects humans but the result was that many areas became, or should I say will become, uninhabitable."

"What kind of infection?" Roy asked.

"A by-product of decades of living in contained, sterile spaces. Charley said it all, I just chose not to listen," Steve said.

"The body's immune system simply went to sleep. It couldn't fight anything and couldn't cope when faced with this new threat. The virus is airborne, carried by small insects, and is nearly always fatal, although once infected it can take years to mutate into the full virus, which is why the vaccine is crucial to protect the remaining population. The problem is that there are no obvious signs of infection while the virus lays dormant in an infected person, which means that they can infect others without even knowing," Silverton said.

"Kallyuke never mentioned this to me," Roy remarked and frowned.

"Kallyuke was careful about who knew about the virus, plus it wouldn't affect you should you ever arrive in their time, which of course you did. You see, your immune system is fully functional and would fight off this virus so why cause unnecessary alarm?"

"What I still don't understand is how we get from a lifesaving vaccine to these Traders smuggling our natural resources forward in time. How did that happen?" Steve asked.

"Some of the scientists went rogue and stole the technology to create another timeline to use it for their own plans. The re-emergence of the virus sparked a rebellion, one faction wanted a change in direction, but instead of trying to salvage a dying planet, they hatched a plan to find a new planet capable of sustaining life, somewhere they could colonise and adapt so they could start afresh."

"What do you mean, like Mars?" Steve asked.

"That's all I know," Silverton replied.

"You seem to know a lot," Steve pointed out.

"I'll say again, that's all I know, nothing else." Silverton paused and then continued, "Aside from the fact that part of their plan involves taking as many resources as they can forward through the timeline to carry out this plan, whatever that may be, which is where we come in."

"And this is where I come in, Charley called me the perfect sleeper agent. Boots on the ground…that phrase keeps coming back to haunt me," Steve said.

"And it will continue to do so."

"I was afraid you might say that," Steve replied.

"The activation of sleeper agents like you is a long-term plan, we can only hope this works."

"What's next?" Steve asked.

"I'm charged with getting us to Paris and to rendezvous with another operative"

"Paris?" said Steve, "I thought you were supposed to get me to London?"

"Need to know basis I'm afraid. We can't tell who is monitoring us and what tech they're using to gather intel. Until we can work that out, all mission information is disclosed at the last minute."

"Right. So, we're just heading off to Paris? And that's that? Do you have any idea what I've been through over the past twenty-four hours?" Steve folded his arms.

"I do, but this is not the time to dwell on that. We have to keep going and ensure that we do everything we can to stop them. Charley was right, as far as we can tell you are the perfect agent. I doubt they would have suspected Kallyuke's plan and with more of you being activated that will only serve to confuse their surveillance operations further and buy us valuable time in trying to close their operations down."

"I only wish I had been invited to the meetings to decide my future." Steve bit his upper lip.

"You'll have to play catch up, and I'm sorry for that," Silverton replied.

"You're not the one that should apologise. And anyway, what about Paris?" Steve asked again.

"There's been a tip-off from an operative working within a cell of Traders. This is an incredibly important breakthrough. You see, we have had little or no visual intel on these people." Silverton clasped his hands together and leaned his elbows on the table.

"When you say operative, am I right in assuming you mean a double agent?" Steve asked.

"Correct. Our contact in Paris received a tip-off from him."

"We have a contact in Paris as well?" Steve asked.

"Keep up, Steve, I know this must be difficult but things are moving fast and we have to act accordingly." Silverton was keen to press on.

Steve stood up and looked down on Silverton. "Do me a favour."

"What's that?" Silverton stood up.

"Next time you lot decide to play with the timeline and fuck with the future of humanity—"

"What?" Silverton asked.

"Do it in a couple of hundred years, that way I don't need to be involved, okay?" Steve said.

"That decision is way beyond my remit. For now, we need to get some rest." Silverton looked at them both.

"What hotel are we booked into?" Roy asked as he yawned.

"No hotel I'm afraid." Silverton reached behind his right shoulder and pressed a small button on the wall. The wall sprung to life and slid open to reveal another corridor, this time lined with concrete. "But we do have this," Silverton said, standing up and gesturing toward the corridor.

"And what exactly is *this*?" Steve stood up to get a better view.

"This is a military-grade bunker that sleeps five people. It has washroom facilities, a kitchenette, and each of the five bedrooms is kitted out with standard grade military rations for a week, along with basic TV.

This, my friends, is your room for the night," Silverton said.

"You want us to sleep here?" Steve took a step back and looked down the corridor.

"It's comfier than it looks," Silverton smiled and winked back at the pair of them.

"Your office is like a bloody Tardis. What exactly is this place, because I bet there is a lot more to it than you're letting on?" Roy asked.

"Standard feature on all military and government facilities, no matter how small, is to have a bunker to ensure key staff survives an attack."

"An attack from what?" Steve said.

"Could be anything, a military coup, an attack from an adversary, could even be an alien invasion, but the first rule of government is to ensure you can govern in a crisis. Each facility has its own bunker. Of course, there is a checklist to say who can come in, but for today we'll make allowances."

"What, you mean like a guest list?" Steve chuckled to himself.

"In any crisis, there needs to be a point of order and a list of priority personnel who can ensure the country can defend itself and rebuild after an attack."

"Who would be on the list for this place?" Steve asked.

"Well, that depends on where they are but it is entirely feasible that if the Prime Minister was in the area they would immediately re-route them to this bunker, at least until an assessment of the attack could take place." Silverton guided them down the corridor. "After that, the next move is down to the severity of the attack and how quickly emergency protocols can be actioned. It's an exact science."

Silverton led the way as they walked down the short corridor.

"There's enough clean water to last for two weeks," Silverton said as they looked in at the tiny kitchenette.

"But only enough food rations for one week?" Roy asked.

"Water is essential for life. In an emergency, you can stretch out the rations to make them last longer but without water, you're virtually incapacitated within days and dead soon afterward," Silverton said.

"This place is self-sufficient then." Roy nodded in approval.

"We have our own power supply too, and emergency comms."

"Okay, so who is in which room?" Steve seemed ready to sleep.

"Just choose, we have a few hours and after that, we need to get to Paris. I'll wake you when we need to leave. For now, grab some shut-eye." Silverton walked into the room nearest the secret entrance.

Steve pushed open the door nearest to him and slumped onto the bed, not bothering to get undressed. He stared up at the ceiling and reflected on the day. Was he starting to get answers to the many questions he had stored up over the years? Why was Kallyuke keen to avoid answering any of his questions? Questions ran amuck in his brain, refusing to allow him to sleep.

He thought of his ex-wife and daughter, Janine and Tanya, though he felt a million miles away from his previous life. What would his daughter think of him now? Would she respect him for who he was, or recoil from this new life?

Slowly his body and mind relented and he drifted into some form of sleep.

Steve tossed and turned in the small bed until he sensed something wasn't right; something was burning. He turned over and held up his left arm, to his horror the lower part was on fire; the flesh turned charcoal black as the flames spread. He jumped out of the bed and rushed over to the small basin, twisted the tap until the water gushed out, bounced off the basin and onto the floor. He screamed out in agony, the flames started to recede, the water seeped into the gaping burn holes in his flesh. He screamed again as he forced his arm under the water in the basin and watched as streams of blood flowed from the open wounds.

Steve woke up as Silverton and Roy barged into his room. He sat bolt upright, staring at his arm. "It was on fire!"

"You must have had a bad dream," Silverton replied.

"But the basin, there's water everywhere, blood. Look!" Steve looked over to the bone dry basin.

Steve didn't know whether to feel foolish or annoyed at himself, but it had been so vivid.

"Okay, looks like there's no need for a wake-up call. We need to get to the airport fast. I have a private jet on standby. We'll be in Paris within the hour."

Steve got up and wandered down to the washroom. He looked at himself in the mirror, stuck out his tongue, and then squint tightly. He was still awake and nothing had happened to him.

"Come on let's go," Silverton was keen to get moving.

"I'm coming," Roy shouted from his room.

Steve took one last look in the mirror then hurried down the short corridor and into the main room.

Silverton grabbed his jacket off the coat stand and ushered both Roy and Steve out of his poky office and down the hallway. They jumped in the car and sped off down the road toward the airport.

"I don't have my passport on me," Steve said while he shuffled through the pockets in his jacket and looked at the aircraft parked on the runway on the other side of the fence.

"You won't need it. I have a special arrangement with security staff at both airports." Silverton drove up to a private entrance gate at the City of London airport.

The security man acknowledged Silverton and waved them through. Silverton opened the window while the car crawled past the guard, "Welcome back Commander Silverton, good to see you again."

"Thanks, and good to see you Frank, is the family okay?" Silverton asked.

"Good as can be, thanks. Have a safe flight." And with that, Silverton drove off toward a huge hangar.

"You're not kidding about arrangements, are you? And *Commander*? I thought you were a detective?" Roy asked.

"I'm a Commander, but when it's required I can be a detective, it depends on what ID I need to use and what level of authority is required. Anyway, once a detective always a detective." Silverton smirked back at Roy.

"You seem to have all the bases covered," Steve said.

"I'm a government agent. We have access to certain privileges, no questions asked and no explanation needed," Silverton replied.

"No wonder Kallyuke likes you," Steve said this time looking at Roy with a knowing glance.

Silverton parked the car in a hangar next to a large white Gulfstream jet. Roy and Steve jumped out of the car, slammed the doors shut, and followed him up to the small set of stairs at the run.

Once inside, they sat down and prepared for take-off. Steve marveled at the plush leather interior of the jet. It even had a drinks cabinet.

"This makes a change compared to your office," he shouted across to Silverton as the jet started its slow crawl toward the runway.

"As I mentioned before, Kallyuke wanted me for my network of contacts, and the fact I can get things done, you know, cut through the red tape."

"Is this jet government-owned?" Roy yelled.

The engines fired up to maximum, the jet scampered down the runway and took off.

"Yes. I use it to get to investigation sites around the world. It comes standard with a pilot on standby at all times, fully fuelled and of course, no questions asked. Just how I like it," Silverton replied.

13

Paris.Present-Day.
The Night Before.

Clint and Matt checked into their rooms at the Hotel Richard. It was a modest hotel, but one that fit their need to lay low whilst waiting for further instructions from Armstrong.

Matt knocked on Clint's room door and poked his head around to talk, "Are you coming then?"

"If we must, but let's be careful, please."

"There's this place down the road called Zero Zero, looks like my kind of place," Matt said with a grin.

"What do you mean it looks like *your* kind of place? Since when were you an expert on twenty-first-century nightlife?" Clint laughed.

"Since now, and try to keep those comments to yourself, I don't want to scare the natives with any talk of time travel. They'll think you're a bit odd," Matt said.

Zero Zero was only a short walk. They entered the club to be greeted by the beats of a DJ playing havoc on the decks.

"They call this entertainment? It's a wonder they're not all deaf!" Clint shouted.

"Just leave me to do the talking, I don't want to spend the rest of the evening listening to you discuss the intricacies of the space-time continuum, and I doubt anyone here does either." Matt pushed his way to the front of the bar.

Matt didn't have a clue about what to order, the colourful drinks menu was a brave new adventure for him. He closed his eyes, randomly pointed at the menu, and ordered two Pina Coladas from the barman. Having paid for them, he turned and wove his way through the scrum of people.

Clint was sitting at a table with two women. He seemed to be talking with them fairly confidently which gave Matt a sense of optimism. Matt walked up to the table and placed the enormous drinks on the table in front of Clint.

"What the hell is this? I asked for water." Clint tried to work out what was now in front of him.

"I had no idea what any of it was, the names were riddles so I just pointed and ordered. This is called a Pina Colada. I think it looks great." Matt looked to the women who laughed at the drinks he had chosen.

"Tastes like some form of refined sugar. It should be okay, I guess," Clint said and continued to drink from the straw.

"What are your names?" Matt shouted across the table to the women.

"Pardon?" one of the women responded.

"Names?" Matt repeated.

"Ah, okay, English…" one of the women looked at her friend, "My name is Estelle and this is my good friend Adele." The other woman nodded at them both in acknowledgment.

"Okay, very good," Matt sensed a joke was being played on them.

"Et tu?" Estelle asked.

"Tu? What do you mean?" Matt asked.

"Your names, what are your names?"

Matt sensed a chance to get even, "My name is Bill, and this is my friend Phil," Matt glared at Clint because he wasn't paying attention. He was far too obsessed with the drink which was now half gone.

"Oh nice, like us you rhyme, where are you from?" asked Adele.

"That's not easy to answer," Matt said while Clint gulped his drink.

A waiter approached the table. "Voulez-vous plus de boissons?"

"What did he say?" Matt asked the women.

"He said would you like more drinks," Estelle said.

"Please, may we have two more Pina Coladas?" Matt spoke slowly and pointed to the drinks, the waiter looked and nodded.

"May we have a drink also?" Adele asked.

"Yes, of course," Matt was not used to how things worked in the bars of Paris, or of any city in this time for that matter. Adele ordered two drinks from the waiter who then chuckled at something she said in French while she glanced across at Matt and Clint.

Minutes later the drinks arrived and punctuated the silence between them, Matt handed over some money to the waiter. The alcohol started to flow, it was a sensation that Clint had not experienced on many occasions and seemed to release him from his tenseness.

"What do you do for a living?" Estelle asked them.

"We work together."

"So, what do you do?" Estelle asked again and chuckled at Adele.

"That would be telling," Matt sipped some of his cocktail.

"Let me guess. Are you secret agents?" Adele asked, she was still laughing at their drinks.

"Not quite," Clint replied, the collection of four large cocktails on the table dominating his view.

"What are you then?" Estelle laughed.

"It means that…" Clint was just about to speak again when Matt jumped in.

"It means that what we do is a secret, and not interesting," Matt said.

"And it means we can't say any more," Clint briefly closed his eyes, he felt himself growing woozy, and the sugar rush was getting the better of him.

"I love men of mystery," Estelle said.

"What do you do?" Matt asked.

"This mainly." Adele was utterly honest in her response, she pointed to the bar and the DJ.

"This?" Matt looked around at the bar.

"We drink, we party and then we do PR," Adele replied.

"What is PR?" Clint slurred.

"What is PR? Are you joking? It means we party with clients and get them press, you know, help them talk to the media, make them look fabulous, famous…and interesting." Estelle took a sip from her drink.

"Should we be talking to these people? After all, I think Armstrong hates the press," Clint looked at Matt.

"Who is Armstrong?" Adele asked.

"Just someone we know," Clint said, "no one of interest."

"Is he a secret agent as well?" Adele persisted.

"No," Clint was beginning to sway in his seat.

"Relax okay? They have no real interest in us," Matt looked at Clint, then he spoke to Estelle, "isn't that right?"

"Oh, you can be assured that is correct. We have no interest," and with that, the women picked up their drinks, left the table, and walked into the other room behind the bar.

Clint and Matt looked at each other, "This isn't going well is it?" Matt said.

"I'm having a great time," Clint slurred his words.

"I think we should go back to the hotel before we get into any trouble." Matt got up and helped Clint to his feet. They walked out of the bar and back to the hotel.

It took Clint several attempts to open his room with the key card, but he eventually succeeded. He fell into his bed and went straight to sleep. Matt opened the door to his room and noticed a white envelope on the floor in front of him; it was sealed but completely blank.

He bent down to open it and take out the piece of paper inside.

Matt read the handwritten note contained inside the envelope, "Now we have a plan."

And with that, he slumped onto the bed and went to sleep.

14

Paris.Present-Day.

At five o'clock the next morning, Clint was woken by a vigorous knock at the door. Matt was ready to go but Clint was not.

Matt banged on the door again.

"Okay! Okay! I'm coming," Clint got up, dragged on some clothes, and opened the door.

"We have to go and fast. I've received our instructions," Matt said.

"What did they say?" Clint asked.

"The two men Armstrong mentioned will be carrying large navy holdalls and will be outside a cafe near the station. We are to establish contact and follow their instructions to the letter."

"And that's it? I mean nothing else?" Clint rubbed his eyes.

"I guess that's all we need to know at the moment. You know how protective Armstrong is about this information."

They rushed out of the hotel and made their way back to the Voltaire metro station.

The train to the Trocadero approached the station and juddered to a halt. They grabbed a couple of seats in the half-empty train as it rattled its way across the city. Clint looked around at the broad assortment of other passengers, all of whom shared the common factor of looking tired of being on the train. Newspapers rustled; feet were tapping away to music while some people just mentally drifted off as they waited to arrive at their stop.

When the train arrived at the Trocadero, Matt and Clint got off and made their way to the foyer.

"Which cafe?" Clint asked.

"I've been told to meet our contacts outside the newspaper stall next to Cafe Kleber," Matt said.

"Bit risky isn't it? Being out in the open like that?" Clint shook his head and frowned.

"Sometimes something that appears to be obvious to us is not obvious at all," Matt replied.

They walked up the stairs of the station and approached the newspaper stand outside the cafe; Matt noticed two men who matched the images Armstrong had shown them in London; they were both carrying large navy holdalls. He walked toward them and nodded. The nod was returned in acknowledgment.

"Not too close," one of the contacts said in a thick French accent as they walked back down the stairs of the Trocadero metro station. "We need to not look like we are a group of people, too many will attract attention, make some problems for us, you understand?"

Matt and Clint backed off but continued to follow their contacts across the busy foyer. One of the men strode off, leaving the others behind; he walked unnoticed through the crowds and down a small corridor off to the side of the main entrance. They signaled Matt and Clint to wait where they were.

Matt wanted to make sure that they didn't look awkward as they waited amongst the crowds, he left Clint and picked up a French newspaper at one of the stalls. He pretended to read it until the stall owner shouted at him to buy it. He paid and walked away.

"You can read that?" Clint asked as Matt returned with the paper.

"No, but that's not the point. The point is that I'm trying to blend in."

Within a matter of minutes, Matt and Clint got the signal to follow the other contact. They maintained a sensible distance, while commuters rushing to get to wherever they were going continuously bumped into them. Despite the human obstacles, they zig-zagged their way across the foyer toward the small corridor. There was an open door at the end. They all went through and pulled it tightly closed.

All four of them stood in a circle. Alain handed Clint and Matt two torches from their holdalls.

"It is time for some introduction, no? My name is Alain and this is Jean-Paul," said one of the contacts.

"I'm Matt, and this is Clint."

"Did you travel or are you assimilated?" Alain asked.

"If by travel you mean *have we come back* then yes. Who is assimilated?" Clint asked.

"I am," Jean-Paul spoke up while he pulled a torch from out of his jacket.

"A new ally in the fight for our cause?" Matt asked.

Jean-Paul nodded.

"What's in the bags?" Clint asked.

"Everything we need to carry out the extraction, including spare bags, plus a few items for extra insurance," Alain replied.

"Extra insurance?" Matt asked.

"We are not here to talk; we are here to do. Each person has their reasons for their choices, I do not question them." Alain paused to look around, "What have you been told?"

"Nothing," Clint replied. "What can you tell us?"

"Paris is unique in as much as these underground tunnels allow access to the soil behind the walls. The catacombs will provide us with access as well." Alain continued, "But even more important is what we found in this soil, diamonds. For some reason, there is an abundance of them."

"How come these have not been picked up until now?" Clint asked, surprised.

"You have to know how to gain access to the right catacombs to start looking. This particular set of tunnels were only discovered recently. There is a drain outside the station that was initially the main point of access," Alain said and shone his torch down into the tunnel and back toward the door they had just come through. "This door has been kept sealed for many years but we were able to trackback to this point of entry using sophisticated scanning equipment sent back to us from our comrades in the future. You see, this part of the tunnel was dug recently as a link into the catacombs but the authorities kept it quiet, they didn't want more tourists flocking to disturb this area."

"That makes sense. Any thoughts on the diamonds and how they got there?" Matt asked.

"We are not sure, their location is erratic and we have to sometimes take large quantities of soil to find even one diamond, but they are there. Especially near the catacombs. These disused Metro tunnels provide us with the perfect access to them," Jean-Paul said and flashed his torch around the tunnel to prove the point.

"And no one knows about them?" Matt asked.

"Well, we can't be sure of that, but we are confident," Jean-Paul replied.

"There is one other possibility about their origins, they could be the buried treasures from the aristocracy, hidden during the revolution. However, the fact that only diamonds are here makes us wonder, but it could explain the locations being near the catacombs," Alain explained.

"Aren't the catacombs full of bodies?" Clint asked.

"Time has taken its toll, there are no complete skeletons but lots of walls of bones and skulls and this also makes us wonder about the location of the diamonds," Alain said.

"How many are there?" Matt asked.

"We are not sure. We did some testing after some initial scans of the area, but that is all. We have a location to test now to see how much is there, that may give us more clues as to how many we can expect to find in other similar locations within the catacombs," Alain replied.

"We'll need to fill those spare bags you have with samples of the diamonds and send them forward for further analysis, just to be sure we are correct in assuming these are what we think they are as this may be a perfect location for further extractions," Matt said. "Will you lead the way?"

Clint and Matt followed Jean-Paul as he took the lead down a long, dark tunnel, their torches offering the only respite from the relentless darkness; Alain remained a few paces behind them. Water seeped down the walls of the tunnel as they progressed deeper underground. Jean-Paul signaled for them to be quiet and stop for a moment, pointing at a light up ahead and the silhouette of someone sitting on a chair. Clint noticed the faint glow of a cigarette that person was smoking. Jean-Paul crouched down to avoid detection and the others followed his lead. Clint could feel the dampness from the floor on the knee of his jeans.

"What is it?" Clint whispered to Jean-Paul.

"Must be some sort of security officer, maybe for staff. I don't know, it may be a new facility but it wasn't in the plans we saw." Jean-Paul was puzzled.

"We need to deal with this. What have we got?" Clint asked.

"I have just the thing," Alain said as he pulled a small gun with a silencer from his bag and passed it to Clint.

"Thanks." Clint held the gun in his hand.

"I didn't sign up for this," Jean-Paul looked at it in shock.

"Just stay here while I take a closer look," Clint said and with that, he crawled along the tunnel floor staying as near to the wall as he could.

As he closed in on the silhouetted figure, he could make out a man in some sort of uniform. His hat was just about visible in the light shining from the office doorway. The man was clearly oblivious to Clint's presence.

Clint got as near as he dared to, he took the gun and slowly pulled back the hammer. The man took a long drag on his cigarette. Clint, fearing the noise would alert the man, took in long shallow breaths of damp air. He crawled a few more inches toward his target.

The man looked across in Clint's direction. Clint exhaled slowly and gradually got to his feet, keeping tight to the wall to avoid detection. He was now about fifteen feet away from the man, but the lack of light meant he was still hidden. The iron support struts protruding from the tunnel walls offered Clint some cover, but he could feel cold water dribble down the slime-covered metal as he stayed as close to the wall as possible.

The man stood up and dropped his cigarette to the ground, stubbing it out with his boot. Clint readied himself. This was his best chance. He stepped away from the wall, raised his weapon, and fired a shot at the man before he could register what was happening. The silencer did its job, and the dull thud of the bullet hitting the man in the head was the only sound. The man stumbled backward, the bullet exited the other side of his head and hit the wall with a thud; the noise reverberated along the tunnel. The man slumped to the ground.

Clint rushed across to the man and nudged him with his foot to ensure he was dead. The others followed. Jean-Paul flashed his torch at the body and glanced down to see blood pouring from the head wound, he then walked a few feet away. A moment later the others heard him retching.

"We need to get this body into the office, and try to clean up this mess as best as we can, do you understand?" Alain demanded.

Matt and Clint grabbed a leg each. Alain was left with the delicate task of carrying the man's torso. They kicked open the door to the tiny office and put the body in an upright floor standing locker. They slammed the locker shut and jammed the door handle.

"What is this place?" Matt wiped the sweat from his forehead.

Alain was washing off some of the blood from his clothes using the tiny sink in the corner of the room. "It looks like a security office, maybe for the guards who patrol the tunnels."

Jean-Paul stood in the doorway wiping the final bits of vomit from his face.

"What are they guarding?" Clint placed the gun back in the bag.

"Probably many things, you know, checking for people who get lost down here, making sure the tunnels don't get used by homeless people, the usual. They've also had issues with groups of people using the catacombs as places for social meetings," Alain replied.

"Social meetings?" Clint asked.

"We need to move quickly, this man will be missed and others will come to find him, we cannot delay." Alain was keen to press on.

With only the beams of light from their torches giving any clue to their location, the four men progressed further into the bowels of Paris.

15

London.2618.

Richard, Tamsin, and Kieran sat on a row of chairs in a stark, white room alongside Stan, the lorry driver. It was like being back at school, Kieran had remarked; this was partly due to the large wooden desk which was situated at the front of the room.

The walls were covered in motivational posters. Each carried slogans espousing messages about change, taking steps into a bold, fearless future, and being part of the new world. The accompanying artwork portrayed the perfect nuclear-style family, they were always smiling, and they were always perfectly dressed as they posed together; the future looked rosy, at least according to the propaganda.

They had been escorted to this room on the eighth floor by the two guards who had accompanied them during their shuttle journey into London. The guards had invited them to take a seat and wait for a man named Eldon. Richard demanded to know what they were doing there but the guards insisted that all would become clear when Eldon arrived.

Kieran jumped off his chair and looked out of the window, he was still excited by his new surroundings.

"Look, Dad, the Shard and there's St Paul's!" he yelled.

"British and built to last son," Richard said while he watched a man walk into the room carrying something that looked like a laptop; the man placed it on the desk at the front of the room.

"Some buildings survived, others didn't, that's how it happens," Eldon said, his wiry frame, glasses, and thinning hair afforded him a homely, familiar look.

"And who might you be?" Richard stood up. "We've been here for hours. I demand answers."

"Demanding is not going to help your cause, and my name is Eldon. I'm here to help you assimilate into our time." Eldon opened the device and typed something on the glass screen.

"You're here to do what?" Richard frowned.

"I'm here to make your life easier by assisting you in your transition into this time, as I said, assimilate."

"Like a caseworker then?" Tamsin said.

"If that is what you would like to refer to me as, then yes, I'm your caseworker."

"Is this the part where you get out some probes and start poking around our bodies?" Stan tentatively asked.

"I feel that someone may have watched too many science fiction movies because that is definitely what we won't be doing," Eldon said and sat on the edge of the desk.

The wall behind Eldon burst into life as the laptop device projected images of the headlines from the M6 crash across it.

"Was that us?" Richard asked, his squinting eyes struggling to focus on the headlines.

"Yes," Eldon replied.

"Paranormal?" Richard shook his head.

"Yes, that is what the reporter called it: the *M6 Paranormal Crash* to give it its full title. They seem to have had a rather vivid imagination, don't you think?" Eldon chuckled as he looked at the headlines.

"Why are you showing us this?" Richard placed the palms of his hands on the table and leaned forward.

"Because you should know what is going on back in your time, in case you think this" – Eldon gestured to the surroundings – "is a hoax."

"I don't think hoax is the word I would use. I said this was an elaborate way to extort money from me, you see back home—"

"Yes, we know. Back home you know *people*. People who would miss you. And you are, what was it… ah yes, a *powerful businessman*. Well, that is behind you now. Long behind you, I'm afraid."

"So, we've just got to wave goodbye to it all? No chance of returning home?" Richard asked.

"As you can see from the headlines, you can't go back, you are at the centre of a major incident, one in which it is reported that you disappeared. To go back would open up all sorts of issues and questions would come with it. This is your home now." Eldon clasped his hands and placed them on his lap.

"You mean that?" Tamsin asked.

"I do. We cannot allow you to simply walk out of a car in a crash scene when there is evidence that confirms you disappeared. There is eyewitness testimony. Therefore, as you were told before, this is your new home. And your future. In due course, the headlines will die down as the interest in your story wanes and you will become old news."

"What if these headlines persist? Then what?" Tamsin asked.

"We have ways of fixing things. You know, making them go away," Eldon peered over his glasses.

"Just exactly how do you fix that?" Richard pointed at the headlines.

"That's our problem," Eldon stared back at Richard.

"Seems to me that this is our problem as much as it is yours, after all, we're living this mess." Richard bit his upper lip.

"All will become clear in the fullness of time," Eldon replied.

"Time is the one thing we appear to have an abundance of at the moment," Richard glared at Eldon.

"And what about our son? He's at school, what about his future? Or doesn't he count in this plan you've hatched?" Tamsin snapped.

"It's okay, mum, I like it here," Kieran spoke quietly as he fiddled with his phone.

"Whether you like it here or not is irrelevant. You need an education," Tamsin said.

"Look, and I mean no disrespect to the truck driver…" Richard spoke.

"The name is Stan," Stan interrupted.

"Stan, okay whatever. But what the hell are we supposed to do here?" Richard asked.

"Well, for a start you'll have a future. And after that, well, the possibilities are endless," Eldon replied.

"You know it took months to find the right school for our son. Keeping him here will be a major disruption in his education." Tamsin stared at Eldon.

"I can see that emotions are running high, and you're right to ask these questions. First, your son will be educated. We have schools. We have everything you need. We have houses, work, schools, and everything else you would expect from a modern progressive society." Eldon gestured to the posters behind him.

"And I suppose we're expected to believe these posters?" Tamsin looked through Eldon at them. "As the adults here we'll have to cope, but our child needs his friends, his routine, and his studies. These posters may paint a rosy picture but taking Kieran away from what he knows is hardly good for him."

"The posters are meant to help reassure people like you," Eldon pointed at the posters.

"What does that mean *people like you?* You mean there are more people like us?" Richard asked.

"There's been a few, call it a casualty of our predicament."

"And what predicament would that be?" Richard asked.

"Opening a timeline has created some incidents, similar to the one you were involved in and inevitably that has caused the occasional accident." Eldon shrugged his shoulders.

"So, you've done this before?" Stan asked.

"Yes," Eldon replied. "My job is to ensure that your transition to this time is as smooth as possible and to give you every chance of making a success of your new lives."

"What happened to the others?" Stan asked.

"After a period of denial and adjustment they settled into this time and, I might add, are living their lives to the fullest."

"You just expect us to accept our fate?" Richard folded his arms and sat back in the chair.

"You have to understand, you disappeared from your vehicles in front of eyewitnesses, and CCTV, and while we can cover most of our tracks there will always be some evidence that we cannot access and erase. Therefore, you cannot return to your time, there will be too many questions and we cannot risk our mission."

"Your mission? What about our lives? What happens to them?" Tamsin snapped back at Eldon.

"Think of it as a new chapter in your lives. I want you to embrace the journey and let me do my best to help your family settle into this time," Eldon said, holding out his hands and then clasping them together.

"And the past? What happens to that?" Tamsin asked.

"That will be taken care of, as I said before we have operatives on the ground in your time who will ensure that as many loose ends as possible are tied up."

"We'll be missed you know, family, friends, businesses will all be asking questions," Richard said as he placed his elbows on the table.

"We have a set of protocols in place to deal with that," Eldon replied.

"Think you're clever, don't you? Got all the answers." Richard looked around for support, none was forthcoming.

"Not really. There are always risks but the fact remains you are safer here than back there facing questions you will be unable to answer," Eldon said.

"Not much of a choice, is it?" Richard shook his head and looked downward.

"There is no choice to be made; you have to remain in this time. And you talk about work, well we need people like you to help us rebuild our history, fill in the many blanks we have, help us piece together our past. Centuries of conflict have caused a lack of knowledge about our past. In a small way, you can help us learn about your time."

"That's not work though is it?" Richard said.

"It's the kind of work that we need, understanding our past so we can avoid the same mistakes in the future is tantamount to creating a better society for all. You will become an important source of knowledge, your life experiences from that time, a crucial time in history are going to help us immensely. Trust me when I say you are better off in the here and now." Eldon changed the image behind him to a sequence of still shots of the new London.

"And you promise there will be no probes?" Stan asked.

"No probes. I promise," Eldon replied and smiled.

"That's good enough for me," Stan said.

"Let me take you on a tour of your new home. Show you how we live in this time and show you all the things we have to offer in this wonderful city. I want to show Kieran the schools. I want to show you all the work we are doing to create the perfect environment for families to prosper. We have different priorities but our goals are the same. We want to develop, and with people like you amongst us, we not only develop, we can also look back at history and learn from those mistakes."

"Just out of interest, what makes you think our time was all about making mistakes?" Tamsin asked.

"I didn't say all of it, but much of what happened in your era became the foundation for the problems that followed. Now, you can become part of our brave new world and take those precious first steps into the future with us." Eldon looked at Tamsin and then glanced back at the posters.

"I think we need to hear him out, after all when you look at it, we can't go back, so what have we got to lose? We either fight this thing and drive ourselves crazy or we accept the situation and make the best of it. That's the kind decision a business leader would make isn't it?" Tamsin looked at Richard.

"Dad, I like it here, I really do, let's stay, please." Kieran stood up and wrapped his arms around Richard's neck.

"I'll be with you every step of the way, making sure you have as much or as little help as you need to make this your new home," Eldon said and slowly nodded his head.

Stan stood up and shook Eldon's hand. "You can count me in. After all these years of listening to late-night conspiracy shows, I never thought I'd get the chance to feature in one. Ironically, I will probably miss it."

"That's it then. We have no choice but to accept your invitation," Richard said, stood up, and held out his hand. Eldon willingly grabbed it and shook it.

16

Paris.Present-Day.

Steve awoke from his nap as the jet's tires bounced on the tarmac at Charles de Gaulle airport. The jet abruptly slowed and then progressed along the runway. It taxied into a large hangar on the fringes of the airport, the noise of the engines boomed around the empty structure as it slowed to a halt.

Silverton stood and stretched. "We need to get to the 11th District, the Bastille region of town right away. We have a car waiting for us."

"I don't get one thing," Steve said.

"And what is that?" Silverton frowned and looked at his watch.

"If this is all about resources, what are they expecting to find in Paris?"

"We're not sure but there must be something of importance here," Silverton replied.

"Let's hope your contact is correct," Steve said.

"Bonjour, Monsieur Silverton, good to see you again," the chauffeur said.

"And you Michel. We need to get to the 11th District as quick as you can please."

"My pleasure," Michel replied.

"Insider intel," Silverton turned back to look at Steve and spoke.

"Explain," Steve replied.

"We have reason to believe that one of their operatives is running a financial services company in London as a front to gain information about locations, you know, from various mining companies that he is looking to invest in. He's using the promise of millions of pounds of investment to gain an inside track on what the potential return could be, but, of course, that is just a cover story. We know the real reason he wants information."

"And with London being one of the biggest financial centres in the world no one will blink an eye at someone waving that kind of money around," Steve replied.

After the necessary security checks, the car exited onto the main route heading toward Paris.

"Clever," Roy said.

"Very. And it's perfect because if this information leads to an extraction it can be dismissed as inaccurate. It simply disappears. No one suspects a thing as the information would not have been in the public domain at that time, so no one is any the wiser. What is more disturbing is how easily this insider information appears to be available to the highest bidder."

"How do you know it is insider information?" Steve asked.

"We have an operative in one of the government agencies reviewing the accounts and activities of this company and it is entirely consistent with others that have been used as a front to gain this type of information."

"So, this operative must be using shell companies that have managed to gain a trading license in London," Steve said.

"Exactly. Plus, they're all incorporated overseas which makes them very hard to track. If one gets busted they simply set up another one and tick the relevant boxes to gain a license."

"In places like Panama?" Steve replied.

"All over the place but yes, Panama has been used as it's almost impossible to investigate the true state of ownership over there. You see, I knew there was a reason why an accountant would be useful to our mission." Silverton smiled.

"I guess I'll take that as a compliment," Steve said.

Silverton looked at his phone to catch up on messages and e-mails. He quickly flicked through the Parisian news sites and noticed that the Champs-Elysees was closed, along with several of the surrounding roads due to protests.

"Have you seen the reports of the protesters along the Champs-Elysees?" Silverton turned to talk with Michel and held up the screen on his mobile phone so he could see it.

"Yes, my friend, I have been watching this story unfold on the news. It's been going on all day. They are protesting about this Carbon Quota System. They should realise that this is pointless, the government will not listen."

"How bad is the traffic?"

"North of the river it is bad, for us it will be okay, I can assure you," Michel pushed on toward the 11th District.

17

Anton sat at the back of a scruffy cafe in the Bastille neighbourhood of Paris. The streets were alive with market traders, impromptu buskers chancing their luck, and tables of fresh produce on display outside the local shops.

Traffic crawled along the packed roads, pedestrians dodged the cars, and the back streets were filled with alfresco diners enjoying a glass of wine on a relatively warm day.

Anton sat alone drinking a coffee and watching the news on the TV perched on a stand that protruded out from the wall opposite him. The noise of the coffee machine and customers barking out their orders did their best to drown out the words of the anchorman, but luckily the ticker tape display that ran along the bottom of the screen showed the most relevant headlines. Steam erupted from the coffee machine and filled the air, forcing the cafe owner to wipe her brow.

Anton drank more of his coffee and returned to his newspaper. The main story on the front page declared *"Anarchie des Quotas de Carbone."*

Anton briefly glanced up to look at the headlines on the TV. It was an endless montage of images of protesters taking over the Champs-Elysees on their march toward the Arc de Triomphe. A reporter covering the story stood on the side while the protesters continued their relentless march toward the famous landmark. He tried to interview some of the protesters, but his efforts were curtailed as people behind him started to shout obscenities at the camera. The reporter tried on several occasions to restart the interview with another protester but he knew it was a pointless task, the obscenities showed no sign of abating and the coverage returned to the studio.

Anton returned to his paper. The front-page story concerned the new policy of the French government, desperate to put something in place to reduce France's dependence on fossil fuels and introduce the Carbon Quota System.

Each time a household purchased carbon-burning fuels they would have to register the purchase on an app developed by the government to monitor this type of transaction. This policy was not without controversy.

It was entirely plausible that a household could run out of its monthly allocation. If that were to happen, theoretically they would be unable to heat the house, drive to work, or cook. Human Rights lawyers had lobbied politicians about this potential flaw in the policy, but the French government hoped that, by pushing ahead and implementing it, people would adapt and begin to change their consumption habits. To allay public fears, politicians had maintained the stance that as the policy rollout began they would never leave any individual without an emergency supply of power should it be required.

Whilst the framework for the plan was being drawn up, poll after poll showed the French were keen to see such a policy implemented, but no other country was taking part in the trial, leaving France as the sole participant; this is what angered the public.

Politicians across all parties were also cautious. They saw the policy as a brave step that, in many ways, had to be taken, but they also saw it as a step into the unknown. They were concerned about how the public would adjust to the changes in lifestyle needed to stay within their monthly allocation.

Alternative energy supplies that would not impact the monthly allocation were still a niche industry and struggled to keep up with demand. This new policy would impact the supply chain even further and potentially push demand for new, cleaner energy sources over the edge. It was this issue that concerned politicians. Watching France slip into end-of-month blackouts as quotas ran out was not the desired side-effect of this new policy.

　　The headquarters of Parisoil Inc, the massive state-owned energy company, was the initial focus of the protester's anger. It was besieged by many of them in the early stages of the march, some of whom were brandishing placards criticising the allocation process. They wanted a re-think from the government about the trial and feared being exploited by this process.

　　Anton glanced back up at the TV. The noise had died down around him and he was finally able to hear the reporter while he spoke to one of the protestors on the Champs-Elysees.

　　The reporter asked why the protester feared the trial.

　　"My concern is that we have no way of validating the tariffs attached to each unit of carbon. We are being told that oil is this much and electricity uses that much, but we have no clear indication from politicians or from the energy companies about what constitutes a unit. If we have no idea, then how can we try to ensure our allocation will last for a month?" the protester made a very salient point.

　　The reporter nodded that he understood and watched the protester being swept off in a sea of people heading for the Arc de Triomphe.

　　Anton returned to his paper and turned to the sports pages.

18

Clint, Alain, Matt, and Jean-Paul progressed toward the end of the abandoned tunnel that started under the Trocadero, taking them right to the edge of the city's catacombs.

Matt decided to take the lead and shone his torch ahead piercing the darkness of the tunnel. He saw a grey, steel door with a padlock secured sliding bolt which now blocked their route.

"Looks like we may have a problem," Matt said and turned back to the others.

Clint, Alain, and Jean-Paul looked on as Matt traced his hand around the door's edges, looking for any sign of weaknesses; there weren't any. He then returned to the large padlock that held the bolt in place. "I've seen these Medeco padlocks before, they're almost impossible to cut," Matt said, shaking his head.

"How come you know so much about padlocks?" Alain asked.

"Hazard of the job I guess. You come across a lot of locked doors in this line of work."

Alain pulled a small jackhammer out of his holdall and passed it to Matt. "Luckily we also came prepared. You may find this useful." He then pulled out a heavy-duty mask and passed it to Matt.

"You came prepared then?" Clint said.

"We also have similar experiences of such obstacles," Alain replied.

Without saying a word, Clint put on the mask and deployed the hammer on the door hinges. Sparks flew into the air then extinguished when the metal from the hinges connected with the jackhammer. The concrete surrounding them was old and had been subjected to years of damp conditions, it soon relented under the continuous blows.

Matt dug the hinges out from the concrete but knew he needed more leverage; he turned to Alain.

Alain reached into his holdall and pulled out a crowbar. "Try this, it may also help," he said.

"You really did come prepared." Matt grabbed the crowbar. He placed one foot against the wall, steadied himself, and jammed the crowbar into the newly created gap between the edge of the door and the concrete frame. The final remnants of concrete encasing the hinges gave way to Matt's attention as he pried the door slowly open. He stumbled back as the crowbar slipped from the widening gap between the door and the frame.

Matt passed the jackhammer and crowbar back to Alain who placed them in the holdall. The door was now half-open. He grabbed his torch, pointed it through the gap, and peered inside. A small atrium lay beyond the door, from which three more tunnels converged. The air was damp and heavy, and Matt was greeted with a stale smell. *The smell of death,* he thought to himself. He climbed through the gap and stood upright on the other side. Condensation dripped from the ceiling, creating a thin film of mud on the floor. He took a couple of paces to regain his footing and continued to look around. He pointed the torch across to one of the walls where he saw a mass of earth, skulls, and the occasional glimmer of light reflecting from something that appeared to be jammed in the earth.

Matt looked back through the doorway to the others, "We need to get moving, this is going to take hours. Be careful with anything you touch. Remember we only want diamonds." He pushed the door further open so they could get the large holdalls through to him.

Clint started to pass them through the gap. He then followed Matt into the catacombs.

Alain was next through the door, followed by Jean-Paul. The ground was covered in small fragments of bone and then there was that stale smell in the air. Alain pulled the spare holdalls out and threw them onto the floor.

"How long?" Matt asked.

"How long what?" Jean-Paul replied.

"How long have places like this been abandoned?"

"This particular area, or at least some of the neighbouring catacombs, were used for some sort of clandestine meeting place up until a few years ago. Until then it remained undiscovered. But some of them date back to the revolution, so you are talking over two hundred years, but of course, that is still open to debate as some have their origins dating back to Roman times. As is the origin of those diamonds," Alain pointed his torch at the crumbling walls of the catacomb and down one of the tunnels. "If you get lost in here, it will not end well for you." The beam of his torch expired long before it reached the end of the tunnel.

"If they're from the revolution, how come they're encrusted in the earth and rocks?" Clint asked as he chipped away at the rocks with a small hammer he took from one of the bags.

"The truth is we have no idea. With some of these tunnels dating back to Roman times they could have been buried here for many years," Jean-Paul said.

"Well, the main thing is to get a decent-sized sample back for analysis to check for purity and to see if there are any more buried in this area," Matt said and flashed his torch around the area.

Clint was impatiently chipping away at a cluster of rocks, he got frustrated, then seemed to give up after he tossed the cluster into one of the large holdalls.

"What was that?" Jean-Paul froze and shone his torch into the tunnel ahead of him.

"What was what?" Clint asked, stopping to look up.

"I thought I saw something moving."

Alain walked up to Jean-Paul and looked down the tunnel. "There's nothing else down here. Now, will you help, because you're not much use to us just standing there?"

"I'm not crazy, there was something there. Maybe an animal, but something definitely moved."

"We have a gun and torches, nothing will happen to us," Alain said, "besides, most of these catacombs have been empty since they were sealed up, which is why the diamonds are still here. If anyone had come down here surely they would have taken them, no?" He shrugged his shoulders.

Matt paced around, he shone his torch onto the floor then up to the ceiling, and then across at the other tunnels. The roof in one of the tunnels had caved in, and another was too small to get down. "I think this area will be suitable to open the timeline, I don't want to carry these bags too far. They are going to be heavy, and besides, this place is far too easy to get lost in," he said.

"Don't you think large amounts of energy will upset the fragile condition of this place?" Jean-Paul asked, pointing his torch at the pile of rubble that had sealed off one of the tunnels.

"I would like to think that they have done their research into the location, but all we need to do is open the timeline and travel through it, no more and no less."

"But what about on the other side? This place will still be unstable when we arrive," Jean-Paul persisted.

Matt had to admit that Jean-Paul had a point. He glared at Jean-Paul. "You don't have to worry about that, everything will be taken care of. Focus your energy on the job in hand."

Matt pulled at a rock toward the bottom of one of the walls and a small smattering of stones fell from the roof. Everyone stopped what they were doing. Matt shone his torch at the roof to reveal dust slowly descending to the floor. He glanced at Jean-Paul who wore a rueful expression.

"Let's hope you're right about that research," Jean-Paul said.

19

Paris.Present-Day.

Michel drove the car around the back of the cafe and into the street directly behind it, parking next to a row of industrial waste bins. The arrival of the car disturbed a group of pigeons who had been feeding on discarded food containers on the road that had spilled out of the overflowing bins. Silverton got out of the car and took a quick look around to check the area before proceeding along the back street, onto another side street, then to the front door of the cafe on the main street. The others followed closely behind him. He pushed open the door and walked over to the man at the back reading a newspaper, pushing down on the top of the newspaper to reveal Anton's face.

"You made good time. The roads are blocked by this protest." Anton stood up and shook Silverton's hand, then Roy's, and Steve's.

"Nothing new there, Paris as we always knew it," Steve remarked as he sat down.

"Not everything in Paris is as you read in your newspapers," Anton said. He was not impressed by Steve's comment and looked down at the table to avoid making eye contact with him.

The waitress walked over, and Anton looked around at them all across the table. "Coffee? Non? Okay, trois cafes, s'il vous plait." The waitress scratched the order on her pad and left.

"It is good to see you again, my friend," Anton said to Silverton.

"Likewise. I just wish it was under better circumstances."

"I never thought this would happen so quickly," Anton said, pointing to the news coverage of the protests.

"We were warned but what surprises me is how many people are taking part. The news coverage I've seen suggests it is in the tens of thousands."

"And that is just in Paris. I hear there are protests in all the major cities across France."

"What has this got to do with us?" Steve asked. "Surely you knew this was about to happen..."

Anton glanced at Steve. "This is where the end begins. Soon, as corruption and fear take over, other streets, towns, cities, and countries will have their own demonstrations. You are witnessing history in the making – our history – exactly as Charley Sandford explained it to me." Anton sipped his coffee.

"You've met him as well?" Steve asked.

"Of course, how do you think I know about all this?"

"What he said is starting to make sense, but at the time it all seemed so bloody unreal. I wish I had...oh, never mind. But how is this connected? I don't get it."

"Excuse me, please," the waitress said in broken English while she placed three cups of coffee on the small table in front of them.

"As I said, this is only the start. What comes afterward is far worse." Anton rubbed a line into the table with his thumb. Roy sipped his coffee quietly, taking it all in.

"What do you know about this? What have you been told?" Steve asked, his voice eliciting an amount of urgency, "and while we're at it, who exactly are you?"

"I'm like you, Steve, part of a group of people supplanted here to help the cause, boots on the ground."

"There's that phrase again, I can tell you've met Charley Sandford." Steve smiled and slowly nodded his head.

Anton leaned back in his chair. "Did Charley Sandford ever tell you about a group of people on a train on the west coast of America?"

Steve shook his head. "Please don't talk in riddles, I've had enough of those to last a lifetime."

"No riddles. In fact, for me, it was the clearest way he could put into context what is about to happen."

"Okay, so *now* you have my attention, what happened?" Steve pointed his index finger upward.

"I don't want to rush anyone," Roy said, "but don't we have something else we need to attend to?"

"Let him talk," Silverton said.

Anton glanced at his watch again. "We have time, an extraction will take hours to set up, and I want to catch them when that timeline is open."

"How will you know it is open?" Roy asked.

Anton smiled. "I have my sources."

"So, getting back to this train," Steve said, "you said it set things into context, how exactly?"

"What happens here will eventually happen all over the world." Anton drank more of his coffee. "You could say this is only the tip of the iceberg, but what Charley told me in Santa Monica put things into perspective. You must first understand that America was one of the last countries to introduce the Carbon Quota System, and they did it only under duress. The UN was fighting a losing battle with governments across the world as they sought to control energy consumption, particularly from fossil fuels. Politicians had to face up to the reality that energy supplies from cleaner sources were in short supply. At times, entire cities would be rationed to the point that the little power available was supplied to the emergency services. The system that had been designed to alleviate the pressure on energy supplies, and the environment, inadvertently created a black market in quota sales."

"When are we talking here? What year? What decade?" Steve asked.

"The next few decades," Anton replied.

"Okay, so far I'm with you," Steve took a sip of his coffee.

"The idea behind the policy was to manage consumption on a per household basis. Each household would have a monthly quota of allowable energy; they would be issued a quota allowance via an app that would measure how much they used. People had to use the app every time they accessed their quota. Once they ran out of allowances, well, that was it for the month. The logistics were challenging, to say the least. Each household would need to have an effective way to measure these quotas against the allowance to allocate the correct amount of energy; this is where smart meters came in. The plan was to gradually restrict the amount of carbon-based energy used in each household, with the overall goal of reducing dependence on fossil fuels to almost zero, while other energy sources were being developed to replace them."

"But we already have these energy sources, surely?" Steve asked.

"As a niche yes, but in reality, these sources were not widely enough available on the scale needed to replace the current energy requirements, and this is the problem. A new supply chain had to be created out of what, at least on the surface, were the good intentions of politicians around the world. For the first time in a generation, everyone seemed to be on the same page. Something had to be done to maintain an effective, clean, supply of energy."

"You talk about something that hasn't happened yet, but you claim that this is our history," Steve said.

Anton took a deep breath, "I know. But going back to the train...there is a route from Los Angeles to Seattle. It was a popular route, not only for tourists but as a means to reach a myriad of smaller towns that lie between the cities. As the Carbon Quota System was being introduced to America, the protests resisting the policy became violent. You see, America had a chance to see how the rest of the world would react to its introduction, and the people could see that this policy was open to abuse and corruption by those in charge of setting the quotas. They didn't like what they saw and failed to see how it could improve the management of energy supplies; after all, America had no energy supply issues at the time."

"I can kind of see their point," Steve said and shrugged his shoulders.

"In some respects, so can I. However, they were about to be held ransom to a system where the local government controlled the levels of allowable carbon consumption per household; they would simply apply to the central government for those allocations. But of course, these allocated quotas didn't always make it to their intended destinations. Some of that quota would be lost or filtered away by the officers in charge of outward distribution to the app. Instead, it was passed through a highly sophisticated network of criminals, who sold it on the black market to the highest bidders and found its way onto jailbroken apps. So, for example, we had situations in France, where schools had no power and the officers in charge of the quotas were taking bribes from the teachers to ensure a continuity of supply. And guess what?" Anton paused to solicit a response.

"The criminal networks were selling this so-called *lost* quota back into the system?" Steve knew where this was going.

"Exactly. Entire streets were in blackout as people failed to pay the bribes needed to release their assigned quota from the hands of these criminals. The American people looked on and thought, no, why would we want this in our country?" Anton drank more coffee and signaled the waitress for a refill. She came to the table and duly obliged.

"Hang on. Who was in charge of this mess?" Steve tapped the table with his fingers.

"That's just it, local government was in charge but it was so poorly executed that there were no monitoring systems in place to ensure the quotas reached the correct destination. The central government was too busy trying to secure alternative energy sources. As far as they were concerned the consumption of carbon-based fuels had to be eradicated at any cost, so all of this abuse simply went under the radar."

"Where did all these quotas go?" Silverton asked.

"As with everything, to the highest bidder. Council elections were rigged so candidates who were effectively bought by the criminal gangs always won seats. Once in power, those candidates siphoned off allocations to criminal networks and whoever else could pay. But even against this backdrop of corruption and blackouts, America had no choice, it had to follow because the rest of the world expected it. After the initial protests died down, and the system was introduced, the country descended into chaos; only on a bigger scale. The public transport infrastructure was one of the very few services where the imposition of any form of quota was rejected. The transport systems had to be protected from this self-imposed rationing to preserve any hope of retaining some form of an economy." Anton drank some more coffee and then looked over to the counter, where plumes of steam rose from the coffee machine. A customer used their hat to waft away the steam as it swirled around in the air.

"The trains…where do they fit into this?" Steve spoke quietly.

"As town after town descended into anarchy, people sought refuge from the ever-growing problems of corruption and violence. Street by street and town by town, groups of people turned against each other as they tried to protect their families and communities from the onslaught of corruption. We're talking about neighbours who had known each other for years, becoming sworn enemies overnight due to the rationing of quotas. Small enclaves of people sprung up all over the place; quite naturally people had decided you were better off being part of a group to protect yourself than attempting to face these new threats on your own. People who had never, at any time in their lives, contemplated joining a gang sought refuge within these enclaves as they vied for power within their region."

"But what about law and order? Surely there must have been something there to protect these people from the abuse," Steve asked.

"It was all breaking down, everywhere in the world. The people charged with enforcing the law had their own households to protect, and many took advantage of their position to seek preferential quotas to ensure they always had power. They argued that they needed this to help uphold the law; after all, you can't fight the bad guys on an empty stomach, eh?" Anton paused and drank more coffee. "This skewed the system and placed further pressures on central government, while it desperately tried to wrestle control of the country back from these enclaves that had sprung up in virtually every state. This type of conflict had no borders, no defined external enemy, and spread from country to country like wildfire. Word got out that energy was the commodity of choice for any self-respecting criminal or warlord. They knew if they controlled the energy supply they had unimaginable power over the people in their region."

"Apart from anyone who sought refuge on some form of public transport?"

"This is the point. But again, many people who worked for public transport networks had families to support, so they had other concerns. Much of the network laid dormant as the infrastructure crumbled; apart from the west coastline from Los Angeles to Seattle, somehow the people who worked the line had kept it going for as long as they could. This train became a refuge for those fleeing oppression, at first only a trickle of people realised there was some form of respite on the trains. As the word spread, it became a stream, and then a river. Refugees could be seen for miles as they sought space on the trains, it was their only hope of survival. There was one train in particular that served this route. The train driver and his staff had worked on it for more than thirty years, he knew every inch of track on the line and knew every town, even down to the stores near the stations. They knew something was going on, as more and more people got on their train, and fewer got off. Luckily this was a long-distance train with a lot of capacity to carry passengers, but soon it became filled to the brim with those seeking refuge. Many were left by the tracks as there was simply no more space. People came from all walks of life; doctors, teachers, office workers, military personnel, you name it. They came with their families and anything they could carry until soon there was no more room. Some simply came with the clothes they wore on their backs."

"But surely this train was dangerously overloaded?" Roy asked.

"No. It was the opposite, people understood that they had to do something to preserve their way of life. They knew they had to pull together. The train driver decided that they would now travel slowly along the track, going from town to town. They were trying to avoid attracting any unwanted attention. They had to preserve what little energy was running through the rails. At night they would turn off all the lights and travel at maybe five miles per hour, but it never stopped. When they did stop, it was in daylight, and only at stations the driver knew were near to local stores. At first, they paid for everything with the money they had left. They ran to the stores, got what they needed, put money in the tills, and left. After the money ran out, they resorted to looting, but they soon ran out of supplies. They weren't the only people looting these towns; it was rife, the supply chains started to systematically fail as the infrastructure crumbled. So now they would stop in the middle of nowhere to hunt and forage for food in the nearby forests. They had to adapt to the world within which they were living, rather than what had gone before."

"How does Charley Sandford know all of this? What's to say he wasn't making this up?" Steve asked.

"I said the same thing, but the people on this train were organised. As time progressed they converted some of the carriages into sleeping quarters and turned one into a school, another into a basic medical facility and another was like a restroom. It became a small town on rails."

20

The Train. 1.01

"It may not be much but it's the best I can find and it is a home of some kind," Jim squeezed down the corridor.

"Given what we've had to deal with, this is a miracle," Lucy was in close attendance as they shuffled down the tight corridor.

"Mind ya' backs! One coming through! Don't block the corridor we've got new passengers moving in every minute now!" Chuck directed the couple to their new accommodation.

"You know they even have a school now so little Sammy can get back to doing some lessons." Jim lifted his young son and beamed a huge smile at the kid.

"Aww...do I have to dad?" Sammy said, looking less than impressed.

"Don't try to get out of it. I think we all need to return to some kind of normality, so yes Sammy, you do. It will do you some good to mix with the other children." Lucy looked at Sammy whose face dropped at the prospect. She craved the life they once had in the leafy suburbs of Bakersfield, but that had been cruelly ripped from them as corruption took hold of the quota distribution system.

"I know that Del and Tom have finished fitting out the med room carriage, it's not great but then, what can you do with a bunch of first aid kits and some antiseptic creams? We'll have to find more supplies because we're desperately short of medication should there be any kind of emergency," Chuck said as he bounded his way up the thin corridor of the sleeper carriage.

"I've drawn up a hit list of essentials, the next time we stop we'll zero in on a pharmacy and see what we can find," Jim said, he knew even his basic medical knowledge was going to be needed even if it would be tested to the limits in the coming months.

"I'll make sure we check on the route to see where the next one is. That's got to be a priority at the moment given what's happening out there," Chuck said, ruefully looking out into the wilds.

***

Paris. Present-Day.

"It sounds like an Ark…" Silverton muttered.

"Maybe it was. They knew things were changing and decided to record these changes with whatever equipment they had at their disposal. They captured images of every town they traveled through, documenting the decline of society as they journeyed northbound and then southbound through the same towns, giving us a unique time-lapsed insight into what happened in those dark years. It was an invaluable source of information for future generations. When devices became full or ran out of power, they were stored in a safe in the engine room. The driver taught several other passengers how to drive the train so they could take turns, ensuring that they would never have to stop unless at a scheduled location. Eventually, the final remnants of authorities protecting the power supplies to the tracks dissipated, and the train came to a halt just north of Sacramento." Anton took another sip of his coffee.

"Then what?" Steve asked. All three men were now engaged in Anton's story.

"Some of the passengers sought refuge elsewhere, thinking that they would be safer in the hills but many stayed and tried to make the best of the situation, using whatever sources of fuel they could find to maintain some form of power supply to the carriages. Then one night, it happened."

"What happened?" Silverton probably knew the answer as he asked.

***

The Train. 1.02

"We can't leave, this is the closest thing we have to a home. We can't just leave!" Lucy shouted at Jim through the open door. He ignored her and continued packing the bags in their small quarters.

"You've got to get over this place. It's finished." Jim paused for a moment to wipe a tear from Sammy's eye.

"I'm scared, daddy," Sammy whined and clung tightly to his teddy bear.

"The moment this thing stopped we became a target." Jim continued frantically packing.

"But we can't give this up. People need us," Lucy implored.

"She's right." Chuck looked in at Jim from the doorway.

"I don't like this any more than you, but we all know how vulnerable we are. I've seen too many examples of what happens to people like us. It's not safe for us here." Jim stopped packing to look up for a moment.

"But it's our home!" Lucy stamped on the floor.

"It *was* our home." Jim closed the argument by leaving the small room, struggling down the narrow corridor with bags filled with whatever personal belonging he could cram into them.

"So, that's it?" Lucy asked as she stood alongside Chuck and Sammy in the narrow corridor.

Jim walked back up to Lucy and leaned in to talk quietly to her. "We have to go. Grab Sammy and let's get out of here while there's still sunlight. I don't want to get lost in the forest."

"Where are we going?"

"Anywhere safe and undercover." Jim had no idea. He only knew that the train had outlived its purpose.

***

Paris. Present-Day.

"They fled with whatever they could carry, to the relative safety of the forest."

"And those who stayed behind?"

Anton shook his head. "The evidence points to an organised gang. According to Charley, who recalled folklore that was handed down through the generations, the gang was on the move. They were probably displaced and angry, like so many others. It seems they came across the train by complete accident; the primeval sense of survival is a powerful source of strength in times of need. They had all manner of weapons, making them unstoppable. No one survived."

***

The Train 1.03

Two men, scruffily dressed with unkempt, knotted hair, and blackened teeth, lay side by side at the edge of the forest looking across the short distance to the stationary train. "See that piece of shit up there? We can take it," one of them said.

Their nomadic existence wasn't a lifestyle choice, it was a quest for survival. Their group numbered twenty people, all adults and the majority of these were male. Their struggle for survival had led to them adapting their dietary needs in line with what they could find; anything was fair game in these desperate times.

"The train?" The other man asked as he spat onto the ground. "You dragged me over here to see a fucking relic? It's years old. What use is it to us?"

"Yes, that fucking train! What the fuck else can you see out there?"

"You've been drinking too much of your own brew, Sam. There's nothing on there but a booby trap, or worse, the fucking Stink."

"The Stink doesn't venture into these parts, and if they did, we'd kick their asses."

"After the last time? They fucked us over big time. Sparrow warned us to back off and leave them to it, but no, you had to have a piece of their action. So, excuse me if I question what the fuck is going down, but I ain't taking no beating." Jack shuffled in the undergrowth; his clothes offered little protection against the debris littering the ground.

"We were unprepared, that's all. Now shut the fuck up. Look through these and tell me what you see, *then* tell me I'm wrong." Sam thrust the rickety old binoculars into Jack's hand.

Jack peered through the eyepieces, taking his time to adjust the focus.

"So?" Sam asked.

"Well, I'll be fucking damned!" Jack removed the binoculars and looked at Sam. "There must be enough rations on that shithouse to last weeks, maybe fucking months."

"Go tell Blane and Dougie to gather the gang, we're gonna have ourselves a party. The Stink is gonna be sick as pigs when they find out." Sam took the binoculars and placed them back in their case.

Within minutes, Jack returned with the gang. They crouched in the undergrowth on the fringes of the forest. Each of them held some kind of homemade weapon, fashioned from the remnants of anything they could salvage. Up ahead, the dim glow of candlelight flickered through the dirty windows of two carriages; the rest were in darkness. Silhouettes confirmed there were people in the carriages.

"There are a few men on there, some women and children too," Sam said as he turned to instruct his gang. "We take the men out first. Only use your guns if you have to, we don't have much ammo and this train doesn't look military."

Sam led the way as they quietly crawled through the overgrown field, getting closer to their prey, then sat up against the large wheels to avoid detection.

One by one they quietly climbed up the steps that led to the first carriage. Sam slowly opened the door to the carriage and looked on with glee as Dougie manoeuvred himself through the half-open door into the darkened carriage.

Sam remained at the entrance and peered in while Dougie quietly walked up the middle of the carriage. He was flanked by row upon row of empty seats and paused for a moment to instinctively check all was clear. Dougie turned to Sam for reassurance as he took another step further into the carriage. Sam signaled him on but this time his boot landed on something which cracked underfoot, Dougie paused again and let out a sigh of relief. Sam noticed something stirred from one row of seats ahead of Dougie but before he could say a word a man wielding a coal shovel jumped out and ran toward him.

"Get off my train, you bastard!" the man shouted as he continued toward Dougie.

141

Sam pulled out his gun and ran into the carriage to help Dougie as the burly man charged toward him. The man raised the coal shovel and was about to strike at Dougie but Sam stood behind Dougie and took one shot. The man instantly fell to the ground and rolled onto his stomach.

Sam crouched down and turned the body face up. He had shot him in the head. He then looked up to Dougie, "Fuck it, if they ain't gonna play nicely kill 'em all."

The others were slaughtered one by one as the gang ruthlessly chased them down through the carriages.

Blood splattered across the dirty candlelit windows of the two carriages. Limp bodies were carried out over the shoulders of the gang.

"Best meat in a long time," Jack tenaciously chewed at a bone, as the gang gathered around the victory campfire; the train was in the background; the candles were no longer burning.

"Don't ever fucking doubt me again, you hear me boy?" Sam stood up, drew his gun, pulled back the hammer, and pointed it at Jack's head. The others around the campfire stopped eating.

"Never, boss," Jack replied.

"That's okay then. Tonight, we eat. Tomorrow, we find a way to preserve what we have left." Jack released the hammer on the gun back to its resting place. Flames from the fire rose into the night sky, casting a shadow across the campsite. Jack's flame reddened face looked relaxed, he smiled to reveal small bits of white flesh caught between his teeth and glanced over at the pile of bodies next to the train.

***

Paris. Present-Day.

"But they never got to the safe and the contents remained intact, providing us with one of the most important collections of images from the dark years." Anton pointed to the ongoing news coverage of the protests. "And none of it is good."

Steve stared at the news channel. "So, this is it then? This is really the start of it?"

"Yes."

Anton tapped the side of his ear and nodded. "We need to go. They are getting close."

"What was that?" Steve asked.

"I've no time to explain now. We have to get to the extraction site, and quickly."

Anton put some money on the table to cover the coffees, looked across to the waitress, gestured toward the money, and then led them out of the cafe and to the Bastille metro station.

As they stood on the train Steve yelled across to Silverton, "Why not take the car?"

"Too easy to intercept, remember what happened last time? I recall that things didn't go so well," Silverton replied.

21

Paris Metro.Present-Day.

"I need you to wait here, just in case things don't go to plan," Silverton said to Roy as they stood in the busy foyer of the Trocadero metro station.

"How can you be so sure about their location?" Steve asked Anton.

"I just can. Follow me. We need to be quick." Anton strode across the foyer and down the corridor toward the door at the end. He pulled a set of skeleton keys from his jacket pocket and used them to unpick the lock, he then opened the door.

"This way." He signaled to Steve and Silverton to follow him into the dark tunnel.

They paused to allow their eyes to adjust to the darkness. Silverton and Anton took out torches, with Anton taking the lead as they made their way down the tunnel, his torch illuminating the seemingly endless route.

"You better be right about this, Anton," Silverton said.

"I am."

"How do you know this double agent of yours isn't feeding you false information?" Steve tripped over something on the ground.

"Just trust me on this," Anton replied.

They walked further into the depths. The air was stale and damp, the lights from the torches serving as their only respite from the oppressive darkness of the tunnel.

"What's that up ahead?" Silverton pointed the torch at the dimly glowing light.

"That must be the security office," Anton said.

"What, here?"

"Yes, here. They are a legacy of the disused Metro stations and tunnels that connect them. They're here in case people get lost in the tunnels," Anton said.

"But how do they get down here in the first place?" Steve asked.

"There are ways. The tunnels and catacombs have become a playground for extreme tourists. The idiots think they can find their way around, only to turn up days later, if they're lucky, starving and dehydrated."

Anton tensed as they got closer to the security room. He and Silverton shone their torches around the immediate vicinity.

"It's clear," Anton declared.

"Hold on. What's that?" Steve pointed to the blackened marks on the wall of the security room.

"I think that could be part of the security guard's brain," Anton said with no emotion.

Steve shook his head. "Did you just say what I thought you said?"

"I did," Anton replied with even less emotion if that was possible.

"But you said it was clear."

"Of any immediate threat, yes."

"He's right." Silverton walked over to the wall and held his torch inches away from the marks. "By the looks of it, they've been there a while."

Anton walked into the security room and picked up a clipboard with a list of times on it. "According to this, there's no scheduled changeover for another three hours, which would explain why this body has not been detected."

"What body?" Steve asked.

Silverton lit up a cigarette and entered the room. Steve followed him inside.

Anton walked over to the locker and pulled at the door handle, "It's been jammed shut."

Anton eventually managed to pull open the door. The dead guard slumped to the floor in front of him, the top of his head covered in a sticky black gloss and shards of fractured skull. "This body."

The heady mix of cigarette smoke, bodily fluids, and dried blood created a sickening smell that made Steve gag.

"How do you know all this?" Steve struggled to get out the words as he took deep breaths.

"Don't ever doubt my contact again, do you hear me? He had to stand and watch this man get shot and couldn't do a thing to prevent it, in case it blew his cover. Can you imagine how that felt?"

"I'm sorry." Steve bowed his head in acknowledgment.

"No, you didn't know, and what's more, when you don't know the whole story sometimes it's better to, as we would say, tais-toi," Anton said and walked past Steve and Silverton and out into the tunnel.

"We need to get moving," Silverton said. "I'll contact someone later that I know in the Paris Police Prefecture to make sure this man, at least in death, gets the respect he deserves." Silverton was keen to get to the extraction site but also mindful of what they had just witnessed.

"We're just going to leave him there?" Steve asked, he took one final look at the body that was now slumped halfway out of the locker.

"You have a better suggestion?" Anton looked back at the body from the office doorway. "We cannot take this body with us and we have no time to go back and alert the authorities now, plus that will completely blow our cover. Let Silverton handle this one, he has the contacts and the ability to cover our tracks. We must remain focused on our mission." Anton summoned the pair of them out of the room.

Silverton, Steve, and Anton continued along the tunnel, their torches cut an erratic line of light into the damp air as they progressed.

***

Matt looked around again, still deciding on where they should set the timeline. He crouched at the mouth of one of the tunnels, took a silver disc from his jacket pocket, and placed it carefully on the floor; it was a phasing unit, similar to the one used by Roy. He removed a palm-sized touchpad from his jacket, tapped the screen, and looked around again. If this went wrong, they could be buried alive, and he didn't want to add to the body count already filling the catacombs.

"This should work." He stood back and looked at the others. "I hope," he muttered.

"You don't sound very confident," Alain said.

"Is that going to work with the arrival location? Aren't we going to get stuck in this catacomb when we arrive?" Clint asked as he walked over to join Matt.

"No, they have made sure that won't be the case, which is why we cannot move from here. I'm working with the location markers they sent me. I don't expect us to be surrounded by skulls when we arrive." Matt looked back at the bags.

"Well, that's reassuring," Clint said with a hint of sarcasm.

"Listen, I've got to set this. Stand back in case there are any stability issues." Matt looked at Clint and slowly shook his head, he knew this was a dangerous place to open the timeline.

Matt then took a few paces back from the device. "Stand back everyone."

He held his breath and pressed the touchpad for the final time.

The phasing unit on the floor sprang to life. A large, crosshatched frame of light filled the space above it and crackled as the rectangle began to fill with a bright yellow light. The ground shook slightly as the density of the light became stronger and brighter. Matt grabbed his sunglasses from his jacket and put them on. The others followed suit. The ground shook again and small fragments of rock fell from the ceiling, but within seconds, the shaking was over and silence resumed.

Alain nodded his approval. "You have done well, my friend, it looks stable."

"We'll test it before we use it." Matt looked around to see if there was anything they could use. He grabbed a skull and cleaned it off with his hand.

"What are you going to do with that?" Jean-Paul asked.

"Send it through. If it makes it they'll send us a signal, and we can start the extraction." Matt took his sunglasses off and looked at the holdalls. The others followed suit, squinting to give their eyes time to adjust to the light.

"How long will it take to get there?" Alain asked.

"Well, given that it's going forward about six hundred years, I guess it could take maybe thirty minutes. But this is not an exact science. A lot will depend on how stable the timeline is beyond what we can see." Matt held the skull in the palm of his hand and tossed it up and down to get a feel for how much it weighed, and then held it close to the portal, using the light to check its condition.

***

The light flooding through the half-open door caused Anton to slow down. He crouched down, signaling the others to follow suit.

Silverton moved closer to Anton so he could whisper. "What do you think?"

"I've seen a lot of things in my time but that light tells me they have opened the timeline." Anton pushed Silverton's torch downwards.

"Already?" Silverton looked at Anton.

"Yes, but that is good because we need to try and capture the device they are using, so we can analyse it, and understand their tech, and how they are enhancing it. That was always part of this mission. We need to get closer, but we need to move slowly. They may have set motion sensor traps."

"What do they look like?" Silverton asked.

"They are tiny. You won't see one and you won't know you've triggered one until there is a gun pointing at your head." Anton moved along the side of the tunnel as they spoke.

"That's reassuring," Silverton said and checked his gun was still in the holster on his hip.

Steve followed behind as they crept toward the half-open door at the end of the tunnel. They pressed up against the wall on the other side of the doorway. Anton could just about make out the silhouette of someone standing at the portal; they appeared to be holding something in their hand.

"What do you think they're doing?" Silverton asked as he remained crouched beside Anton.

"I'm not sure, but that opening is a timeline, using that amount of energy to do that in a place like this is a huge risk. See what he's doing…" Anton pointed to the person in front of the portal.

"What the hell is that in his hand?" Steve asked, nudging closer to the door.

"I think they're testing the timeline with it," Anton said.

"Testing it? How?" Silverton asked.

"They'll send something—"

149

He froze as the figure pushed the object into the wall of light. The crackle of electricity filled the room and sparks flew out of the portal, illuminating the air in front of him; the object was completely absorbed into the light.

"What the hell was that?" Steve said.

"The timeline can't be stable. It must have reacted with whatever that object was," Anton replied.

"Fucking great!" Steve whispered as loud as he dared.

The portal began to swell outwards from the frame and fill the immediate area.

"This is our chance," Silverton said, carefully getting to his feet and drawing the gun from his holster.

"No, we need to see if this portal will work." Anton pushed Silverton back down to the ground.

"How much more evidence do you need? That thing, whatever it was, is gone."

"We need to be patient. If they send an object back they will know this timeline is stable, but it could take a while."

"Who would send something back?" Steve asked.

"The extraction team at the arrival site. This will have been planned for a long time, right down to the smallest detail. This location is not an accident, it will be secure on both sides."

"Define a while, and what if you're wrong?" Silverton asked.

"I don't know, minutes, maybe hours? Anyway, we have no choice, we must wait." Anton held his hand up and glared at Silverton.

"Why wait?" Steve frowned.

"If this portal is successful then they will lock down these settings so they can recreate the same conditions for future extractions. If that's the case, then any device encoded with the settings will transmit the same unique waveform signal, an identity stamp that should be consistent across other extractions they attempt. If we can track this signal it means we may be able to detect other potential extractions by setting CCS to detect these specific waveform signatures as they happen. Think of it like a fingerprint."

"And what if they change the signature? We could be looking for the wrong fingerprints, surely?" Steve asked.

"We know they've had problems before, in China for example, and would have learned from those mistakes. The waveform settings they are using for this extraction will be unique. If this timeline is stable then I'm confident they will want to retain these settings." Anton paused for a moment, "I think."

"I hope you're right," Silverton said.

"So do I." Anton turned to look at the glowing wall of light through the doorway.

The waiting dragged on; Silverton looked at his watch. Anton stretched his legs like a Russian dancer and Steve slumped against the wall.

A small tear appeared in the wall of light as a bright, spherical-shaped object broke through the surface; sparks emanated from the area surrounding the sphere. The person in front of the light reached out to touch it, and then seemed to change his mind and backed away.

Anton crawled as close as he dared to the doorway. "The timeline is stable," he whispered.

Anton looked on silently as the man stepped in front of the sphere. It became free of the portal and was now suspended in the air. Again, he reached out to touch it and sparks flew as his hands made contact.

"Yes!" the man shouted; his eyes lit with the glow of victory.

Anton watched as the man triumphantly grasped hold of the sphere at head height in his outstretched hands and then turned to the others. The sphere was so bright that his hands glowed orange and his veins were now clearly visible within the confines of his flesh, creating a network of red rivers beneath his skin.

As tempted as he was to get closer, Anton remained crouched down by the doorway and watched as the situation unfolded.

The sphere then rose out of the man's hands and hovered in front of him, illuminating his face and casting his shadow back toward the portal. The number 27 was now visible on the surface of the sphere.

The man turned and looked at the others, "It's worked! It's fucking worked! Look!" his voice became excitable and he clenched his fists together.

The brightness of the sphere started to recede and the man stepped closer to it, the word "minutes" now appeared next to the number 27. These gradually faded out to be replaced by a series of words being written into the surface of the sphere.

Anton could see that the man was beaming with excitement as he looked back at the others and shouted to them as the words slowly appeared in front of him.

"It says that the test has worked, that they have received the skull, that the extraction site is now fully secure and…" the man waited impatiently for the final text to display, "...that we can proceed to the next stage. That means we can send through some of the diamonds as a final test to ensure stability." He then rushed over to the bags and grabbed one of them.

The sphere was now floating next to the portal, seemingly keeping a watch on what was happening.

Anton turned back to look at the others, "It's worked," he said.

"How long do you think it will take to get across the timeline?" Clint asked Matt who was now standing by the portal with the holdall.

"Well, I guess that's what the twenty-seven minutes meant…" Matt said shrugging. "Isn't that the case?" he asked, looking around for answers.

"I think that could be correct. I timed it at fifty-seven minutes. If you allow time for them to examine the skull and send this sphere back then it makes sense, but of course, that is for one small object… not a holdall full of diamonds," Alain said. "And this is not an exact science, is it?"

Jean-Paul walked over to the portal and tentatively reached out to touch the sphere with his index finger. "It feels weird, sort of warm, but with no texture to it. How does it retain that shape?"

Matt shrugged. "All I care about is this thing has given us the all-clear to continue with the extraction."

22

"They're using that sphere to communicate with the extraction team. I've never seen this type of device before," Anton whispered to Silverton. "You see? That way they don't have to use any earth-based comms systems and that means—"

"Their movements are untraceable. There will be no location-specific signal for us to track, apart from the waveform signatures you mentioned earlier." Silverton looked at Anton.

"They are undoubtedly improving their technique," Anton said, nodding slowly.

"Learning from their mistakes," Silverton agreed. "This is not a good development."

Silverton pushed back his jacket and clasped the gun in his holster. He slowly cocked it, being careful not to make a sound. Pulling the gun out, he took aim through the doorway.

"What the fuck are you doing?" Anton raised his voice as loud as he dared.

"Following orders. You have yours, I have mine." Silverton gestured with the gun for Anton to get out of the way.

"On what authority are you acting? Whose orders? You can't do this," Anton pleaded, but Silverton just stared at his gun.

"Believe me when I say my orders have been signed off at the highest level," Silverton said.

"How come we know nothing of your orders?" Steve asked.

"Need to know basis, we couldn't risk jeopardising the mission. We had to be sure that there were no outside influences that could impact the mission."

"So, what exactly are your orders?" Steve asked.

"Apprehend the target and neutralise the portal," Silverton replied.

"By using a gun? I cannot believe that would be sanctioned," Anton said, shaking his head.

"Neutralise the portal by any means possible," Silverton repeated the order.

"Neutralise the portal with a gun? Are you crazy?" Steve hissed from the other side of the doorway. "This is a fucking tunnel. Shoot that in here and there's no telling what will happen. I may be a newcomer to your world of timelines and fucking intercontinental spy games but even I know this is not a good idea. You need to rationalise your orders with our current surroundings. This is not the place to be using that thing." Steve narrowed his brow and pointed at the gun.

Silverton lowered his gun. "This has to stop. If the extraction is a success, can you imagine the repercussions? They will be in possession of all the information they need to replicate this extraction whenever and wherever they want. Other attempted extractions have either failed or the intel has proven incorrect. This is the perfect storm. We can't let this happen – *I* can't let this happen." Silverton stood just far enough from the doorway to avoid detection and took aim at the portal.

"If you shoot near that portal we have no idea what will happen. Remember what happened in China," Steve said.

"He's right, that portal is basically a huge wall of energy. We have no idea what you will unleash if you fire at it," Anton said.

Silverton was in no mood to compromise. "And if we let this happen? Then what? They will stop at nothing to carry out their mission of smuggling the resources they need forward in time. Do you understand the impact multiple extractions like this could have on this time? That's a risk we are not willing to take. So, whilst it may look drastic to you, this is the only way I can see my orders being carried out to the full."

"We can deal with it, I can assure you, but leaping into the unknown is not the kind of risk we should take, especially given our proximity to the city," Steve replied and let out a deep sigh when Silverton lowered his gun and crouched down.

Matt stood next to the portal, "You have to record this" he said pointing to Jean-Paul. "They need to understand what happens on this side of the timeline. It is vital that we document it."

"How will they receive it?" Jean-Paul asked.

"I'll upload it into the sphere and then send it back through the timeline," Matt replied.

"How do you know that will work?" Jean-Paul questioned.

"I saw the prototype of this baby back home. It is a remarkable piece of technology, far beyond what we could ever imagine, or believe was possible," Matt replied and looked admiringly at the sphere.

"But record it with what?" Jean-Paul said.

"This," Matt took a small video camera out of his jacket pocket and passed it to Jean-Paul. "It's primitive, but it will do what we need it to do. I don't want them to miss anything. They need to understand how this portal reacts with the diamonds."

"You want me to use this?" Jean-Paul examined the camera.

"Yes," Matt replied.

Jean-Paul held the small camera in his hand, he pointed it up to the ceiling to get an idea of how the lens worked and then panned around the immediate area. Matt was caught in the frame at one point but almost totally in silhouette.

"You need to move across," Jean-Paul said while he waved Matt away from the portal.

"I'm not important. This is what I want them to see." Matt pointed to the portal, "And what happens when we send the diamonds through."

Matt stood a few feet away from the portal, holding up one of the bags. Jean-Paul backed up to the doorway until it was only a few metres behind him.

"I need more light, hang on a minute." Jean-Paul grabbed a small torch from an inside pocket of his coat while Matt looked on impatiently.

"Come on! Damn it, why do you need more light now? You just told me to move because of the light!"

"It's a different kind of light. Do you want this to be done correctly or not?" Jean-Paul insisted.

Jean-Paul shone the torch into Matt's eyes.

"Not there!" Matt shouted back.

Clint and Alain were looking, each holding a bag of diamonds. "This had better work," Clint said.

Jean-Paul steadied the camera in one hand and held it close to his left eye keeping the torch pressed against his right temple. "Okay, we're filming."

"This is the first bag of diamonds we are sending," Matt said while looking into the camera lens. Suddenly Jean-Paul's free eye widened, he focused on something that was caught in the beam of the torchlight beyond Matt and in the doorway behind him; he pulled the camera away from his left eye.

"What is it now?" Matt snapped.

"Nothing. I got something in my eye."

"Don't give me that shit, you stopped filming. What did you see?" Matt took a couple of steps toward Jean-Paul.

"Nothing. Are we going to get on with this or not?" Jean-Paul waved his hand to direct Matt back into position.

"Something's not right." Matt dropped the bag and turned around. He took out his torch and shone it through the doorway into the tunnel beyond and then back again, across the floor and around the door frame before stepping closer. He pushed the door out of the way as best as he could and then pointed the torch into the tunnel ahead.

"Right," Matt said. Having satisfied himself that there was nothing to be seen, he turned around and took a few steps toward the glowing portal, "Let's continue," he said.

Jean-Paul held up the camera and gestured that he was about to start filming again. Matt looked disinterested and kept looking toward the doorway. "Will you focus on the camera please?" Jean-Paul asked.

Matt tried to focus on the camera but continued to glance back at the doorway. Jean-Paul was becoming increasingly impatient with him. "Just forget it!" Jean-Paul snapped.

Matt stared back at the camera and waited for Jean-Paul's cue to continue his speech. He was interrupted again, this time by the crunching sound of the door being wrenched open and the sight of Silverton rushing through with his gun pointing directly at him. Without saying a word Matt jumped out of the firing line leaving Jean-Paul in front of Silverton.

"NO!" Anton leapt through the doorway and pushed Silverton's arm just as the bullet flew out of the barrel and toward the portal.

The bullet whistled past Jean-Paul and punctured the portal next to him. The glowing wall of light ruptured and expanded outward, enveloping Jean-Paul and dragging him into the portal. As the wall of light contracted back into the frame, Matt reached out to try and grab him but it all happened too quickly. All he could grasp was the camera from his outstretched hand. Jean-Paul was lost in the void of the broken timeline.

Clint and Alain looked on, transfixed. Silverton rushed forward and rugby-tackled Matt to the ground.

Anton and Steve stood in the doorway blocking one possible escape route. Alain dropped the holdall and made a dash past the ruptured portal into the tunnel behind it, but it was blocked by rubble. Silverton clambered to his feet, Anton moved forward and stood over Matt, ensuring he didn't get any ideas. Alain turned around to see Silverton striding purposely toward him; Silverton took aim with his gun and shot Alain in the leg.

Alain fell to the ground, screaming in agony. Silverton grabbed him by his jacket collar, dragged him past the portal, and pushed him to the ground next to Matt.

Anton bent down and punched Matt in the face. "That is from Jean-Paul," he said while looking toward the decreasing wall of light.

Clint dropped his bag and held his hands up. Steve grabbed the holdall and took him by the arm, leading him back to the group assembled next to the portal.

Anton looked at the portal. "Where are you, my friend?"

Silverton stood over them all, waving his gun around. "Well, this is a cosy little gathering, I never—"

Before he could finish his sentence, Silverton was thrown to the ground and the gun spilled from his hand. A deep booming sound emanated from the portal; it was so loud that the ground shook violently, small rocks and dust began falling from the ceiling coating them with dust and debris.

The incessant booming grew louder and the light within the portal started to crack. The ground shook violently beneath them. Steve lost his balance and tripped over Clint, hitting his head against one of the ancient skulls on the floor. Anton tried to crawl over to him but his progress was slow against the onslaught of rocks and dust falling from the ceiling. Steve shook his head and signaled to Anton that he was okay.

"What the hell have you done?" Matt shouted at Silverton, but he was drowned out by the noise.

The shards of light within the portal fractured and imploded inward, sucking the sphere into the black void. The booming sound became unbearable and everyone tried to shield their ears with their hands.

Matt seized his chance, along with Clint, who had grabbed a nearby holdall. They staggered to their feet and struggled to the doorway, rocking and swaying as the floor vibrated. Anton tried to reach out and grab them while Silverton was frantically trying to find his gun amongst the loose debris, unaware of their attempted escape. Alain couldn't move, blood gushed from the open gunshot wound in his leg. He looked on in frustration while Matt and Clint bounced their way through the doorway.

Silverton shouted at the pair as they ran into the tunnel. Anton and Steve staggered to their feet and gave chase down the tunnel.

The empty frame of the portal collapsed into the phasing unit and the relentless noise abated. The ground finally stopped shaking, allowing Silverton to locate his gun amongst the loose rubble and stand up.

He pointed the gun at Alain. "Get up," he said while reaching down to pick up the phasing unit which was now partially hidden amongst the rubble.

"Don't shoot me," Alain begged.

"I already have." Silverton waved the gun at him.

"Don't do it again," Alain shouted.

"Don't run away, then I won't shoot you again." Silverton grabbed Alain by the collar and pulled him to his feet.

"What are you going to do with me?"

"First, you're coming with me, then it is up to them." Silverton pushed Alain through the doorway.

"Them?" Alain asked.

"You'll find out soon enough. Now keep walking, and don't give me another excuse to shoot you."

Silverton gestured the way with his gun. Alain limped down the tunnel with Silverton in close proximity.

23

Paris Metro.Present-Day.

Matt and Clint ran through the tunnel toward the door that led back up to the Trocadero metro station. Steve and Anton were gaining but were still a few hundred yards behind them.

"How far?" Clint panted as he struggled with the exertion of carrying the holdall.

"I don't know, but we've passed the security office so it can't be far. Come on!"

The sight of the door gave them the extra impetus to push on. Matt barged into the partially open door and fell into the short corridor that led back to the foyer. He scrambled to his feet, and Clint followed him. They stood next to the door to catch their breath and regain some sense of calm. Matt pushed the door back in place and tried to jam it closed but it was no use.

"Let's go," Matt uttered, struggling to catch his breath.

"Where are we going?" Clint asked.

"Let's get back up to the road, there's more cover there," Matt replied.

"What about the Metro?"

"I don't fancy being trapped on a train, besides there's nowhere to hide or escape to if we need to make a quick exit."

Matt and Clint calmly walked through the crowded station.

***

Silverton pushed the gun into Alain's back. "Keep walking or I'll—"

"You'll what?" Alain didn't seem to care.

"What I don't get is why the fucking hell you are bothering with all of this?" Silverton asked.

Alain stumbled through the tunnel. "Because we have to." He was breathing heavily with the pain.

"You don't have to. You just want to create chaos." Silverton pushed Alain forward.

"You have no idea what you're messing with. You're being played, and you don't even realise it. Open your eyes, man. Stop being pathetic and seek out your own answers."

"You can save all that shit for Kallyuke. He'll be interested in hearing your thoughts."

They walked past the security office, pausing for a moment to observe the lifeless body of the security guard. "Was that your doing?" Silverton asked.

"I'm not a killer."

"Maybe not, but Kallyuke will be concerned that you have a trigger-happy friend."

"Kallyuke won't listen. He thinks this is about him. He thinks all we want to do is destabilise his power base and... oh, never mind, what's the point, you've already made up your mind, haven't you?"

"The only thing I have made my mind up about is that this has to stop – and stop now," Silverton replied.

"You think this will stop us?" Alain stopped walking and turned to face Silverton. "This is just the beginning – child's play – pretty soon we'll be launching wave after wave of extractions. We will stop at nothing to find an escape route off this planet."

"Are you crazy? First you dream up some plan to plunder the catacombs of Paris and now you expect me to believe you planned all this just to escape the planet? You're common thieves, and just because you can travel through time to steal your plunder from the past doesn't change that fact."

"Sometimes the endgame isn't always apparent from the start," Alain replied.

"Don't play games with me," Silverton snapped.

"No games, none at all."

"But why? What are you escaping from?" Silverton, for a moment at least, was prepared to listen.

"You really need me to answer that? I tell you what, when you next decide to visit our time, take a moment to open your eyes and understand what you see. I mean *really* see, not what they want you to see, and decide for yourself." Alain resumed his painful walk toward the exit.

Silverton was a few steps behind him, he lowered his gun to his side. "What do you expect me to see?"

"If you look properly and keep an open mind you'll know what I mean. Shouldn't be an issue for a smart guy like you."

They continued walking through the tunnel in silence. Silverton was deep in thought.

***

Steve pushed open the door at the end of the tunnel, and he and Anton paused for breath in the stark bright light.

"We've got to go," Steve said, trying to regain his breath.

"What about Roy?" Anton asked.

"He's here somewhere but we have no time to find him. Let Silverton explain what happened. We cannot allow these people to escape."

Steve found a second wind, and they hurriedly navigated through the rush of commuters in the foyer and ran up the stairs. Anton reluctantly followed and they now stood at the top of the stairs looking for clues.

"Where did they go?" Steve asked as he surveyed the immediate area.

"Not sure. They won't be heading that way though, too much attention," Anton pointed toward the Eiffel Tower.

"Let's try this way then," Steve said and pointed down the Avenue de President Wilson. He started to run toward it via the connecting road while Anton followed, puzzled by where Steve was getting all his energy.

"What's going on down there?" Steve pointed in front.

"Where?" Anton puffed out his cheeks as he tried to keep up with Steve.

"There's something going on, I can hear shouting," Steve quickened his pace in an attempt to get closer to the source of the commotion.

"Is it them?" Anton shouted back.

"I don't know but something is going on down there!" Steve started to sprint past the crowds with Anton trying to stay in close attendance. Steve ran onto the road, keeping close to the pavement to try and avoid the other pedestrians. Anton tried to keep up but clipped the heel of a man who stood in his pathway as he made his way toward the road. The man went flying, his briefcase smashed open and papers flew out onto the pavement. Steve glanced back to see if Anton was okay only to see that he was now only a few yards behind him.

A short distance ahead, Steve could see a man waving his fist and shouting at a white van parked on the side of the road. He watched as the man tried to pull on one of the doors to keep it open but an outstretched arm from inside the van pushed him in the chest; the man fell backward onto the pavement.

"It's them! I'm telling you!" Steve shouted to Anton as they closed in on the scene.

"How can you be…" Anton ran out of breath.

"I just know, call it a hunch…." Steve kept running, they were now yards from the van.

Steve approached the van and started to bash on the side of it with his open palm but it was too late; the van pulled into traffic.

"Shit! Did they just get into that van? Tell me that didn't happen!" Steve shouted.

"Fourre-tout bleu?" Anton asked the man who was gingerly getting to his feet.

"Oui," the man replied as he pointed to the van.

"It's them," Anton turned and spoke to Steve.

They both watched helplessly as Clint and Matt sped down the road.

"I have an idea," Anton shouted as he paced down the road.

"What?" Steve was focused on the van as it made its way down the crowded road.

"Here!" Anton shouted back to Steve.

Anton moved quickly to pull a driver out of another white van that was waiting at the side of the road, "Nous avons bison de voter camionette, c"estune urgency, il set un policier d"Angleterre," he said to the driver who was now standing on the roadside.

"What?" Steve stood there.

"Get in!" Anton yelled.

"What did you say to him?" Steve said jumping into the passenger's seat.

"I said we have an emergency," Anton replied, engaging first gear and speeding off .

"What else did you say?" Steve was not convinced.

"That you are a policeman from England." Anton stared ahead trying to plot a route to catch up with Clint and Matt who were in the van which was now weaving through the traffic ahead of them on the Avenue de President Wilson.

"Can you catch them?" Steve asked.

"This is my hometown," Anton said and briefly smiled at Steve. If anyone knew the streets, Anton did.

"Fair point." Steve nodded and held on to the base of the seat.

* * *

Silverton finally made it to the short corridor with Alain who was bleeding heavily.

"I'm going to put away my gun so we don't cause a scene, but make no mistake, if you try anything, I *will* shoot you."

He nudged Alain forward and they entered the foyer. Commuters brushed past them, some of them gasped at the sight of the gunshot wound, parting the way for them both to get to the stairs. Silverton flashed his badge to the onlookers and surveyed the area trying to locate Roy.

The parting of commuters attracted Roy's attention.

"What the hell happened to him?" Roy approached them through the crowd of commuters, completely unnoticed by Silverton.

"Let's just get out of here before we arouse too much attention." Silverton pointed to a policeman standing near the ticket booth. They started to climb the steps.

"What happened? And where are the others?" Roy asked again.

They stood away from the entrance to the station, nearer to one of the back roads that fed into the Trocadero.

"It went wrong, badly wrong, apart from managing to grab this," Silverton pulled the phasing unit from his jacket. "Take it back, tell them to analyse it for wavelength patterns, or anything else that's traceable. And take this man for interrogation, tell them they used some form of secondary comms system – a sphere. I don't know what it was. I've never seen anything like it.

167

They were filming it as well. It was like fucking Hollywood down there."

"Hang on, a sphere? What sphere? You're not making any sense." Roy threw his hands in the air.

"You saw it, you tell him," Silverton turned to Alain.

"I'm not saying anything." Alain shook his head.

"I need you to take over from now on," Silverton said to Roy.

"It's no problem, I know what to do."

Silverton shoved Alain closer to Roy, who glared at him, "Just so you know, where we're going you won't get a lawyer to help you."

"Whatever," Alain said.

"What are you going to do?" Roy asked Silverton.

"I need to find the others. I have a bad feeling that something else is going to happen." Silverton exhaled and puffed out his cheeks.

They turned down a small back street away from all the hustle and bustle of the city and made two turns before heading down into a dead-end street. There were a few old cars parked on the side and some large rubbish bins that were filled to their breaking point. The smell of rotting food mixing with the steam from the extraction fans poking out of the walls made for a disgusting cocktail. Silverton tapped Roy on the arm and signaled his approval with a slight nod of the head.

"What are you going to do with me?" Alain glared at Silverton.

"That's for us to worry about," Silverton replied.

Silverton watched over Roy while he pulled out a phasing unit from his jacket and pushed the button. A bright light surrounded them both and within an instant they disappeared. The swirling steam was now the only evidence that something had just happened.

Silverton walked back into the crowded streets and set off in pursuit of Anton and Steve.

***

Steve drew a sharp breath as Anton aggressively negotiated the huge roundabout that led them onto the Avenue d'Iena.

"Where the fuck are they going?" Steve shouted.

"Fucking circles, you can tell they are tourists, they drive like fucking clowns!" Anton gripped the steering wheel and planted the accelerator into the floor.

Traffic littered their path but Anton found enough gaps to squeeze through as he weaved across in a desperate attempt to catch up to the other van.

"This is not good," Anton said.

Steve concentrated on clinging to the door handle. "You've nearly got them!"

"I told you this is my hometown!"

Steve squeezed the door handle tighter as he saw the van in front swerve out of the way of an oncoming bus hitting a road sign in the process.

Anton was closing in as they approached a major junction, to their left the Eiffel Tower came into full view.

"Don't do it! Don't fucking do it!" Anton shouted as the van in front cut left across the junction and the oncoming traffic, forcing the cars to brake heavily. The van continued onto the Pont D'Iena. A chorus of horns could be heard from the stationary vehicles.

"Hang on!" Anton tapped his ear slightly, nodded and shouted across to Steve.

Anton took the same sharp left and guided the van through the traffic that was now backed up where the first van had cut through. He swerved across the lanes and turned onto the bridge narrowly avoiding the scattered road signs.

"The road is closed!" Steve shouted.

"I know!" Anton shouted back.

The Eiffel Tower was directly ahead of them. Anton hit the gas and managed to pull alongside the other van, he swerved toward it and the two vehicles momentarily collided. The sound of metal on metal filled the air.

Pedestrians scattered in all directions, but Steve noticed one man remained on the side of the road with his camera pointing toward them.

Steve's attention was then drawn to another man who stepped onto the road in front of them with his arm raised.

"What the fuck is…" Steve shouted but his words were cut short by a piercing bright light that flashed toward them. Steve was surrounded by inky darkness. He shivered as a familiar sensation washed over him.

As the steam subsided from the engines mangled in the wreckage of the two vans, some witnesses slowly started to approach the scene. One witness was taking pictures of the vans, and another noticed that the back doors on one of them had flung open in the collision, revealing a large holdall buried in the bread and pastries. It was half open and, upon closer inspection, he discovered that it was full of rocks that were glimmering in the sunlight. He reached over and heaved the bag closer so he could have a better look.

Police, who were patrolling the area ,came running toward the crash scene, accompanied by the sirens of emergency services vehicles in the distance. One of them pulled out some yellow police cordon tape from his belt and started to surround the vans with it.

The man who grabbed the bag managed to blend back into the growing crowd of witnesses, sensing an opportunity to slide off unnoticed. He carefully took one of the rocks from the bag to have a closer look. He brushed it against his jeans to try and remove some of the dirt revealing some form of crystal rock under the muck. He tried to slink away from the scene, but one of the other witnesses noticed him and the holdall he was carrying. The witness shouted at him to stop and called him a thief but he ignored the witness. He placed his finger on his lips gesturing at them to be quiet but the witness continued to shout at him. The man quickened his pace and headed toward the Eiffel Tower.

"Arretez de voler!" the witness shouted.

The man looked downwards as he started to jog and pulled the peak of his baseball cap down to try and disguise his face. He could hear the witness continue to shout in the background as he progressed further away from the crash scene.

The shouting alerted a nearby policeman to what was happening. The man panicked and started to run toward the Eiffel Tower, but his progress was hindered by the heavy bag. The officer shouted at him to stop but he continued to run. The man ran past a group of startled tourists who realised what was happening and ran in all directions as the policeman gave chase, shouting at him to stop.

The man was now directly under the Tower and running toward a small area of roadworks in the distance. The policeman shouted again to try and make him stop but that was the last thing on his mind.

Two officers on the other side of the Tower heard the shouting from their colleague and looked across to see the man running toward the Champ de Mars. They started running to try and apprehend him.

The holdall was getting heavier with every step and the man started to slow down as he got closer to the road. Not thinking straight, out of the breath and now staggering, the man quickly looked around to see the three officers getting closer. He tried to jump over the roadwork that blocked his path but he caught his foot on one of the signs and fell into the shallow trench dug by workmen earlier that day.

The navy holdall split on some sharp metal object and the contents spilled out into the trench. The man had managed to twist his ankle and was now lying on his side in agony. He looked up to the sky and took a deep breath as the policemen converged on him pointing their guns at his head.

"You were told to stop!" one of the policemen said as he placed his gun back in his holster, realising that the man was no longer a threat. He reached down and pulled the man to his feet while the other two officers stood guard. The man slumped to the ground in agony.

"What is in the bag?" the officer asked.

The man looked down to the ground, ignored the question and spat on the road. The policeman took the hint and called for an ambulance.

"You will be taken to the hospital, but I must warn you that you are under arrest," the policeman said and he continued to read the man his rights.

24

Santa Monica.
A Few Months Earlier.

"You can't hide from this, Steve. This is you, whether you like it or not. You are part of this and you know what? You are the most important part," Charley said.

Steve slumped into the tatty chair in Charley's makeshift portacabin. "So you keep saying. But you keep talking about time travelling smugglers. I'm having a tough time trying to keep up with you, let alone believe you."

"This map shows the locations of all of the infants we supplanted into this." Charley turned the screen around. Steve glanced at it but wasn't really paying much attention. "You see here, and here?"

Steve made a point of ignoring the screen. "What is it you expect from me?"

"Some enthusiasm."

"For twenty-six dots on a screen? And what *are* these...dots? No, let me guess, people like me?"

"Don't bust my balls, this is difficult enough." Charley thumped the table with his fist.

"Well, I'll tell you what, I won't bust your balls on the condition that you can show me some solid proof of what you're telling me. How does that sound?"

Darkness once again engulfed Steve.

25

Paris.2618.

Steve stood in front of what was left of the Eiffel Tower.

"What the hell happened here?" Steve looked in awe at the struck down wreck of a once proud Parisian landmark.

Kallyuke ceased his furious pacing and stopped in front of Steve. "This was the eye of the storm, the part we couldn't explain to you, but you can see it with your own eyes now. It is a testament to all that is wrong with war. Where no boundaries are set, and where no place is sacred in the quest for victory."

Steve wiped his brow on his sleeve. The sunlight was blistering and the heat overwhelming. "It's sickening to think this will happen one day. Never in my wildest nightmares did I imagine this was part of the future."

"Did anyone think to stop these people before they got to the street?" Kallyuke pointed to the two men lying on the ground, face down, with their hands tied behind their backs with plastic ties and their feet bound together. "It would have saved us all this mess and the inevitable fall out that Silverton will have to now clean up."

Anton remained silent.

"If Silverton had refrained from using his gun we wouldn't be standing here."

"He was following orders," Kallyuke snapped.

"Whose orders?" Steve looked at Kallyuke.

"My orders. He was the failsafe. Stop the mission at all costs if it cannot be effectively controlled.

You failed to control it therefore he acted," Kallyuke chided and then glared at Anton. "Go and get your leg fixed."

"Perhaps next time the orders could be shared. Anton and I had no idea what he was up to. In fact, aside from observing the situation it wasn't clear what we could do to prevent the attempted extraction," Steve's eyes remained fixed on Kallyuke.

"Well if *you* had spent more time listening to Charley Sandford, instead of ridiculing him, we may not be in this mess. This is yet another distraction from what we should be doing: breaking up this gang of criminals."

"It wasn't his fault. I tried to stop Silverton from shooting the portal, it was too risky. All that happened afterward was as a direct result of Silverton's actions," Anton said.

Kallyuke glared at him. "What did you just say?"

"I said if Silverton had not been aiming for the portal—"

"He wasn't aiming for the portal! I wanted him to neutralise those responsible for the extraction, you fool. Before any of this mess could happen," Kallyuke pointed to the prisoners and resumed pacing.

"So, it was an assassination then?" Anton asked.

"No, I wanted them alive."

Anton strode purposefully toward Kallyuke. "This is not the mission as I understood it. If you want to assassinate someone, get your own people to do it. Don't involve me."

"No one said anything about an assassination. I ordered Silverton to neutralise them so we could interrogate them. They were of far more use alive than dead," Kallyuke replied

Steve stepped forward. "Look, what happened is in the past now, but what if there are people like them turning up all over the place. How do we deal with that?"

"By going straight to the nest. We take off the head and work downward from there." Kallyuke turned and stood toe to toe with Steve.

"And where is this nest?" Anton asked.

"Silverton has some intel on it. These people will help us confirm our hypothesis, then we can make our move," Kallyuke said and turned to look at the prisoners.

"It's a pity he didn't have intel on Jean-Paul," Steve said.

"We didn't want to compromise his safety," Anton said. "He was crucial to us tracking them down and trying to stop that extraction. Believe me when I say his loss is hard to stomach. There are times when we can trust no one."

"Let's hope there aren't many more times like that," Steve replied.

"How did you know about Jean-Paul?" Kallyuke was confused by this.

"Anton tried to stop Silverton shooting at the portal, or so I thought; Jean-Paul was right in the firing line if anything happened, which of course it did. And then Anton hit Matt saying...what was it?" Steve said.

"*That is for Jean-Paul,*" Anton repeated, slowly shaking his head. "I didn't realise you could hear that."

"He was an excellent double agent. We spent a lot of time ensuring his cover was rock solid, but such are the risks…" Kallyuke shrugged his shoulders.

"Such are the risks?" Anton threw his hands in the air.

"He knew the risks the minute he agreed to sign up," Kallyuke argued.

"We have another problem as well, don't we?" Steve said. "Another potentially fatal crash scene with no bodies. In the centre of Paris. That's bound to raise some questions, wouldn't you say?" Steve shrugged his shoulders.

"That has been taken care of," Kallyuke said, dismissing the problem. "It is more important to get these two men to the interrogation unit."

"I thought places like that would have died out centuries ago," Steve said.

"Then you still have a lot to learn about us. Prisoners are still prisoners, irrespective of what year it is, and they need to be dealt with accordingly." Kallyuke replied and then signaled to the guards to pick up the prisoners.

26

Paris.Present-Day.

Clouds gathered over Paris, along with a brisk wind. The flashing lights of the emergency services vehicles lit up the area with metronomic regularity.

The crash scene was a hive of activity as the local police tried to keep order. Witnesses were doing everything they could to catch a glimpse of the bodies in the vans but the police were now in control and were directing the ambulances to park next to the fire engine that had arrived earlier on the scene.

The plastic sheeting from a large, white forensics tent flapped in the wind as fireman battled to attach it to the frame; it was positioned next to the vans and would serve as cover for the bodies when they were removed.

More people approached the crash scene, with some of the onlookers pushing against the yellow tape, stretching it to its limits as they attempted to get closer to the vans to look inside. However, they were being urged to move back by the police who were very keen to ensure people were prevented from obtaining any images of the victims.

"This is a mess isn't it?" said one of officers to his colleague while they kept guard.

"It is, and so close to that as well," the other officer pointed toward the Tower.

"What do you think he is looking at?" the officer pointed at a man who was intently studying his camera.

"I have no idea but no doubt it will be online somewhere soon, you know what people are like," the other officer remarked with a smirk.

Francois got out of his car on the other side of the police cordon, stubbed out a cigarette on the ground and walked toward the officers who were guarding the police cordon. "Who are you?" he asked as he flashed his badge.

"Officer Debuchy, sir," the officer immediately replied.

"And you?" Francois looked at the other officer.

"Officer Flamini sir," he replied.

"Why are these people so close to the vehicles and where are the paramedics?" Francois asked.

"They are by the vans now looking at the victims," Flamini replied.

"We're doing our best with the people," Debuchy said.

"Do better then," and with that Francois walked over to the vans.

Entering the white tent, Francois asked, "Who's in charge here?"

"We are all working together on this but as such, I guess, I am the lead paramedic. My name is Brigitte, who may you be and how can I help you?" She held out a rubber glove covered hand.

Francois shook her hand and showed her his badge, "Francois Blanc. Nationale."

"I see, and what brings a member of the Nationale out to a routine crash like this? This is hardly the work of a criminal mastermind," she asked while the rest of the paramedics continued to examine the bodies in the background.

"I don't really know. I tapped into the police radio transmission and heard them talking about some sort of light. It felt like something major could be happening, you know how you sometimes get a hunch about something, eh?"

"Sorry to shatter your hopes, and your hunch, but this is just a routine crash," Brigitte replied.

"Okay, so what about them?" Francois nodded toward two of the crash victims as they were placed on the stretchers by the paramedics."

"Oh, there's nothing we can do for these people I'm afraid." Brigitte hastily shook her head.

"They're all dead?" Francois asked.

"Yes, all dead," she said.

"But looking at the condition of the vehicles, this was hardly a high-speed collision, do you have any idea what they died of?" Francois lit another cigarette.

"Not yet, we need to get the bodies back to the mortuary for examination, then we can learn more about the circumstances in which they died," Brigitte said.

"Where are you taking them?" Francois asked.

"Cognac-Jay Hospital," she said.

"Please, do this for me, no questions asked. Take the bodies directly to the Pitie Salpetriere hospital, please," Francois took a drag from his cigarette.

"But that's—"

"I know it's a big favour to ask, but the best pathologist in France works there and I want to ensure that no stone is unturned during the autopsies. I'll get clearance with no questions asked." Francois was insistent.

"You've really got something in your head about this crash, haven't you?" Brigitte asked.

"Call it a detective's instinct."

"I have a similar set of instincts. Tell me, do you not think this is a bit strange? This isn't a high-speed motorway. Look at the condition of the vehicles, they're not so bad, yet all four people died. Isn't that slightly unusual? Surely at least one would have survived, maybe even briefly," Brigitte said.

"Guesswork can be dangerous. My instincts do tell me there is something unusual about this crash, but until we have all the facts, it is difficult to quantify what that may be," Francois said and then took a final look at the bodies before the paramedics loaded them into the ambulances.

Francois lit another cigarette and stood by the vans. The gathering crowds were a nuisance and interrupted his thinking. He wandered out toward the edge of the police cordon and stared up at the Eiffel Tower and then turned to look back up the road toward the Trocadero. He wanted to focus on what may have happened by mentally reconstructing the events of the crash in his mind. As he turned back again he paused briefly thinking he caught a glimpse of a familiar face in the crowd. The person in the crowd turned away and shuffled off. Francois shrugged his shoulders and carried on surveying the crash scene. He then noticed Brigitte approaching.

"They don't understand why they have to divert the bodies," Brigitte said, pointing at the paramedics now sitting in the ambulances.

"As I explained previously, the pathologist at that hospital is the best I know so if anyone can find out what happened to those bodies then he is the one I trust to do it." He stubbed out his cigarette on the ground.

"You know I also don't deal in guesswork Monsieur Blanc. Like you, I also deal in facts," Brigitte stood square on to Francois as she spoke.

"And your point is?" Francois shrugged his shoulders.

"Well, I had a very short opportunity to examine the bodies, and you know the first thing I noticed?"

"I don't, but I have a feeling you're going to tell me."

"Rigor mortis."

"Rigor mortis?" Francois reached for another cigarette from his jacket pocket.

"Yes. Rigor mortis. It normally takes hold in a dead body after about four to six hours, but in these bodies it is already apparent. That shouldn't be possible. Don't you find that strange?" Brigitte folded her arms.

"As I have said, I put my trust in the pathologist at the Pitie Salpetriere hospital and as you've said, you've not established anything about the circumstances surrounding their deaths."

"You don't need to carry out an examination to see that rigour mortis is taking hold, you can tell by simply lifting them onto the stretchers."

"Let's make a deal right here," Francois paused to light the cigarette in his hand and took a long drag on it. "Your involvement in this case now ends and you will say nothing more about it. The bodies are on their way to the hospital and my people will now take control of this investigation. Does that sound like something you can do?"

"Of course, I understand."

"I'm glad we understand each other." Francois shook Brigitte's hand.

27

Paris.2618.

"Take them to Unit 1 of the Captivus Zone in North West Sector 1.0, prepare them for interrogation as well. I don't want to lose any time." Kallyuke strode around the two prisoners and then paused to look up at the Eiffel Tower. He was clearly not happy with what had happened and cast his mind back to the last issues.

He looked over to Steve, "How many this time?"

"Pardon?" Steve was caught in a mental no man's land while he tried to take in this new version of Paris.

"How many people do you think witnessed the crash? You know that the aftermath of the incident on the M6 got a bit out of control. I take it you've seen the reports by Mark Collins on the incident?" Kallyuke stopped for a moment and looked at Steve.

"Mark Collins? Never heard of him, what do you mean reports? I've not seen anything." Steve was surprised by this new revelation.

"First, let's get in the shuttle, we can talk about it on the way to London. Anton, I told you to get your leg fixed. I don't want you bleeding all over the place," Kallyuke said and then ushered Steve and Anton into the shuttle. The guards escorted the prisoners onto the other shuttle.

Anton limped to the back of the shuttle and reached for a MediKit in one of the compartments. He pulled out a thin, pen shaped object and leaned against the back of one of the seats. He raised his cut leg so he could arch around, he then pointed the object at the wound and squeezed it. A thin black liquid discharged from the tip. He administered the liquid along the length of the wound, and it was immediately sealed, and stopped bleeding as the liquid solidified.

Both shuttles blasted off into the silent heat of the Parisian skyline. They flew slowly over the city and into the sunset heading for London. Steve settled back into one of the sumptuous seats and drank some water that had been placed on the table by one of the Kallyuke's staff. Anton limped back and sat next to him across the aisle and settled back to take advantage of the respite and grab a short nap. Kallyuke sat opposite Steve, observing his every move like a cat ready to pounce on its prey.

"This Mark Collins guy, what did you mean by reports?" Steve asked.

"They're calling it the *M6 Paranormal Crash*. Can you believe how naive these people must be to get drawn into a so-called report with that title?" Kallyuke was dismissive of the reports.

"Well, it's not every day that a bunch of people disappear into a bright light and appear six hundred years in the future, is it?" Steve said.

"Maybe not, but these reports are shoddy at best. They're based on hearsay, there's no quotable witnesses, and no substantive evidence to support the man's claims. Clearly, he's just bumbling around trying to assemble a set of facts that he can make into the most sensational report possible. So far the reports have only been carried by the fringe media so it hasn't gone very far…yet." Kallyuke smiled, he knew that the damage to their mission would be minimal.

"Yes but people have a tendency to believe what they read in the media," Steve suggested.

"That's because people are gullible, they don't question, they simply agree with what they're told and lap it up time and again."

"Can I see the reports?" Steve asked.

"When we get to London," Kallyuke said. He was keen to put this to one side for the moment.

Steve peered out of the window, looking at the devastation below. He started to understand the sheer scale of damage and destruction heaped upon Paris in the ensuing years after the initial protests over the quota system.

"So, Anton was right," he muttered to himself.

"Anton is always correct, trust me, I know," Anton said, waking from his light snooze. He smirked then promptly folded his arms and settled back into the seat and dozed off again.

"Are you referring to the Carbon Quota System and the effect it had on people?" Kallyuke asked.

"Yes. But I had no idea how devastating it was," Steve said.

"Seeing is believing, and of course you are in a privileged position to see the effects of a poorly planned policy and what it can do to the human race," Kallyuke sounded almost proud by this.

Both the shuttles were in close proximity and were crossing over the English channel which had now been reduced to a parking strip for the many ships that were abandoned and rotting, swaying meaninglessly in the tide.

"What are those ships doing down there?" Steve pointed out of the window.

"Very little. You can't set sail and do trade with the world's markets when you have no fuel to run your fleet. Most of these ships are commercial vessels that would have carried millions of tons of goods around the world, but when the policy makers enforced their rules, the fuel ran out. In protest they simply dropped anchor and left the ships to rot," Kallyuke explained, raising his eyebrows.

"Wasn't very clever was it?" Steve looked at row after row of ships of all shapes and sizes.

"If you ran a fleet and you had no way of keeping those huge engines turning then what else could you to do? People had very few options. Some owners tried to scrap them in the hope of recovering some money back into their businesses, but of course with so many maritime operators doing the same thing, the market became saturated. What you see down there is a worthless collection of scrap metal. I believe there were similar places in the twenty first century, deserts I believe, only for decommissioned aircraft."

"Yes but they were decommissioned due to age and old technology, not because some policy resulted in a lack of fuel to fly them," Steve replied.

"Politicians of that era were notoriously fickle. What they did, they tended to do for the populist vote, good policies got left behind in all the hyperbole."

"What makes you so different?" Steve asked.

"I've never said to anyone I'm different or correct in what I stand for. I just want to create a better world for us, given what we have left to work with."

"But not everyone agrees with you, if Charley Sandford is to be believed."

Kallyuke leant forward and rested his arms on the table. "You're in the middle of something that you don't quite understand yet, but the answers are tantalisingly close. Questions about who you are and what you are there to do, in the context of time, will soon become clear. Until then, observe and learn about this, your real home."

London was quickly on the horizon and the shuttle carrying the prisoners veered off in another direction heading toward Northwest Sector 1.0.

Kallyuke stood up and walked into the cockpit; after a few moments he returned to his seat opposite Steve. "I've asked them to do a pass of the city so you can see the effects of order, and not chaos on society. This will act as a comparison to the carnage you saw in Paris."

London came into view and Steve absorbed as much as he could through the window. The city was bright and vibrant, and he could just about make out the people rushing along the huge streets. Then he looked across and saw buildings that he recognised, the Tower of London and the Shard were still standing tall.

"Is that really the Tower of London?" Steve asked.

"It is, really," Kallyuke nodded and smiled.

"And the Shard? I would have thought that years of conflict would have destroyed them."

"Contrary to what you may think and to the many filmmakers of your time, there was no great apocalypse. Anton was right. What happened to this planet was the culmination of years of many smaller conflicts, some of which were essentially gang wars between people living on the opposite sides of a particular street. There was no World War Three, it simply never happened."

Anton stretched out his arms and slowly opened his eyes. "Where are we?"

"London. We will be landing at Central 1 soon. I'm just showing our new guest what a wonderful place London has become."

"You mean he's been here before?" Steve asked of Anton.

"Anton was initiated months before you, so he has had more time to acclimatise. We had problems trying to extricate you from your situation, so we had to manufacture certain scenarios to get you to Santa Monica. That way we knew we would have your undivided attention, though of course, Charley Sandford said that you were possibly the most obstructive of all the people he had met."

"What scenarios?" Steve pushed Kallyuke on this.

"Well, for a start there are the e-mails, we had to use a method of communication that would grab your attention, but also not appear to be some kind of trick. But you were already halfway there, weren't you?" Kallyuke sat back in his seat.

"How do you mean halfway there?"

"Well, you knew something was not quite right, didn't you? What was the trigger...perhaps you were frustrated by the technology of that time, or did you find yourself laughing at the repeated claims of the many so-called time travelers that made the headlines? You knew they were fake but somehow you knew it was possible. Steve, we are a lot closer to you than you may think, after all, you are one of our prized assets. We were watching everything."

"I'm nobody's asset. And yes, I was always on the outside looking in and questioning things, but that was always part of my make-up, even at school. It's one of the reasons I became an accountant. Figures offer very little room for variation; they are what they are; precise instruments of mathematics."

"Come on, Steve, Don't try and kid yourself. When you got on that aircraft to meet Charley Sandford part of you knew this was it, the beginning to a series of the answers you so badly craved, and that is why you are here today. You simply had to know, irrespective of the cost. It is your human desire, your thirst for knowledge that needed quenching and we are now continuing that process." Kallyuke drank some water.

"I suppose if I hadn't gone then I may have gone insane," Steve said and momentarily closed his eyes. He knew that his family was also caught up in the fallout. "Look I don't want to talk about this. I'm here because of who I am, but the whys and wherefores are an irrelevant by-product, they're not important anymore. I have to accept this now." Steve let out a long sigh.

"Fighting it will turn you inside out." Anton reached over and placed a reassuring hand on Steve's arm.

"I think we shall change our landing location. I'd like to land near the River Thames. We can take a short walk through the streets, experience at first hand the brave new society we are building." Kallyuke said and clasped his hands together.

***

Roy stood in a military medical facility on the outskirts of London. The room was stark with white walls and had only one bed in it, which was surrounded by guards and equipment.

"There's no permanent damage. The bullet is out now and he will be able to walk unaided within two hours, once the casing unit takes effect. You know what, I haven't seen one of those in years, a friend of mine had an antique pistol and accidentally shot himself in the arm. How did this happen? Who on earth manages to shoot themselves in the back of the leg?" the doctor looked at Alain who was now sitting up in bed.

"Thank you for that assessment," Roy said. "Now if you don't mind I need a moment alone to talk with the security guards." Roy looked at the door.

"Is he under arrest? For shooting himself?" the doctor was persistent.

"Sort of, but this is official business and I've got to talk with someone about the arrangements," Roy gently nudged the doctor to the door.

"I can take a hint. You may as well sign for him now." The doctor held out a small rectangular DigiPad that Roy duly signed. The doctor left the room.

"What's going to happen to me?" Alain's breathing quickened.

"You, my friend, are going to experience a
whole new level of hospitality courtesy of Northwest
Sector 1.0," Roy rubbed his hands together as he spoke
to Alain.

"You may as well kill me now," Alain replied.

"Why would I want to do a thing like that? I like
to help out from time to time bringing people like you to
justice," Roy said.

"What do you know about justice?" Alain asked.

"Well, I know one thing, never get caught trying
to fuck with the future because this is what will happen
to you," and with that Roy nodded to one of the security
guards who took out a small stun gun, pointed it at
Alain's neck and pulled the trigger, knocking him
unconscious.

"Get him to Sector 1.0. They can decide what to
do with him. I need to get back." Roy walked out of the
room, brushing past the doctor who was waiting outside
the door. He walked up two flights of stairs and out onto
a small landing pad on the roof. There, waiting for him
was a small shuttle with the door already open.

"I need you to take me back to the same place in
Paris where you picked us up. I have some unfinished
business to attend to." Roy climbed in the back of the
shuttle and it took off into the clear sky, heading back
toward Paris.

***

The shuttle transporting Kallyuke, Anton and
Steve landed next to the River Thames on a small
landing pad near to the Tower of London.

"What's happened to Tower Bridge?" Steve
climbed out onto the pavement and looked across at it.
Tower Bridge momentarily disappeared from view, "I'm
sure I just saw it flicker."

"It was destroyed. What you see in front of you is a perfect, holographic reconstruction," Kallyuke replied.

Kallyuke and Anton joined Steve in looking at the digital version of Tower Bridge.

"Why on earth would you do that?" Steve asked.

"There are certain things that are done in the best interests of the people, you know, to help boost or maintain morale. A vibrant, stimulating environment is crucial in helping us rebuild the world we want to live in. A world where there is no fear, no poverty and where people work together to help create a brave new society," Kallyuke declared.

"Is that your dream, or is that the rule around here?" Steve was skeptical.

"Anyone is free to leave. There is no door preventing them from leaving the safety of this and other cities around the world. They can try and go it alone, but there is no protection from the dangers that lay in wait. You won't find any law and order out there, only chaos, disease and crime. You saw the state of Paris with your own eyes, " Kallyuke said and then paused for a moment to regain his breath. "I tell you this much, I am determined that the 27th century will go down in history as the century of peace and prosperity for all."

"That's a rather bold claim isn't it?" Steve suggested.

"Look around you. These people – this city – is thriving under these new conditions. We may have rules, but any civilised society has rules in order to govern." Kallyuke pointed to the clusters of people walking along the perfectly manicured streets.

"Or control," Steve muttered as he turned away from Kallyuke.

The people walking past seemed happy enough, and the streets were immaculate. On the surface of it, life looked good. "Tell me this much, how did you manage it?" Steve asked. "How have you succeeded where, for centuries, so many others have tried and failed?."

Kallyuke looked puzzled. "Succeeded at what?"

"All this. It can't have been easy given what other people are plotting." Steve wanted to know more, like was this immaculate display for his benefit?

"We learnt a long time ago that if you create an environment and a supportive strategy that encourages people to cooperate and develop together, then you are already on the way to overcoming one of the biggest obstacles faced when creating a brave new society; that of alienation. Alienation is a mindset that is a breeding ground for discontent and violence, and we will stop at nothing to prevent its spread."

"You're saying that alienation already existed, and you're trying to crush it, or is alienation another word for rebellion?" Steve stared intently at Kallyuke.

"Don't try to put words into my mouth, it won't work. There is no rebellion because there is nothing to rebel against. However, don't take my word for it, I encourage you to spend some time amongst us so you can draw your own conclusions, after all, seeing is believing." Kallyuke gestured to the people going about their daily lives.

"You have to understand this is all new to me. A few months ago, I was an accountant for a firm in Manchester, now I'm looking at the city of London, six hundred years into the future and being told that everything is perfect and wonderful and you are creating this…*brave new society.*" Steve made finger quotations to emphasize the point. "This is why I'm questioning everything I see and what I'm told. As you've said, that is my nature and it won't change. Seeing, I'm afraid, is not always believing."

"Let us walk and give you time to see the new London as it is now. It will help you come to terms with the fact that you are indeed, now home." Kallyuke put his arm on Steve's shoulder to direct him along one of the busy streets. "Anton, we'll meet you in a short while at the Central Control Room."

Anton nodded and wandered into the crowd.

"How are your guests acclimatising to the so-called perfect world they are living in?" Steve asked.

"Guests?" Kallyuke tilted his head and frowned.

"You know, the ones that had to remain here after the M6 incident. How are they getting on? Are they enjoying their new lives in utopia? I seem to remember that one of them was particularly adamant that the whole thing was a scam. Has he calmed down yet?"

"I haven't heard anything to the contrary, so I guess they are fine. After all, as you say, they are now in utopia. I know I'd much rather be in the here-and-now than back in their time with all that is to come."

"But they don't know that do they?" Steve said.

"They probably do by now," Kallyuke replied while they continued to walk through the streets. "They have been assigned someone to guide them through the assimilation process. They could become valuable members of our society."

"Do they have a choice in the matter?"

"A limited one, but if they wanted to return they could only do that under our terms."

"Your terms being what?" Steve was curious.

"A scenario that wouldn't undermine our chances of success and avoids any awkward questions. Preferably one that means they are kept away from the public eye."

"Not much of a choice then, is it?"

"Maybe it isn't, however, it is a choice, just one that I wouldn't take."

"And how come you know so much about me?"

"You are *our* asset. We created the life you led in that time and had to ensure that you were prepared for what was to come. You made it easy for us to monitor you. In fact, as the years progressed, it got even easier. What you don't realise is just how much information you put out there about yourself for us to analyse. Data that was sent and shared across the world in an instant, data that helped us put together a profile of how you were developing." Kallyuke laughed at the thought of it.

"You mean information posted online that was secured behind firewalls?" Steve asked.

The sun shone brightly onto the street and bounced off the pristine buildings that lined their walk through the city.

"Yes, the information you posted freely. I'm afraid your so-called firewalls were no match for our technical abilities. Even now, we are harvesting billions of pieces of data from that time in our attempt to rebuild the archives. We want to rebuild the knowledge of our past to discover who we once were. The people of that time were obsessed with the online world. It is an absolute gift and we accept it willingly." Kallyuke held out his cupped hands.

"So, you're snooping? Stealing data? Is that how this brave new society is being built, on the foundations of theft? Correct me if I'm wrong but isn't hacking still illegal? I would have thought after all these years that would be a thing of the past, but obviously it isn't," Steve said.

"Hacking may be illegal in your time, but we don't play by your rules."

"What rules do you play by then? Is all of this part of an elegant facade to divert me away from what is really happening? Is this another Tower Bridge? A carefully constructed illusion?" Steve asked, pointing to the pristine buildings and the people who they were passing as they walked through the immaculate streets.

"You have a lot to learn, and in case you're wondering, we're *not* stealing anything, we are simply harvesting what is out there and ensuring that this priceless archive is not lost forever. We will not make the same mistakes again and we *will* build this archive, for all of our sakes and for the generations to come, who, I might add, richly deserve to have a past they too can be proud of."

"It sounds like you're stealing, even if your motives are understandable. Morally and ethically, it seems difficult to justify your actions."

Kallyuke let out a sigh, looked up to the sky and then looked at Steve. "We don't *need* or seek anyone's justification. We simply want to have a past that we can hand down to future generations and I'll stop at nothing to make this happen. We have to protect the future." Kallyuke shook his head.

"And what if stopping at nothing risks more lives?"

"We don't play with life. We are simply trying to enhance it. You could learn a lot from the data we've harvested. The museums for example, they are now able to recreate accurate holographic versions of vast collections of lost treasures from art galleries around the world. This has only been made possible through this work. Art that had been lost for centuries is now on display in this city. Do you not think that art and culture is an essential part of a thriving society?"

"I do, but morally, art has to stand up for itself and not be tainted in any way, or that undermines the value it brings, surely you can understand that?"

"You keep using the word moral like it's a stick to beat us with, however, a society that is culturally enriched is a place where people want to live, develop and contribute. Isn't that the goal of any community, at any point in time? I believe it is." Kallyuke nodded in agreement with himself .

"I don't doubt what you're doing, I just don't buy into the methodology of how you obtained these treasures."

"It's not just digital recreations. We've embarked on a plan to retrieve culturally significant artefacts that were either lost or stolen during the wars and conflicts of that time. Some were hidden by dictators as they fled power, others were placed in vaults by wealthy collectors to protect them from theft; vaults that were long considered destroyed or looted."

"And you're able to locate them, how?" Steve was intrigued.

"We've deployed a highly skilled group of people who have pieced together clues leading to the whereabouts of thousands of pieces of lost art and other artefacts. You may have read newspaper reports and heard rumours about the lost Nazi trains filled with loot, the Swiss bank vaults filled with all manner of valuables, and there's more, thousands of locations in fact. This will take years to complete, but it will help us recreate new museums that in turn will aid our understanding of our past."

"I'm an accountant. The rumours have passed me by."

"You *were* an accountant," Kallyuke replied.

"This also appears to be very true."

"Some of these artefacts haven't seen the light of day for centuries. Despite what you think, there is a lot of good coming from this undertaking."

"You don't strike me as someone who is keen on looking at the past." Steve wanted to stop and take in the surroundings but Kallyuke kept nudging him along.

"To build a future based on fairness and equality, you need to understand the mistakes from your past." Kallyuke sounded like he had rehearsed that line.

They continued to walk further into the pristine city but an uneasy silence fell between them.

Steve broke off for a moment and strolled toward the windows of the row of shops they were walking past. Inside one of them he saw a huge array of groceries from fresh fruit and vegetables that adorned the counters to the walls that were covered in pots all clearly labeled with various names of herbs and spices. He recognised most of the names on the labels.

They continued to walk through the streets of New London and Steve observed snippets of what life was now like. People ambled into view while they went about their business; but it felt contrived, like it was some form of show; a performance. Even if it wasn't.

"Despite the issues, the timeline opened up new opportunities for you," Steve said, breaking the silence.

"It allowed us to fill in the blanks that currently exist. We've also been experimenting with architecture and the city layout. The streets and buildings have been created to resemble what went before. Anyone can build glass towers, but that is not what we wanted for New London. We want this city to have a soul and be the blueprint for other cities." Kallyuke kept ushering them through the street.

"So ,you're building a giant theme park." Steve dismissed Kallyuke.

"No, we're building an environment, a place to live."

"But why that particular time in the past?" Steve asked.

"Many reasons, the tipping point between the proliferation of technology and the accessibility of information collided with a cultural springboard that meant you leapt beyond the norm and weren't afraid to embrace and explore your humanity. Unfortunately, the dark ages came soon after that. Society collapsed and imploded and the rich cultural heritage you cultivated for years simply disappeared."

"Do you fear a return to that time? Is this a knee jerk reaction to ensure there is too much at stake to go back to those days?" Steve said.

"I fear that returning to it may be signing our own death warrant. This is why we are trying to create what you see here and need everyone to pull together in this journey."

"Charley said the food here was bland and flavourless and that in our time, the flavours and choices we had made him jealous. I've looked through the window of one of these shops and there seems to be a tremendous choice of groceries, nothing like I expected. Was Charley lying to me?"

"No, he wasn't. We've been focusing on rebuilding the variety of our food supplies. It was narrow for a long time, through the necessity to feed people." Kallyuke stopped outside one of the shop windows with a huge display of food in the window. "There were two major issues; a lack of land to cultivate crops and a lack of variety. In the early stages of the rebuild, we had to grow what we could to survive but this city has a huge resource that lay untapped for centuries."

"And what would that be?" Steve asked as he watched someone pick up a bag full of groceries from one of the shops and walk out without paying for them.

"There are about two hundred and fifty miles of disused tunnels under this city. It used to be the London Underground, you're probably aware of it. Much of this has been salvaged and along with the stations, we've gained access to a significant amount of land that we converted for farming. It's not perfect, but it is safe, and we can control the environment to suit the crops using technology we've been developing for a while. We're also using the timeline to bring forward seeds to grow crops that have long since disappeared from our time. This is another major project we are undertaking.

Sourcing land outside the city is a particularly hazardous activity at the moment."

"In what way?" Steve asked.

"There is little law and order outside the city's perimeter," Kallyuke said as they continued to walk toward a large steel building that stood proud at the end of the street; it looked odd, almost out of place.

"You mean there are people who live outside the city? When we were in Paris, Anton told me about a train that ran on the West Coast line of America. He said the people who sought refuge on it were all eventually murdered by a roaming gang. I wouldn't have thought anyone would dare to live outside the city, the risks would be too high," Steve briefly stopped and stared into another one of the packed grocery shops.

"We have an issue with rogue groups that are scattered around the world, and it won't go away anytime soon. These groups have evolved over many years. They are a product of the gradual breakdown of society. They refuse to accept what we are creating here, preferring to live by their own rules, but they are poorly equipped to survive in such a hostile environment. They don't have adequate shelter and their food supplies are erratic. Then there are the splinter groups, smaller collectives of people, some of which are bound together by the virus; you know this virus was the primary reason for opening the timeline, don't you?

"Yes. I know."

"We had to locate key compounds for the vaccine we were developing. These are now completely eradicated in our time so we had no choice but to find a time where we could locate them, what with antibiotics having no effect. The timeline was created in an attempt to hunt these down and they were eventually located in the twenty first century," Kallyuke said.

They approached the entrance to the large steel building.

"So, *you* caused the issues you face with these Traders?" Steve stood next to Kallyuke while he punched in an access code into a small panel to open the door to the large steel building. The door slid open and they walked into a huge foyer. Kallyuke strode toward another door with Steve in close attendance, he stared at a sensor and the door opened; it was a lift and it immediately sprung to life.

"It is a side effect, but it was never intended that way. The scientists who worked with us on creating the timeline saw an opportunity to seize control of the technology for their own motives and split off to continue with their own agenda. We were powerless to stop them. We had no idea that this would be a consequence of the work we were undertaking to control the virus. If we had known, I would never have taken the risk," Kallyuke said.

"And sacrifice any chance you had of saving people from the virus?" Steve replied.

"That was our dilemma, the virus has spread unchecked amongst people who are living in the enclaves. With no access to medical care, they are simply rotting to death. Another complication is that the virus can lay dormant for years, so we are developing new screening mechanisms to try and detect it, even at that primary stage. But this virus is still proving to be resistant to the initial vaccine we developed which will create another major issue. It leaves us with very few choices in our attempts to keep the spread of it in check." Kallyuke wrung his hands together in frustration.

Steve nodded. "I've read that the way a virus reacts to a vaccine is hard to predict. One of my friends worked in a lab developing various medications and she was always stressed about the actual results versus the modelling predictions." Steve thought back to those long lost days when they had friends over for dinner parties.

"We will keep developing the vaccine until we succeed. That is our only choice otherwise we risk losing millions of people to this virus and damning millions more to a lifetime of misery because we cannot allow them within the cities. The risk of infection is too dangerous."

"So, you just let them die?" Steve asked.

"We are looking at other ways of dealing with this," Kallyuke sighed.

"And what would that be?" Steve dreaded the response.

"One option is to build or reclaim another city for the infected, an area where they can live in safety but also a place where we can control the virus and hopefully develop a cure for them."

"That's if they want to go there," Steve said.

"This is very true." Kallyuke looked down to the floor and stayed silent.

The lift door slid open. "You know, this building was reclaimed and renovated. We use it as our headquarters. It seemed pointless to destroy it," Kallyuke proudly explained.

It was a short walk to the large double doors that opened into the huge control room. Anton sat at the large table, deep in conversation with another man.

Behind them the screens were covered in headlines, but only one story was being displayed and the headline read, "M6 Paranormal Crash" by Mark Collins.

28

Paris.Present-Day.

Francois looked across to see Debuchy deep in conversation with the tourist who managed to capture something earlier on his camera. He noticed how Debuchy became visibly excited as their conversation progressed and how he kept looking at the screen on the tourist's camera.

Francois wanted to find out more so he approached the tourist, extinguishing another cigarette on the way. He lifted the tape and summoned the tourist onto the other side, "What it is that you have on the camera that has got my colleague so animated?"

"It's easier if you just look." The tourist held out the camera to Francois.

Francois took the camera and watched the footage on the small screen, then glanced at the two vans. Now that the bodies had been removed, ASPTS officers were examining the vans. "Excuse me, sir, but does this camera have a slow motion mode? I need to have a closer look," Francois handed the camera back to the tourist.

The tourist shrugged his shoulders and then examined the camera again.

"Debuchy!" Francois shouted over to the officer who was busy talking to the other witnesses.

"Yes sir," Debuchy stopped and walked over to Francois.

"Make sure those officers get DNA swabs from anything in those vans capable of holding any form of DNA sample, do you understand me? However small it may be. No part of those vans must be left untouched,

and they are not to move them until this is done."
Francois pointed repeatedly toward the police cordon
zone which contained the vans.

"Yes sir." Debuchy walked off to relay the
message to the ASPTS officers.

The tourist returned the camera to Francois and
pressed play. The footage ran in slow motion and they
watched the crash unfold frame by frame. The tourist
paused the screen without warning.

"See this, see their faces, watch next, the man
comes," he said to Francois, then pressed play again.

The next few frames showed a man appearing
out of nowhere walking into the road in front of the
oncoming vans. His back was turned to the camera so
they couldn't see his face. As the vans got closer, the
footage became shaky as the tourist was trying to hold
his nerve as he knew this was a dangerous situation he
found himself in.

The screen turned completely white as a bright
light enveloped the vans and the man who stood in front
of them. The light receded and the image of the vans
returned as they veered off into the side of the bridge
and crashed.

"Just rewind that please, sir, just for a moment,
right after that light subsides from the screen," Francois
asked.

The tourist obliged. "And pause now," Francois
said pointing at the camera.

They looked at the screen in complete silence.
"Do you see it as well, sir?" Francois asked.

The tourist nodded.

"I need to keep this camera," Francois said, "at
least until we can download the file onto one of our
computers and analyse the footage. I can assure you it
will be perfectly safe. Officer Debuchy will get your
details and take a brief statement, and in the next few

days, we will call you into the offices to make a formal
statement; are you staying in Paris for long?"

"I am here for the next five days, but I need my
camera back before I go, it has a lot of family memories
stored on it."

"Of course, it will be perfectly safe in our hands,
and may I have your name, sir?"

"Will Deschamps."

"Okay, Monsieur Deschamps, wait while I get
Officer Debuchy to take your statement and thank you
for your cooperation with this matter."

Francois walked over to Debuchy who was busy
talking with some witnesses and had a quiet word in his
ear. Debuchy looked over at Monsieur Deschamps as
Francois placed the camera in the evidence bag that the
officer held open for him.

"What are they saying?" Francois asked.

"You won't believe it."

"Let me guess…they saw different people in the
vans after the light dissipated."

Debuchy slowly shook his head as he spoke,
"Yes, that is it, but that is impossible."

"We have it on camera, it's not a very clear
image but I think we can get a positive ID on these
people. In the meantime, I need you to ensure that all the
CCTV cameras in this area are secured and we get
copies of the footage. They may hold more clues, and no
one sees them apart from the investigation team. I don't
want any unnecessary panic."

"But if it's not a clear image, how can you tell
they're different people?" Debuchy was even more
confused.

"Easy, after the light all of the four people in the
vans are white, before only three were, but I don't want
a word of this spoken to anyone do you understand? The
press will be all over this given the location, so I don't
want to give them anything else to put into their

reports," Francois held his finger up to his lips to silence Debuchy.

"Of course, sir."

"I'm going to get all the details of these three witnesses you have spoken to, so we can follow up and secure formal statements, are these the people?" Francois pointed to a group of people talking amongst themselves as they discussed the accident.

"Yes," Debuchy replied.

"Okay, in the meantime, please get Monsieur Deschamp's information and a brief statement, and please, not a word, the press will be all over this like a swarm of locusts if we let anything about this slip out, okay?" Francois was insistent.

Francois lit another cigarette to calm his nerves and got out his notepad. He was old school and found the reliance on technology annoying; a pad was more than enough to cope with the job in hand. He walked back to the three witnesses. "I need all your details that way we can follow up with formal statements at the station. Please can I have your names, addresses and contact numbers," he said.

The first witness came forward and started to talk to Francois, "My name is Bethany Sagna," she said, but something distracted Francois as he scribbled her name onto a sheet of paper from his notepad. A large white van with a satellite dish was making its way through the crowds and heading for the crash scene. TV Paris Central was written on the side of it in large black letters. Francois knew this would be an issue, he completely ignored the woman as she continued to talk and slowly walked toward Debuchy who was now talking with Monsieur Deschamps.

"I need you to take over," Francois said as he continued to eyeball the van.

"But I'm dealing with this…" Debuchy said.

"I don't care, get Flamini to help out, he's not doing much." Francois pointed to Flamini who was talking with the ASPTS as they collected samples from the vans, "I think I'm about to meet an old acquaintance."

The van stopped a few metres away from the cordon and then Evelyn Martins opened the passenger door and stepped out. She was a tall, glamorous, journalist and had been the main crime reporter of the prime time news show on Paris Central for many years. She was well known to the public and not afraid of courting controversy in her quest for a story. She was assertive, well-liked and someone who knew exactly how to get the best from witnesses and the authorities alike.

She walked up to Francois, who was still on the other side of the tape and pointed her phone under his nose. "I got calls from two different witnesses that claim the people in that crash changed…the people in those two vans were different after the light to the people who were in the vans before the mysterious bright light appeared. I struggled to believe them but I'm also told that someone recorded it, is that true? Are you willing to go on the record for my report please? Can I see this recording because if it's true, this will be a story of global importance and you know how I like those kind of stories," she persisted by pressing the phone as close as she dared to Francois' face but he was an old hand when it came to dealing with the press and gently pushed it away.

"I did wonder how long it would take before you surfaced, but even by your own brilliantly presumptive standards, this is a new low in journalism," Francois stubbed out his cigarette in front of her as he tried to rebuff her claims.

A small crowd of people gathered around them as the game of cat and mouse continued. Evelyn pushed on the police cordon tape to get at Francois.

"But I take it this is what you are being told by the witnesses you have spoken with or am I telling you something you don't know? I know that makes you very mad," Evelyn said with a grin. She was not going to give up on Francois. She felt that she had him on the ropes, and, despite his calm look, she knew we was growing furious on the inside.

Evelyn first crossed swords with Francois five years earlier on a copycat murder case; she managed to stumble across a witness who had a key piece of the puzzle that was missing from the enquiry and eventually led the police to the killer. Francois had ignored the witness on several occasions, dismissing her as delusional and someone who would do anything for publicity and money. Evelyn gave the woman an interview slot on a special crime report. An arrest was made within a matter of days based on her public testimony. Francois had never forgiven her for this public humiliation.

"Nothing has been confirmed and nothing will be until we have carried out a full review of the evidence and the witness statements, so please leave me to get on with the job of reviewing the crime scene," Francois replied.

Evelyn was persistent and again reached over and poked her phone under Francois' nose in another attempt to get him on the record. "What can you tell me about what happened here? There must be something that you can tell us. Why would an apparently minor crash attract the attentions of the Gendarmerie Nationale? This is hardly the crime of the century is it? Or is there something you're not telling me?"

Francois spoke through gritted teeth, "Don't cross the line otherwise your already shitty career will be over," he snarled.

"Can I put that on the record?" Evelyn chuckled.

"You can try, but you will regret it. Now stand away from the crime scene and allow my team to do their work."

29

Paris.Present-Day.

The clouds were thickening above the city and a bolt of lightning erupted into the air and was followed by a low grumble of thunder. Evelyn looked around in search of another angle. She spotted two witnesses ducking under the cordon tape and shuffling along the pavement as they left the crash scene. This was her chance, and she chased after them. She signaled across to the cameraman who was standing by the open sliding door of their van. He grabbed the camera and ran after her.

"Excuse me monsieur, can I speak with you for a moment about the crash and what you saw? I am from Paris Central news," she shouted at the back of one of the witnesses.

The witness slowed and turned toward her. "I've been told not to repeat anything, I'm looking for my wife. I have no time to talk, sorry."

"Who told you not to repeat anything?" Evelyn asked.

"That man," the witness said and pointed through the crowds toward Francois, who was still busying himself at the crash scene.

"The police can't stop you from talking to a journalist, you are a witness." Evelyn put a reassuring hand on the witnesses' shoulder, just as the cameraman caught up with them and looked at his light meter. The gathering clouds grew darker.

"If we're going to do anything we need to do it fast. I don't like the look of these clouds," the cameraman said, as he set up the tripod and placed the camera on it.

"So, what do you think?" Evelyn turned back to the witness.

"Are you sure?" the witness asked. "I'd sure like to be on the telly."

"One hundred percent. This isn't a police state and there's nothing they can do," Evelyn said.

"Okay, as long as you're sure, I'll talk," the witness replied.

The wind started to pick up, the white tent at the crash scene was flapping in the background.

"Stefan, are we ready to start?" Evelyn asked the cameraman who was busy adjusting the settings on his camera.

"Ready when you are."

Evelyn stood next to the witness, "I shall start by asking your name and then we can go from there. Don't worry if you make any mistakes, we can edit it afterwards. What is your name by the way?"

"Philipe Thomason."

"Right, are we ready yet?" Stefan was getting cross, he looked up at the sky and quietly cursed.

"Yes, let's go for it," Evelyn composed herself, Stefan passed her a microphone.

"Right, we're rolling." Stefan looked through the viewer at the pair of them.

Evelyn looked at Philipe and started to speak, "I'm standing at the scene of what is being described as a mysterious crash involving two vans that took place only hours ago, near the Eiffel Tower on the Pont D'lena bridge. After talking to several people, I have been able to track down a witness to this strange incident. First, can you tell me your name and what you were doing here?"

"My name is Philipe Thomason and I am here on a short sightseeing break with my wife, Anne." Philipe sounded assured.

"And in your own words, can you explain what you saw this afternoon?"

"We were walking toward the Eiffel Tower when we heard this horrible screeching noise. I turned around and saw two vans driving up the Pont D'lena bridge toward us, they kept knocking into each other. I knew something was wrong when the people on the pavement were running to get away from them."

"Then what happened?" Evelyn wanted to push on to the money shot and was conscious of the gathering clouds.

"Then I saw something very strange. A man walked out in front of the vans and there was a light, a very bright light. I remember covering my eyes but being just about able to make out the people in the vans. They appeared to travel through this light."

"So, you could clearly see the faces of the people in those vans moments before the light?" Evelyn knew this was a crucial point to make.

"Yes, I could," Philipe replied without hesitation.

"What happened next?" Evelyn pushed on with the interview.

"When the light subsided, the vans appeared to be locked together at the front, maybe with the bumpers or wings and veered into the side of the bridge."

"And what was strange about this?" Evelyn knew she had to keep pushing Philipe into a corner with her questions so she could get the crucial facts on the record.

"Immediately before the crash and after the light had subsided, I noticed that the man was no longer standing there and also something else that was quite strange," Philipe said and then paused for a moment. He couldn't quite believe what he was about to say on camera. He broke from the interview. "Are you sure I will be okay saying this on the recording? I don't want to get into trouble, you know. I'm just a yacht salesman from Antibes."

"I promise that you will be fine, all I'm asking for is the facts, the truth, and nothing else," Evelyn nodded at Philipe as she answered.

"Guys we need to get moving, this weather is not good," Stefan pointed to the clouds.

"Okay, so in your own words please, what did you see immediately before the crash?" Evelyn jumped back into journalist mode.

"The people in the vans, they were different, they were different people to the people who were there before the light," Philip shook his head as he spoke and looked down to the ground.

"And you are sure of this?" Evelyn asked.

"I am one hundred percent sure, you see, after the light subsided, the four people in those vans, their skin colour was white, but before the light one of them was black, he was definitely black," Philipe looked straight at the camera.

"And you are sure of this because we have to be clear." Evelyn nodded again as she pushed Philipe on this point.

"I am one hundred percent sure that the people changed in those vans, their faces were also different, like they were sleeping," Philipe said.

"Can you explain what you mean by that statement?" Evelyn asked.

"Before the light, the people in those vans looked like they were shouting and waving their arms, but afterwards, when the light went, nothing, like they were asleep," Philipe said with authority.

"And you are sure of this?" Evelyn sought confirmation.

"I have no doubt about what I saw," Philipe reiterated.

"Thank you very much," Evelyn turned to face the camera, "that was Philipe Thomason, a witness to some extraordinary events that led up to the crash today near the Eiffel Tower. Stay tuned to Paris Central for more updates on this breaking story."

"And that's it," Stefan indicated that he had finished filming. "We got lucky with the weather. Let me get the equipment back to the van before that luck runs out." Stefan quickly packed everything away and walked briskly to the van.

"Thank you for doing this," Evelyn shook Philipe's hand.

"What will happen now?" Philipe asked.

"It will go back to the studio where we'll edit it and it will make the news bulletins later tonight," Evelyn said and then noticed Francois loitering in the background.

"Anything else?" Philipe asked.

"I need you to sign a release form so if you can wait for a moment, I will go and get one."

"Please be quick, I don't want that officer seeing us talking," Philipe said and nervously tapped his foot on the ground.

Evelyn returned with the release form and a clip board for Philipe to lean on. He squatted down on his haunches, quickly scribbled down his e-mail address and signed the form. She folded up the form and placed it in her bag. Francois casually strolled toward her as she pulled out a cigarette and placed it between her lips. Francois seized his chance and lit the cigarette for her with his lighter.

"Thank you," Evelyn's eyes widened upon seeing it was Francois.

"Broadcast that interview and I will ensure you never work in journalism again," Francois said putting his lighter back in his jacket.

"And how will you do that? He spoke the truth," Evelyn shrugged her shoulders.

"The world does not need to hear the so-called truth from one crazy person. I will get twenty interviews that dispute that man's account and undermine everything you stand for in journalism. After all, the majority opinion carries weight and you have no one else to back you up." Francois held all the cards and he knew it, he just wanted to ensure that Evelyn was aware of this fact.

"Let me get this straight, if I broadcast this interview you will create, I think that is the right word, or is it fabricate, twenty other witness interviews to try and ridicule this one man's account. That's a bit severe isn't it? Even by your own lofty standards, what has got you so rattled?" Evelyn was in no mood to compromise, "And this time I want the truth."

"We need time to review the evidence, which may shed a completely different light on what happened," Francois said.

"You hope or you think? And can I get this on the record while we're at it?"

"This is off the record. What they are saying is simply not possible and until I can get any form of evidence to support this one way or the other I insist on a media blackout."

"Media blackout for a silly little car crash? I've never heard of such nonsense."

"We don't need rumours based on crazy witness statements making their way into the public domain. It will attract a media frenzy that is not helpful for our investigation."

"Twenty-four hours. After that I broadcast." Evelyn took a long drag on her cigarette.

"No promises, no time limits and you can only broadcast that interview on my say so or I will ruin your already dodgy career. Do I make myself clear?"

"I want the exclusive though, you have to give me something in return, you owe me." Evelyn took another drag on her cigarette, spots of rain started to drop onto the ground.

"I don't have to give you anything, but I will ensure you are given notice of when you can broadcast that interview." Francois walked off without giving Evelyn the chance to reply.

Evelyn took the last few drags on her cigarette and extinguished it on the ground before walking over to the van to join Stefan. Stefan was sitting in the back, reviewing the interview on one of the screens whilst searching the internet on another.

"Well?" Stefan asked.

"We can't broadcast it yet," Evelyn stood by the sliding door entrance to van.

"That's crazy, why not?" Stefan asked.

"Because they'll counter it with fake testimonies that will make ours look like Philipe Thomason is lying. Remember the last time that happened?" Evelyn was referring to the drug addict witness in a murder case.

"I do, and look what we did, and look at the outcome," Stefan said, knowing what she was referring to.

"But that was different, there are things about this crash that are not making sense, and we have little or no evidence to support this man's testimony. If they do counter our interview, we have no way back. Believe me, I don't like to lose but I know when to sit tight and this is one of those times."

"There may be another option," Stefan said.

"Okay, you have my attention."

"Well, the description Philipe gave during the interview got me thinking, so I've done some research

215

into crashes where witnesses reported a bright light. There aren't many you know, and when you drill down to the details there is actually only one incident that truly fits what may have happened here," Stefan smiled and pointed to the sky.

"Really?" Evelyn was eager to know.

"Yes, really. If we could prove this incident was not a one off, that there may be a pattern, however far-fetched it sounds, it would add weight to the report and to Philipe's witness statement."

"What did you find out?" Evelyn asked.

"Look at this," Stefan pointed to the screen.

There, displayed in big letters was the headline *M6 Paranormal Crash* written by Mark Collins, it was now spreading all over the world as more web sites indexed the report.

"A conspiracy website?" Evelyn was skeptical.

"Just read it," Stefan tapped the screen.

Evelyn climbed into the back of the van and started to read the report. Word by word she got closer and closer to the screen, her hand reached out and traced each line as she continued to read. She then stopped and looked at Stefan, her mouth was open wide but no words would come out.

"Exactly my thoughts," Stefan said.

"And this is the only other crash that is remotely similar to what happened here?" Evelyn pointed at the screen.

"Yes," Stefan replied, "but you know what made me think?"

"What?"

"Well, none of the mainstream media outlets seem to be covering the story and yet when you read this report, it's similar to what happened here; it's as if people are scared of the truth getting out," Stefan said.

"What do you know about the reporter?" Evelyn asked.

"Not much, but I did find a Twitter account he has used, @mcollinsblog so maybe try to contact him via that?" Stefan put two thumbs up.

"Good, I think this may offer us another option." Evelyn pulled out her phone, looked up Mark Collins' Twitter account, and sent him a short direct message introducing herself and referencing the report he had written about the M6 crash.

30

Paris.Present-Day.

The crowds were now dispersing from the crash scene and the recovery trucks had arrived to remove the two vans.

Francois was hovering around, talking with the ASPTS officers while they loaded up their vehicle with various samples taken from the two vans. "Have you got everything?" he asked one of them.

"We have DNA samples from the van but we will need the owners DNA to rule them out of the enquiries."

"I shall send someone to pick them up." Francois was keen for delays to be kept to a minimum. "Contact me the minute you get any results please." Francois handed the ASPTS officer one of his cards.

"You're not very good with faces, are you? I have one of those from the last crime scene we worked on together." She smiled and climbed into the back of the dark blue van.

Francois just stood there and nodded while the officer pulled the door closed and the van drove off. The rain was getting heavier and the rumble of thunder cannoned off the surrounding buildings.

Debuchy and Flamini took down the police cordon tape and directed the two recovery trucks so that they were as close as they could get to the vans. The white tent was quickly taken down by the fireman and folded into the back of the fire engine.

Normality returned to the area as the crowds went about being tourists and the vans were dragged off for further examination. The fire engine drove off leaving Officers Flamini and Debuchy with a pile of paperwork to sort out and submit to Francois.

Francois walked over to them while they picked up the remaining yellow tape that was blowing in the wind. "Good job today. I want your reports and statements by tomorrow morning, 11:00AM latest."

Debuchy sighed and continued to clear the area of yellow tape. Flamini took a card from Francois and nodded his acknowledgement.

Francois walked to his car, got in and drove across the bridge and down Avenue de New York. He felt worn out but knew this was just the start of a very complicated case that would draw on all of his department's resources.

***

Roy and Silverton sat outside a cafe, under the canopy, in the Montmartre region of the city. Silverton was smoking a cigarette and looking at his phone, scouring for news about the crash; nothing had been reported so far.

"Francois Blanc of the Gendarmerie Nationale, the minute I saw his face I knew I couldn't get close to the crash scene," Silverton's words were punctuated between drags on his cigarette.

"Why?" Roy asked.

"Well, for a start, I'd like to know why he was there in the first place. Officers from that department tend to specialise in far more serious cases. After all, whilst we know there were some extraordinary circumstances behind the crash, I'm not so sure that he would. I mean how could he?"

"Maybe he was in the area?" Roy asked.

"These officers don't just go to an incident because they are in the area, trust me on that." Silverton stubbed out his cigarette in an ashtray that was now full of extinguished butts; most of them belonging to him.

"How do you know him?"

"We met on another case. I was seconded by the British Government to work with him on another of Paris' crashes, though it was slightly higher in profile. He's a meticulous detective and knows his stuff. He never looks at a case in a straight line, he prefers to get to the motive via channels that feed into the central enquiry. Which is exactly what this case doesn't need."

"Let's see, eh? Maybe your friend isn't as good as you think he is," Roy replied trying to reassure Silverton.

"Possibly, but there's nothing we can do here. I suggest we get to London. Drink up and we'll grab a taxi to the airport. I'll make sure the aircraft is prepped and ready to fly."

Silverton left some money on the table to cover the bill and they set off to find a taxi to take them to Charles de Gaulle airport.

31

London.2618.

Steve paused momentarily to look up and try to absorb the information being displayed on the large screen in the control room. "What exactly can you see here?" Steve asked, his voice echoing around the room.

"Everything." The man sitting across from Anton stood up. "We can see everything and more. CCS is a vital cog in the wheel, but so is the technology of that time. The sophisticated nature of the satellite systems are crucial in helping us carry information back to our time."

The man stepped forward to greet Steve. "My name is Sayssac, and you are Steve Garner."

"You know what? I think I'm slowly getting used to people knowing who I am before I've met them." Steve greeted Sayssac with a certain reticence.

Anton stood and held out a hand to greet Steve. He was limping slightly. "Glad you could make it. I thought you'd got lost."

"We had a little catching up to do, six hundred years is hard to explain away in ten minutes. You know what it's like." Steve smirked.

Sayssac continued, "Kallyuke issued instructions that we harness everything that we can to learn, and to monitor Trader activity. This is the nerve centre of that operation, and very few people are privileged enough to enter due to the sensitivity of our missions. We cannot afford to have people thinking they can simply come here and make a request for data. We are not in the business of tracking dead relatives, for example."

"So, what are you in the business of? Surely you don't need all this technology to stop a bunch of smugglers?" Steve asked.

"We have another issue to deal with, Steve, something that became apparent only recently and is threatening our progress," Anton said. "We suspect a life form made contact with the renegade scientists and is aiding them in their quest to leave Earth. This life form appears to be supplying them with a new form of organic technology. At least that's what we think but we cannot be sure."

Sayssac jumped in, "And it's really quite remarkable tech as well. We managed to capture some examples of this technology from one of their abandoned bases; this is truly groundbreaking stuff. It would take us decades to replicate."

"Well, why didn't you say so? This was bound to happen at some stage, I mean, we've had time travel, secret agents from another time, so why not an alien life form, eh?" Steve mocked.

"Don't be so flippant," Kallyuke retorted. "By choosing that path they have denied us some of the finest scientific brains we could call on to help rebuild this planet."

"Maybe they have ideas of their own. Why not let them go?" Steve asked.

"Because the trade lines that are sucking resources from your time to aid their escape are creating a paradox and impacting on our time; we cannot allow that to continue. Look at this screen, and you'll see what I mean."

Kallyuke pointed to the giant screen showing the locations of all the known extractions, along with a series of images depicting the deterioration of Earth. It revealed a gradual decline with much of the planet descending into a brown colour, denoting the decline of life sustaining territories. Next to each image of the planet numbers denoted the decline in the human population along with an extinction count of species lost in each phase as the planet gradually deteriorated.

"Hang on, I've seen this before. Charley showed me this." Steve walked closer to the screen.

"Every time they are successful with an extraction it impacts on us. They have to be stopped," Sayssac said.

"So why not shut the timeline?"

"Because the technology is not fixed. We close one and they open another and another and another, until we make a mistake and something goes terribly wrong," Kallyuke said.

"Like a major paradox?" Steve dared to ask.

"Yes. Up until now, and with foresight and planning, this has been avoided, but our luck is running out. I'm concerned they will make a rash decision. The impact could be devastating for us all," Kallyuke said.

"What do you know about this life form? And when exactly was First Contact?" Steve asked.

"Very little. All we know is that the renegade scientists are exploiting their technology in order to escape Earth," Kallyuke was brief in his response, appearing to brush aside the question.

"If the risks are so great, why not negotiate a truce?"

"With who? They have no desire to negotiate because they have no desire to abort their mission, plus we have no idea where they are. They move their operations from one region to the next to avoid detection. So, you tell me, what are our options?" Kallyuke laughed off the suggestion.

"And now we have this." Sayssac pointed to the headlines about the M6 Paranormal Crash. "These incidents cannot continue. You understand that, don't you?"

"How has this Mark Collins got hold of all this information?" Steve pointed at the report emblazoned on the screen, "and *paranormal*! I don't remember anything paranormal happening."

"Maybe not to you, but to those who don't know any better, paranormal is the catch-all word to explain away incidents like this, and it grabs the headlines as well," Sayssac said.

"Besides, this man, whoever he is, is playing a dangerous game, and he probably doesn't even realise it. At the moment, these reports are on the fringes of the media, conspiracy web sites, but it's only a matter of time before mainstream media covers this story." Kallyuke looked concerned.

"Do you know anything about him?" Steve asked.

"Nothing. Until these reports surfaced, he wasn't even on our radar. But this kind of careless reporting will not help us track down *this* man." Kallyuke pointed to an image of a smartly dressed man. "We know him as Terence Armstrong, or at least that is the identity he is using at the moment. He uses a sophisticated network of financial services companies in London to gather information from various sources that may lead to potential extractions. He's hidden behind this network for several months, which means we have to be careful how we deal with him. Up until now, his activities have largely been under the radar and fairly restrained which has made him even harder to track down. Mark Collins' report may change that. Armstrong might see the report as a motive to increase their efforts, especially if he thinks the noose is tightening around him and his group. I'm not saying that will happen, but it is a consideration. We need to get to Armstrong before he gets an itchy trigger finger; and we need to get to Collins too." Kallyuke thrust out a finger pointing at the image on the screen.

"But if you know where this Armstrong character is, why don't you just take him out? Surely with all this technology at your disposal you can do that?"

"It's difficult because he is a moving target. If I felt we could do it without arousing suspicion then believe me, we would. For now, we need to try a subtle approach. You see, sleeper agents like Armstrong are well connected, embedded deep into the eco-system of London's financial services industry. He knows where to show his face, and where to make himself known to establish the right contacts. If something happened to him, then people would notice and we have no idea what trail of clues he has left that could lead people back to us and disrupt what we are trying to achieve. We cannot have that, the risks are far too great," Kallyuke explained.

"This seems way over my head, it's like a Cold War era scenario and I'm not sure I'm the right man to help sort out whatever mess you have got yourselves into." Steve shook his head and looked down to the ground.

"You're not operating alone, there are people out there to help and guide you through this…" Kallyuke replied.

"Yes, there are people. People who get us caught up in traps on motorways. People who ram into vans in the centre of Paris and then disappear. People who seem to appear at any moment with yet another piece of information that I'm told I simply must take on board. Do you have any idea how that feels, to get to know that the very basis of your existence was a fake, a total set up?" Steve looked straight back at Kallyuke.

Kallyuke sighed heavily, "There will be moments of doubt but right now you represent one of the best chances we have of halting this operation in its tracks."

"You know there was this kid back on the motorway. He behaved like someone in a sweet shop when we arrived in this time. He was running around, taking pictures and just relishing the moment. It was as if he was taking part in his own private science fiction adventure, and you could see the joy on his face. His innocence had taken over. Contrast that with the behaviour of his parents, particularly the father, who was angry. He didn't want this, he just wanted to get home."

"So, what are you trying to say?" Kallyuke asked.

"I guess what I'm trying to say is there are times when I feel like I'm the father figure. You thrust me into this and yet you don't have any idea who I am or how I would react. You ask me what I'm trying to say, doubts, that's what I have, doubts." Steve closed his eyes for a moment.

"And that is entirely natural, but you are now part of this and I promise you every support will be made available to help you achieve our goal," Kallyuke clasped his hands together.

"Let's hope I meet your expectations. For all our sakes. I still harbour many unanswered questions," Steve replied.

"Which, in time, we will answer." Kallyuke nodded his approval.

Sayssac shifted back to the headlines. "Collins' reports have some basis in fact, but I'm surprised at how quickly they saturated the fringe media, given the subject matter. The headline is obviously devised to attract maximum attention, but it is sensationalistic. The coverage should quickly burn out, but we must monitor this man's activities, maybe try to bring him onside and manipulate him into reporting what we want him to write."

"You want to influence a journalist? That's a plan that is riddled with holes. Journalists are careful

226

about what they publish. What makes you think you can manipulate him? You don't even know him. He could be part of their plan, you know, a diversion to distract us," Steve interjected.

"It is a possibility, but why would Armstrong want to attract unwanted attention to his activities?" Sayssac asked.

Kallyuke stepped in. "Think about this; your era is littered with claim and counter claim and diversionary events intended to deceive the public and keep them away from the truth; who wrote the reports that spread the word about these events? Who published them in the public domain? It was the journalists, and the media that were manipulated by those in positions of power, people who would stop at nothing to get their intended message out there. Leaders of the global superpowers were hell bent on enhancing their credibility and increasing their approval ratings at the expense of others. Why do you think you have such a sophisticated network of conspiracy sites? Whether you believe them or not, they exist, and for a good reason. They are constantly being fed huge tranches of information, and that information has to have a source, and even the slightest basis in some kind of fact. If you look beyond the narrative the politicians and the military want you to believe, then you'll understand why these sites exist. And this is why Mark Collins could become a vital part of our operations."

"But only if we can get him onside," Steve cautioned.

"Yes, of course, I understand this part is crucial. But now we have a voice into that time, and someone who is being followed by the media, so we must maximise this opportunity for all our sakes, and more than likely his as well," Sayssac said.

"And you're perfectly placed to help us achieve that goal. He's apparently based in Manchester, your hometown, and is more likely to trust someone from his own town than an outsider, am I correct?" Kallyuke raised his eyebrows.

Steve paced up and down in front of Kallyuke. "In all this…this craziness, I still haven't had an explanation from you." Steve paused to look at Kallyuke. "How did I become part of this? You've been making demands of me for a while now. It's only fair that you tell me what I am part of before I seriously start to go crazy," Steve's voice slowed.

Kallyuke turned to Sayssac, "I need some time alone with Steve to discuss this."

Sayssac looked over to Anton and nodded toward the doors. "I think you and I have some research to do." Anton followed Sayssac out of the room.

Steve pulled out one of the large chairs that surrounded the black oval table and sat down. Kallyuke stood a few feet away from him.

"Everything you knew, or thought you knew, is now considered your past. Your future is with us." Kallyuke looked at the large screens on the wall, his voice filled the room.

"The first of many big unanswered questions. If that's the case, how did I get here? I mean, how did I get *here*, now?" Steve pointed to the chair he was sitting on.

"You mean in literal terms? I don't think I need to answer that question surely?" Kallyuke replied.

"I want to know how I became embroiled in this plan of yours. Charley made little or no sense in Santa Monica. Not until what happened on the M6. Now, I'm sitting in this place you call the future, but this is your future, not mine. I'm still not sure how I fit into all this." Steve felt he deserved those answers after all that had happened to him recently.

"As you know by now, you were supplanted at birth into the late twentieth century. We embedded you into society so we could develop you into the perfect

228

agent, someone that no one would suspect – a part of the community, someone with roots in that time—"

"Someone you could control," Steve bit back.

"Control is not my preferred terminology. I prefer to use the word *mould.* You were part of a mission that had been meticulously planned for years, executed to ensure that we had some way of stopping the destruction and havoc that others are now creating. We needed a way to counter their activities, and to operate in that time without detection; this is why the plan was so perfect. People would have no previous knowledge of your identity. You were completely under their radar. We had to take this course of action because we suspect there is a mole amongst our ranks. Someone is leaking sensitive information to the rebel scientists, compromising our operations and the identity of the people we have strategically placed on Earth," Kallyuke said, glancing back at the screens.

"But what I still don't know, is who was I before all this? Why choose me, and what about my parents? What happened to them?" Steve pushed.

"When we found you, we concluded that you were an orphan."

"You mean my parents are dead?" Steve asked.

"We assumed they were. There was no conclusive evidence to suggest they were alive."

"What proof did you have?"

"We found you along with several others in an abandoned medical facility on the northeast coast of America. You were all in the intensive care units. It's a miracle you were found alive, given the state of the place."

"What do you mean? What about the doctors?" Steve was confused by this. "Why would a medical facility be abandoned in the first place?"

"The area was notorious for lawlessness, sectarian violence. The medical facility was in a demilitarised zone, but the truce that governed that facility had broken down. We entered to rescue survivors. The majority of people fled."

"Just fled?" Steve said.

"You have to understand, societal structures that you take for granted no longer exist here. Rules and the people to maintain those rules don't exist outside of the cities. The northeast coast of America was particularly badly hit. Hundreds of groups were fighting for control of the region and this was the inevitable fallout of those skirmishes."

"So, if what you're saying is true, I'm American?" Steve asked.

"I suppose in the past you would have been considered American, but borders, as you know them, no longer exist," Kallyuke tried to be as sensitive as he could, but that was not in his nature.

"You said there were others at the facility. How many others, and are they all part of this group you put together? What about Anton?" Steve asked.

"Anton was not found in that facility, but there were others, and we decided they were the perfect candidates for this mission. Had you not been discovered, you would have probably died, so in many ways—"

"What? You thought you were doing us a favour? For saving our lives? You thought that gave you the right to own us? Control us?"

"No, it was not like that. We wanted to give you a purpose. All twenty-six of you. You were the perfect fit for our plans – plans that were already in an advanced stage, we were just missing the final pieces of the puzzle."

"Us?"

"Yes."

"So, what happened to my parents?" Steve asked again, determined to get an answer.

"We don't know. In fact, we know very little about you, only that you were rescued when you were a few days old and that none of you were affected by the virus—"

"And that none of us would be missed by anyone. No wonder we were perfect. There were no tracks to cover, no awkward questions and no consequences." Steve shook his head as he spoke.

"No, it wasn't like that."

"Then what was it like?"

"You've got to understand, this was not by design, far from it. It was sheer luck that we found you. I'm afraid there were many thousands who were not as lucky as you."

"Lucky! You call this lucky? I've spent most of my life questioning things. Was I really this person I thought I had become? I felt like I was living a parallel life, that somewhere there was something more, something I was missing. I'd spend days turning myself inside out questioning even the most basic things people took for granted, like computers or mobile phones, and laugh at how rudimentary they were. Do you know how that sounded to me…in my head? I couldn't dare speak out because if I did I would have been sectioned, then what would have happened with your wretched plan? Fucked! I don't think lucky is a word that adequately explains this existence." Steve slammed his fist onto the oval table.

"I know this has been a long and painful process for you, but you are amongst friends now. You are now in the place you belong. This is that parallel life you always thought existed."

"And what about my life in the past?"

"That life was planned to bring you to this point. Everything around you was there to ensure we could nurture you through to this conclusion. The orphanage you were taken to as a baby, the people who brought you up..."

"You mean my adopted parents?"

"Yes. Everything was planned, and they were a part of this plan. Their contribution helped to ensure its success."

"Are they from this time or that time?"

"Some are. Some gave up their futures to ensure we could influence what was happening in the past, help steer it away from the destructive route it is now taking by watching over you and the others. Ensuring you were safe. Ensuring you were at the right place at the right time."

"It didn't quite work on the M6 though did it?" Steve smirked.

"Sometimes even the best plans can go awry," Kallyuke replied.

"You don't give a lot away, do you? How about we reminisce about the olden days?" Steve jabbed.

"Much of what went before is firmly in your past, and it needs to remain there. You need to remain focused on the here and now. This is your life." Kallyuke furiously pointed to the floor.

"But I have a family. Giving them up is not a negotiable part of any plan you may have for me."

"You were the only one of the twenty-six to do so. It made things very difficult for us," Kallyuke said.

"So why didn't you stop that, I mean you claim to have this select bunch of people out there who were watching over us, why not stop that part of my life?"

"There are limits. You fell in love at a young age, settled down and became what many people aspire to become, a family man. We had no way of dealing with it in a way that would maintain our anonymity and ensure you were still of value to us," Kallyuke shook his head.

"Value?" Steve raised his voice.

"Yes, value. Because believe it or not you were an investment in time and resource. Keeping our distance yet watching over you was the only way we felt we could deal with the situation."

"And what about what I've put my family through in the interests of your so-called mission, what value are they to you?"

"That is hard to answer."

"That's because they are of no value, they are collateral damage."

"No. That was never my intention!" Kallyuke raised his hands.

"I guess I have to take your word for it. Meanwhile there they are, six hundred years in the past and with no clue about who I really am. What if I decide to talk to them about it?"

"And say what? You yourself have said you feared being sectioned, how will talking with them avoid that scenario? You'd be deemed an unfit father and lose everything" Kallyuke replied.

"At this moment, I don't feel like I have a lot to lose," Steve looked down toward the floor and shook his head.

"It wasn't easy activating you. Charley Sandford was convinced you would turn your back on all this." Kallyuke frowned.

"That wasn't an option, but I won't turn my back on my family."

"Of course not. Charley was concerned you may commit suicide with all the stress, but you didn't, you were stronger than that."

"You and Charley needn't have worried. It was never a consideration. I have many reasons to live and continue this journey." Steve dismissed Kallyuke's fears emphatically.

"It crossed his mind, that is all I will say on the subject," Kallyuke replied.

"So where does my family fit into all of this? I can't leave them there, not if the world is on the brink of disaster."

"We will deal with them, I promise you, but for now we must deal with the issues we are currently facing. I can assure you that no harm will come to them until I can work out a plan to safely bring them forward in time. Of course, that is if they want to join you," Kallyuke sensed Steve was calming down.

"They will, trust me on that," Steve said and nodded his head.

"Let me show you something that will help you settle into your new life." Kallyuke sat down in one of the chairs next to Steve. He tapped onto a matt black area of the table which ignited a three-dimensional image of the Shard. Kallyuke pointed to a floor near the top and expanded the floor to reveal a large apartment.

"Do you think you and your family could live here?" Kallyuke continued to point at all the rooms.

"You seem to forget that I'm divorced," Steve replied.

Kallyuke continued to expand the rooms in the massive penthouse apartment. "Of course, well if that's the case, we can arrange something for your ex-wife as well. We want you all to be happy and feel like you belong."

"Her name is Janine, and my daughter's name is Tanya."

"Rest assured, we can make the accommodation arrangements as required."

"Simple as that?" Steve chuckled slightly.

"You are an important part of what we are creating. We want those at the forefront to be rewarded for the risks they have taken."

"That's a pretty fancy place, it must cost a fortune." Steve kept looking at the floor plans of the apartment.

"You don't understand, do you? Money is no longer required," Kallyuke said.

"You're correct, I don't understand."

"Our plan for this brave new society included removing the tools of war within our new cities, tools that had so badly let us down in the past. We wanted to avoid the pitfalls that beset previous attempts to reboot society, namely money and religion. They were responsible for dividing communities, fueling hatred and weaponising those who wanted to enforce their opinions on others. They have no place here."

"So, you banned them?" Steve asked

"No, we removed the need for them to exist. We educated people about the way we felt our society should develop, and they decided that our lead was correct and compatible with what we were creating. Through education and, as you would say, enlightenment we replaced them with far greater goals."

"That's a bold statement to make, to remove components that have been pillars of humanity for centuries. It smacks of prohibition to me."

"We had to make bold decisions. We had to cross the frontiers of humanity to ensure that we had every chance of preserving life on this planet as we envisaged it should be; peaceful and prosperous for all. Prohibition never entered our thought process, nothing was enforced, it was voluntary."

"But what about the human soul? Doesn't that need to feed off the hope that religion offers?" Steve asked.

"We weaned ourselves off the gods of war and destruction. We learned, many generations ago, that they were representing something we no longer strived to emulate. We wanted greater empowerment, we wanted coping mechanisms that were no longer reliant on what went before; above all we wanted to look forward, that is why these relics from the past have simply dissolved from view over time."

"I can't and won't question you on the morality of any of this, but I am intrigued to learn more," Steve said.

"There is nothing to stop you from understanding and learning about how we have tried to shape our new society. I implore you to immerse yourself in this life, see for yourself how we are trying to build a better future for all of us."

32

Paris.Present-Day.

The rain lashed down from the grey Parisian sky. The Pitie Salpetriere hospital was a hive of activity as people armed with clipboards and tablet computers rushed down the numerous corridors. The public announcement system was constantly in use informing people of ward waiting times and security information.

The hospital mortuary was in the basement, at the end of a long bleach-white corridor. The double doors opened into a stark, white room that was harshly illuminated with fluorescent lights.

Jacques sat on a stool, hunched over a table, reading through a bunch of notes. The four bodies from the crash were lined up next to each other. He momentarily paused and peered over his glasses to check they were still there, for some reason.

Jacques was the lead pathologist, a man in his late fifties who had presided over many autopsies. He thought he had seen everything – until now.

The morgue assistant, Laurence Dubois, walked in holding a clipboard. She was in her mid-forties, a sprightly woman, with ambitions of one day becoming the lead pathologist of the hospital. She had worked with Jacques for many years, so much so, that they were like a couple, constantly arguing over whose turn it was to get the coffee. "I finally got those reports," she said.

"So, what do we know about them?" Jacques asked whilst rubbing his tired eyes behind the lenses of his glasses.

"They were all involved in the same accident, near the Eiffel Tower earlier today, and declared dead at the scene. That's about it really."

"Any identification on the bodies?"

"None that has been noted." Laurence shuffled through the pages on the clipboard.

"So, we have four bodies, with no identification. That's not what I want to hear near the end of a busy shift." Jacques removed the sheet covering one of the bodies. "And what do we know about the crash itself?"

"We have notes to suggest that witnesses observed a bright light that enveloped the vans before impact. We also know that it was a relatively minor crash. Two vans apparently came together, and then collided into the barrier on the bridge approaching the Tower."

Jacques continued with his initial sight examination of the first body, a white male. "If this was a crash, why is there no sign of bruising on the body?" He lifted up the arm of the victim. "And if there was a bright light, would there not be some burn marks?"

"There are no notes to suggest what the source of the light was, and according to this, neither of the vans was driving very fast."

"Even so, there should be some evidence of trauma, even if it was a broken finger."

"There may be evidence in the vans that will help us understand what happened."

"Well, let's see what forensics can dig up on that, but I'm intrigued by this light. What do we know about it?"

"Nothing. They've redacted some of the notes." Laurence shrugged. "This may sound strange, but I was handed these reports by an officer from the Nationale."

"The Nationale are involved?" Jacques looked puzzled. He took off his glasses and wiped them on the corner of his white coat.

"I didn't really stop to think and ask why. He was talking with the paramedics and just handed them to me."

"Let me see that." Jacques took hold of the clipboard.

Laurence pointed to the page in question and Jacques now looked through the page with redacted notes. "I've never seen anything like this before either. Okay, let me do a quick examination." Jacques returned the clipboard and looked at the body again, then moved to the next body, and then the third.

"None of these men are showing signs of trauma," he said, removing the sheet covering the fourth victim. "And guess what?"

Jacques looked across at Laurence. "Neither has that body?" Laurence guessed.

Jacques shook his head. "You do have the correct reports?"

"Of course." Laurence frowned at Jacques.

"Then something isn't right. I need to make a call to see what I can find out." Jacques picked up his mobile phone from the worktop on the side.

"From who?" Laurence asked.

"The man who sent these bodies here. This is not the closest mortuary to the crash, after all." Jacques held the phone up to his ear.

"I was wondering why they were sent here."

"I was asked a favour. Oh, hang on…sorry." Jacques turned away from Laurence and spoke quietly, "I know what you said but this is not normal. Yes, you know what I mean. I want to meet for a drink…when?…Now. I don't care for excuses. You asked for a favour and now I am asking for one." Jacques paused and cupped his hand in front of phone.

Laurence gathered together some clear plastic sample bottles out of one of the glass cabinets and turned to Jacques. "I'll take their blood and get it to the lab tonight."

Jacques nodded in agreement while still on the phone, "Right…okay…yes the usual place, your round I believe?"

Jacques finished the call and placed the phone back on the worktop.

Laurence was busy collecting blood samples from the victim's arms, she momentarily looked up at Jacques who had taken off his white coat and replaced it with his jacket. "That sounded quite serious, who was that?" she asked.

"That was the man who arranged for these bodies to be sent here, I've asked to meet him for a drink. I'm not happy about this, not after the last time. I don't want any unwanted attention from the media. Luckily, he is more than capable of ensuring that will not be the case."

"I'll continue collecting samples."

"Thank you, we need to determine the cause of the death for the certificates, so anything we can discover from the results will help."

"But surely, the crash was the cause of death?" Laurence was surprised by Jacques. "I mean, they were all alive before the crash."

"Possibly, but until we know for sure, I don't want anything signed off or those bodies released to the relatives, that is if we can find out who our four guests are."

Jacques swung open the mortuary door and discovered two police officers on either side of the doorway. "What are you doing here? I don't recall asking for police presence outside my mortuary."

"We've been asked to guard the mortuary," one of the officers replied.

"For what reason?"

"You have twenty-four hour protection for the time being," the officer replied.

"Protection from what?" Jacques frowned at the officers.

"That's classified sir," the officer replied.

Jacques slowly walked back into the mortuary.

"I thought you were going?" Laurence said.

"We appear to have two policemen guarding the mortuary. I don't know why," Jacques said.

"What?" Laurence looked up at Jacques, almost removing the needle from one of the victim's arms in the process.

"You heard, now listen, I'm going to get some answers but make sure they do not enter the room. They have no requirement to be in here." Jacques stuttered slightly. "I'll let you know what I find out, but for now everything is normal as normal can be."

"As normal as having redacted reports, bodies with no signs of trauma, and a police guard can be, yes, I suppose it is," Laurence laughed nervously.

Jacques nodded and strode past the officers without saying a word.

Laurence finished collecting the samples and placed them in a medical bag to drop off at the laboratory. She wheeled each body into the cold storage room, ensuring that the sheets covered the bodies before turning off the lights. She then took off her white coat, replaced it with her jacket and left, carefully locking the door on her way out.

The mortuary was in darkness. The two police officers remained sitting on chairs on either side of the doorway.

"Bon nuit," Laurence said, but neither officer replied.

Laurence walked up to the laboratory, opened the door and placed the bag of samples on the worktop next to a very busy looking Sam, the lab technician.

Sam barely stopped to look up and muttered the word, "Hello."

"Sam, I need a big favour. Can you get these results back to me by tomorrow?" Laurence asked.

"Why did I have the feeling you were about to say that?"

"Because you know me too well," Laurence smiled and winked at Sam.

"I'll do my best. Is this for that crash?" Sam looked up from an array of small glass sample vials.

"How did you know?"

"There are rumours going around about the Nationale being involved. I got the samples they've recovered from the crash scene. I think they're from the vans, just some blood and some skin tissue," Sam said and then looked around for the sample bags. "Ah yes, here they are, got told it was an emergency. So should I add this to the same batch and come back to you with all the results?"

"That would be great, thanks Sam, I owe you one," Laurence replied.

"You know, one day a drink would be nice," Sam muttered to himself while looking at the samples.

"Maybe one day, but you need someone young and innocent. Not old like me," she said with a laugh, acknowledging Sam's persistence in trying to date her, though in her mind, it was all in jest.

"What's with the Nationale getting hold of this case? That's a little bit much for a crash isn't it? Or are they – let me guess – not saying much?"

"You guessed it. We're to get on with the job and not question, but in this instance I have to agree with you. It seems somewhat over the top. No doubt they'll have their reasons." Laurence was in a hurry but also keen to appear polite; she edged closer to the door.

"And I know, before you say it, you have to dash. With a bit of luck, I'll have these results for you in

242

the morning." Sam looked resigned to another shift sitting alone over a desk full of samples.

"One day, I promise you will find a good woman who deserves you."

"Yes, and until then, if you want me, you know where you can find me," Sam winked at Laurence as she opened the door and left.

33

Paris.Present-Day.

Jacques sat at a table in the Cafe Barge, playing with a large glass of brandy, swilling the contents around and occasionally taking a sip. He noticed Francois walking through the door and held up his hand to signal him over. Francois took a seat and gestured to the waiter for service.

"Une bière, si'l te plait," he said to the young waiter.

A glass of cool beer was quickly delivered to the table, along with a bill for the drink.

Francois reached inside his jacket for his wallet but Jacques pushed it away. "My turn," he said as he placed some money on the table.

"Is this your way of accepting you overreacted to the favour I asked?" Francois seemed slightly perturbed as he took a swig of his beer.

"No. I still have an issue with the bodies in my mortuary." Jacques took a gulp of his brandy. "And what's with the two officers? I presume *you* parked them outside?"

"The officers are a precautionary measure. I wanted to make sure that no one comes or goes into that morgue without clearance. That's all."

"You could have warned me." Jacques frowned.

"And said what? That I'm sending two officers to guard the place. We're talking about it now, so what's the problem?"

"I'm a man of medical science, someone who believes in facts and evidence over rumour and unsubstantiated claims." Jacques took his glasses off and

244

rubbed his eyes, he then placed the glasses back on his face and squinted as he focused on his glass of brandy.

"Of course, my friend, that is why I wanted those bodies sent to your hospital. I know of no other pathologist in Paris who would do a more thorough job of examining them. Now, what's caused you to sit here and gulp your brandy?"

Jacques started playing with his brandy glass again. Peering over his glasses to look at Francois, he said, "I don't think they died in that crash. In fact, I'm struggling to understand how they died, and until we get the results back from the bloods I'm not going to able to sign off the death certificates, not with anything that would make sense." Jacques ordered another brandy.

"Hang on a minute, I saw those bodies being wheeled into the ambulances, none of them were alive. And they were in those vehicles. I saw them with my own eyes," Francois said.

"They may be the bodies from that crash, god forbid they got mixed up somehow. But nothing I've seen so far suggests they died due to any injuries sustained in that crash."

"So, you can't say for sure what caused their deaths?" Francois was now gulping his beer.

"Correct. Until we get the results back from the lab I cannot say, but the bodies…" Jacques' second large brandy arrived on the table, stopping him in his tracks.

"What's wrong with them?"

"What?" Jacques was lost in the haze of his drink.

"In all the years I've known you, I've never seen you this worked up about something."

"I've only had the chance to do an initial examination but I cannot see any injuries that are consistent with what we would normally see in a crash victim. There are no bruises, no broken bones, nothing. They look as if they died in their sleep or maybe from organ failure. I don't know, maybe even a heart attack. But there is no visible evidence of trauma that is consistent with injuries sustained from a crash." Jacques attacked the second glass of brandy with enthusiasm.

"Maybe a further examination will show—"

"Why are there redacted sentences on the reports?"

"I can't tell you." Francois took another gulp of his beer.

"You know about them? You see, that makes me wonder as well, these initial reports from the crash scene are a useful reference when we write up our conclusions. I need to know what you are covering up, then maybe I can understand more about the circumstances behind the deaths of those people," Jacques leaned across the small table.

"I think covering up is a strong statement."

"Then tell me what you redacted." Jacques was not giving up.

Francois looked down. "I can't."

"Why not?"

"I can't tell you until we have corroborated the evidence, and at the moment, there's a complete blackout on the crash until this happens. No one outside of the immediate investigation team is allowed access to the initial reports, including the paramedics reports, along with any unsubstantiated witness statements that may have found their way onto the said reports. I especially don't want any leaks to the media. That would be disastrous at this stage of the enquiries."

"What has you so spooked? A small time crash is hardly a case for the Gendarme Nationale. What the hell is going on?"

"As soon as I know, my friend, I will tell you. Until then, I need you to focus on the autopsies. They are crucial to my enquiries."

246

"We go back long enough for me to know that you are unsure about what exactly happened."

"There's been a few weird things that have sort of fallen into place around this crash that make it a slightly bigger deal than it should be. Stuff that at first sight you wouldn't credit as being connected. This is strictly off the record though, okay?"

"We are friends. I'd like to think that we can trust each other." Jacques took a further sip of his brandy.

"You know the first thing that got me thinking?" Francois said.

"What?," Jacques replied.

"Well, I can't be sure of this, and like I say it's off the record, but I was inside the police cordon and watching the crowd when I was sure I saw a police officer from England. I can't be sure, but I was convinced it was him. I was also convinced that he saw me because he appeared to freeze when our eyes met. Foolishly, I got distracted and turned to talk with someone; in a flash, he was gone."

"So, I'm not the only one whose seeing ghosts. Who was this officer?"

"A man I worked with a few years ago. He was sent by the British secret service. His name was…" Francois paused for a moment. "That's it…Detective Roger Silverton."

"And what does he do? And more importantly, what would he be doing at this crash site?"

"He was a special agent within the British Police, his specialty is… and please don't laugh…"

"As if I would," Jacques was already grinning in expectation.

"He used to work for the British Military – in the UFO department."

"He investigates little green men? Come on! Now I'm laughing!" Jacques was smiling ear to ear.

"No seriously, the British military had this department set up to investigate UFO sightings and try to substantiate the claims. Of course, nothing really came of it and I think he was moved over into a specialist department in the police force instead."

"So how come you met him. Were you working on a UFO sighting in Paris? Were there any green men on the loose? And if so, why didn't you send them to me for an autopsy, *now* that would have been fun."

"As it happens, there was an incident a few years ago, a sighting above the city, but no, that was not the reason we met. It's classified I'm afraid and will be for a long time."

"You mean I can't know until I'm too old to remember to ask or care about it?" Jacques smiled.

"If you put it that way, then yes."

"Maybe he was just a curious tourist, or it was a case of mistaken identity," Jacques suggested.

"No. I seldom get it wrong, and he left as soon as he saw me, which made me think. In the same way you believe those bodies didn't die in that crash, I am positive that it was him, although I have no idea why he would be in Paris; and no I don't buy the curious tourist thing."

"Well, maybe you can check the CCTV footage from the cameras on the Tower. Maybe you will get lucky and get a positive ID."

"Thing is, if it is him, what on earth is a British police officer doing snooping around my crime scene? And how did he know to be in Paris at that precise moment in time?" Francois scratched his head.

"Perhaps you are reading too much into it," Jacques said, staring at Francois.

"I'm a police officer, I don't do coincidence, as you well know."

"So, what else has drawn an officer of the Nationale to this crash?"

248

"A security guard has been found shot dead in the disused tunnels under the Trocadero."

"I've not heard about this? Where did the body go?"

"I ordered a media blackout until I can find out what the hell is going on and if there's a connection. It may be tenuous, there may be no connection, but the proximity to the crash means I have to at least investigate the possibility. The body is in the Pompidou at the moment. I'll try to get it transferred to your mortuary, but this appears to be a straightforward shooting. What is not apparent is the motive. You know that motiveless killings always make me uneasy, so I sent down a colleague of mine, Oscar Mercier, to check out the area."

"And what did he find?" Jacques asked.

Francois took a large gulp of his beer.

"Now it is you that is drinking fast eh?" Jacques laughed at Francois.

"It wasn't what he found there, but further inside the disused tunnels of the labyrinth." Francois started to play with the cardboard beer mat on the table. "It turns out that at the end of one of these tunnels is an access door that leads into the catacombs. The door was smashed open. Whoever wanted to gain access knew exactly what to bring to get through that door. On the other side, we have a potential crime scene."

"Potential?" Jacques repeated.

"Well, that's just it. There's evidence of activity down there, rocks that look like they've been recently disturbed, and of course there are piles of skulls. But some of these skulls look like they've been burnt. Now, Oscar is many things, but he isn't one for hyperbole and this really got him spooked. I mean, this place has probably been sealed up for years, so to find out that there has been a break in and then to see that some of the skulls may have been tampered with..."

"What are we talking here?" Jacques asked.

"I don't know, some form of sick ritual maybe? Who knows…but here's another piece of a puzzle that doesn't quite fit."

"You mean there's more to this?" Jacques' eyes widened.

"Yes, I was told that immediately after the crash someone removed a bag from one of the vans and ran toward the Champ de Mars. Luckily, there were police on site. They gave chase and managed to catch the man after he fell into some roadworks. But the bag split resulting in a lot of the contents scattering into the roadworks."

"Where's the connection? What am I missing?"

"I don't know yet. Oscar has managed to secure the bag that was stolen from the van and we've got forensics examining it."

"What was in it?"

"Rocks. We don't have the results yet, but I would place a large bet that the rocks from that bag match up to the rocks that were disturbed in the catacombs. It looks like our friends have stumbled upon some buried treasure; you know the legends about buried valuables in the catacombs? From the aristocracy?"

"This could be the connection?"

"Possibly. If my theory is correct and these rocks are from the catacombs then how did these people find something that had been hidden away for decades? Think about it…if this is correct they knew exactly where to go." Francois ordered another cold beer.

"Perhaps they have some new evidence to suggest there was a haul of treasure hiding there, an old map, maybe found in an attic?" Jacques suggested.

"Okay, let's go with that theory. If that was the case, then why only take one bag of rocks? And another thing, who was chasing them? A rival gang?"

"I'm beginning to see what you mean."

"Even in this early stage of the investigation there are already many unanswered questions, and that's before we get to the issues you've raised about the bodies. The tests you are carrying out, well it is entirely possible, that these could prompt even more unanswerable questions."

"I think I've had enough of this mystery for one day my friend," Jacques said, standing up and depositing money on the table for the drinks.

"I'll know more once I get the lab tests back on the rock samples, when forensics come back on the vans and of course when you get your results. I take it you've sent blood samples to the lab?"

"It's all in hand, I will call you the minute I get the results, but for now I bid you farewell. Enjoy the rest of your evening, and mind the rain," Jacques ruefully looked outside. The rain cascaded from the thick, grey sky.

Francois stood to shake Jacques' hand and watched his dear friend leave the cafe; leaving him to enjoy the final sips of his beer.

* * *

Evelyn stood in the arrival area of the Charles de Gaulle airport. The rain from the previous day had been replaced by a bright morning sun that was shining through the large terminal windows. She was nervous about meeting her guest.

As more passengers slowly filtered through the electric doors into the arrivals lounge, she held up a placard with a name on it. A smartly dressed man with a small suitcase walked through the doors and stared at all the placards as other passengers rushed past him and settled on the one brandishing his name.

"You must be Evelyn Martins, Paris Central News," Mark said, tilting his head to get a look at the placard.

"Mark Collins?" Evelyn replied excitedly,

"Yes." Mark held out a hand and shook Evelyn's hand. She then discarded the placard in the rubbish bin that was right next to her.

"I am so pleased to meet you. Thank you for flying over at such short notice. I know you must be busy with everything that is going on. Is there any more news about the M6 crash by the way?"

They made their way to the exit.

"Just the usual game of cat and mouse with the police, and don't be silly, anything to help a fellow journalist, call this an extension in my line of enquiries," Mark said while they walked to the exit and to the nearby car that was parked outside the terminal.

"I read your reports. They were fascinating, it sounds unreal. I think the incident near the Eiffel Tower may have some connection to the one on the M6, there seems to a lot in common."

"From what you say there are certainly similarities, the bright light is definitely a common factor, but this evidence you have…"

"The witness testimony?" Evelyn replied.

"Yes. I can't believe they stopped you from broadcasting it."

"Believe me, they can do that, and they have done this on another case I was investigating, but I have no choice because they will undermine the report publicly and ruin the channel's reputation…or at least that's the threat."

"Sounds like the police are trying to bully you away from the truth. They only tend to act like that when you are too close to something sensitive. I need to have a look at what you have so far. That will give me a better idea of what we're dealing with."

Evelyn unlocked her vehicle. Mark threw his small suitcase in the back seat and jumped into the passenger seat.

"How about we get you checked into the hotel I've booked for you, grab some coffee and then we can go and pay a visit to the crash site?"

"Sounds perfect," Mark was beaming as Evelyn started the engine and drove toward Paris.

"Is this your first time in Paris?" she asked while they drove down the A3 highway.

"To be honest, and I'm ashamed to say this, but yes, it is, although depending on what we discover over the next couple of days, possibly not my last."

"That is a distinct possibility," Evelyn said.

"And hopefully this isn't the last time we get to meet as well," Mark said and winked at Evelyn.

"Just remember what you came here to achieve and stick to the plan," Evelyn smirked.

34

London.2618.

Sayssac pushed open the door. Kallyuke and Steve turned around to look as light cascaded into the room. Anton followed him as they strode with purpose into the control room.

"This had better be good," Kallyuke said, using a hand gesture to collapse the three-dimensional frame of the Shard building.

"Anton and I got to talking about something that was niggling in the back of my mind, and as it turns out, also in his mind." Sayssac stood opposite Steve and Kallyuke looking down on them.

"You see, the bodies we sent back are from here…" Anton pointed to the ground to emphasise the point.

"We are fully aware that they are from here," Kallyuke said.

"They are from *here*!" Sayssac endorsed Anton's view.

Headlines on the screen were now flashing up with more pages filled with Mark Collins' reports. The news was spreading like a virus.

"They lived here, in a city that has clean air, no pollution. And I am sure it's standard procedure to carry out blood tests…" Anton was cut short.

"…exactly. And any blood tests will return results that are consistent with someone living in this time. Their blood will be pure. Abnormally pure." Sayssac's eyes lit.

Kallyuke and Steve both got to their feet.

"What are you talking about?" Steve butted in.

"We sent back some bodies to replace yours, in the two vans," Kallyuke said.

Steve jerked backwards in shock, "You did what!"

"We had to. It was the only way to cover our tracks. We couldn't risk yet another crash with no victims in the vehicles. This was our only option," Kallyuke replied.

Steve took a few paces away from the others. "Let me get this straight, you're telling me that you sent back four people in time so they would die in that crash in Paris? Is that correct or have I missed something?"

"They were already dead," Sayssac replied and let out a sigh.

"How?" Steve scrunched his brow and shook his head.

"They were criminals, people who had committed heinous crimes and were sentenced to death. They were merely paying their debt to society, in a way that would serve a greater purpose," Kallyuke's monotone response was chilling.

"But I thought this was a brave new society without a need for the tools of war?" Steve threw up his arms.

"It is not entirely without flaws. We still have a criminal fraternity operating in these times but there are laws in place to deal with them. We needed to secure the crash scene as best as we could; limit any further issues. This seemed like a logical solution," Kallyuke said.

"So, you bumped off these four people and replaced us with them?"

"Did you have a better idea?" Sayssac asked.

"Maybe avoiding the crash in the first place would have been a good start," Steve stated.

"That wasn't possible. I was under instruction to ram the other van to avoid anyone being arrested by the police. After all, dead people cannot talk…" Anton said.

"But their blood can," Steve said. "And I don't remember instructions. When did you receive these?"

Anton pointed to his ear.

"Anton received a communication implant a few months ago, something we managed to capture from one of the scientist's bases," Kallyuke said, turning to face Sayssac. "When did you discover this potential complication with the blood?"

"While you and Steve were in conversation, I took the liberty of talking with our forensics division and they gave me this." Sayssac held out a small, silver, oblong device in the palm of his hand. "We were supposed to inject each of the bodies with this serum before we sent them back. They just didn't have it ready in time. An oversight on their behalf."

"I thought you could control time," Steve scratched his head.

"There are limits," Kallyuke stared straight back into Steve's eyes.

"Obviously," Steve replied.

Sayssac held out the silver syringe. "The chemicals in this serum would have made their blood samples reveal normal results, completely indistinguishable from someone living in Paris in the early twenty first century."

"And avoided the inevitable barrage of awkward questions," Steve said.

"Yes, questions that most people will not be able to answer. Now, we start with the unexplainable thing all over again as enthusiastic reporters try to fill in the gaps. Gaps that we know don't exist," Sayssac said as he pointed to the screen now adorned with the M6 Paranormal Crash reports.

"Planning went a bit awry here, didn't it?" Steve smirked.

"We had very little time to set this up. Clearly, mistakes have been made, but we couldn't afford for any of you to be held in police custody. The risks to our ongoing plans could have been catastrophic," Sayssac said.

"It seems like the risks have just increased," Steve sighed.

"What are our options?" Kallyuke asked.

"This serum will still work on the bodies," Sayssac said, holding up the device.

"But they're dead, even I know that shouldn't be possible," Steve said.

"There's been a lot of progress in medical science since your time, it will work," Sayssac replied.

"And how do you propose we get that serum into the bodies? They will be in a morgue by now," Steve said.

"Do you know how many morgues there are in Paris? How are we supposed to find them?" Anton subtly shuffled back a few steps.

"They were taken to the Pitie Salpetriere Hospital," Sayssac said.

"And we need you to administer the serum," Kallyuke said.

"How do you know they are at that hospital? Or is that a silly question," Steve asked and looked up slowly shaking his head.

"Silly question. We have ways of tracking them," Kallyuke said.

"But I have no idea how to inject a body!" Steve replied, growing agitated.

"The syringe is automated." Sayssac held it up so Steve could see it more closely. He pressed a button and the screen lit up with the numbers one, two, three and four now prominently displayed. "Hold this end against the skin, then press the numbers, each will administer the exact dose to bring their blood into line with someone of that time. The syringe is encoded to your fingerprints so will only work when you use it. Just a little added built-in security we thought may be necessary."

"Sounds so easy," Steve said expecting more instructions.

"It is. We just need to cover our tracks," Kallyuke said.

"So, next problem, how do I get into a morgue undetected?" Steve folded his arms.

"That's the easiest part. We can send you into the morgue directly from our time. No one will know you have been there. You will have time to inject the bodies and then return to our time," Kallyuke said. "No one will be the wiser."

"I had a feeling you would say that," Steve uttered and took a deep breath.

"That's because the process of crossing over into your new life is now taking hold of you. This is what you know, instinctively," Kallyuke replied.

"Dare I ask what happened to the man Silverton shot?" Steve asked.

"Let's just say he's cooperating at the moment." Kallyuke's reply was ominous.

Steve didn't want to know any more.

"I think we should push on with this plan and get to Paris," Sayssac raised his hands and faked a quiet clap.

"I'll organise that now. Do you have the location coordinates?" Kallyuke asked.

"Yes, I'll feed them into CCS so we can pinpoint the exact location," Sayssac said.

Kallyuke turned to face Steve. "This is very important. I know this takes us off course for the time being, but we must secure the integrity of those bodies and ensure nothing is left open to suspicion. This cannot be allowed to derail our plans."

"Then I guess I have no choice," Steve reluctantly replied.

"You *were* an accountant from Manchester, but now *you are* one of us," Kallyuke proudly declared grabbing Steve's arm.

35

Paris.Present-Day.

"Is the traffic in Paris always this crazy?" Mark clutched hold of his seatbelt. A mass of cars crisscrossed in front of them and the sound of car horns interrupted their conversation as they progressed slowly along the Ave de New York alongside the River Seine.

"This is nothing." Evelyn seemed positively enthralled by the huge amounts of traffic. "When Paris is this busy, it is alive. And when it is alive, I can feel the pulse that radiates off the streets."

"Do you live in Paris?"

"Of course. You don't think a reporter for Paris' most popular news station is going to live anywhere else, do you? Anyway, where do you live? London, no?"

"No, I'm afraid not. I work in Manchester, reporting is a passion of mine," Mark replied.

"A passion, how do you mean?" Evelyn asked, glancing at Mark.

"I currently do this when I can, but with this story who knows what may happen? Hopefully, one of the newspapers in London will sit up and take note. No one else seems bothered with it." Mark shrugged his shoulders and smiled.

"This is true. So, tell me, how did you get to know about the crash on the M6? It was not near Manchester was it?"

"My brother was caught up at the back of the crash."

"Oh wow, was he hurt?" Evelyn's eyes widened.

"No, he was late for an appointment but wasn't hurt. I was heading to a meeting in Staffordshire when I got the call. He was quite a way back, but he saw the light. I tried to interview the officer in charge but got very little out of him. I knew then that they were either covering something up or unable to explain what had happened." Mark paused and took a deep breath. "I decided to stick my neck out, write up my report and publish it online."

"Didn't that concern you?"

"In what way?"

"Well, if your report was ridiculed, your career would be as good as finished."

They eventually arrived on the Pont D' Lena and were sitting in traffic, crawling toward the Eiffel Tower which was now in full view.

"That thought never crossed my mind. I knew from the little I found out that I had to report what I believed had happened. I wasn't concerned about the implications, or how it may come across."

"You know, as a reporter, especially in this climate, we have to ensure that everything we write is watertight. We cannot publish anything without statements to substantiate our claim in case the courts award against us. Objective, investigative reporting has become almost impossible. So much is going unreported now; so many people are getting away with things that shouldn't be allowed. The courts have turned on us, and whilst I know people are entitled to privacy, that privacy should not extend to the point where they know they can break the law and get away with it by hiding behind press privacy laws."

"You mentioned in your e-mail that you recorded an interview with a witness. Why couldn't you broadcast that?" Mark asked.

"Why? Because a member of the Gendarme Nationale told me they would counter it with something to undermine my witness statement."

"Freedom of speech, eh?" Mark raised his eyebrows.

"Exactly, and I couldn't take the risk. Besides, if the station heard about the threat they would have pulled the report and hauled me in front of the boss," Evelyn said while they continued to crawl toward the Eiffel Tower.

"The problem I had was people were willing to talk, but not go on the record, which is why all the witness statements are anonymous," Mark explained.

"And what do you hope to achieve here?" Evelyn finally got to a small street around the back of the Eiffel Tower and parked the car.

"I think I can solve the problem you mentioned in your e-mail," Mark said.

They both got out of the car and started to walk toward the imposing Eiffel Tower.

"How?"

"Well, I can take your witness statements, remove the names of the people you spoke with to circumvent the lawyers, and publish them on my blog," Mark smiled at the thought.

"Mark, these people aren't playing. If you publish this stuff they'll—"

"They'll what? Knock on my door in the middle of the night?"

They continued their short walk toward the Tower.

"Frankly, yes, they will, and worse," Evelyn grabbed Mark's arm.

"People like this are all talk, they can't do anything like that." Mark was confident this was the case, at least in front of Evelyn.

Mark steered them toward an ice cream van. He purchased two large ice cream cones with chocolate flakes and turned back to face Evelyn. "Ice cream?"

Evelyn took the ice cream and started eating it. "I thought we were going for breakfast?"

"Answer me this, has anyone spoken to the owners of that cafe?" Mark pointed across the bridge to a small cafe with a neat arrangement of tables outside. He finished off his ice cream.

"I'm not sure, why?"

"Look at it. It's the perfect spot for a witness to see the whole event. You said they crashed here?" Mark pointed to some black tire marks on the road and the exposed bare metal on the railings where the vans had crashed. There was little else to suggest that there was a fatal crash at the location.

"Yes," Evelyn was still battling with her ice cream, it started to melt and dribble down the side of the cone covering her fingers.

"There may have been witnesses to the crash sat in that cafe, the view is unobstructed," Mark said and started to walk toward the café. Evelyn followed him.

Mark kept looking back, sizing up the distance between the crash site and the cafe. He paused for a moment at the traffic lights, which enabled Evelyn to catch up.

"You don't think this place is too far away?" Evelyn asked.

"We won't know until we ask," Mark replied while they scampered across the road.

They walked up to the small arrangement of tables outside the café, where a woman in her sixties was wiping the tables, checking the salt and pepper pots to ensure they were full and emptying the ashtrays. A light breeze chased its way past. Mark and Evelyn stood patiently, waiting for the woman to notice them. For some reason, she kept ignoring them. Evelyn shuffled for something in her bag and Mark coughed to get the woman's attention.

"Excuse me, madame, English?" Mark tried to politely interrupt her table cleaning routine.

"Yes, English is okay. What do you want?" her response was short.

"Can we ask you some questions about the crash that took place over there yesterday?" Mark pointed across to the crash scene.

"Don't you people talk to each other?" the woman snapped back.

Mark tried to feign ignorance. "I don't know what you mean."

"I said, why don't you people talk with each other? One of your colleagues has already been here to ask questions," the woman stopped what she was doing, looked up, and folded her arms.

"A policeman?" Mark asked.

"An English policeman came by last night; said he was part of some special investigation team. I told him it was all magic," the woman said as she started to frantically clean up one of the tables.

"What was his name?"

"How should I know? He left quickly, seemed like someone was after him," the woman barged past Evelyn and Mark. She moved on to another table and continued with her cleaning routine.

"What was magic?" Evelyn asked.

"You know, I heard the rumours. I'm not stupid," the woman threw her cloth onto the table and stared at Evelyn.

"We wouldn't dare suggest you were, madame. I just want to know what you mean?" Mark persisted.

"The rumours talk of the people in those vans changing after the light, and there was a smell, it's magic I tell you," the woman replied.

"What kind of smell?" Evelyn asked.

"Like lightning, when it hits water; a strange smell in the air," the woman was making even less sense to Evelyn and Mark, but they knew they had to persist.

"And you think that was connected to the crash?" Mark asked.

"What do you think?" she spouted.

"Do you have any CCTV?" Mark asked.

"Why would I need cameras? We're a cafe, not a bank," the woman returned to the table in front of her. "Anyway, I heard that someone had recorded it. Ask them for help. I have nothing here." The woman picked up a pepper pot and shook it. Grey dust sprinkled in the air and she set the pot back onto the table.

Evelyn looked at Mark and signaled that she wanted to leave by pointing toward the road. Mark took the hint.

"Thank you for your help," Mark said as he left the cafe in pursuit of Evelyn.

"You come here and ask all these questions, but you don't order anything," the woman shouted as Mark and Evelyn walked along the pavement.

"What's wrong?" Mark asked as they crossed the road, heading back toward the Eiffel Tower.

"That woman can connect both of us to the crash investigation. She knows your face and probably mine, and I don't want anything to lead the police to my front door. I've got enough problems to deal with." Evelyn was obviously agitated.

"But she may go on the record?" I was so close to getting her to agree—"

"To what? Going on the record about magic? Like that's going to help, anyway, she's already on record," Evelyn said as they stood under the Eiffel Tower.

"She is?" Mark asked.

Evelyn took a small Dictaphone out of her handbag and played back some of the scratchy interview Mark had just tried to conduct with the cafe owner.

"That's brilliant, but we don't have her name," Mark replied.

"Neither do any of the witnesses on your reports, but that hasn't stopped you so far. If you want to do this, then we do it properly. I'm not having you risk your neck for some half-arsed report that has nothing to do with what happened. We can review this later. I want to have a look over there." Evelyn pointed beyond the crash site. "Oh, and by the way, she owns the cafe, getting her name won't be a problem."

"Good point. And what's so important about that?" Mark looked in the direction that Evelyn pointed.

"A man stole a bag from one of the vans at the crash scene, he was caught over there. I want to see if we can get close and find out what was in the bag."

As they approached the police cordon an armed officer walked toward Evelyn. He spoke very quickly in French, making her stop in her tracks and grab Mark by the arm so he couldn't get any closer.

"That sounded a bit dramatic. Did he mention you by name? What did he say?" Mark asked Evelyn whose nails were now digging into his arm through his jacket.

"He said that my picture has been circulated by the investigating officers from the Nationale and that they're instructed to prevent me from coming any closer to this or any other police cordon connected to the crash."

"Can they do that? This is a public place…?"

"I told you these people mean business. We have to be careful. This is not a game. They will step close to the edge of the law to prevent us gaining access to witnesses and anything else connected to the case,"

Evelyn led Mark under the Eiffel Tower and back to the car.

"They are trying to prevent you from doing your job," Mark replied as they climbed into the car and slammed the doors shut.

"That is the way it is I'm afraid."

Evelyn turned the key in the ignition and they drove off.

36

Paris.2618.

Steve sat opposite Sayssac and Kallyuke in the shuttle as it flew toward Paris.

"Remember, you only need to touch their skin with the tip of the syringe," Sayssac pointed to the relevant end of the syringe.

The shuttle glided over what was left of the Parisian skyline, its metal shape catching reflections from the piercing sunshine.

"How will I get there?" Steve asked.

"With this." Kallyuke held up a phasing unit.

Steve leaned forward to get a better look, "I've not used one of these before."

"It's easy. It's been programmed with the location coordinates for the morgue. Once we arrive at the drop zone, you'll need to make your way down to it using this. We won't be able to get you any closer. This device will direct you." Kallyuke placed it on the table between them. "Press it here, and it will send you back to the correct point in time. Once you have completed your task, press it again, and you will return to our time; everything is pre-programmed."

"And remember, when you arrive you will be inside a mortuary cold room," Sayssac said.

"Can't I leave that room once I've completed the injections?" Steve asked.

"It will probably be locked from the outside and I cannot take the risk of you getting caught in the main autopsy room. You should return from that location," Kallyuke said.

Steve drifted away from the conversation and looked out of the window to the scene below. Paris was a mess of buildings overgrown with plant life and mangled metal from the various structures that now littered the ground.

"Okay, we're here," Sayssac said.

The shuttle slowly descended. The doors slid open and light-filled the shuttle cabin. Steve lifted his arm to shield his eyes. In front of him was what was left of the Pitie Salpetriere Hospital. The walls of the main hospital entrance had been wrestled to the ground, reduced to rubble under the strain of years of abuse from the vines that were left unchecked. Windowless frames littered the remaining walls and debris from years of conflict was scattered around.

"This will act as a compass. Place it in your hand and the pointer will give you directions. In addition, you have a readout for distance," Sayssac said placing the phasing unit into Steve's hand. "Guard it with your life," Kallyuke added.

"Aren't you forgetting something?" Sayssac held the syringe in an outstretched hand. Steve grabbed it from Sayssac and placed it in his jacket pocket.

"We will see you back here soon," Kallyuke said.

"How we will communicate?" Steve asked.

"I want a comms blackout to minimise the risk of this mission being scuppered," Kallyuke said.

Steve walked slowly toward what remained of the hospital entrance while the shuttle doors closed behind him and it quietly took off into the sunlight.

Entangled tubes of rusting metal, the carcasses of old desktop computers mixed with shards of glass and wheelchairs littered the dilapidated entrance. Steve had to pull them apart so he could gain access to what was left of the main foyer. Glass crackled under his boots with every step and shattered into tiny pieces; the sound of his footsteps echoed around the now deserted, hallways.

Steve held the phasing unit in the palm of his hand and it pointed north along one of the corridors, indicating he needed to travel forty metres. He looked ahead to see what lie in store for him and could just about make out a staircase at the end of the corridor. The ground underfoot was damp and littered with medical waste that had survived for centuries; syringes, discarded bottles of tablets, and rubber medical gloves were among some of the debris strewn across the floor; the hospital had the appearance of being abandoned in haste.

Steve reached the top of a staircase. The phasing unit now indicated minus thirty metres which meant he had to descend into the bowels of the hospital.

The light reduced as he descended each flight of stairs. By the time he reached the thirty metre target, he was in almost complete darkness. Steve took a moment for his eyes to adjust. The device now showed that he needed to head along the straight corridor for fifty metres.

The corridor reeked of a sickly sweet smell that he couldn't quite place but found repulsive. He began to wretch and took deep breaths. The air was chewy and got to the back of his throat, triggering his gag reflex. Water dripped onto the floor from the ceiling, dispersing into puddles. Steve tripped over something, it felt soft, even malleable, and stood out from anything else he had trodden on so far; he didn't want to stop for a closer examination so he kept moving.

The device indicated that he had covered fifty metres. He now stood in a large double door frame beyond which sat the mortuary. A chill ran down Steve's spine and he shuddered to think about what lie ahead. He tried to remind himself that the mortuary was empty and had been for many years.

He inched forward until he stood in the exact place demanded by the phasing unit. A glowing red button appeared in the middle of it. Steve touched it and was immediately enveloped in a bright, white light.

37

Paris.Present-Day.

The door frame of the cold room in the morgue of the Pitie Salpetriere Hospital glowed brightly as intense white light filled the room; the light stretched into the main room of the mortuary. Steve had arrived and could see his warm breath scatter into the room in the subdued, glowing, night light.

"Right let's do this," he muttered, taking the syringe from his jacket pocket.

Nerves got the better of him, he dropped the syringe on the floor but crouched to gather it. Steve got up to be confronted by four bodies, lying side by side and all covered with a white sheet. He took a deep breath and pulled back the sheet from the first body to expose the arm. He held the top of the syringe against the pale white skin, as instructed. The screen on the syringe sprang to life, displaying four buttons on it. Steve touched the first button and watched the serum enter the veins in the victim's arm. The veins glowed bright orange under the skin, as the serum traveled quickly into the body.

The sight had an almost hypnotic effect on Steve, but he had to remain focused and get on with the job.

He moved on to the next body, squeezing in between the trolleys, pulling back the sheet to reveal a pale white arm. He injected it. Again, the serum rapidly invaded the victim's bloodstream; then onto the third body. A routine was beginning to form.

Steve started to breathe heavily as he approached the final body, he knew he was nearly done.

He was just about to remove the sheet to expose the arm when he heard the door to the main room burst open.

Two armed officers, Perez and Legrand, pushed open the cold room door as Steve poised over the final body, with the syringe in his hand. They pulled their guns and pointed them directly at Steve.

"Arrêter maintenant!" Legrand shouted.

Perez quickly turned on the main lights in the room. Steve squinted as his eyes adjusted to the stark whiteness of the room.

The standoff continued.

Steve dropped the syringe on the floor and threw his arms into the air. "Don't shoot!"

Perez approached Steve, kicked the syringe away from him and toward Legrand, who picked it up, shook it about, and then pressed the dark screen but nothing happened. He tossed it over to Perez.

"What the fuck is this?" Legrand shouted in English while Perez continued to examine the syringe.

"What the fuck are you doing in here?" Perez barked at Steve.

"Don't play with it!" Legrand shouted to his colleague. "It could be a booby trap!"

Perez looked startled at the suggestion. He threw it on the ground near the door.

"You! Get down on your knees, hands behind your back!" Perez yelled and pointed his gun into Steve's face. "Call it in, I've got him covered."

Legrand slipped out of the cold room to make his call, returning a moment later.

"What did they say?" Perez asked.

"They will call Francois Blanc. Given what has just happened, I expect he will be here very soon," Legrand replied.

"Did they believe you?"

"I don't think they had any choice, security surrounding this place is so high at the moment that they cannot take any chances."

"Let's move the suspect into the main room, this place gives me the creeps," Perez glanced around at the bodies and then escorted Steve into the main room. "On your knees and don't make me use this," he said waving his gun in front of Steve's face.

Steve remained silent as the minutes slowly ticked on.

In a sudden flurry of activity that punctuated the stillness of the room, the doors flung open and Steve observed a tired-looking woman as she walked into the mortuary. It was now the early hours of the morning.

Steve was on his knees, hands behind his back, Perez stood over him, pointing his gun at Steve's face. Legrand was pacing up and down in front of them.

"Who are you?" she looked at both of the officers.

"I am officer Legrand, and this is Officer Perez."

"So, let me ask you this, what are you doing in my morgue and who is this? Laurence folded her arms.

"Perez heard something, maybe it was nothing he thought, we checked it out, then this," Legrand said.

"So, you're telling me this man broke into the cold room?" Laurence spoke quickly to the officers.

"Yes madame," Legrand replied.

"How did he get in?" she asked.

"We don't know, he won't speak," Perez kept his focus on Steve.

"Well, that's just fucking brilliant, have you seen the time?! I thought you two were supposed the guard the place! And what is this?" Laurence pointed to the syringe that lay on the ground at the entrance to the cold room.

"We don't know, he was holding it in his hand when we caught him," Legrand said.

Laurence crouched down next to it and took out her smartphone, she subtly activated the camera and took a picture of it.

"I don't think you should do that madame," Legrand said.

"It is my mortuary, so I will do what I want. Do you know his name?" Laurence asked.

"No, as I said, he won't speak," Legrand replied.

"Well, perhaps you should focus your efforts on establishing who our guest is, and what he was doing in my cold room, rather than observing me," she said.

"Perhaps, but they should leave that to me," a voice came from the entrance to the mortuary.

"And who might you be?" Laurence snapped at the two men who just entered the mortuary.

"My name is Francois Blanc of the Nationale and this is my colleague Oscar Mercier," Francois and Oscar brandished their badges for Laurence to see.

"I see," Laurence said.

"I'm heading up the investigation into the crash near the Eiffel Tower," Francois said.

Francois walked into the cold room, leaving Oscar in the main room of the mortuary.

"Isn't this a bit small time for the Nationale? You guys only put an appearance in when there's some politician involved with a mistress or some kind of fraud. It's not often we see you scratching around our humble domain."

Francois wandered back into the main room.

"No madame, this is definitely not small time." Francois shook his head in disapproval and he turned his attentions to the uniformed officers. "I thought you were guarding this place?!"

"We were, sir," Legrand replied.

"So, where were you when he broke in?" Francois asked.

"We were outside the entrance," Legrand said.

"You let him through?"

"I tell you that no one gained access via the entrance," Legrand replied.

"You didn't see him until you broke into the cold room? Is that correct?" Francois asked.

"Yes," Legrand confirmed.

Francois turned to Laurence. "Are there any other access points to this mortuary?" he asked while looking around the room.

"No. One way in and one way out," Laurence said and pointed to the entrance. "That one."

"Then explain how he got into this room undetected," Francois asked the officers.

"We can't. We heard a noise and investigated. The suspect was standing over one of the bodies, holding that thing in his hand"

Francois looked at the syringe laying on the floor at the entrance to the cold room, he turned to Laurence. "Do you know what that is?"

"I have no idea. I'd need to examine it," Laurence replied.

"Not yet, please. It may have prints that we can use," Francois said. "And what has the suspect said?" Francois turned to the officers.

"Nothing. He hasn't said a word, apart from when he shouted *don't shoot!*" Perez replied.

"So, he's English?" Francois asked.

"We don't know if he's English, all we know is that the only words he shouted were *don't shoot,*" Legrand replied.

"Did you detect an accent?" Francois asked.

"Not from two words, and it was said in a panic, so there was no way of detecting an accent," Legrand said.

276

Francois drew breath. "Right, I want you both to resume guarding the entrance, no one gets in or out without my authorisation." He turned to Laurence. "This is now a crime scene. You will instruct the relevant departments that no further deliveries can be made to this mortuary until further notice. Until we know how this man gained access, and what his motive was for doing whatever he did to those bodies, this mortuary is out of service."

"Okay, but Jacques will not be happy with this," Laurence said and dialed the front desk.

"He will understand, I know Jacques very well, trust me on that."

The officers resumed their position outside the mortuary and Laurence finished her call to the front desk. "No more bodies will be sent to this mortuary until we give them the all-clear."

"Good, now let's try and ascertain what happened here," Francois looked at Oscar.

Oscar had assumed the role of guarding Steve. He pulled his gun out for added security and smirked at Steve. "Thought you'd break in and play with the dead people, did you? You people make me sick."

"Have you touched this thing?" Francois asked Laurence, while he looked down at the syringe.

"No," Laurence was running out of patience as tiredness took over. She slumped onto one of the stools perched by the worktop and rested her head in her hands.

Francois crouched down and placed the syringe into a clear plastic evidence bag. "Search him," he said to Oscar.

"You heard my colleague, stand up and put your hands above your head," Oscar ordered Steve.

Steve looked around and assessed the situation, he was in no mood for heroics so complied with Oscar's request. Oscar frisked him from top to bottom and then back up again. He removed the phasing unit from Steve's jacket. "What's this?" he asked, holding it inches away from Steve's face; Steve remained silent.

"Give me that," Francois snatched off Oscar and put it into an evidence bag. "I'll get these to our forensics teams to see what they make of them."

"Now put your hands out front," Oscar ordered Steve and then cuffed him.

Francois paused for a moment to try and get a sense of perspective as to what happened. He walked around the cold room where the four bodies lay, and then back out into the main room of the mortuary. He kept turning the same things over in his head. "Why? Why mess with dead bodies? And why those exact bodies?" he spoke softly to himself.

Laurence stood at the entrance to the cold room. "Some people get a kick from it," he said.

"Too crude, I'm not sure this guy is about that, he was caught standing over one of the bodies, not messing with them in *that* way," Francois went to light a cigarette.

"Sorry not in here." Laurence quickly pointed out the no-smoking sign on one of the walls.

"Where is Jacques?" Francois asked while carefully placing the cigarette back in the box.

"He will be here soon. He lives further away than me. I'm always the one that gets the first call in the event of an emergency, but this is probably a first for me," Laurence said.

"It's probably a first for us all, and until he decides to speak we have no idea what motivated him, it's not every day you wake up and decide to break into a mortuary. Who knows what his state of mind must be," Oscar said in a seedy tone, glancing back at Steve.

Oscar was still keeping a watchful eye on Steve but had placed his gun back into its holster having noted Steve's wilful compliance thus far.

Francois was pacing up and down, thinking. He paused for a moment and glanced across to Steve. He wanted to get the opinion of his friend Jacques. The wait, combined with the lack of nicotine, made each minute seem like an hour.

"Sometimes, time just stands still," Francois mused to himself.

Steve looked over and smirked at Francois.

"You think you have something to smile about?" Oscar asked but Steve offered no reply, "You're in a whole world of shit, my friend. But you keep smiling, that's fine."

The door to the mortuary swung open. "Sorry, I got here as quickly as I could, now, can someone tell me what the hell has happened here? And, what is this man doing in my mortuary?" Jacques was out of breath as he entered the main room of the mortuary.

Francois turned around to greet him. "Don't worry about it, as for him, it's looking like he broke in to play with the bodies -- the ones from that crash."

"The crash near the Eiffel Tower?" Jacques removed and rubbed his glasses and squinted. He narrowed his eyes as he looked across at Steve.

"I told you there was something strange about it, but this is off the scale now," Francois replied, eager to hammer home the points he made in the cafe the day before.

"What's so strange?" Laurence asked.

Jacques looked at Laurence. "Francois thinks there's more to this crash than meets the eye. And I'm beginning to think he may be correct, and this man may have some of the answers to help us understand what happened."

"These items may also hold some clues," Francois held up the evidence bags.

"What are they?" Jacques asked.

"We have no idea, and he won't say a word. I'm going to send them across to ASPTS to see what they can uncover," Francois said and then he held up the two clear bags to the fluorescent light and studied them.

"That one there, what's the point at the end of it?" Jacques tapped the bottom of the evidence bag that contained the syringe, "Let me see that."

"Don't take it out of the evidence bag," Francois said passing it to Jacques.

Jacques took a few moments to hold the syringe tight to the plastic bag. He then pushed a finger against it to see if there was a reaction; nothing happened. His eyes followed the sleek lines of the main rectangular shape down to the small black triangular tip at one end.

"I don't know for sure, but if I was making an educated guess, I would say this is some kind of syringe. Don't send it to ASPTS just yet, I'd like to examine it more closely."

"How can we find out for sure?" Laurence asked.

"Has anyone touched the bodies since he was caught?" Jacques asked.

"No," Francois replied.

Jacques walked over to the cold room, he brushed up against Steve and tripped ever so slightly. Steve pulled back quickly, flexed his hand, and swore at Jacques.

Oscar drew his gun from the holster, Steve fell silent and stood straight with his hands out in front.

"I'm sorry about that, it must be the static from these cheap shoes," Jacques lamely joked. He rubbed his fingers and put his hands in his trouser pockets. "Okay, I want to take this one step at a time, Laurence, will you draw more blood from the bodies please?"

"Why?" Laurence frowned.

"You'll see," Jacques said and walked over to Francois. "Do we know how this man got into the cold room undetected in the first place?"

"No, as I said, he won't talk." Francois was obviously not happy about this and glared at Steve.

"So, we have some unanswered questions then, perhaps the new set of blood along with the previous ones, coupled with the DNA results from the crash scene may hold some clues that will help us solve this mystery," Jacques said.

"You're starting to sound like me," Francois chuckled.

"Probably worse, medical evidence tends to be more or less an exact science, but this incident adds to what is becoming a very unusual case. Like I said, hopefully, the results from the new blood tests will help unravel what the hell is happening here."

"We need the test results as soon as you can please. We have to justify holding him in custody and those results could make all the difference," Francois said.

"How long can you hold him?" Jacques asked.

"Well, under normal circumstances twenty-four hours, but I think I can persuade the powers that be to allow us to hold him longer, maybe forty-eight hours," Francois replied.

"We'll do our best to ensure the results are back before that time," Jacques said.

"Fine, keep in touch. We will take him to the station and get the evidence off for evaluation," Francois said.

Oscar pushed Steve past Jacques and Laurence and out into the corridor, "No tricks my friend, just walk and keep quiet."

"I will be in touch very soon," Jacques said.

Francois followed Oscar and Steve up the long corridor.

Jacques waited until they were out of view and then pulled something out of his trouser pocket. He placed it into a small plastic container he grabbed from the worktop and sealed it with a lid.

"What are you doing?" Laurence watched Jacques.

"And you think I would wear cheap shoes?" Jacques chuckled.

"What are you talking about? What has that got to do with anything?" Laurence was lost.

"What time is it?" Jacques looked at the clock, it was 6:00AM. "My God, I need coffee and lots of it. Is there any left in the pot?"

"Forget the coffee. Let's rewind for a moment. The shoes, what did you mean by that?" Laurence walked over and switched on the coffee pot.

"The cheap shoe comment from earlier, you see that was just an excuse, there was no static at all. I used it as an excuse to pinch the suspect's skin."

"Skin? Are you suffering from a lack of sleep?"

"Not at all, I'm hoping that I can use that skin sample to get a positive DNA result, although I'm aware it may be contaminated."

"You crafty old—"

"Less of the old, please. And there's no time to waste. Can you take it to the lab with the new blood samples?" Jacques was visibly excited by his unusual technique.

"But any result would never stand up in court, where's your proof that it was from the suspect?" Laurence asked.

"I haven't got that far yet, but at least we may have more of an idea who our suspect is, his identity may flag up on the DNA database," Jacques said and winked his approval at Laurence.

"In all the years we have worked together, I never knew you were such a devious, downright

282

deceitful but cunningly clever man." Laurence was still guardedly impressed with Jacques' actions.

"I've always said it's the older ones you have to watch! Now, where's that coffee?" Jacques was feeling proud of his ingenuity.

38

Paris.Present-Day.

Evelyn parked her car outside the Tourisme Avenue hotel on the Avenue de la Motte-Picquet and rushed into the foyer where Mark Collins was waiting for her. "So, was it good here?"

"Functional with a hint of luxury, plus they served a great breakfast," Mark replied following her back out to the waiting car.

"Good, I know how you English people love a full breakfast," she said.

They both climbed into the car.

"What's the plan then?" Mark asked.

"First, I think we head over to the offices, review the evidence I got from the crash scene and talk about how this can be used without getting either of us into hot water." Evelyn put her foot down and quickly drove across town. She wanted to make the most of the limited time they had together.

TV Paris Central's offices were modest but clean and situated on Rue Muller. Evelyn navigated her way there in no time at all and quickly parked. Mark followed her up the compact staircase to her office on the second floor.

"So, this is where it all happens?" Mark said, regaining his breath. He wasn't as fit as he should be.

Evelyn walked over to the coffee machine. "How do you take your coffee?"

"Milk please, with one sugar." Mark gawked at the numerous still shots from the various investigations Evelyn had been involved with. "How long have you been reporting for these guys?" He spotted a picture of

Evelyn standing next to Nicolas Sarkozy on the steps of the Grand Palais. She was holding a microphone under his nose.

"You know what," Evelyn shouted across the office while preparing their coffees, "I think it must be about ten years now, or maybe eleven…I think…it's a bit of a blur."

"Eleven years doing this?" Mark looked at another still shot, this time Evelyn was interviewing a woman he didn't recognise for a television show, the caption running along the bottom of the image read *"The Evelyn Martins Special Report."*

Evelyn spotted Mark eyeing the image. "That was the interview that pissed off the Nationale, you know, Blanc."

"Oh really? Why was that?" Mark took a hold of his coffee.

"That woman was a drug addict. I interviewed her on my show. It was a copycat murder case and was all over the newspapers, massive coverage. The investigating officer was Francois Blanc of the Gendarme Nationale. He repeatedly ignored my attempts to get him to take her testimony seriously, so he gave me no choice. She had some important evidence – evidence the police were ignoring. So, we took her under our protection, sat down with her for a few weeks, and helped her regain enough confidence to go in front of the camera and repeat certain parts of her testimony. We weren't pushing her. She was very fragile. It was enough to get the police to sit up and pay attention, but not enough to jeopardise their investigations."

"And did it work?"

"Yes. After we broadcast her interview, Blanc got in contact and requested that we help him revisit her testimony, but this time in private, at a police station. Of course, by then the damage to his reputation had been done because in the eyes of the public he was prejudiced and selective when it came to witness statements."

"So did the case get solved?"

"It did, but instead of Blanc standing up and claiming all the credit, we got a lot of plaudits from the public and the police department for playing a major part in helping solve the case. But it only served to antagonise our relationship with the Nationale, and especially with Blanc. Here we are, over five years later, and Blanc still has a vendetta against the station and against me in particular."

"The police and the media always appear to have a frosty relationship," Mark commented.

"It is a crazy world at times. Maybe that is what appeals to me with this job, the lack of knowing what tomorrow may bring," Evelyn said and drank her coffee while leading Mark to her desk and pulling a chair across for him.

Mark sat down and peered inquisitively at Evelyn's computer screen, which was full of images of his report into the M6 crash. "You know, I never thought that report would lead me to Paris."

"Like I say, it's that lack of knowing what each day will bring that provides me with the adrenalin rush, and for me, that's a major reason to get up in the morning," Evelyn repeated and then tapped the keyboard and brought up her interview with Philipe Thomason, the witness whose testimony she was now unable to broadcast.

Mark picked up a framed picture showing Evelyn and another man standing arm in arm. "Significant other?" he asked, showing Evelyn the picture.

"No, I'm afraid that in this job you tend not to get much time away from work. The men in my life drifted away." Evelyn brought up the interview with

Thomason onto her screen while Mark placed the picture carefully back where it was.

Evelyn switched screens to show the reports that Mark had written, which were spreading fast and being translated into almost every language on the planet.

"I'm confused, you call it a paranormal crash in the report and yet you have no proof of anything paranormal, why?"

"The power of the headline."

"I don't know whether to admire you or be scared of you. You come across as a bit of a loose cannon," Evelyn said. "And we cannot afford a mistake in the current climate of scrutiny facing our industry."

"I still want to write this report," Mark said with a serious tone. "I'll take your witness statements, write up the reports and release them as if they are from my own investigations. No one will know any different. I'll even allow you to check them over before I post them to my blog."

"But what if they trace it back to me? What if they trace you?"

"And do what exactly?" Mark questioned.

"You are a bit naïve, aren't you? Don't you know what happens to journalists who uncover politically sensitive stories? Have you heard of Gary Webb? Don't you know about the case of Anna Politkovskaya, the Russian investigative journalist? There are countless more examples of journalists who have fallen foul of various vendettas, many of them political, and this is one battle I'm not sure you would want to take on, because you cannot win," Evelyn said and frowned.

"Yeah, but this story is too good to pass up on. If I don't write about it someone else will. Please believe me when I say I can handle myself. I live in Manchester." It was obvious that Mark wasn't giving up on this story.

"Oh please," Evelyn laughed that off.

"And I'm a mean negotiator," Mark said and held out his hands to pray.

"You really want to write about this don't you?" Evelyn was impressed but equally concerned by Mark's determination.

"It's not about the police or anything they've done wrong. For all we know they genuinely have no idea what is going on, so what harm can I do? I'm not going to undermine anyone and I certainly won't be mentioning the issues you've faced with that bloke you mentioned."

"You mean Francois Blanc," Evelyn added.

"I won't mention him. I'll simply take what evidence you've secured and write up a report that tells the public what we know at this stage. What harm can it do?" Mark shrugged his shoulders.

"The man in that picture," Evelyn said, gesturing to the photo in the frame that Mark picked up earlier. "You never asked who he was."

"I kind of got the hint you didn't want me to know."

"He was a colleague, a dear friend, and for a while a lover." Evelyn looked longingly at the picture. "That was taken near Antibes four years ago. It was one of the last holidays we took together."

"What happened?" Mark asked.

Evelyn took a tissue from her bag. "He was a tenacious journalist with an inquisitive mind. I knew no one like him. He would stop at nothing to get to the truth, but..." Evelyn paused to wipe a tear from her eye. "He went to Columbia to trace the origins of the drug trade, you know, the Cartels and how the trail of destruction began over there and finished in the ghettos of Paris. He wanted to show the impact it was having at all stages of the trade until it reached the addicts."

"That must have been some undertaking."

"It was, but he felt sure the story would help us understand how we could tackle the trade and help stop the tidal wave of people falling victim to drugs and the violence in the ghettos. Of course, this meant he had to take incredible risks. He knew I was afraid for him and that I stood against the risks he was willing to take, but he wouldn't listen to me."

"I feel like I shouldn't ask, but what happened to him?"

"Claude…" Evelyn picked up the picture. "Claude was found dead in a shack on the outskirts of a small town called La Calera. The police reckoned that the interview he was conducting with some small-time Cartel member went badly wrong. He must have touched on something he didn't want out in the public domain. He shot Claude in the head."

Evelyn wiped the tears from her face, placing the picture back on her desk.

"I'm so sorry, I had no idea."

"How could you know? But this is why I am cautious about this story, and I'm mindful of your safety. There are bad people out there, people who get upset when a journalist knocks on their door at three in the morning because that is the only time they know they can get a response, and these people can bite hard."

"I will be careful, I promise you, but I do know what I'm doing." Mark sought to reassure Evelyn by holding her arm for a moment.

"I hope so, for both our sakes. So, what about you?" Evelyn wanted to move on from Claude.

"What about me?" Mark replied.

"Any significant other in your life?" she inquired.

"You're kidding, aren't you? I mean, I've tried a few times but the women I meet don't really understand me." Mark shook his head.

"As in…what you're doing?" To Evelyn, this was familiar territory.

"I suppose so, I don't seem to have the time to dedicate to a relationship at the moment, so I just tend to meander through relationships."

"We all do that from time to time," Evelyn replied.

"So, getting back to this," Mark said. "If you give me your interview with Thomason and the recording from the cafe, along with what you know, I should be able to write a report up. What do you think?"

Mark reminded her of her early years in journalism, she was always striving to uncover the truth and would stop at nothing to get to the heart of the story.

"Okay, but we must be careful. Names, places, everything must be carefully constructed to avoid any issues for us both." Evelyn placed the palms of her hands on the desk.

Mark was visibly excited. "We can create the link based on the bright light, that seems to be the common link between the two incidents."

"And, don't forget we have allegations of the people in the two vans changing in Paris and the occupants never being traced from the M6 crash. That's another strong link," Evelyn added.

"Will you send me what evidence you have collected so far, this way I can review it in Manchester?" Mark asked.

"No," Evelyn shook her head. "But we shall spend time reviewing the files here before you go back to Manchester. That will allow you to make enough notes to write the report. How does that sound?"

"It seems fine, but why not send me the files?" Mark pried.

"If I send the reports, we run the risk of them being tracked and that could put you at risk. But also, these pieces of evidence are the property of the studio. I could get in big trouble for releasing evidence for what could be another major story."

"But you've been warned off broadcasting them by this Blanc character."

"He won't be able to hold us back indefinitely, and when your reports surface, we will have a lot more leverage to justify broadcasting the interview."

"So, you're using me then?" Mark teasingly tried to take the upper hand.

"I prefer to say we are working together, for our mutual benefit. Wouldn't you agree?" Evelyn smiled.

Mark grinned and held out his hand in approval, "Okay, it's a deal."

They shook on it and as Evelyn fetched more coffee, Mark began jotting notes on his pad.

***

Jacques burst into the lab and sat opposite Sam.

"These are only the preliminary results. I'm still doing more work on the samples," Sam said.

"And what do they tell us?"

"The blood samples Laurence gave me last night, before the break-in, are strange – very strange. It's as if the blood was taken from people who had lived in a bubble. The samples were pure. There's nothing to suggest they lived in, or were from, anywhere like a city or town, or anywhere. There is nothing to suggest they have been breathing our air. It's as if they've been walking around with an oxygen tank strapped to their backs."

"All of them?"

"Yes. But here's where it gets weird, they all had traces – high-level traces I might add – of Succinylcholine."

"Seriously?"

Sam handed the report to him. "The levels suggest these people wouldn't have been capable of walking, let alone driving."

Jacques glanced over the report. "According to these results, they would have been almost unconscious. Are you suggesting that this happened postmortem?"

"Possibly. But as you know injecting Succinylcholine into a dead body defeats the objective, it would have no effect. But the second set of blood samples has given us some equally strange results." He leaned forward across his desk, "I've been told the suspect was caught standing over the bodies and that he had some form of syringe. Is that correct?"

"The object hasn't been officially identified, but yes, that is a possibility."

"Well, if that's the case I think he only managed to inject three of the bodies. From the second batch that Laurence took, three of the new blood sample results were what I would consider normal, but still with traces of Succinylcholine."

"So, whatever that device was doing – no – that shouldn't be possible." Jacques scrunched up his face in confusion.

"I'm afraid there's more," Sam added. "The fourth result was the same as in the first batch. I can pretty much guarantee that he failed to inject whatever was in that syringe into the last body."

"Why would he try to manipulate their blood?" Jacques asked.

"Maybe he was trying to cover his tracks."

"From what? And for what possible reason?" Jacques squinted.

"Reasons that I would rather not think about," Sam bit the inside of his lip to stop himself from speculating.

"The bloodstream should have been incapable of absorbing anything," Jacques argued.

"The results say otherwise."

"This is unbelievable." Jacques removed his glasses and swept the sweat from his brow.

"It gets stranger."

"Stranger?" Jacques guffawed. "How can it get any stranger?"

Sam shuffled through his notes. "I had two samples from the forensics team at the crash scene. One of them was a blood sample from a seat base I've been told was damaged in the crash."

"And you have a match?"

"No. There is no match to the blood Laurence gave me, and this time the blood looked normal, so if that's the case, do we have a fifth victim who is on the run? I've put out a notice to all the hospitals in the surrounding area to see if anything turned up, and so far, nothing."

"Could the sample have been there from before the crash?" Jacques asked.

"It's possible. But I think we have to assume that is not probable. The integrity of the sample was good so that would mean it was recent."

"This can't be happening…" Jacques stared downwards at the table.

"It is happening and I've saved the best until last," Sam smiled a sadistic smile as he spoke. "I wasn't sure about the ethics of this but I did it anyway. You see, forensics obtained a small sample of tissue from the grab handle in one of the vans. I was able to get a reasonable DNA sample from it, but there appears to be no link to the blood samples that Laurence provided."

"So, we have a sixth person?"

"Perhaps not," Sam said.

"Oh?"

"I will pass these results on, but there appears to be a complication. That sample you *obtained* from the suspect…well, it's not a full result, but his DNA looks like a close match to the DNA on the grab handle in one of the vans."

"The man found in the cold room was in one of the vans?" Jacques' mouth fell open.

"If the DNA sample can be fully verified, I believe so. I need another sample to be sure though."

"But according to witnesses, there were only four people. Now you're saying there were six?" Jacques asked.

"He may not have been in the van at the time of the crash, but he was there at some point." Sam folded his arms. "I need to carry out some more tests to be certain, but in the meantime, Blanc is expecting you at Rue Pierre Lescot police station. He wants an expert there."

***

"Don't let those notes out of your site." Evelyn pointed to the bag that Mark was clutching tightly to his lap as Charles de Gaulle airport came into full view.

"I won't, I promise," Mark took a deep breath.

They arrived outside the departure terminal.

"Don't forget, I want to see this report before you hit the button, okay?" Evelyn was insistent.

"I won't let you down, I promise," Mark said jumping out of the car with his small suitcase and travel bag.

"It's been a pleasure to work with you so far. Let's make sure that, for both our sakes, we have long careers after this," Evelyn tightly shook Mark's hand.

"I think we will," Mark said and leaned in and kissed Evelyn on both cheeks, and then left for the check-in desks.

Evelyn stood for a moment as if entranced, watching Mark mix in with the crowds heading for their flights. She was quickly pulled from her trance by the loud honking of a horn. It was an angry police officer shouting at her to move on. She climbed back into her car and drove back to Paris.

39

Paris.Present-Day.

Jacques retreated to the row of seats set against the wall on one side of the busy police station foyer to wait for Francois. Minutes passed before Francois pushed through the foyer to greet Jacques.

"I know you must be tired, but we have little time and I need this evidence to secure an extension of the custody period," Francois said as he shook hands with Jacques.

Jacques got up and followed Francois through the corridor into a small office at the back of the station.

They were about to sit down and review Sam's notes when Oscar burst into the office. "I'm sorry, but I need you both in the interview room along with the evidence otherwise we are going to run out of time."

Francois looked at his watch, "Are you sure?"

Oscar glared at Francois who understood that to be a yes. Without delay, they filed out of the small room and followed Oscar down the tight, dimly lit corridor; they stood just outside the interview room to compare notes.

"What do you want me to say?" Jacques asked.

"I need you to go through the results in front of the suspect and hope that he starts to open up, or at the very least prove that this evidence is compelling enough for us to secure more time," Francois said and then paused. "I'm waiting for an analysis of the footage a witness took at the scene, but that may not be here in time."

"Do you have time to go through the results before we commence?" Jacques asked.

Francois pointed to his watch, "We have very little time so we need to do this as we conduct the interview."

"What has the suspect said so far?" Jacques asked.

"Nothing, apart from asking for a drink," Oscar said.

"Do we know who he is? Did he have any ID on him?" Jacques asked.

"He had nothing on him at the time of arrest apart from the syringe and that other thing we took off him. We think that he's English, but it's hard to detect an accent when someone doesn't speak."

"Are you sure it's a good idea to disclose these test results to him?"

"It might break his silence," Francois replied.

"Well, let us commence," Jacques said brandishing the bundle of results in his hand.

Francois unlocked the door to the interview room with his security card and gestured for Jacques to enter, along with Oscar.

Steve sat on the other side of a long dark table that had one end pushed against a wall. On one side of the room was a huge mirror. The fluorescent lights caused Jacques to squint as he adjusted to the sheer brightness. Francois inserted a new cassette into the tape recorder at the end of the table and took the middle chair, opposite Steve. Oscar sat to his right and Jacques to his left.

Francois placed the evidence bags containing the syringe and the silver disc on the table. Steve eyed the bag but sat motionlessly.

Jacques pressed the record button on the tape recorder. "For the record, the interview will commence at 12:30PM on the 15th of May. Present at the interview are officer Oscar Mercier, Jacques Courtois, who is the lead pathologist at Pitie Salpetriere Hospital, myself

Francois Blanc, and the suspect, who has refused to disclose any details about himself."

Francois placed his elbows on the table and clasped his hands together. "Are you now willing to disclose your name?" he asked Steve.

"No comment," Steve replied.

"Okay, first, how did you gain access to the cold room of the Pitie Salpetriere Hospital without my officers realising?" Francois asked.

"No comment," Steve replied without hesitation.

"Our forensics team managed to extract the tiniest sample from the tip of the triangular shape at that end." Francois pointed to the syringe in the evidence bag, "It's an odd mixture of some nasty substances, including lead. Why exactly were you injecting dead bodies? And can you tell us what was in this syringe? For the tape, I am now holding up the evidence bag containing the syringe for the suspect to see."

Francois placed the evidence bag back on the table in front of Steve.

"No comment," came the reply from Steve.

"Injecting a dead body would be pointless, or at least that is what you would think," Jacques continued to address Steve. "However, the lab results from the blood samples have thrown up some interesting questions. You see, my assistant, Laurence, took some blood samples on the evening that the victims arrived in the morgue. These were sent to the lab for tests before you were caught in the cold room. Did you tamper with those bodies using this syringe?" Jacques carefully lifted the evidence bag containing the syringe and waved it around in front of Steve.

"No comment," Steve replied.

"This looks like a very sophisticated piece of equipment. If this proves to be what we think it is, a syringe, then I can state that I've never come across anything quite like this in my career. Where did you get this?"

"No comment," Steve replied.

"Is this a military device?" Francois asked.

"No comment," Steve looked up at the light, let out a long sigh, and folded his arms.

"The first set of blood test results taken by my colleague differ from the second set we took after you were caught in the cold room. The initial results showed the blood to be pure, perhaps almost too pure. The second set showed the blood to be more in keeping with what we would expect. Did the contents of this syringe change those results?" Jacques placed the syringe right in front of Steve.

"No comment," Steve replied.

"Of course, one of the blood test results remained consistent to the first set. Did you manage to inject them all or did you miss one?" Jacques asked.

Francois and Oscar slumped back into their seats as Jacques presented the evidence.

"No comment," Steve said and let out another sigh.

"God, what the hell have we got here?" Oscar buried his head in his hands in disbelief. "You need to start coming up with some answers, and quickly my friend," he spewed and pointed aggressively at Steve.

"Whatever you were attempting to achieve, it failed by the simple fact we had already taken samples and you failed to inject the fourth and final body. So, in my morgue, at this very moment, there are three bodies that have been tampered with and one that remains as it was when it was delivered," Jacques explained as he leaned forward and stared at Steve.

"Do you know any of the victims in that morgue?" Francois asked and leaned forward as well.

"No comment," Steve stared straight back at Francois.

"Next we move on to the DNA results. Now, this is twofold. First, we'll look at the samples lifted at the crash scene by the ASPTS team. The blood found on the metal piece of the seat base has no match to the blood samples from the four victims currently lying in the morgue. Do you know what happened to the bodies from that crash?" Jacques sat back to watch the reactions of Oscar and Francois.

"No comment," Steve replied.

"Then there is the other sample of DNA from the door handle of the same van, again not a match for any of the victims in the morgue."

"Who are you working for?" Oscar asked.

"No comment," Steve again replied.

"We do have to take into account that both of the samples obtained could have been present before the crash," Jacques cautioned. "But you may also remember I brushed into you in the mortuary. From that, I managed to obtain a tiny sample of your skin, just enough for a DNA test. This DNA result may not be an exact match, as it may have been compromised in the way that I obtained it, but it is, in the opinion of the lab technician, a close enough match to the DNA secured from the door handle in one of those vans."

"So how do you explain this result?" Francois asked.

"Again, no comment," Steve said and smirked.

"You may have been in the van earlier? Maybe you got out before the crash? That would explain why traces of your DNA were found on the door handle. Regardless, according to the evidence you were in that van. Can you explain this?" Jacques again pushed Steve on this point.

"No comment," Steve replied.

"We can place you in the van and the cold room. What were you covering up and who are you working for?" Oscar asked.

Steve stared back and took a sip of his drink. "No comment" he muttered.

"How long do you think you can keep this up?" Oscar leaned closer to eyeball Steve.

"Perhaps the final results from our tests may jog your memory," Jacques said, tapping his fingers on the table. "The four bodies we have in the morgue have another thing in common from the initial blood tests. They all contain levels of Succinylcholine that, in my opinion, and that of the lab technician, would render them incapable of driving. In fact, we believe that they would have been either dead or heavily sedated at the time of the crash, given how much of it they had in their bloodstream. Do you care to explain why this might be the case?"

Oscar and Francois stared at Steve awaiting his response.

"No comment," Steve replied.

"However, this leads me onto yet another problem I've had with the victims, something that has bugged me from the very first minute I set eyes on them. If they were involved in a crash, then why are there no physical marks on their bodies. As you seem so interested in them, can you explain this to me?" Jacques asked.

To everyone's surprise, there was a stern knock on the door.

"What is it?" Francois shouted.

A uniformed officer partially opened the door and peered around to look into the room. "I think you should come and see this," he said holding up an iPad.

"This had better be more than important Leclerc!" Francois barked and abruptly stood up, the noise of the chair scraping across the floor filled the interview room.

"It is, I promise you," Leclerc replied.

"For the record, the interview will now be paused," Oscar said and pressed pause on the tape recorder.

Francois left the room and stood in the corridor next to Leclerc while he tapped away at the iPad.

"What is so important that we have to break off from the interview?" Francois asked as they leaned against the wall of the corridor.

"I've been in contact with the relevant authorities and managed to secure some CCTV footage from one of the cameras near the Eiffel Tower. This particular camera captured the moments both leading up to and after the crash, including the moment when the bright light flashed across the road. I've spent some time comparing this to the footage captured by the witness you spoke with at the crash scene."

"You mean Will Deschamps? The footage from his camera?" Francois clarified.

"Yes, and a side-by-side analysis of what they captured reveals some very interesting facts about the people in those vans. Look here." Leclerc opened a pre-prepared screen that had the CCTV footage and the witness footage, side by side, frame by frame. He pressed play and set the playback speed to one quarter.

"So, talk me through this, what are we looking at here?" Francois asked.

"I've started this from the beginning of when Deschamps started filming, so you can see what he would have seen versus the camera from the Tower." Leclerc kept the footage rolling but slowed it down to one-eighth speed. "This is the part where it gets interesting," he said pointing at the screen.

"I'm almost afraid of what we're about to see." Francois held his breath in anticipation.

Leclerc paused the footage for a moment. "As you can see, quite clearly, here, we have all four occupants in full view. Luckily for us, the footage from the Tower is slightly clearer," he said pointing to that side of the screen.

"Can you clean it up?" Francois asked.

"I did. Now look at the face in that van on the right on the passenger side," Leclerc froze the frame, then he zoomed in on the face.

Francois looked at it closely, and then at the other footage captured by Deschamps, which was frozen at the same time, all the faces were blurred in comparison.

"Do you see what I see?" Leclerc asked Francois.

"And these clock times are correct?" Francois pointed to the times indicted by both sets of footage.

"One hundred percent. I've bookmarked this frame, but there's more to this as we will see." Leclerc continued to play the footage at one-eighth speed.

Francois looked closer at the screen. He was mesmerised by what he saw, the bright light now dominated both sets of footage. Leclerc allowed the footage to progress for a few more seconds, the brightness subsided, he then froze the screen again and zoomed in on both vans clearly showing the faces of the occupants.

"I'll ask you again, do you see what I see?" Leclerc asked.

"That's impossible." Francois shook his head. "Take us back to the first bookmark with the image of the passenger, before the light, please," Francois demanded.

Leclerc took it back to the frame as requested and hit pause.

"This is backed up isn't it?" Francois wanted to confirm, as this evidence was crucial to their inquiries.

"For sure. I did that before I came in here to show you," Leclerc replied.

"Good, you've done well Leclerc. Let me take this now," Francois said, took hold of the iPad, and returned to the interview room.

"Perhaps it's best I come into the interview room with you," Leclerc suggested. "I know how to operate this software and one wrong button press…"

"….yeah, you're right," Francois agreed. "But follow my lead."

"For the record Officer Blanc has returned to the interview and is joined by Officer Leclerc," Oscar said as he pressed play on the tape recorder.

Francois settled into his chair while Leclerc pulled a chair up to the table.

"Recognise this face?" Francois said shoving the iPad in front of Steve.

"For the record, Officer Blanc is showing the suspect an image of a face on an iPad," Oscar said.

"No comment," Steve replied.

"So, you don't want to say anything to me about how you came to be in one of the vans before the crash?" Francois didn't care what Steve had to say, or what he didn't have to say; he wanted answers.

Francois turned the iPad around. "Take it to the next point after the light dissipates," he told Leclerc, who immediately followed the instructions.

Francois then turned the iPad around so that Steve could see the screen. The others remained quiet, the only sound was the ticking of the wall clock.

"Do you see what my problem is here with this image? You see, despite what you may think, and I have no idea what is going on here, and how you managed it, but all our occupants are now white...clearly, we can see this here," Francois said and pointed to the screen again, gesturing for Steve to look at it.

"No comment," Steve said, sitting motionless.

Francois looked at Officer Leclerc. "Thank you for this, it has been most helpful. Make sure this is kept in a safe place and off-limits to anyone, and I mean that, no one else can see this until I give clearance."

Leclerc picked up the iPad and left the room.

"For the record, Officer Leclerc has left the interview," Oscar dutifully noted.

"That's where you were immediately before the crash, wasn't it? There was a bag stolen from one of the vans. A large blue holdall. What were you doing down there?" Francois asked, assuming Steve was connected to what occurred in the Catacombs.

Steve was silent.

Francois folded his arms and looked at Steve. "I don't suppose you want to tell us what you were doing down there, and who shot the security guard?"

Jacques took off and wiped his glasses with some tissue.

"These weren't just any rocks, were they?" Francois said to Steve. "Some of those rocks contained diamonds, didn't they?"

"You're nothing but a thief, aren't you?" Oscar stood up and looked down on Steve to try and intimidate him into talking.

Francois turned his attentions to the silver disc in the evidence bag. It had been somewhat ignored, but given all the revelations from the DNA samples, blood tests, and now the video footage, it was hardly surprising. He picked up the evidence bag and tried to press what appeared to be a button on the top of the device.

"Don't press that," Steve said.

"Ah, so finally we have a response," Francois said. "Have we touched a nerve?"

"No. But I can assure you that it would be unwise to touch that," Steve spoke again.

"How so?" Oscar tried to push Steve on the point.

"Just don't. That is all," Steve kept to the minimum number of words.

Francois looked across to Jacques and Oscar and signaled with a nod that he wanted to talk with them away from the table. "Perhaps we should take some time to talk. For the record, the interview is suspended," he said, and with that, he stood up, grabbed the two evidence bags, and paused the tape recorder.

Jacques and Oscar followed Francois out of the room and closed the door.

Steve was alone. He sat motionless in the chair staring at the clock, watching as time slowly ticked by.

"This guy is not right in the head, he's playing us for suckers and we're falling for it," Oscar ranted and waved his arms around.

"How can you be sure?" Jacques shrugged his shoulders.

"It's obvious, look at this, all of this, it's a trick, some kind of clever prank. I don't know how they're doing it but I guarantee you next week it will be on YouTube and some arsehole will be making a fortune from it and laughing at our expense. I'm telling you, man, this is all shit, an elaborate prank." Oscar was quite emotional and was still waving his arms around the tight corridor to emphasise his point.

"I don't agree," Francois said. "If this is a prank, then how come we have all these unanswered questions?" Francois shook his head.

"And if it was a prank, how do you fake medical science? Those people were not crash victims, as I stand here now, I am telling you that fact," Jacques said and threw his hands in the air. "Francois, you've known me for years and you know I'm not prone to exaggerating things. On occasion, you've accused me of playing down evidence, but this time, what happened, it's not possible. Take it from me. It is simply not possible. There is, as far as I'm aware, no medical explanation that can explain what happened to those bodies that are lying in my morgue. I tell you this, plain as I stand here now."

"Emotions are running high, and this man is not helping," Francois said in an attempt to calm the situation.

"Not helping? You're joking, this guy is a one-man fucking prankster!" Oscar stomped his foot.

"We are not going to solve anything arguing amongst ourselves. We need to stay focused and try to pry out of this man some form of sense that will help us understand what happened. Let us try to keep an open mind and use our collective knowledge to get to the bottom of this case. Because despite what we may think, or indeed want to think, this is just another case that needs solving, and that man is probably our best chance of achieving that goal," Francois replied.

"Now come on, you know you have had your doubts," Jacques wanted to remind Francois of their meeting in the cafe, but before he could say another word he spotted a woman in a dark navy suit walking briskly toward them.

"Who's in charge here?" she asked in an English accent.

"Pardon me, madame?" Francois asked.

"I said who is in charge, surely that is not too hard a question to answer," she spat.

"That depends on who is asking," Oscar said.

"Don't try and play games with me. I want to know who is in charge of this case and who is interviewing the suspect in there," she said nodding toward the door.

"Apologies, there was no intention to play games, I merely wanted to ascertain if you were in the correct part of the station. I am in charge madame," Francois replied.

"And who might you be?" she asked.

"Well, I may ask the same of you first," Francois replied.

"My name is Helen Smith. I am the suspect's lawyer and I demand to see him in private," Helen spoke sternly.

"I am Francois Blanc of the Gendarme Nationale, and your suspect is quite safe at the moment but I cannot allow you a private conversation until we can ascertain what he is capable of, that is, given what we know so far," Francois said.

"He may be quite safe officer, but I can assure you that his rights are currently being infringed. Under French law, he's entitled to a private meeting with his lawyer. I demand that his rights are upheld and you grant me that time now," Helen raised her voice.

"We have reason to believe your client may be capable of doing things," Francois said.

"*Doing things*? Ha! That's a new one. And precisely what kind of things do you think he is capable of *doing?* After all, he is currently locked up in a police station interview room," Helen chuckled.

"We have reason to believe that he managed to break into a morgue undetected, despite the presence of police officers at the only entrance to the place, and somehow manage to escape the scene of a crash without injury," Francois spelled out his concerns.

"Hardly the stuff of miracles is it? And I suppose you have proof of this?" Helen asked.

"Yes, we do. He was caught in the cold room of the Pitie Salpetriere mortuary by my officers and he was caught on camera placing him in one of the vehicles involved in the crash near the Eiffel Tower. So, now do you see my problem?" Francois asked.

"Hardly a danger to the public though is he? I mean, we all know how sleepy cops can get halfway through the night when on a long job, surely, it's not beyond the realms of possibility that he managed to slip past them undetected, is it? And besides, that doesn't remove his right to a private meeting with his lawyer. That is the law. I take it you do know the law, don't you?" Helen frowned at Francois.

"Yes madame, I can assure you, I do know the law of this country very well." Francois nodded slowly.

"How did you know it was at night?" Oscar picked up on one point made by Helen.

"Excuse me?" Helen was caught off guard.

"How did you know the break-in at the morgue took place during the night? You just said that we all know how sleepy cops can get halfway through the night when working a long shift, how did you know the break-in was during the night?" Oscar repeated the question.

"I'm just guessing, and anyway, none of this removes his right to a private meeting with his lawyer, as I've said, it is the law here in France," Helen brushed aside Oscar's point.

"Please be assured that I'm well acquainted with the law madame, but also, may I point out the fact we don't even know his name," Francois said and raised his eyebrows.

"I can clear that up for you right now," Helen said.

"You can?" Francois' eyes widened. "Go on, what is his name?"

"My client's name is Steve Garner. He is a British citizen. So now that we have established his identity and nationality, I demand to have a private meeting with him immediately," Helen retorted.

"What was he doing in a morgue in Paris?" Oscar asked.

"When I get a chance to talk with him I just may be able to clear that up for you," Helen snapped back.

"What assurances can you give me?" Francois asked.

"Assurances for what precisely?" Helen wore a puzzled expression on her face.

"That nothing will happen to him, after all, we have only just found out his name," Francois replied.

"Well, surely the collective power of the Gendarme Nationale, added to the fact that my client is seated in an interview room in the middle of a police station should allay any fears you could have, or is there something *you're* not telling me?" Helen rebutted.

"No madame, there isn't anything we're not telling you, in fact, we have very little we can tell you." Francois looked to the ground, "We have two items recovered from the cold room of the mortuary that are unidentified, and a man who won't speak with us. Aside from that, we have very little to add apart from DNA, blood test results, and some CCTV footage."

"I expect to have access to all of this evidence as we progress," Helen said.

"Of course," Francois replied.

"You realise that any recordings you have made during the interviews you've illegally conducted with my client are inadmissible in court?" Helen skipped past the other details that Francois had mentioned.

"I understand," Francois stared at Helen.

"Your client has hardly spoken to us since we arrested him, clearly you have trained him well," Oscar said.

"Then you'll not delay me any further. Please allow me access to my client as per the laws of your country. Perhaps after that my client may decide to talk with you," Helen said.

Francois used his security card to open the door to the interview room. He held it partially open to stop Helen from entering. "You have thirty minutes, and believe me when I say, I'm watching you like a hawk."

"May I remind you that this is a private meeting, you have no right to do that," Helen nudged open the door to see Steve sitting alone.

Francois led Helen into the room and pulled a chair for her to sit down. Steve sat, unmoved by Helen's presence.

"Answer me this, how did you know he would be here if we have been unable to log his name with the front desk?" Francois said standing in the doorway.

"He's a resourceful British citizen. He has any number of ways to contact the Consulate," Helen brushed aside Francois' question.

"But there are many police stations in this town, why come here?" Francois persisted.

"There aren't many with an unnamed British suspect being held in custody who won't talk though, are there?" Helen quickly replied.

"This is true, still, I have to wonder how you managed to find him. This is just one more reason why I am cautious. I don't know what may…" Francois was cut short.

"...What may what? Happen next? I have many reasons to believe this man has been mistreated during his time in custody. Let's hope that Steve Garner proves me wrong on that particular point, otherwise you may be called on to face some uncomfortable questions from the British Consulate. That's what may happen next. Do I make myself clear?" Helen quipped and then removed a small Dictaphone from her bag and placed it on the table.

"Very clear," Francois replied.

"Good," Helen said.

"You will record your interview?" Francois asked.

"Yes, but since you have wasted some of my time, I can see that I now have only twenty-six minutes to talk with my client," she said and looked across to Steve who shuffled uncomfortably in his chair.

"Perhaps so, but I think that will be enough. Take it from me, he's not very talkative," Francois said.

Francois turned and left the room, closing the door behind him. He stood in the corridor in front of Oscar and Jacques, put his index finger to his lips, and thought for a moment.

"Oscar, please go and find Leclerc, tell him to take the DNA results from the van along with the DNA Jacques obtained and see if there's a match to a Steve Garner. We now know his name and that he is a British citizen. I want to see if there's anything on Interpol's database. He may have previous indiscretions. We might find something that may help us understand what we are dealing with here."

"I'll get the files e-mailed across now from the lab so you'll have them," Jacques said to Oscar.

"And what about the lawyer?" Oscar asked.

"As she said, his right is to have a private meeting with his lawyer, there's nothing we can do about that. But we may just find out something else about him that could help us piece together who this man is and what he was doing in Paris, I don't believe robbery was the motive," Francois said.

"Why not?" Jacques asked.

"Just a hunch. That man doesn't look like he's done anything wrong in his life," Francois said.

"Looks can be deceptive, as we know, but let's hope your hunches are correct eh?" Oscar said as he walked off to find Leclerc.

"Who are you?" Steve asked Helen.

"That's not important right now. What is important is that I'm here to help," Helen stood on the opposite side of the table looking down at Steve.

"They have footage of me in the van just before the timeline…" Steve began to talk while Helen skulked

312

around the interview room with a roll of duct tape in hand that she had taken out of her small bag.

"Shh," she said, pausing momentarily to look over at Steve. She then placed a small length of black tape over the CCTV camera on the wall in the corner of the room.

"What are you doing?" Steve asked as Helen continued to look around the room.

"Covering our tracks," she replied. "And don't worry about the footage, Silverton will sort that out for us," Helen continued.

"How do you…" suddenly things were clicking into place for Steve. "Of course, do you…?"

"Don't speak, please, we already have enough issues to clear up here," Helen placed her finger on her lips.

Oscar caught up with Leclerc who was seated at his desk continuing to analyse the footage from the crash. In the background there was a bank of small TV screens displaying various parts of the police station; one of them was blank, the screen was labeled EC1. Oscar and Leclerc were oblivious to this, being far too preoccupied with the frame-by-frame progression of the crash.

"Okay, what do you need now?" Leclerc asked sensing he was about to be tasked with more work.

"I'm going to forward you the DNA results from earlier, can you run a check with Interpol using these and also the name Steve Garner?" Oscar asked. "We need to see if this man has any priors."

"Excuse me, but who is Steve Garner?" Leclerc asked.

"That happens to be the name of the suspect in the interview room," Oscar replied.

"You mean, he's talking now? Maybe you should show him the footage again, see if he'll talk about what happened," Leclerc suggested.

"Don't waste your time, he's not talking, but his lawyer is. She's the one who told us his name," Oscar said.

"What lawyer?" Leclerc looked at Oscar.

"The one who just arrived, in fact, moments after you left." Oscar paused for a moment. "Come to think of it, we didn't even ask for any ID, she was so insistent on seeing her client, she bullied Francois into submission."

"That doesn't sound right," Leclerc replied.

"I'm telling you, that is what happened."

"Listen, there's only one way in and one way out, via that corridor I just walked down and I didn't see anyone walk past me. I could be wrong, but…let's check the front desk. They'll have a record of her arrival." Leclerc dialed the front desk on his phone.

"Are you ready?" Helen stooped over the table in front of Steve and looked at the Dictaphone.

"I don't think I ever will be, but let's do this," Steve said and braced himself.

Leclerc slowly hung up the phone and stared at Oscar. "According to the officer on duty, no one has signed in at the front desk for hours."

"You're kidding!" Oscar jumped to his feet and looked at the bank of TV screens. "What's wrong with that screen?" he said pointing at a blank screen labeled EC1.

"Nothing, I don't think anyway," Leclerc said, stood up, reached over, and repeatedly pushed the on and off button several times to see if that would inject some life into the screen.

"What's happened to it?" Oscar shouted. He reached for his phone and started to dial.

"It's working, the screen is fine, it's just the camera," Leclerc frantically fiddled with the control panel on the screen.

"Is it…?" Oscar asked.

"Yes!" Leclerc stopped messing with the control panel, he knew the screen was not the problem.

"It must be nearly thirty minutes," Francois paced up and down the corridor.

"I know, this is painful," Jacques looked up from his seat. "Can you slow down? You're making me dizzy."

On the other side of the door, Helen was ready. "Let's go," she said and pushed a small button on top of the Dictaphone.

"Look at the screen," Leclerc pointed to screen EC1, the edges of the display were now glowing brightly.

"Get in there!" Oscar shouted through the phone to Francois.

Francois had barely answered the phone when his eyes were drawn immediately to the bright, glowing light that seeped out from beneath the interview room door.

"Hurry!" Oscar ran down the corridor and barked his order to Francois.

Jacques jumped up from his chair and Francois scrambled to find his security card to gain entry to the interview room. Leclerc and Oscar were closing in on them.

Francois burst through the door to be greeted by nothing. The room was empty.

Oscar came to an abrupt halt, slamming into the frame of the door, and then followed Francois and Jacques into the room. Leclerc just stood in the doorway, looking in at what was left.

"Where the fuck have they gone?" Francois said and checked under the table in desperation.

"She wasn't a lawyer!" Leclerc barked out in between breaths.

"How do you know?" Jacques yelled as he continued to search every corner of the room.

"Because the officer on duty said no one has checked in for hours," Leclerc replied.

"If that's the case, then how did she get in unnoticed?" Francois stopped and looked at Leclerc.

"Don't you see? There's a pattern emerging! Look at the facts, a bright light, people then change or disappear, can't you see? Look at the crash, look at the bodies, everything about this is very much on the fringes of what we understand, or like to think we understand. Everything we know so far, all the evidence we have seen before us, challenges what years of training, experience, and common sense have taught us," Jacques said.

The search of the room stopped.

"What are you trying to say, that this is all some kind of supernatural event?" Oscar yelled at Jacques.

"I think only a fool would suggest there *wasn't* some kind of unexplained happening at play here, something we cannot pin down, we can't see it, and it's partly due to those hardened years of experience between us," Jacques calmly replied.

"He's right, there's an emerging pattern here, and none of it is easily explainable. Look at the facts, all we have left now are those items, and that footage from the crash. But we have no suspect, and it would appear we now have an accomplice to trace," Francois said and then looked over at Leclerc. "Will you keep running those checks with Interpol and add Helen Smith to your list to check as well. It's highly unlikely that is her real name but let's see, maybe we will get lucky. In the meantime, we'll check this room for prints and anything else."

"I'm on it now."

"And Leclerc."

"Yes?" Leclerc stopped in the doorway.

"Say nothing to anyone," Francois pointed to his lips.

"Okay sir," Leclerc turned and walked up the corridor.

"What are we going to say about the suspect?" Oscar enquired.

"For now, we say nothing, do you understand me? Nothing," Francois replied.

"We can't just say nothing, the duty officer will be expecting him back in the cell soon." Oscar was right.

"What do you suggest? That we tell them the truth? That some unknown woman posing as a lawyer turned up and demanded to see the suspect, and that somehow, before we knew it, they disappeared into thin air? Is that what you want me to say because if I say that, then I can assure you we will be stripped of our duties…indefinitely," Francois replied and threw his hands in the air.

"No of course not." Oscar looked down to the ground shaking his head.

"So, we have to keep quiet about it, that is until we can come up with something that makes sense and doesn't make us look like we're losing our minds," Francois insisted.

Oscar reached up and removed the black tape from the CCTV camera, "I'm guessing this is what caused the issue with the camera then."

"Oh great…" Francois said.

Oscar placed the tape in an evidence bag he had in his jacket. "One of the screens, the one monitoring this room, wasn't working, or so we thought, but it turns out someone covered the camera with this duct tape."

"That may contain fingerprints," Francois pointed at the bag.

"I know, that is why I put it in the bag. I'll make sure it gets to the forensics lab for tests," Oscar replied.

"Get the interview tape as well. We may get a trace based on his voice," Francois pointed to the machine at the end of the table.

"Okay." Oscar pressed eject on the machine and placed the cassette into a box.

"Right, I think we finish up here, try to make some sense of what just happened, and see if this duct tape holds any more clues alongside the evidence we already have. And no talking to the press because they will have a field day with this," Francois said.

The three men walked out of the interview room and closed the door.

"I'm going back to the hospital. I'll let you know if the samples in the lab throw up any new results," Jacques said while he shook the hands of both Francois and Oscar, and then made his way back to the foyer.

Oscar led the way back to the office where Leclerc was still reviewing the crash footage.

"Not a word of this to anyone," Francois said to Leclerc, as he slumped into the chair at his desk.

Oscar looked at the screen monitoring EC1, it was now working clear. "Clever," he said to himself. "I'm taking this to forensics."

"I'm going to try and come up with some kind of story to at least buy us some time. In the meantime, if either of you have any ideas or new evidence let's keep tight and not say a word to anyone else," Francois uttered and then surveyed his messy desk.

An hour or so of silence had passed, Francois was still busying himself with the pile of papers on his desk, while Leclerc sat wearing headphones replaying the same piece of audio over and over again. He was scribbling down notes, then pausing the audio and examining what he wrote, and then comparing it to the replayed version of the audio.

Leclerc removed the headphones and turned to look over at Francois who was several desks away from him. "You know, we may have no visual evidence but there is some audio, albeit not very good, but we can hear them."

Francois stopped what he was doing, sat up straight, and immediately looked at Leclerc. "Seriously?"

"Yes," Leclerc replied.

"Can you make out what they're saying?" Francois stood up and approached Leclerc's desk.

"I think so, it's very fuzzy and of course, she did partially cover the microphone on the camera with the tape, but the suspect seemed concerned about the footage. I'm sure he used the word timeline, but I can't be one hundred percent certain, here, have a listen."

Francois put on the headphones and Leclerc played him the audio track. He stared upwards, trying to focus on what they were saying, then his eyes lit up, "Silverton!"

"Pardon?" Leclerc looked quizzically at Francois.

"The face that I thought I saw at the crash scene, it's him!" Francois shouted.

"And?" Leclerc was lost. "Who are you suggesting, this Silverton person?"

"She mentions that name in this audio track. I'm not going crazy. I thought I saw him. I just couldn't understand why he would be there," Francois said, nodding to himself.

"I don't follow," Leclerc said.

"It's a long story, but I met this Silverton character many years ago during another case. He was head of a special investigation unit in London, but later in his career, I heard he was moved to another unit that specialised in investigating UFO sightings. You know, some sort of government spook that was there to, how can I put this, quiet things down if they got of hand, in the interests of the public and all that shit."

"You mean *cover-up*," Leclerc rolled his eyes.

"Kind of...yes, but this unit was quite small. I think they wanted him out of the way for whatever reason, probably because of that other case I mentioned. After that, well, we didn't speak again and then I saw him at the crash scene. It sounds like Helen Smith, whoever she really is, says that Silverton will sort it out in direct reference to the point that Garner makes about the footage, just before the bright light occurs," Francois explained, clenched his fist and shook it.

"Are you suggesting the British UFO service, or whatever they may be called, has something to do with this crash?" Leclerc frowned.

"I don't know. It can't be ruled out though. Until I do some more investigating, not a word of this to anyone, do you understand me?" Francois demanded. "We don't want any more complications."

Leclerc understood.

"Timeline," Francois muttered the word to himself.

"Excuse me?" Leclerc asked.

"Timeline. You said the suspect used that word, yet we have no context for it because he stops speaking. What can that mean?" Francois sat back in his chair, looked up to the ceiling, and crossed his arms.

40

Paris.2618.

The police interview room was now, like so much of Paris, a remnant of the past. Layers of dust that had built up over the years stirred and rose into the dark space. A piercing light began to fill the room, followed by the appearance of two silhouetted figures in the middle of the maelstrom. As the light subsided, Helen and Steve stood in the dark room trying to make out their new surroundings.

"Of all the places to wind up, it had to be this place," Helen said.

She gingerly shuffled around the room, her outstretched hands serving as ballast as she attempted to get her bearings.

Steve coughed. "Damn. What the hell is in this place?" He said, kicking over some debris that was lying on the ground.

"I wouldn't like to guess, but for the moment, come and help me with this," Helen said as she stood by a tightly sealed door.

Steve used her voice as a guide and started to walk slowly toward her, his outstretched hands helping him navigate.

"Stand back!" a voice shouted from the other side of the door. Steve and Helen stepped back toward the middle of the room as the door smashed open. Two security guards stood in the doorway, beckoning them to follow.

Steve squinted as light streamed into the room and waved away the dust filling the air in front of him.

"We have to go, and quickly, we have instructions to escort you to the shuttle," one of the guards said.

"How far away is it?" Steve asked.

"It's next to the Eiffel Tower."

"How come it's over there?"

"Security reasons. It was safer to land there," the other guard replied.

They escorted Steve and Helen through the wrecked police station and onto the overgrown streets of Paris. Out in the open air, it became clear that something wasn't right. An atmosphere pervaded the streets, accentuated by the stillness. Shards of sunlight streamed through the broken buildings and onto the ground. The silence embracing the city was occasionally punctuated by sounds that bounced off the derelict buildings. Every panel of glass on the Grand Palais was shattered, reducing the once proud monument of Parisian commerce to a rusting wireframe. It was a stark contrast to London's skyline.

They walked along the Avenue de New York, which stretched out for miles in front of them. A Golden Eagle swooped majestically from one of the twisted lamp posts lining the avenue. This was its territory now, and it didn't care for the people walking within its hunting grounds; they were the intruders. Steve stooped to avoid contact as the eagle made a final dart to the ground to snatch its unsuspecting prey. The eagle flexed its enormous wings and flew off into the distance, clutching a large rodent in its claws.

The two security guards took the lead, their weapons drawn; they were clearly concerned about something.

"If this isn't safe for the shuttle, why is it safe for us?" Steve whispered to Helen.

"It's too enclosed here and favoured by hijackers. A shuttle would be easily overwhelmed," Helen said.

"You're not making me feel good about our situation."

"You don't have to worry, these security guards are armed, they will cope with anything we're likely to confront."

They progressed ever closer to their destination. Steve was trying to take it all in whilst staying vigilant. The streets were littered with the rusting wrecks of cars, many of which appeared to have been adapted with amour plating. There wasn't a single building that had escaped the ravages of war and the searing heat offered no respite.

"Do I get the feeling we're being watched?" Steve asked as he glanced into the shells of the abandoned buildings; there were plenty of places to hide.

"Stay close to the security guards. We'll be fine," Helen replied.

"That sounds like a nice way of saying that we are?" Steve quipped.

"Just keep walking," Helen said. "There's nothing to worry about. If we're being watched, it's probably just a small group who wandered into the area by accident, possibly drawn by the promise of shelter."

"How come you know so much about all this?" Steve said as he looked around.

"Because when people were telling me things, I was listening, rather than trying to discredit them."

Point taken, thought Steve.

"The Dictaphone you used, that was a bit James Bond, wasn't it? What's next? A hairbrush that can send morse code?"

"Sometimes you have to improvise, and besides, it's something any self-respecting criminal lawyer would carry. Most importantly, the idea worked."

"So exactly who are you? I mean, do I get to know the real you? You're not just a lawyer, are you?" He turned to look at Helen. "If you're a lawyer at all"

"It may surprise you to learn that I am just like you – one of the collective – one of the twenty-six."

"So, how come you got to bust me out of the police station? Aren't we supposed to be the chosen ones, protected at every step by mysterious chaperones that appear from nowhere to guide us through life?"

"Now you're being silly," Helen said as they walked past a series of burnt-out school buses.

"Maybe I am, but you haven't answered the question." Steve was intrigued by Helen. She came across as this steely, cool woman and that always raised his eyebrows.

"What can I say? They wanted someone with brains, someone who could talk their way into the room, and most importantly, someone who could get you out of there. They obviously thought I was that person, and it looks like they chose wisely." Helen smiled at Steve.

"I guess a pretty smile doesn't hurt, either? I mean that with the utmost respect before you shout at me!" Steve said, realising he had to qualify his statement.

Helen laughed. "Whatever are you trying to suggest?"

"Nothing, I promise. I'm just a confused man on a voyage of discovery, and probably on the verge of a nervous breakdown. God, that sounded cliché. You know what I mean. Half the time I'm questioning what the hell is going on, and the other half I find myself, well…here, in the middle of Paris in some kind of urban hell. This is not normal for an accountant – sorry, a former accountant. We like things boxed off, t's that are crossed, i's that have dots. Do you understand what I mean?"

Helen smirked. "I think so. You just have to stick with it, let things shape the world around you. In time, it will all make sense."

They saw the Eiffel Tower up ahead as they walked along the last stretch of road. The broken monument still had the power to shock Steve. His mind wandered back to his previous life. He yearned to see his family again, but he feared that could be a long way off.

"You must have friends in high places," Helen said, shaking Steve out of his daydream.

"In what way?"

"Well, it's not every day that the Gendarme Nationale lose a suspect from the confines of their own police station, especially given that we didn't leave via traditional methods. There will be clues…clues that could lead straight to our respective front doors."

"I don't let things like that worry me now," Steve said.

"What happened to crossing the t's and dotting the i's?"

"Perhaps I'm letting things shape this new world like you said. It will make sense in time, and perhaps I have to allow that process to happen."

The shuttle was in clear view up ahead. A symbol of the future amongst the destruction.

Kallyuke was pacing up and down in front of the shuttle.

"I'm trying to reinvent myself as a sort of happy-go-lucky, super-spy guy from the future. I think it must be my age, besides, people like him appear to have all the answers. I just do what I'm told," he said, pointing toward Kallyuke.

"Either that or you are becoming one crazy motherfucker who likes to live life on the edge. That's hard to reconcile as I know of no other accountant who lives like that." Helen laughed.

"That's exactly it, I'm a crazy motherfucker. You know, I like the sound of that! The accountant was Steve of the past – this is Steve of the future; the new me."

"I'll settle for a dose of sanity at the moment," Helen stared back at Steve.

They were getting closer to the shuttle. As well as Kallyuke, there were two more security guards in attendance.

"More security guards. They are taking no chances," Steve whispered to Helen.

"You seem to forget what happened here recently," Helen replied.

"If we're being technical about it, that happened about six centuries ago," Steve said.

"Don't be technical" Helen replied, "Who knows who has been tracking us. We have no idea who is out there at the moment. Maybe it's against your newfound laissez-faire approach to life, but I think it's better to be safe than sorry."

They approached the shuttle to greet Kallyuke who paused for a moment and looked at the pair of them.

"Welcome back, albeit not in the circumstances that I expected or wanted," Kallyuke said.

"I would second that," Steve said.

"The decision to break you out of that police station wasn't an easy one. We could have left you there, but upon reflection, to rescue you was the correct decision. It was a calculated risk and one that we had to take. There's too much time and resource invested in you to walk away now," Kallyuke paced in front of Steve and Helen.

"Well, I'm glad you did." Steve looked up to the deserted sky, and then at Kallyuke. "We need to talk."

"Follow me." Kallyuke ushered them into the shuttle where they sat around one of the tables. Helen sat next to Steve and Kallyuke sat opposite them. "Tell me, what is on your mind?"

"The bodies you switched…did it not occur to you that they were all white? That's a bit of a miscalculation on your part, isn't it? Surely, you could see the flaw in that plan?"

"Let's get one thing straight. There will be mistakes made. That is an inevitable consequence of what we are doing here. I'm aware of that, and make no excuses or offer any apologies, and yes that was an oversight." Kallyuke folded his arms. "Decisions made in the heat of the moment can quite often have unwanted consequences, but those are the risks we take, and I stand by those decisions."

"Then we have to make better decisions, don't we?"

"We will," Kallyuke said.

"Because now we have the CCTV footage of me in one of the vans that was captured from the camera on the Tower. On top of this, I find out during the interview that you drugged the bodies with something called Succinylcholine. Don't you think these things through?" Steve shook his head.

"We had to make a decision, and that was a solution. It wasn't perfect, I know, but at the time it was our best option."

"Evidence like this doesn't get missed. Everyone has a damn smartphone. People film crime scenes all the time. There are CCTV cameras everywhere, filming everything we do. There are no places to hide. Autopsies can trace almost any suspicious chemical in a dead body, as we now know, let alone the cocktail you had me inject into those bodies. The shit that just went down in Paris…they will be onto us if we're not careful. And believe me, when they catch up to us, we will have a lot of explaining to do, most of which we cannot explain without sounding insane. The twenty-first century can't be your experimental playground. The tech they have at their disposal will eventually track us down. I'm not prepared to spend the rest of my life trying to explain this away in some secure mental unit because of your carelessness. What happened here was a risk too far." Steve pointed vigorously to the ground.

"We are many steps ahead of these people, both in terms of the tech we have at our disposal and also in the way we can circumvent even their best officers, without them knowing what is happening around them. They can guess, but when it comes down to it, can you imagine an officer of the law standing in front of a judge and trying to coherently explain what really happened in Paris, on the basis of a hunch?" Kallyuke was ebullient as ever. "It simply will not happen. Not one officer is going to risk their career, their reputation, and their pension, to try and expose our operations. Of that, I am very confident."

"That may be the case, but we are leaving a large audit trail for them to follow. We have to stop making it easy for them," Steve said.

"What do you mean by an audit trail?" Kallyuke sat back and frowned.

"It's an accountancy term. It's a trail that leads someone to something that you may not have found out if the individual or company hadn't been careless. They're like clues, unwanted information that can add up to help solve an investigation. That's all I'm saying," Steve said.

"And what are they going to say if they uncover a shred of truth? Do you think they're going to want information leaking out into the public domain? Of course not, they'll cover it up and bury it, like they always do. That is why we have people like Silverton working with us. They help perpetuate the myth, cloud over any clear view to the truth with diversions and create alternative versions of what happened to help cover our tracks," Kallyuke replied.

"Thank you for introducing me to Helen as well," Steve looked across at her.

"That was a calculated risk, a good decision. We couldn't afford to take the risk of you recognising someone in that interview room, it would have jeopardised the plan. You would have given it away, even if you think you wouldn't have done so. Your subconscious would have let you down. Perhaps you should give us more credit," Kallyuke said. "And you should thank this woman for getting you back in one piece before anything else happened to you."

"I understand everything that you've said so far," Steve leaned forward to stare at Kallyuke. "I'm just not sure we need to leave such a blatant trail for them to follow, after all, why make it easy for them?"

"Even if they follow the trail, their investigations will buckle under the weight of skepticism, and a lack of concrete proof."

"I hope you're right," Steve muttered.

"We have so much to accomplish, so much to learn, and so much more to do to protect our future, and I apologise if, at times, you feel lost. However, in time, all of this will one day make sense. I promise you that." Kallyuke stood up to shake Steve's hand.

"Ironically, it is time that seems to be making a mess of things," Steve said quietly. He stood up and was now eye to eye with Kallyuke.

Kallyuke grasped his hand and shook it rigorously. A biting pain spread through Steve's palm, progressing into the muscles and tendons. He yelped, looking down in horror to discover his hand was now glowing bright orange. Helen sprang from her seat and stood several steps away. A searing heat embedded itself into the palm, he retracted his hand from Kallyuke's grasp. Steve cried out as the glow spread through the veins in his arm.

"What the fuck have you done to me?" Steve shook his hand in the air to try and cool it down. The glowing subsided.

"I've given you a magnificent power. You have the whole world right there…"

Kallyuke pointed to Steve's hand, under the surface of the skin something was embedding itself into the muscle tissue, merging into the fibres of the bones and becoming part of his hand.

"What the fuck is it?!" Steve said, examining his hand.

"In time, you will thank me," Kallyuke smiled.

"Tell me what the fuck this is!" he shouted.

"Do you know what this is?!" Steve looked across to Helen as his breathing quickened.

"She knows nothing about it. And for your information, it is the latest development of CCS. You may remember Charley Sandford told you about this in Santa Monica. That is if you were paying attention."

"CCS? You mean Charley's little cube, the one he called the all-seeing eye?" Steve slowly started to calm down; the pain subsided.

"Yes. You now have it, there, in the palm of your hand," Kallyuke reached over and carefully tapped Steve's palm. "You are the first to have access to this new technology. We were able to adapt the organic technology we captured from one of the abandoned bases. It really is fascinating stuff."

"Now I'm a fucking guinea pig?" Steve barked. "I have no choice in the matter?"

"No, you're not, and yes, you have choices," Kallyuke replied. "But what you are, is part of this new and exciting development. In time, as you adjust to it, CCS will start to interface with your brain giving you

330

the ability to access it and communicate with us. Your eyes will become conduits into the world, you will be able to store and transmit information via this miracle called CCS. Imagine how that can help us when faced with these difficult decisions that require immediate attention?"

"And what happens if I don't want to keep sending this stuff? What happens if I want some time alone, away from all of this? Then what do I do? Wear a blindfold!" Steve was angry and skeptical.

"Not at all, in time, you will be able to control this, and simply switch it off."

"You keep using the words in time…"

"Because you are still adjusting to all of this, and *in time,* you will succeed."

"Irrespective of the amount of time I have, I'm not sure I will ever adjust to this," Steve said, examining the palm of his hand.

"You will come to rely on it. One day, it may even save your life." Kallyuke was undeterred by Steve's concerns.

"So how do I get rid of it?"

"What makes you think that you will want to get rid of it?"

"It's nice to have the option," Steve said.

"Give it time," Kallyuke said. "This is a significant technological breakthrough."

"Time?"

"Yes."

"And what's in it for you? You don't strike me as someone who does something without some form of payback."

"This is about pushing the boundaries of technology, not about any form of payoff," Kallyuke said.

"So, you can guarantee that you won't use this against me or my wishes?" Steve questioned.

"You will be in control of it and have the ability to make decisions about its deployment, so yes, I can guarantee that." Kallyuke paused. "We must get back to London, Sayssac wants a face-to-face meeting with us in the morning."

"Do you know what it's about?" Helen asked.

"I'm not sure, but in the meantime, you both need to rest. I think it's about time Steve got to use his new apartment," Kallyuke said.

"I'll second that," Steve said and nestled back into the seat, covering his hand with his sleeve, just in case.

The shuttle took off into the bright sunlight heading toward London and leaving behind the stillness of Paris.

41

London.2618.

Steve peered out the window as the shuttle arrived next to the Shard. The sun was brighter than ever, the reflection bouncing off the glass structure was almost blinding in its intensity. The shuttle remained completely still as a covered walkway extended five metres out from the 80th floor of the Shard and sealed against the door on the shuttle.

"We're secure," a voice announced from the cockpit. The shuttle doors opened to reveal the short walkway to the entrance of the Shard.

Steve got to his feet and shuffled past Helen. "What floor is this?" he asked Kallyuke.

"The 80th, home to one of the best apartments in the building, if not the city, and it is all yours," Kallyuke smiled.

Helen looked across to the exterior of Steve's new apartment. "Very nice, I see that someone is going to have the best view in the city."

"That thing in your hand, the thing that you appear to despise," Kallyuke said. "Think of it as a guide to your new home."

Steve looked at the palm of his hand, nodded, and took the few short steps across the walkway to his new apartment.

The door to Steve's new apartment opened.

Helen looked on with envy. "When do I get a place like that? Or is that just reserved for him?"

The walkway retracted from the shuttle back into the building.

"Soon. I had to keep him on our side and this was the best way I thought I could achieve that," Kallyuke replied.

"So, now you're bribing him? How long do you think that will work before you need to resort to something else to placate him?" Helen retorted.

"I don't know, but we need him now, more than ever like we need you all," Kallyuke said. "Plus, I have another idea that I think may help him adjust...we just need to explore all the variables before we put a plan in place to deliver on that promise."

Helen sat back to ponder what that plan may be.

Kallyuke let out a sigh of relief as he sat back down and the shuttle continued on its journey.

                              ***

No sooner had Steve looked around his new surroundings when he heard a stern knock on the door.

"Beware of distant acquaintances bringing gifts," Richard stood at the door and held out a bottle of what looked like whiskey.

"Someone seems a bit more relaxed. What is that stuff?" Steve pointed to the bottle.

Richard looked at the bottle, "This, my friend, is as close to whiskey as they can get. It's okay and more importantly, it has the same effect."

"Well, don't just stand there, let's give it a try." Steve ushered Richard into the main room of his apartment and Richard was instantly drawn to the view from the large windows.

"Wow, they didn't mess around with you then did they? What's it take to get a place like this?"

"Who knows, but for now I'll just take it as it comes I guess." Steve held out two glasses.

Richard filled them with the brown liquid. "A toast to new beginnings."

   "To new beginnings, whatever they may be,"
Steve said and raised his glass.

42

Manchester.Present-Day.

The less than salubrious end of Deansgate in Manchester was home to the office of Mark Collins. It was all he could afford and had the feel of an office belonging to a man who was running out of time, ideas, and money.

"Shit!" Mark shouted at the discarded letter lying open on his desk, the word "REMINDER" was printed in red at the top. He stood up, turned around, and opened one of the large windows to let in some fresh air. Traffic buzzed past on the road below. It was a busy place at any time of day but had the redeeming factor of being close to where he needed to be to attend client meetings.

The office was filled with battered old filing cabinets and shelving units, all of which were overflowing with files and binders. There was an old, flea-riddled couch set against the large window on the other side of the poky office. A small table with a kettle, some mugs, and tea bags sat in the corner near the door; with a plastic bottle of milk on it that was starting to turn.

Mark switched on his computer to check his e-mail.

The usual mix of unwanted demands, spam, and offers of work filtered into his inbox, then he spied a message from Evelyn Martins congratulating him on his recent report and supplying a few amendments of her own, along with a warning not to use his name on the final version.

Mark walked over to the kettle and checked it for water. It was his lucky day; there was just enough to make a cup of coffee. He switched it on and wandered back to his desk. He pulled up his Blogger account and copied the report into the site. He added the Twitter handle @mcollinsblog and his name and send. There was no way he was going to let someone else take the credit for all of his work.

The kettle finished boiling and Mark walked over to make some coffee. After pouring in the water and stirring in the instant coffee granules, he reached for the milk. It dropped into the coffee, lump by lump.

"Maybe this isn't my lucky day after all." He attempted to stir the gooey mess floating on the top of the coffee. A beep from the computer signified that he'd received a notification.

"That was quick."

Mark walked back over to the computer. He was pleasantly surprised to see the report he had just posted was being read and syndicated into conspiracy websites across the world. Word was spreading.

He opened his email and set about sending a reply to Evelyn with links to the report.

***

Evelyn finished reading the revised version of the report and smiled. She knew that Mark wouldn't be able to resist using his name. "Let the games begin," she whispered to herself.

She got up and walked over to the coffee machine to grab a fresh mug when her phone rang. She ran back to her desk, thinking it may be a lead for one of the other investigative reports she was working on.

"I hope, for your sake, this fucking shit report has nothing to do with you," the voice barked through the phone.

Evelyn recoiled in her chair and held the phone away from her ear. She took a deep breath before answering. "What on earth do you mean? Who is this?"

"This fucking report. It's all over the fucking web. You don't think we monitor these things?"

Evelyn tried and failed to get in a word while the verbal rampage continued.

"The last thing I need is a fucking queue of mad idiots outside my office, claiming they know something about this crash when they clearly haven't a clue. These idiots are just out to make a name for themselves. I warned you before and I stand by that warning. If I find out this Collins character is your patsy, I will destroy what is left of your miserable fucking career, do I make myself clear?" And with that, the caller slammed the phone down.

Evelyn replaced the phone on the receiver. If someone was rattled then Mark's report must have touched a nerve. She sat back, smirked to herself, and looked on while the report spread across the world.

43

London.2618.

Sayssac stood alone in the control room, the huge screens in front of him filled, time and again with the headline M6 Crash Report – Suspected Link to Paris Crash Being Investigated; the story was spreading – and spreading fast.

"I know what you're going to say," Kallyuke said as he swept into the control room with Helen and Steve closely behind.

Sayssac turned around. "And what is that?"

"We must get to him and try to manipulate him to our way of thinking, but, you must also know he is very close to the truth, dangerously close. The last thing I need is this Collins character running riot on the internet causing us even more issues. Kallyuke tightly clenched his fist.

Steve was slightly hungover and worse for wear. He read the headlines in detail. Helen did the same. They knew that Mark Collins was capable of blowing their cover as much as anyone else. Sayssac gestured for everyone to take a seat and join him around the large table.

"Someone had a drink last night then," Helen looked at Steve.

"It's not what you think, the whisky they use here is, shall we say, a bit basic," Steve tried to defend himself. "Besides, Richard, an old friend, dropped by for a drink. I've hardly seen him in nearly six hundred years you know, and as you can imagine, we had a lot of catching up to do." Steve momentarily closed his eyes.

"Really, well you do surprise me," Helen said sarcastically.

Steve steadied himself and walked toward the table, he reached down to scratch the palm of his hand; he was still in some discomfort after having the CCS device forcibly installed into his hand.

"I'm aware of the fact we should try and get to him, but this is the perfect diversion for the next stage of our plan," Sayssac said quietly to the three of them. "In my opinion, we shouldn't be hasty in trying to make contact. Whilst all of this is going on, and the incidents are buried in an avalanche of spurious headlines, we can make our next move completely under the radar."

"Possibly, but you realise this man is capable of putting something out there that could lead anyone right to our operations, whether inadvertently or not," Kallyuke said and bit his upper lip.

"I think that is a risk worth taking," Sayssac replied.

"Risks have to be carefully calculated," Kallyuke rebutted, glaring at Sayssac.

"Hang on, you think you can manipulate this man into your way of thinking?" Steve slowly shook his head. "How exactly?"

"Everyone has their price," Sayssac tapped his index finger against the palm of his other hand.

"You think that we can simply reach out to this guy, throw him some sort of a bung, and then he'll come join our merry team? Bit of a risk isn't it? I mean, you go on about blowing our cover, this smacks of doing exactly that," Steve said and threw his hands in the air.

"Bung?" Kallyuke enquired.

"Bung. Bribe. Money." You know, a brown envelope full of beer tokens." Steve rolled his eyes back and shook his head.

"We wouldn't need to use such a crude mechanism to achieve our goal," Kallyuke said.

"So what mechanism are you going to use? Luncheon vouchers?" Steve sarcastically quipped.

"You're being hysterical. You seem to forget that you are part of our collective, you are here because you believe, not because of money."

"I'm here because I'm part of this right from the beginning. This guy is a journalist, and as far as I'm aware, journalists have to be squeaky clean now. There are guidelines, ethics, all of these will fly in the face of the mechanism you will use to try and corrupt this man," Steve argued.

Sayssac stepped in. "No one used the word corrupt. We prefer to suggest that he will see the light and can be persuaded to follow our version of events."

"See the light? This could backfire – spectacularly," Steve said.

"Sometimes the risks are worth taking," Kallyuke replied.

"Even if those risks jeopardise our cover?" Steve asked.

"There are always ways to reinvent our cover," Kallyuke said.

The screens on the walls flickered off and then back on again; Kallyuke glanced at Steve, but he was oblivious to any connection with what had just happened.

"So, if this is the case, what is our next move?" Steve asked.

Sayssac coolly announced that Armstrong had tripped himself up.

"Armstrong is becoming paranoid, even slightly careless. His offices are guarded twenty-four hours a day and he's sleeping in the quarters reserved for staff. He rarely strays beyond the front door, which means that certain patterns are beginning to emerge, patterns which were not immediately recognisable. But these patterns are now clues pointing to Armstrong's whereabouts."

"How do you know this?" Steve looked at Sayssac.

"We have our sources. There is a huge social calendar that revolves around the City of London, a diary full of meetings. There are various official dinner engagements and other social events that are rigorously documented in the media. Those who attend these events are talked about as much as those who don't," Sayssac replied.

"What is your point, and how does this help us track him down?" Kallyuke asked.

"My point is that we've managed to intercept the lists of attendees to these events over the past few months, and there has a been one company conspicuously absent from them. This company has been almost synonymous with these events in recent months. As a result, I did some digging," Sayssac said.

"Well go on, we're all waiting." Kallyuke folded his arms.

"Armstrong has managed to maintain a public profile in very private places, therefore avoiding any unwanted attention or arousing suspicions concerning his real motive to penetrate the inner sanctum of London's financial services sector. He's won favour with key influencers and movers from the world of politics, finance, and industry, so much so, that he was on the list of attendees to be present at the next Bilderberg meeting." Sayssac smirked.

"How do you know this?" Steve asked again.

"As I said, we have our sources," Sayssac smirked.

"Evidently so." Steve raised his eyebrows.

Helen sat quietly and absorbed every word that Sayssac spoke.

"But by dropping off the social scene so dramatically, he has inadvertently alerted the suspicions of people we had monitoring their front companies. Any one of these companies could have led us to our man. It was pure luck that one of the companies we were monitoring cross-referenced to one company that had disappeared from public view," Sayssac said and looked across to Helen and nodded slightly.

"So, he used the front company to gain inside information? Is that what you're suggesting?" Steve asked.

"Precisely. Being part of the inner circle, he would be privy to reports and sensitive information before anyone else, which would allow him to plan their next move."

"And you're sure this is his current location?" Kallyuke asked as he pointed to the map of London now displayed on one of the screens.

"We've been working relentlessly on this in the background and we've had the location monitored for a while now. We are convinced we are closing in on the target, and now, our intelligence confirms it," Sayssac said with confidence.

"What do you suggest is our next move?" Helen asked.

"We have to get to him and fast. This may be our only opportunity to capture him and unravel their operations."

"And what about the risks? How do we cover this one up? People like him don't simply disappear, especially if you say he's moving in very powerful circles," Steve rubbed the palm of his hand again, this time a burning sensation took hold.

"We have our methods, as you well know," Kallyuke said with a grin.

"I'm not sure this guy is going to simply throw his hands in the air and surrender when we come storming through that front door," Steve rebutted and threw his hands in the air.

"Maybe so, but you simply don't know how he will react. There are different methods for different scenarios. We need to be fluid in our approach," Kallyuke spoke softly.

"And you think now is the right time to execute this?" Steve asked.

"There is now a greater urgency to stop Armstrong, priorities, and risks are a moving target, and if Sayssac is correct, and he is in hiding, then we can extract him with the minimum of fuss."

"Extract? An interesting choice of words," Steve said.

"Don't play with words. This could be a massively important breakthrough," Kallyuke said and turned to Sayssac. "And you are sure he will still be at this location?"

"He's not moved out of the place for weeks now. He has security guards permanently stationed around the premises, suggesting he's been spooked by something."

"It doesn't make sense. Why go to all that effort to create a back story, construct this elaborate network of contacts, and then go into hiding?" Steve asked.

"Perhaps he thought people were onto him?" Helen said. "Maybe he wanted to kill off any potential heat he thought he was attracting."

"That doesn't fit. I mean, who could be onto him and for what?" Steve asked. "There was one thing you mentioned earlier, Bilderberg, are you sure of this?" Steve looked at Sayssac.

"Yes, we are. We know his line of business, and we know that some of the most powerful people in business are present at this conference. There's no media coverage permitted, so it is the perfect place to do business."

"I see where you're going with this, and I think you could be onto something," Helen agreed.

"Agreed. I can see why Bilderberg is perfect," Steve said, nodding in approval.

"It is unless you've managed to piss off another attendee," Helen said.

"That could be a possibility. Don't forget, there have been many high-profile extractions, including the one in China, which resulted in the loss of an entire village. Maybe one of Armstrong's companies unintentionally crossed swords with the wrong people – people who could be attending Bilderberg," Kallyuke suggested.

"But all of this is largely coincidental. If this man is still at that location we can strike a major blow to their operations, and hopefully halt their progress," Sayssac said and thumped the desk.

"So, what's the plan?" Steve naively asked.

"I can see no other way, you and Helen will need to bring him back; preferably alive," Kallyuke insisted.

"And what if we can't bring him back alive?" Helen asked.

"Then you know the alternatives," Sayssac said.

" We're running out of time. Real time. If we don't act now, well, who knows what our future will be," Kallyuke said.

"Unfortunately, Kallyuke is right," Sayssac spoke softly. "Such has been the impact of Armstrong's operations, that we must act now before something major transpires."

"I'm not a killer," Steve said.

"Silverton will be there and briefed beforehand. He will have the authority to act accordingly."

"Oh, of course, Silverton. I should have guessed his name would surface before long." Steve rolled his eyes.

"He's our insurance policy, in case things don't go to plan," Sayssac confirmed.

"Well just remember what happened to that so-called insurance policy in Paris and where it landed us, or should I say where it landed me," Steve replied.

"This is the opportunity we have been waiting for, we cannot delay any further, we have to grasp it with both hands, while we still can," Kallyuke reiterated with a clenched fist.

"And what about the aftermath?" Helen asked.

"Silverton will attend to any loose ends. He has the contacts, and the expertise to deal with the fallout," Sayssac said.

" Let's hope your confidence in him isn't misplaced," Steve retorted.

All of this was beginning to sit uneasily with Steve. He didn't share the mindset of the others and was still wondering why Kallyuke was so adamant that the so-called rogue scientists couldn't just leave the planet of their own accord. However, Steve kept his thoughts to himself. He was also unsure about Helen, and about whether his new implant was tracking his every move or thought; he didn't know who he could trust.

"Then we are all agreed, the plan is set, time to get busy," Kallyuke said and loudly clapped his hands.

"I have the location coordinates and timings set, we should adjourn to the shuttle," Sayssac said.

"We don't have any say in this?" Steve asked as they stood up.

"What's there to say? The plan has been agreed upon. This appears to be our most sensible course of action, and possibly our only option," Kallyuke replied, obviously trying to quell lingering doubts.

"I have a shuttle on standby, waiting for us," Sayssac said.

"You really don't hang about do you?" Steve said.

"Ironically, we don't have time to hang about. Sometimes decisions have to be made and action immediately taken," Kallyuke replied.

They adjourned to the awaiting shuttle on the launch pad. The four of them sat in silence while the shuttle quietly cruised to the drop off location

Helen busied herself reading some notes while Steve looked out of the window at the barren landscape they were heading toward. It wasn't long before the shuttle landed and the doors opened to reveal a part of London that was both deserted and untouched.

"This place hasn't changed much has it?" Steve said stepping out into the daylight, "I mean, why couldn't they allow us to travel from a more central location? Why here?"

"Audit trail? Remember?" Helen said following Steve out into the board daylight.

"Okay, no need to rub it in!" Steve laughed.

Kallyuke stood with them for a moment. "I cannot emphasise how important this could be to all of our futures. I know you may not agree with our methods, but in time, I'm sure that even if you can't agree, you might at least come to understand them."

Steve looked at Kallyuke and slowly nodded, acknowledging Kallyuke's words.

Helen stood close to Steve, "Time to go."

She pushed the button on the phasing unit in her hand, almost immediately they were both enveloped in bright light and disappeared into nothingness. Steve felt alone again, surrounded by the infinite cold inky blackness of the journey.

44

Somewhere in the late
26th Century.

Steve sat like a child, cross-legged and nervous. He was warm, which was counterintuitive to how he had felt just moments ago.

He looked around to get his bearings. In front of him were buildings, all of which were on fire and ravaged by flames that were tearing through the small town; it was surreal, like some kind of trick his mind was playing on him. Then he remembered this was his mind. But was this a trick?

Steve instinctively wanted to get up and run toward the fire. He wanted to try and help the people running through the streets, screaming, as they scrambled to avoid the collapsing buildings; but he couldn't. Instincts told him that he wasn't really there, that this was just a window into another world...but whose world? The feelings of helplessness flood into his mind as he watched people fall and burn to death right in front of him.

The chilling sound of flames licking the wood, the crackle of wooden structures falling to the ground, accompanied by the glowing embers that rose into the night sky, made Steve shudder with fear. He felt connected to what he was seeing, but he couldn't figure out why that would be the case.

Though he tried, he couldn't turn away. He was captivated by the bombardment of images and continued to look on in horror.

Amongst the panic, he noticed a couple sitting calmly on their porch, looking outward, into nowhere in particular, while the raging fire engulfed their house. The juxtaposition of this image, compared to terrifying panic elsewhere, had a calming effect on Steve. It felt like the answer to a question he had never thought to ask was now being offered to him.

The woman then turned to look directly into Steve's eyes and he was filled with dread; there was something horribly wrong with the image. He cried out in anguish and tried to stand up and run toward the couple, but he couldn't move. He watched helplessly as flames engulfed them. They made no effort to escape.

Glowing embers swirled into the air, dancing into the sky as the house collapsed into a pile of burning wood and rubble. The fragile frame of the porch was the only thing left standing.

Steve sat, completely transfixed, feeling like he had seen a ghost from the past.

45

London.Present-Day.

A tornado of bright light swirled on the deserted, barren landscape. Dust flew into the air as Steve and Helen arrived.

Steve blinked and was momentarily transported back to the fire. He blinked again, shaking his head and waving his hands to try and rid his mind of what he saw.

"What did you just see?" Helen asked.

"I'm not sure, but can we please get out of this place? I don't have a good feeling about it," Steve gathered himself and looked around. "Did we travel anywhere because this place looks the same?"

"Of course, we have," Helen replied.

"So much for progress…." Steve followed Helen as they walked past discarded shopping trolleys, large black rubbish bags that spewed their contents onto the ground, and large, empty food containers.

This wasn't the London of hope, of the brave new society, this was reality, the real London, where much of it was left behind to fend for itself.

Helen marched toward a taxi that was conveniently parked on one of the few roads in the area; the engine was running. Steve had a sense of Deja vu as they approached the vehicle. Helen opened the door and they jumped in the back of the taxi. A familiar face greeted them.

"I bet you thought you'd seen the last of me, hadn't you?" Roy looked back over his shoulder at Steve.

"I never doubted that you would surface again, after all, reliable taxi drivers are so hard to find these days," Steve said with a smile.

"Well, good news for you guys, you can relax now. Just sit back, enjoy the scenery, such as it is, and we'll be at our destination in no time. Oh, and feel free to read this dossier." Roy tossed over a large A4 envelope of documents to Helen.

Helen opened the envelope and pulled out the contents. It was an A4 folder packed with details about their target, Terence Armstrong. She became engrossed, blanking out everything else while she delved into the pages. Steve sat and stared into nothingness. He momentarily glanced down at the papers, wondering what could be so interesting, and noticed the FCA stamp on each of the pages.

"FCA?" Steve asked.

"Yes, why do you ask?" Helen looked up for a moment as she shuffled through the dossier.

"Well, unless I'm much mistaken those are official reports from the FCA, is that correct?" Steve asked.

Roy progressed slowly through the traffic; London was packed full of buses, trucks, and cars, all fighting for supremacy on the roads.

"My contacts stretch deep into the Financial Conduct Authority, they provide us with hugely important intelligence. They were key to us uncovering the location of Terence Armstrong," Helen said without looking up.

"So that meeting back then, I mean, you know what I mean. The meeting we just had, Sayssac…" Steve stumbled through his words.

"Yes, I knew exactly what he was talking about, these are just the detailed notes."

"Looks like you have got it all worked out," Steve said, continuing to look out the window.

They crossed over Tower Bridge. Steve thought back to a meeting he had with Kallyuke and the hologram of Tower Bridge that existed in the future.

"Anyway, this is important," Helen butted in, disturbing Steve from his thoughts. "According to this, Armstrong was born in Switzerland to an English father and a Swiss mother. His father, Thomas Armstrong, was part of a small but not insignificant banking family, with interests spread across the major financial centres of the world; hedge funds were their specialty. Terence was educated in South Africa and New York City, later graduating from Harvard with distinction. His parents were killed in a car crash soon after while holidaying on the French Riviera at their beach house near Beaulieu Sur Mer. Terence inherited the businesses but he was ill-prepared for it and cracks appeared in the otherwise slick operations of the family business."

"That would mean that Terence Armstrong isn't from the future – you know, one of us," Steve concluded.

"Perhaps, but this is only what we know. There could be many secrets lurking beneath the surface."

"You think he could be like us?" Steve asked.

"It's a possibility," Helen said and continued to read from the file. "Armstrong descended into a downward spiral of drugs and depression. He struggled to reconcile leading the family business after the loss of his parents. Whilst they were never a close family, he was an only child, so had few people to turn to during the grieving process."

Helen took a breath and then continued, "Armstrong went to ground. He became reclusive and trusted no one apart from an inner circle of business contacts. It was during this time that he came into contact with some dubious people. They offered him business opportunities that brought him to the attention of the FCA. The FCA uncovered a maze of shell companies and trading names that were connected in some ways, but not in others. But at every turn Armstrong was clean. His name wasn't on the list of directors. However, his name was never far away from them, buried in offshore funds that had tenuous associations with these companies. Armstrong shook off his reclusive habits and started to be seen at all the major financial services dinner events and even courted limited publicity. He wanted to show the city he was a legitimate businessman by being seen in the company of other great businessmen from the worlds of finance and politics."

"Why the change? Do you think contact was initiated," Steve asked.

"We have no idea, but then things started to happen. First, we had the failed extraction in China, to name just one incident, then all of a sudden we began to see a pattern. Armstrong's shell companies must be hiding something, they are gaining him access to confidential information about case-sensitive operations before they go to the market," Helen said.

"You mean mining companies?" Steve caught on quickly.

"Yes."

"Clever, the perfect cover then?" Steve said.

"He's getting insider information before anyone else, yet this information is meant for investment purposes only, nothing else, but guess what? In some instances, not all I hasten to add, because he's far too clever to leave a trail, these so-called claims by the mining companies are found to be incorrect. Estimates of reserves are then found to be vastly overstated, in some cases, there's nothing there at all, it's all been extracted, and guess who are the only losers?" It was obvious that Helen knew her stuff.

"Armstrong's investors?" Steve suggested.

353

"Absolutely, but that's the risk you take he would say. And because there's no media coverage, which means avoiding any embarrassing headlines, no one is any the wiser. Anyway, who's going to be interested in an investment company making losses? It is part and parcel of the risk that goes with the territory. Armstrong simply walks away without anyone pointing the finger of suspicion at him."

"And the fallout continues behind closed doors."

"It does because there are always questions to answer. Sometimes the fraud team will get involved due to a shareholder complaint, but how can they prove anything? Armstrong uses several different companies to avoid arousing suspicions of foul play, making it almost impossible to mount a case. The complainants don't even know what to say, other than their investments have disappeared, but that alone is not enough to build a case. And in the midst of all of this chaos, Armstrong simply slips out of the back door with nothing to answer for. As far as he's concerned, you win some investments you lose some…"

"Meanwhile the resources are being sent forward in time."

"It's the perfect plan because it's virtually impossible to prove. Where do you start?" Helen posed.

"So, is this the real Terence Armstrong, or is this an imposter supplanted here?" Steve asked.

"We don't know and until we can obtain a DNA sample from him, we won't know for sure. All we know is that this man is central to the rogue scientist's operations. Stopping him would put a major dent in their plans," Helen replied.

Roy took an abrupt turn and entered an underground car park in the middle of a familiar street in the centre of London. The tires screeched to a halt and he parked in one of the many empty bays, "Okay, we're here."

"How did I guess," Steve said as he got out of the car to be greeted by Detective Roger Silverton.

"I trust your journey was a pleasant one?" Silverton held out his hand to welcome Helen and Steve.

"It was fine." Helen shook Silverton's hand.

They walked in silence, following Silverton into the lift and to his office. He pushed open the door, switched on the lights, and ushered everyone in; it was just as cold and unwelcoming as Steve had remembered.

One of the walls was now home to a corkboard covered in page after page of the reports by Mark Collins; the headlines M6 Crash Report - Paranormal Activity Cited as Possible Cause and M6 Crash Report – Suspected Link to Paris Crash Being Investigated adorned the reports.

"He's done it again," Silverton said. "Clever man, isn't he?"

Steve took a closer look at the reports. "Where's he getting all his facts from?"

"Some are clearly from here." Silverton pointed to his head. "But he seems to have the ability to sex up his reports with just enough pizzaz to demand people's attention."

Steve turned to look at the table.

Helen took another large document from the envelope Roy had given her earlier, unfolded it, and placed it on the table. Silverton shuffled off and turned on the new coffee percolator. "I got tired of crap coffee, and we had some spare budget to play with. Anyone want some?"

A universal yes was the reply.

"This is the network, the nerve centre of this company." Helen gestured to the company in the middle of the page. It was surrounded by a series of arrows that pointed to boxes with various company names in them. An image of Armstrong was in one box in the middle of the page and all roads led to him.

Silverton shuffled over with two coffees, handing them to Helen and Steve, he paused to look at the page then returned to grab the other two coffees, handing one to Roy.

"What do you think?" Silverton took a large gulp of his drink. "It's good, though it should be, it's Indonesian Kopi Luwak coffee, the finest coffee you can buy," Silverton said.

Roy pulled his face. "I've heard about this, but isn't it…? I heard that it is…"

Helen looked at the contents of her mug.

"You heard correctly," Silverton said, "The drinks budget for the year has been well spent."

"Excuse me but what exactly is this coffee because I'm almost too scared to ask judging by Roy's expression," Steve looked nervously at his mug.

"Kopi Luwak coffee beans are partially fermented in the digestive system of the Sumatran Civet Cat, apparently it gives them a unique chocolatey hazelnut flavour; at least that's what I'm told. This is the first time I've tried it. What do you think?" Silverton smiled at them all.

Steve shuddered, he took a sip from his mug, "Let's just say it's a taste I'll try to acquire."

"Basically, you're all drinking cat shit," Roy placed his mug back near the percolator. "I'll stick to the instant stuff I think."

Helen continued to drink without hesitation.

"There's simply no educating some people." Silverton looked at Roy who was now waiting for the kettle to boil.

"So, this is the nest, is it?" Steve pointed to the layout of Armstrong's network of companies.

"You could say that, although this is more like a series of tentacles spreading out with each one having its own ecosystem that makes each part self-reliant in case any other part of the network is closed down," Helen said while looking at the map.

"And our man is right here," Silverton said pointing to the location on an old map on the wall.

"He's very clever. I mean the FCA tends to close down first and ask questions later in light of what has happened over the past few years," Steve said. "Though I've had limited dealings with them."

"But you need a solid case to back that up, which is what they've lacked at every turn." Helen tapped the box containing Armstrong's image.

"We need to move as we have a limited window of time. I've spent weeks observing his movements and whilst he's clever, he's a creature of habit and that habit includes spending time at his favoured Park Lane offices, right here on Mount Street. He'll move there from his current hideout south of the river," Silverton said as he pointed to the map on the wall again.

"Just how many offices does he have?" Roy asked.

"A few. He'll rotate them to avoid detection, but this one in Park Lane is the main front office. It's a swanky address so impresses the clients," Silverton continued. "Helen will assume the role of an FCA officer carrying out a routine, but unannounced audit; a perfectly normal function of the FCA and something he will no doubt be aware can happen at any time…"

"Which of course he cannot object to otherwise he risks losing the business. This will allow me to gain access to the premises without arousing suspicion and I can trigger the phasing unit and take him forward in time for a meeting with Kallyuke," Helen said.

"You think it's going to be that easy? Don't you think this plan is a bit simple?" Steve asked.

"The simpler the plan, the less chance there is for anything to go wrong," Helen replied.

"We can assume that, but what if things go wrong?" Steve pushed them on this point.

"What can go wrong?" Silverton asked Steve.

"Well, for a start, what if he recognises Helen? And isn't it a bit obvious that on the exact day he happens to be in that particular office we show up for an unannounced audit of the accounts?" Steve raised his eyebrows.

"It happens all the time, the FCA's main protocols will be followed. How do you think they stop people from breaking FCA regulations in the first place? If they gave notice of an impending audit any evidence could be buried. Besides, that is not our main aim, we are simply there to capture Armstrong," Helen said and glanced down at the image of Armstrong at the centre of the document.

"It is not possible for anyone to recognise Helen. Like all of you, your activation process and deep cover program mean he will have no idea about her true identity; nor yours, of course," Silverton said and gestured toward Steve.

"What about the break-out in Paris? Don't you think Interpol will be on the lookout for us? We're the main suspects in an escape that took place right under the French police's noses. That means there's a risk, albeit a small one, that there could be images from the CCTV cameras in that interview room of me and Helen in circulation on some database somewhere," Steve said.

"He's got a point you know," Roy said and nodded in acknowledgment.

"That's impossible…" Silverton replied.

"How can you be so sure?" Steve snapped back. "And what if Armstrong can access data in the same way that Kallyuke has indicated we can? I mean, and I say this in his words, the security systems protecting our online data are no match for the kind of tech that they have available. What if they have the same kind of tech at their disposal?" Steve asked.

"It's impossible because there are no records of either of you on Interpol's site, whether that be the public-facing site or the restricted site that is for official access only," Silverton said firmly.

"How do you know?" Steve asked.

"How do you think I know? I checked. Don't forget, being a Government agent gives me certain privileges and also access to certain databases, so you're perfectly safe and still very much under the radar. Why do you think Kallyuke trusts me to deal with these things?" Silverton walked over to the table to join the others.

"And you're forgetting one other final point," Helen butted in.

"What's that?" Steve asked.

"I covered the CCTV cameras with tape. There's no chance of either of our faces being caught on camera," Helen said.

"There's no way the French police will go public about what happened. They don't have any evidence to support what they even dare to think may have happened. If they went to Interpol, they would be laughed out of the building," Silverton said.

"Interestingly enough, someone else said something very similar, you're either well-rehearsed or truly believe what you're suggesting. Either way, I guess we have no choice and have to push forward with the plan," Steve said, backing down.

"Just do your job and let me do mine. It's the only way to stop these bastards in their tracks before it really is too late," Silverton said.

"So, are we ready now?" Roy asked impatiently.

"If we're all in agreement, I suggest that Helen travels with me in the lead car. I'm on official Government license plates so that will ensure we don't get stopped for any reason. Helen will set up the target and complete the extraction. You and Roy stay close as a back-up in case anything goes wrong."

"According to you, nothing can go wrong, so why the change of heart?" Steve smirked.

Silverton shot Steve an annoyed glance but didn't respond.

"And what's with the use of the word extraction all of a sudden?" Steve asked.

"I guess I must be thinking in their terms," Silverton said with a wry smile.

Silverton switched out the light, they left the offices and made their way to the underground car park.

***

The offices of Paris Central TV were unusually quiet. Journalists were scattered far and wide across the city covering various stories that seemed to be erupting in the aftermath of the riots outside Paris Oil's headquarters a few days earlier.

Evelyn sat at her desk, sipping coffee and looking at the unfolding coverage of Mark Collins ' reports. Stefan walked in and sauntered off to one of the editing suites. Bruno Durand, the station editor and the man where the buck stopped, walked in a few minutes later; Evelyn had not looked up at all, she was transfixed by the screen in front of her.

Bruno quietly approached her desk, "It's rare to see my number one journalist so quiet." He sat on the end of her desk. "Something tells me that there is something wrong…"

Bruno Durand had been the station editor for many years. He was a veteran of the Parisian news scene for thirty years. He belied his advancing age with dashing good looks and a quick wit that caused him as many problems as it solved. He was a family man, someone who tried hard to avoid taking his work home,

but he was mindful that these were hard times for
journalists in the city.

Evelyn sat, impassive and staring at the screen.
"Let me ask you this, and we've worked together for
years now so I think I can trust your judgment…"

"I'm glad to hear it," Bruno chuckled.

Evelyn slowly turned to look at Bruno, he
suddenly realised this was serious. "Is it right to coerce
or encourage, or at least not stop another journalist from
writing an article that you know could get them killed?"
Her tone was deadly serious.

Bruno blinked slowly, drew breath, and replied,
"I always say that we should live by two rules: speak the
truth and don't feel guilt. We're journalists, and
sometimes the ripple effects of our work spread beyond
our control, and sometimes the consequences of that
work can, at least in the heat of the moment, appear to
inflict pain or embarrassment. But irrespective of the
costs, if the facts are true and the story is in the public's
interest then it should be told. Above all else, the
integrity of journalism must be maintained, otherwise,
we will lose the trust of the people and that is not a place
I want to go any time soon."

Bruno paused and looked at Evelyn's screen.

"Yes, that is the story to which I'm referring."
Evelyn observed Bruno's glaring eyes almost pierce the
screen.

"Ah the crash, the one next to the Eiffel Tower,
so tell me, why didn't you run that story?" Bruno
wanted to know more.

"Francois Blanc," Evelyn replied in monotone.

"I see. And by that you mean he was giving you
heat about running this story?"

"The usual threats. You know what he's like."

"I do. I also know that his bark is almost
certainly worse than his bite. He has to play by the rules,
but he cannot threaten journalists and get away with it.

This is a free country and he, more than anyone, knows how the law works. Who is Collins?"

Evelyn turned to look at the screen, "He's a journalist in Manchester, England. He's been covering a crash on one of their motorways that was very similar to the one near the Eiffel Tower so I—"

"Let me guess, you got him to write up this story using some of the evidence you acquired at the crash scene?"

"Yes." Evelyn, in a funny way, almost felt ashamed that she'd betrayed her journalistic instincts to publish the story.

"Look, I'm your boss, but I'm also your friend, and you know how we operate here. I don't encourage this kind of behaviour, but when I look at this report, I ask myself; would I want this on our channel at such an early stage? I mean…paranormal is a polarising word to use in a report of this type, especially without solid evidence. Using that word can either make or break a story of this kind, rapidly."

"So, you're not annoyed with me?" Evelyn asked.

"It's difficult to be annoyed because I'm not sure that we could run the story given the amount of speculation in that report. We need hard facts to support our reports, so when the likes of Blanc show up puffing on a cigarette and angling for revenge we can pack them off with a coffee, a smile and a fuck you very much, now get out of my office."

Evelyn smiled for the first time in what seemed like a while. "You don't think he'll go after Collins?"

"If I know Blanc as well as I do, he'll be pissed off and his packet of cigarettes may not last the morning, but he'll soon realise he may actually yield some results from that report being published."

"He rang when the story broke," Evelyn pointed at the ever-growing list of sites carrying Mark's report.

"Of course, he did. Much like anyone in his position, he wants to make you think he'll make good on the threats. But this is France, we have rules and we have rights, so there should be no doubt in your mind that he will have to adhere to them, especially as he's a cop as well. There are no special rules for the Gendarme Nationale; despite what they may think."

Bruno watched as Evelyn let out a long sigh. "I have to go to the editing suite," he said. "Stefan is working on a report. Let me know if you want to talk some more, but above all, don't worry." Bruno stood up and walked off toward the editing suite.

Evelyn sat back and rested her hands on her lap. She felt more at ease, but she was still cautious about what may happen in the coming weeks. The story was spreading fast and was out of her control. Both she and Mark had set the ball rolling, controlling the momentum was something neither of them had the power to do.

***

"You know the drill, let's keep it simple, get this job done and get the hell out before anyone knows what's going on," Silverton said to Helen.

The sky was grey and the clouds laden with rain. Helen looked over to the other side of the road and pointed to a particular street, "That's the one," she said not thinking that Silverton would know this.

Roy kept a reasonable distance behind Silverton to allay suspicion. The silence in their car was shattered by the shrill ring of a mobile phone. Steve scrambled to find it in his jacket and answered; the call was from Janine.

"Where are you and when do you plan to see your daughter again?" Janine shouted. Steve held the phone away from his ear.

"I can't talk right now, sorry," Steve whispered. "Give my love to Tanya and I will call you soon, I promise." He hung up on Janine and switched the phone off.

"You need to be careful with that thing, it will get you caught," Roy said nodding at the phone.

Steve ignored him and cast his mind back to simpler times when his life was about his family and providing a safe place for them to live; he still yearned for those days but knew they would never return.

"It's there," Helen said and pointed toward Mount Street.

"I know," Silverton replied.

Silverton turned the car onto Mount Street and looked around to see where he could park. Helen jumped out of the slowing car. The smartly dressed Armstrong was standing at the top of the steps to his plush offices, "He's there!" she shouted back into the car.

A black limo brushed past Helen and pulled up outside Armstrong's offices; a tall, lean bodyguard got out to open the door. Armstrong peered over his expensive sunglasses, surveying the area while he purposefully walked down the steps toward the limo. He was carrying a slim briefcase. Helen heard the screech of tires and stood flush to the wall, as Silverton's car barreled past her and headed for the limo.

Armstrong froze halfway down the steps, the bodyguard looked back to see where the commotion was coming from. He looked on as Silverton's car mounted the pavement and smashed straight into the bodyguard, tossing him into the air like a rag doll. The bodyguard slammed head-first onto the pavement and was killed instantly. The car slammed into the limo next, the force of the impact knocking it sideways; Silverton's car then veered toward some railings at the side of the street and crashed through them. The car stopped, balancing precariously over the stairwell access to a basement apartment, the rear wheels still turning as they hung in the air, smoke billowing from under the bonnet. The howl from the engine slowly died down and the wheels slowed.

Silverton scrambled across to the other side of the car and crawled out via the battered passenger door. He was covered in blood and glass and tumbled to the ground before getting to his feet.

The driver of the limo shook his head to regain his senses. Helen ran toward a transfixed Armstrong. The driver got out of the car and pulled a gun from his shoulder holster; Silverton, stumbling toward the driver, saw this and drew his gun, shooting the driver dead before he could make his move. Armstrong panicked, he tried to get back into his offices but couldn't evade the attentions of Helen. She grabbed him by the shoulders. His briefcase went flying, smashing open on the pavement. Papers flew out into the breezy London streets.

Roy and Steve turned onto Mount Street. "What the fuck?" Steve looked on at the unfolding mess.

" Don't move or my friend will shoot." Helen signaled to Silverton who was now slumped on the bonnet of the smashed-up limo, limply pointing his gun toward Armstrong. "Get on your knees and slowly place your hands behind your head!" she ordered.

Roy and Steve jumped out of their car, partially blocking the road. "What the fuck went wrong? Simple plan you said!" Steve yelled at Silverton who was visibly in pain and breathing heavily.

Steve strode purposely toward Armstrong; Roy was in close attendance. Helen approached Silverton to check if he was alright. Silverton waved her away with his gun, he didn't want Armstrong thinking he could try and escape.

"I'm okay, I'm okay!" Silverton shouted at Helen.

Armstrong regained his composure, and as instructed, he slowly descended to his knees. He was still facing the bright red doors of his offices. He inched one of his hands toward his inside jacket pocket and slowly pulled a small gun from inside it without anyone noticing. He subtly pointed the gun away from his body and pulled the trigger; a tiny round discharged silently from the short barrel.

Without warning, or making a sound, Roy fell to the ground.

Silverton shot at Armstrong but his arm shook at the crucial moment and the bullet just grazed one of Armstrong's thighs; Armstrong didn't react in any way to the wound.

"Next shot! I'm warning you!" Silverton continued to breathe heavily.

Helen walked over to Armstrong, dragged him down the stairs, and pushed him face down, into the pavement, "What have you done you son of a bitch!" she shouted.

Armstrong silently stared back at Helen.

Steve turned around and rushed over to see what was wrong with Roy and crouched down to check his pulse; he was still breathing.

Armstrong tried to crawl along the pavement, leaving a trail of blood from the wound in his thigh, but Helen kicked him in the back. "You're going nowhere," she spat.

"You think I care?" Armstrong turned and defiantly looked up at her.

Steve now stood over Armstrong and watched as Helen crouched down and reached inside Armstrong's jacket, "Don't be foolish," Steve warned.

"Or what?" Armstrong spat back at Steve.

"Next shot," Silverton shouted.

Helen pulled out the small gun and held it in the palm of her hand, "What the fuck is this?!"

Armstrong smiled sarcastically, "You really are behind the times aren't you? And in so many ways as well... who'd have thought it?" He laughed while he lay on the ground.

"Get on your knees, and this time, no more tricks," Steve grabbed Armstrong by the arm and pushed him to his knees.

"What happened to Roy?" Helen asked.

"Oh, don't worry about him, he'll be fine," Armstrong dismissed her concerns. "He's been stunned with a new toy we've been working on. Clever little device. The round tracks the victim via their DNA. It just happened to have that man's DNA on file for some reason. I guess you could say it was pure luck." Armstrong chuckled to himself.

"You expect us to believe that?" Steve asked.

"I don't really give a fuck what you believe, the fact is, your man over there is taking a well-earned rest thanks to that weapon." Armstrong smirked defiantly and spat on the floor.

Silverton clambered over to join the rest of them, his head was bleeding badly. "I need to get this place cordoned off," he said, staggering to the boot of his vehicle, and pulling out police cordon tape and a portable flashing light. He then staggered over to Roy's car at the entrance of Mount Street and used it as the marker to seal off the street. He unraveled the cordon tape in front of the car, secured it on a lamp post on one side, and wrapped it around the railings on the other side of the street to form a basic cordon.

"I think I'm bleeding," Silverton said, pausing for a moment and touching the wound on his head. He returned to his car and grabbed the first aid kit from the boot to patch up his wound.

"Join us, Steve," Armstrong said.

"What?" Steve shook his head.

"You heard me – join us. We need people like you, thinkers, people who will help our cause and protect our way of life."

Steve paused. "You must be confusing me with someone else."

Armstrong opened the palm of his hand for Steve to see. "No, I'm not." He smiled. "Sometimes using only your eyes to see can be a mistake."

Steve recoiled. "How the fuck did you know my name?"

"We know everything, Steve. It's time to embrace what you have and join us. Don't be naive for the rest of your life," Armstrong spoke slowly with an almost hypnotic quality.

"How fucking dare you? I'm not naïve."

"You need to remember your past," Armstrong said.

"What are you talking about? I do remember my past," Steve retorted.

"I mean your real past, not this past. Think Steve. Think. Find the real you." Armstrong used his free hand to tap his temple.

"What's going on?" Helen asked. She looked over her shoulder to see that Roy was now slowly getting to his feet.

"I'm simply trying to show your friend here that maybe we aren't so different," Armstrong said.

Steve shook his head. "Your actions are destroying our world. I don't want you to ever think I would be a part of this, or that we are in some way connected."

"Do you even know what you're saying?" Armstrong was persistent given his parlous situation.

"This whole thing was about saving lives, controlling a deadly virus, not stealing, or as you would call it extracting. That was never on the agenda," Steve replied.

Armstrong shook his head. "Have you heard yourself? Are you really that stupid? Do you think the people of this time have any use for what we're taking?

In thirty years, the only thing they will be concerned with is survival. They will have no use for what we want. That is why we are taking it and taking it very carefully."

"China?" Steve had to ask.

"I cannot defend what happened there," Armstrong admitted.

"What about the virus?" Steve was determined to find out more.

"Can't you see that it's being used to control you? And you're all falling for it!" Armstrong continued, "The virus was under control years ago. The plans to destroy it are at an advanced stage. The serum has been developed and tested positive, but they're using it to suppress you…holding you back in the grip of fear for something that doesn't…"

"Oh, fuck off! I don't have time for this bullshit! Can we get the hell out of here and get this fucking coward back to where he belongs?" Helen shouted.

"Strong words…" Armstrong muttered.

"Wait! I want to hear what he has to say, so continue, while you still have this opportunity."

Armstrong was bleeding heavily from his leg but spoke in a relaxed and controlled manner, "Let me tell you what you probably don't know. When we first worked on creating the timeline, together I hasten to add, the only thing we wanted in exchange for our cooperation was access to the NASA archives; archives that would have been used to help us regain important scientific knowledge that was lost during those dark years. Archives that could have helped us all secure a future on a new planet, but that wasn't in Kallyuke's plans. The fact that First Contact was covered up in 2009 and that NASA chose to launch a series of false flag diversions to ensure that the story remained buried meant we could obtain the source code to reboot the International Space Station in our time knowing that most of the technological information we needed was already in situ."

"Are you telling me that you intended to hack into NASA's mainframe and that was your sole reason for helping create the timeline?" Steve circled Armstrong.

"We had a more sophisticated route in, hacking was not our preferred method, that was too messy and risked leaving evidence of our presence, which was something we wanted to avoid. No, we had an inside source, a corruptible individual that we had been working on for a while, someone who could have helped us with our mission. You have to understand that NASA buried the data files on the station for a reason. They didn't want to risk a leak of any level from a ground-based intel source, so the files remained up there under maximum security with limited access; save for the odd president and of course, highly connected members of the business community who sought to exploit the technology. We saw those files as an opportunity to learn, explore, and engage, but Kallyuke was against all of this. He saw it as a threat, something that could endanger his plans," Armstrong grimaced through the pain but didn't want to stop talking.

Silverton was in the background making phone calls, occasionally glancing over at Helen, Armstrong, and Steve.

"It doesn't add up," Steve declared.

"What do you mean it doesn't add up?" Armstrong asked.

"What I say, it just doesn't add up. If what you say is true, I can think of no logical reason why anyone would deny the scientists access to those NASA archives to help forward your plan," Steve said, now feeling unsure.

"The Brave New Society, remember it?" Armstrong replied through gritted teeth.

"What about it?" Helen asked as she found herself being slowly sucked into the conversation.

Roy was still groggy, but he managed to walk over and stand next to Silverton who was busily making calls to arrange for the location to be cleansed.

"This was meant to be the perfect world, created for perfect people. A place for people who posed no risk of contaminating others with the virus. A place where the chosen few could cultivate a brave new society that could finally live at peace with each other, or at least, that was the pitch, so I'm led to believe."

"Again, what about it? I don't get your point," Helen asked.

"It's hardly perfect, is it? The truth is, you use holograms to portray an image of perfection and yet underneath the surface lies an entirely different world, one that your leaders are very keen doesn't see the light of day," Armstrong saw how Helen and Steve were being drawn into the conversation; they were both guardedly curious.

"But what you seem to be forgetting in all of this is that these aren't the people sucking the life out of our futures," Steve said.

"Maybe not," Armstrong replied, "but we are facing up to the facts."

"And those are?" Steve finally stopped circling to look directly at Armstrong.

"This planet is dying; life will soon be unsustainable, and to preserve the human race we must look to other worlds, or face extinction," Armstrong said.

"Just for a moment, let's pretend that I believe all of this, then what?" Steve remarked.

"Are you kidding me?" Helen looked across to Steve.

"If we act now, we can save the future of the human race," Armstrong replied.

"And if we don't?" Steve regretted asking the question as soon as he opened his mouth.

"We are finished. Earth will not sustain life for much longer. We need to act while we still can," Armstrong replied.

"Look at him! He's playing you for a fool! Don't be taken in by any of this!" Helen yelled at Steve.

And with that Armstrong calmly looked to the ground, with his hands still behind his back, and took a deep breath. He became enveloped in a bright white light. Helen shouted at him. Silverton turned to see what was causing all the commotion. Armstrong faded from sight and into a vacuum of nothingness. Steve stood there, still captivated by what Armstrong had said.

"Shit! Shit! Shit!" Helen ranted as she stamped on the ground, "We had him right there!" She pointed to the palm of her hand.

Silverton now stood shoulder to shoulder with Steve. "We've fucking lost him…" he pointed to the markings on the ground.

"How did he do it?" Helen looked at the ground.

"How the fuck should I know? You were the ones supposed to be guarding him!" Silverton wiped his head wound with the sleeve of his jacket.

Steve felt duped by Armstrong. "That's why he kept us talking, he was planning his escape. He's too clever, he won't go forward too far, he knows that if he arrives in Park Lane in 2618 he'll get arrested. I bet he changes location using that thing in his fucking hand and that is why he kept talking…"

"If you knew all this why the fuck didn't you do something?" Helen asked.

"Because I wanted to hear what he had to say, do you understand how important that information could be for us?" Steve bit back.

"And you want to believe it? He was buying time to escape. Can't you see that?" Helen threw her arms in the air and looked to the sky.

"We need to win the war of words, Sayssac is right…" Steve muttered as he crouched down to examine the spot where Armstrong had been kneeling moments earlier.

"Excuse me?" Helen said.

"Sayssac is right. We have to control the war of words. We can blow this operation wide open without firing another bullet. Oh, and while we're at it, what the hell is this gun he was talking about? The one that tracks its victims via their DNA?" Steve looked at Silverton and Roy. "Imagine what might happen if they obtain the DNA database?"

"Look, guys, I don't want to disturb whatever conversations you're having here but we've got quite a crowd building over there." Roy pointed to his car and the makeshift police cordon. "Can we tell them to fuck off, or something to that effect?"

Silverton shook his head and slowly closed his eyes. "Don't worry about them, this area will be cleansed in a matter of an hour, by which time they'll have nothing to gossip about."

"Where is Mark Collins based?" Steve turned to Silverton.

"He's been hard to track down, but I think his office is in Manchester," Silverton replied.

"Then we'll go there, and do what Sayssac suggested," Steve said.

"Am I missing something here?" Silverton frowned at Steve.

"Kallyuke and Sayssac discussed something during our last meeting, the idea of manipulating the media, controlling the journalists behind the headlines. Mark Collins is the man we need to get to achieve this." Steve looked around at the mess.

"I'm not sure this is a good idea, especially after what just happened here. Who knows how much more shit we can create," Helen said.

"Just a minute, you want to attempt this without authorisation?" Silverton asked.

"After this debacle, I think it's best if we work under our own initiative. After all, what can go wrong?" Steve sarcastically pointed to the wrecked limo and Silverton's car.

"And you think that by going on a lone wolf mission, which, if it goes wrong, could have serious implications, you can correct the mess we have here?" Helen threw her hands in the air.

"Collins 'reports could be a way to hit back at the Traders and upset their operations. I want to put that theory to the test. I think right now that is our best option," Steve said.

"And what about our cover?"

"If we can make this stick, and create enough shit for these people, that won't be a problem for us," Steve said and folded his arms.

"If you're going to take the heat for this, I'm not going to stand in your way," Helen said.

"We need a car," Silverton said to Steve.

"Are you fit to drive?" Steve asked.

Silverton touched the small, makeshift bandage on his head. "I'll live, and besides, you're not going anywhere without me by your side."

Silverton knew that as he got older the wounds would take longer to heal and that he would spend more time behind a desk rather than out in the field. But when the chance presented itself, he seldom backed down, and ensuring that Steve got to Manchester in one piece was one of those opportunities.

"We'll stick to the back roads this time," Silverton replied.

"Yeah, fine," Steve agreed.

"Two officers will arrive here soon. They are here to cleanse this situation." Silverton looked at the mess, "If anyone asks what happened here, refer them to me, I'll take care of it. After the officers have completed their work they will take you where you need to go."

Roy took in a deep breath and squeezed his eyes together, the effects of the DNA round that struck him earlier were still evident.

Two unmarked police cars swooped onto the scene. An officer from the first car jumped out and raised the police cordon tape allowing the vehicle to drive inside the cordon. The second car parked next to the tape. Two officers sat in the car while one approached Silverton for instructions.

"I want all three vehicles impounded and dealt with per our usual protocols. You need to cleanse the area to our usual standards as well. Nothing can be missed," Silverton said and wiped the blood off his brow.

"Are you okay, sir?" the officer inquired.

"It's nothing, I'll be fine. You just focus on the job in hand and make sure these cars are dealt with in the usual manner," Silverton said.

"Even my car?" Roy asked.

"Yes. It will be all over the CCTV footage. We can't take the risk of it being connected to this incident, so we'll deal with it in the usual manner, you know, make it disappear."

"You don't take any chances, do you?" Roy conceded.

"Not when it comes to this, no."

Silverton continued with his instruction, "Ensure that the ambulance crew is aware of their destination. If asked, explain that this was a high-level hit that went wrong and that we are carrying out investigations, but warn the crew this is classified. Don't talk to anyone who claims to be from the press, no one should know what happened here as it wasn't called in." Silverton was concise with his instructions.

"Yes sir," the officer replied.

"I need your car as well," Silverton looked at the car the officer had just arrived in.

"Here are the keys," the officer tossed Silverton the keys without hesitation.

"Let's go," Silverton looked to Steve.

"And that's it?" Helen asked.

"What else do you need to know?" Silverton asked.

"What do we do now?" Helen again asked.

"Pray that we pull this off," Steve said.

"You should know that we are not particularly religious people," Helen said.

"Then just hope that Sayssac was right," Steve said and got into the unmarked police car next to Silverton who was adjusting the driver's seat. The doors slammed, the officer raised the police cordon tape to allow them out, the other car backed up to give Silverton enough space to squeeze through and they sped off down the road.

"How come you checked out Mark Collins?" Steve turned to Silverton.

"First rule of surveillance, know your enemy, understand what they're capable of and try to track them down," Silverton negotiated the London traffic.

"And then what?" Steve asked.

"Work out how to neutralise their effectiveness," Silverton replied.

Roy and Helen were left in limbo as the officers set about cleansing the scene.

"Great, so we just wait here?" Roy ambled off to find somewhere to sit down.

"I guess so," Helen replied.

46

Paris.Present-Day.

Evelyn took a bite out of her sandwich. It was lunchtime and the office was buzzing with journalists scrambling around with phones in hand, shouting across the room as they formulated their news reports.

By contrast, Evelyn was relatively calm, her report was done and the lawyers were carrying out their usual due diligence checks before it went to broadcast.

She picked up the phone, "Mark, hello, how are you?"

"Is this Evelyn?" Mark replied.

"Why of course, how many French journalists do you have contacting you now that you are a famous reporter?" Evelyn teased.

"Sorry, the line is bad, I'm in a bar…"

"Is now a good time to talk?" Evelyn was hesitant.

"Yes...sorry...yes," Mark stuttered and walked to a quieter end of the bar. "That's better, I can hear you now."

"Look, it's fine, I can ring another time if you're busy," Evelyn held the phone in front of her face for a moment and frowned.

"No, honestly, I can talk. I was just catching up with a friend," Mark replied.

Evelyn looked at her screen again, "Your reports are spreading everywhere."

"Yes, I know," Mark sounded smug.

"Off the record," Evelyn said quietly.

"Yes."

"Do you want to write another one?" Evelyn opened a notepad on her desk, the page was headed Pitie Salpetriere Mortuary. "This time about the morgue where they took the bodies."

"Okay, now you've got my full attention. Let me get to the office and call you back." Mark looked at his watch, "Are you around in about an hour?"

Evelyn looked at the unfolding carnage in the office, broadcast deadlines were approaching fast. This was signified by an array of escalating conversations, waving arms, and a queue at the coffee machine of overtired journalists seeking an injection of caffeine to get through the day; it's a healthy profession, she thought to herself.

"Of course, I will be, we're just breaking a story over here so it's madness."

"What story is that?" Mark wanted to know.

"Oh, some heavy political shit, but I can't say anything because we're under embargo until the lawyers are cool with it. Trust me, this is big." Evelyn still got a buzz from the job and this was obvious by the tone in her voice.

"Okay, look, one hour I promise," Mark fed off the buzz. He took a swig of his beer and went back to join his friend.

47

Manchester.Present-Day.

"I have to ask you this." Steve looked across to Silverton who was concentrating on driving.

"What?" Silverton kept looking ahead at the road in front.

"Are you a believer?"

"Of what?"

"UFOs."

"I'm driving, so sometimes my focus is on the idiot in front of me trying to beat the world record for braking on an A-road."

"Sorry, I just wondered. So many people talk about it, there are movies made all the time and the TV channels are packed with so-called experts trying to sell their latest book about some bizarre sighting on Mars or the Moon. This shit is a daily occurrence now, but is it all white noise? You know, bullshit?"

"What if I told you some of that white noise was there to preoccupy minds that would otherwise stray onto our patch?"

"That wouldn't surprise me at all."

"It's funny because that's how I came into contact with Roy. He's one of the few people to come into contact with a verifiable UFO."

"You don't really believe that, do you?"

"You asked, I'm telling. It was a few years ago. I got a call from the military top brass over at Lossiemouth, an RAF base in Scotland. They'd been having some issues with their comms and they'd intercepted a radio pulse wave that, over a period of time, was signaling regularly. They thought it was some

kind of interference. Anyway, it got referred to HQ.
Then I got called into action and asked to investigate it."

"So how did Roy get involved?"

"Roy is a very intelligent man. His specialism is
monitoring, illegally, military and police radio channels.
He'd picked this signal up and ran it through some of his
equipment. Even with his basic tests, he knew this
wasn't terrestrial."

"Meaning it was extra—"

"Extra-terrestrial, yes, from a source that could
not be verified or identified."

"So, what happened next?"

"What I now know, but didn't back then, is that
Roy is a tenacious son of a bitch and was also an expert
in mapping out these kinds of radio signals and the
probabilities of sightings thereafter."

"So, the signals are like a prelude, a warning to
a sighting?" Steve asked.

"Not always, but in some cases, yes. So I get the
call and before I know it I'm on a military helicopter on
the way to the base at Lossiemouth. When I get there,
who should I see at the gates?"

"Roy?"

"Yep. He was on public ground and entitled to
be there, but his presence was noticed by the top brass.
They were nervous. They wanted to know who he was
and what he was doing there. I met with Roy and he
invited me to his tent. Bear in mind it was pissing down,
the wind was howling and his tent was packed full of
hardware. He showed me a visual interpretation of the
radio signal being tracked at Lossiemouth, then
compared it to one that was first tracked in Eastern
Australia in 2007; they were almost identical. But in
Eastern Australia, there was no follow-up signal or
subsequent sighting. Roy's theory was that this was an
aborted attempt to communicate with us. He felt that a

visitation would have happened had we responded. You can only imagine what I was thinking."

"Did you think he was crazy?"

"No, my default setting with people is to take them at face value and work from there. You know why?"

"I don't, but I have a feeling you're about to tell me."

"Well think of it this way, you have to be a serious UFO hunter to invest in all that equipment. I mean it wasn't military…oh fuck, get off the road!" Silverton stamped on the brakes as the car in front slowed.

"You have no patience. They were just slowing down to turn onto that road," Steve defended.

"Next time we use the fucking M6."

"We both know what happened the last time we tried that."

"It may almost be worth taking the risk," Silverton uttered.

"I'm not sure Kallyuke would agree."

"Well, neither he nor you are driving! Silverton rolled his eyes and exhaled deeply. "Anyway, Roy's equipment wasn't military standard but it was good, like a professional metal detector versus a beachcomber. This stuff could trace the tiniest signal and lock on to any source to disprove the most obvious reasons that something wasn't extra-terrestrial. Roy was good – better than good at this stuff. And the mapping info about Eastern Australia had me hooked. So, I convinced the top brass to let him onto the base, obviously with limited clearance, and on the condition, he was escorted at all times."

"And they agreed to that?"

"Yes, because that particular base wasn't as sensitive as one of the nuclear submarine bases, and it was well known in the local area. It provided a lot of employment so it wasn't a big deal. It's when Roy got talking with the comms team, that's when things got interesting."

"You mean when he had access to the military-grade equipment on the base?"

"Exactly. Between them, they managed to map out a sequence for the signal and lock into a potential location source. It was actually quite scary."

"Are you able to tell me where the signal came from?"

"It was never confirmed publicly, but we had a lockdown to one of Jupiter's moons – Ganymede."

"Didn't they cover it up?"

"Yes, they did. They covered it up for years because NASA, who had worked with the Australian Space Agency analysing the data, had no idea how to pitch this one out. Signals from one of Jupiter's moons, however faint, were not on the agenda. At least, not on the public agenda."

"Was it the same signal?"

"Off the record?"

"Who am I going to tell? After all, I think you have quite a lot of sensitive information about me. Think of this as a quid pro quo situation."

"With this one, even I was concerned."

"So, was it?"

"Yes it was...thing is, Roy was as concerned as the staff at the base. I mean the comms guys shit themselves. We had a fucking signal from potentially the same spot that had been tracked years earlier in Eastern Australia in 2007. Whatever sent the signal still wanted to make contact with us. The problem was that no one knew what the signal represented. Was it a greeting card, a call to arms, or a warning? We hadn't a clue."

"I don't remember seeing any of this anywhere though."

"No, you won't. Roy and I pushed out a diversion via his YouTube channel at a time when there weren't many people spinning that kind of shit online. Luckily, it found a ready audience of believers. So classic diversion stuff, the press swarmed on his channel and left us alone to deal with the real story."

"What was the diversion?"

"Oh, we cooked up a story that the military had somehow tapped into an encoded NASA signal from one of the Voyager missions, and that being classified, we had no idea of the source. Roy made that one up and the military approved it for broadcast."

"What's the real story?"

"The signal is still present, even to this day, but no one knows what it's saying. It was during that process that I realised I could trust Roy as one of my outlets for anything that needed, how can I put this…"

"Covering up?"

"I prefer to use the words smooth over in the interest of the public."

"What about Oumuamua? What are your thoughts on that one?"

"You mean the so-called cigar-shaped object they discovered?"

"Yes, I mean one minute this thing could be a sign of alien life, the next minute they're tripping over themselves to say it isn't. What's the story with this one?"

"I'm not sure, it could be a cover-up. The experts they've lined up to denounce it as evidence of alien life seem to make a pretty compelling case."

"And you believe them?"

"I'm not close enough to the case to make a judgment call either way. But they could be diverting the public's eyes away from it, even if only to give themselves more time to analyse the data."

"Ever the diplomat," Steve said and smirked.

"Sometimes I even surprise myself, but you have to dig deep if you want to keep things away from the mainstream media."

"Which is why I think Sayssac is right about Mark Collins."

"We'll see. From what I remember, this guy didn't strike me as a professional, more of an opportunist who got lucky. Either way, he's managed to concoct a story that has grabbed the headlines, so maybe Sayssac is right."

"We can't afford to keep chasing these people around the timeline because sooner or later more accidents are going to happen. There will be more Richards, and there's a risk that something catastrophic could result from these mishaps."

"I agree, but we have to be careful about who we befriend in our quest to stop these people. You never know what may come of it."

" Don't overcomplicate it." Steve smiled.

"Wasn't that my line?"

"Yes, but this time it's my idea. I say we sit down and explain what we want him to do for us."

"You think it will be that easy? Don't forget, Roy was concerned about the implications of what may happen if information about the radio signals leaked into the public domain so he agreed to be complicit in the cover-up. We may not be so lucky with Collins, and worse still, he may spot an opportunity to make money out of this. That could leave us in a compromised position."

"You're overthinking this."

"You know what I mean. Roy was already on our side. Let's just hope the same can be said of Collins," Silverton said and glanced briefly at Steve.

"We just have to convince him."

They were now approaching the outskirts of Manchester. "We'll check into a hotel and prepare for tomorrow. How about that place?"

"That shithole?" Steve said.

"What's wrong with it?"

"You want a list?" Steve pulled a face as he looked at the proposed accommodation.

"It's out of the city centre and inconspicuous. What do you expect?" Silverton tapped the steering wheel.

"A place where I'm not going to catch a disease from the bedsheets."

"Now who's overthinking? I'm going to park and get us a couple of rooms."

"Fine. I'll wait here."

"You do that."

Silverton parked outside a small hotel and got out of the car. Steve sat tapping his fingers on the dashboard.

"I got us two rooms on the ground floor. It isn't pretty but it's low-key and means we can rest easy. I vote we go over there for something to eat."

"Where?"

"Over there." Silverton pointed to a small Indian restaurant.

"Another shithole? You amaze me. All this government money at your disposal and you manage to choose not one, but two shitholes."

"May I remind you that this is supposed to be your town."

"You may, but I've never eaten in this neighbourhood. I have no idea what that place is like. I mean look at it – it looks like a disaster with a menu attached."

"What's wrong with it?" Silverton asked.

"If you must know, I just don't travel this far south of the city."

"I think you're being a bit harsh."

Steve stepped out of the car and followed Silverton to the restaurant. They entered and were greeted by a smartly dressed waiter who showed them to a table that was set against a brightly decorated wall. Steve immediately grabbed the drinks menu.

"Something to drink?" the waiter asked.

"God I need a drink of something…I'm going to order a whiskey…may I have whiskey, single malt if you have one please, thanks." Steve pored over the menu and then ordered.

"I'll just have a beer please," Silverton said.

The drinks promptly arrived at the table and the waiter stood, pad and pen in hand waiting for their food order. Steve ordered a lamb Bhuna along with some rice, while Silverton ordered a Tandoori mixed grill and Naan bread.

"Good choices gentlemen, and to drink with your meals?" the waiter asked.

"Bottle of house red wine for the table please, and two glasses," Steve said and placed the menu back on the table.

"One glass will be fine. I'll have another beer please," Silverton said.

The waiter shuffled off to the kitchen and then returned to the table with a bottle of wine and placed one glass in front of Steve. He opened the wine and offered the chance to taste it first.

"Just pour, I'm sure it will be fine," Steve lifted his glass toward the bottle of wine.

Another waiter arrived with Silverton's beer.

Soon afterward the food arrived.

"Let me ask you this…you're a cop, right? Or you were…" Steve heartily tucked into his food while Silverton picked at his.

"We established that a while ago," Silverton replied.

"Oh, by the way, this food isn't too bad, a bit on the spicy side but not too bad...I'm pleasantly surprised...you eating that?" Steve nodded toward the half-eaten Naan bread.

"I'm fine."

"Do you mind if I...?"

"Be my guest. Now can we please get to the point?" Silverton placed his elbows on the table.

"Yes, sorry, wine always makes me ramble..." Steve refilled his glass to the brim and used the Naan bread to wipe up the remaining sauce on his plate.

"And whiskey?"

"Turns me into an asshole. Well, according to my ex-wife. I mean, she was a good woman, but she could list any number of dinner parties that I fucked up with a few shots of the good stuff and a Bob Marley record. Thing is...people are so fucking square...you wanna talk about fucking house prices and your pension...just fuck off to work and do that shit...dinner party chat should be about shit...life...not fucking money...anyway sorry..."

"I get the feeling your wife was right."

"And what about your wife? Is she a complainer when the booze sinks in?"

"My ex-wife you mean."

"Oh, I see...I didn't realise."

"You didn't ask." Silverton took a swig of his beer.

"Okay, I tell you what, let's drink to our ex-wives eh? Let's raise a glass and celebrate our newfound freedom."

"I think you may be celebrating a bit too much..." Silverton carefully placed his cutlery on the plate next to the half-eaten food.

"I'm sorry, you've driven and you've been good and all that shit, but as I was saying...before today, had you ever shot a man? I mean had you ever killed someone whilst on duty?" Steve chewed on the last remaining piece of lamb Bhuna and discarded his cutlery on the plate.

"Where did that question come from?"

"Well, now we're buddies and all that, I think I should know who I'm working with."

"Buddies may be a bit strong."

"Okay, have it your way, acquaintances, so have you?"

"Once. It was the hardest decision of my life," Silverton looked over to the waiter who was standing by the bar. "I'll join you in a whiskey…Waiter, could you send over two whiskeys please?"

The waiter promptly arrived with two tumblers of whiskey, "Are you all finished with your plates?"

"I think so, yes." Silverton nodded to the waiter.

The waiter carefully balanced the collection of plates on his arm and left for the kitchen. Steve and Silverton picked up the glass tumblers.

"Cheers! How's that wound by the way?" Steve took a sip from his glass of whiskey.

"It's okay, the whiskey will help…" Silverton took a large swig from the glass and placed it back on the table.

"You see, now we're getting somewhere. So, who was it and how did it happen?"

"The hardest thing is pulling the trigger. Up until then, it's all bravado in the station. People might say what they'd do, and how easy it would be, but until you do it, look someone in the eyes and pull that trigger, you have no idea."

"Who was it?"

"A drug dealer…or should I say, runner. Young man, maybe twenty, in the suburbs of Croydon. I mean they had issues, name me a town that doesn't, but things were getting out of hand. The drug gangs of London were moving out into new territories and we got the heads up about this gang operating on one of the smaller estates. You know how it starts, one gang brings knives, the next gang brings machetes and the final gang to the party…well…they just happen to bring guns to take all the others out."

"And before you know it…"

"Yep, sooner or later someone was going to get killed. This particular night was a bastard of a shift, the one from hell that we all dread. I was in the special armed response unit called in to try and help control the flow of drugs on the streets, you know, beef up the presence and make them think twice about dealing. But this gang didn't give a shit. They baited us to get a reaction. Then during a raid, one of their runners pulled a pistol on me as we searched a flat…I had no choice, but that look, the look on his face as he realised I was preparing to shoot…I'll never forget it…he took one bullet to the chest and died at the scene, paramedics couldn't do a thing."

"How did you feel?"

"I felt sick. I took weeks off for stress. I went to see the boy's parents months later and spoke to them during the inquiry. The strange thing is, they knew I had no choice, they had seen their son go downhill for months with this gang and knew he was already dead; it was just a matter of time before they got that knock on the door to confirm it." Silverton took another swig from his glass.

"They sound very brave."

"They were. And in truth, the kid didn't deserve to die, but as with all of these things, these people get indoctrinated. They get brainwashed and swept away by all the money, the prowess amongst their peer group, and the respect from other dealers as they set out to prove they are the strongest gang in town…then before you know it, it all ends up in a wooden box and that's it…in the click of a finger their life is extinguished…the world won't miss them, but the family goes on grieving for the son they lost…"

"It sounds tragic, but it's not an unfamiliar tale."

"I swore I wouldn't carry another gun but look at today…What would have been the outcome if I wasn't armed?"

"I've never seen anyone shot before today…apart from on the television, and, of course, I saw that body in Paris. I heard you shoot the guy in the Catacombs but I didn't see it."

"When you see their eyes, that look of fear…it's that knowing look…that's when you know."

"Did you retire from the force after that?"

"You'd make a good policeman...and no...I took a desk job after the inquiry. I decided I wanted a quiet life. I think it affected me more than I expected. Soon afterward, the booze kicked in, along with bouts of depression."

"It took its toll then."

"It did, and eventually, it took my marriage. Don't get me wrong, she was a fighter, she fought for us and fought to save our marriage but I was too stupid and often too drunk to see it. I can't blame her."

"So how did you end up here? That's one hell of a jump."

"It isn't as big a jump as you may think. The force knew I had a keen interest in all things paranormal, especially UFO sightings. There was one famous case I was investigating during my spare time – the Alan Godfrey case in Todmorden."

"The alien abduction case..."

"Yes, that's the one. That place is a bit of a UFO hotspot."

"It was the location of the Adamski case too." Steve held up his glass.

"Not many people have heard of that one."

"I have a passing interest in these things. It's still unsolved though, isn't it?"

"It's unsolved to the extent that they don't know what the cause of death was, they couldn't explain how a body that had disappeared for five days had one day's worth of facial hair growth."

" Don't forget the unidentified substance on the neck as well. The one that caused the burns…"

"There's been a development with that," Silverton raised his eyebrows.

"Oh really?" Steve tilted his head.

"Yutu 2 has uncovered an ointment-like substance during its exploration of the Moon."

"You think there's a link?" Steve asked.

"Possibly. To this day the substance found on Adamski's body remains unidentified."

"And you think this could be it?"

"All I'm saying is that I'd love to get the chance to analyse two samples side by side and see if there's a connection."

"And if there was?"

"Whoa there, I'm not jumping to any conclusions."

"But there could be, within your grasp, proof of alien life."

"That's a hell of a jump," Silverton smiled and slowly nodded his head.

"But it's possible."

"Anything is possible when dealing with these types of cases. I know that case like the back of my hand – both cases. It was while I was investigating them that I got a visit."

"From the Men in Black?" Steve teased.

"Almost. The UFO investigation department paid a visit. They're a little-known unit buried within the military. Turns out they'd been made aware of my work and offered me the chance to turn my interest into a dream job of sorts."

"So, a fresh start then?"

"I needed it because this was about the time of my divorce, so it felt right. It felt like I was turning a new page – a new chapter in my life – so I took the job."

"How did you wind up here, opposite me?"

"We have a mutual friend."

"Really?"

"Charley Sandford."

"Funny how his name seems to pop up in most conversations I have about this shit," Steve laughed.

"Charley Sandford is an intermediary. Someone who was sent to test my knowledge and see if I was open to helping in their cause."

"Where did you meet him?"

"At the site of an alleged UFO sighting, the exact location is classified and will be for some time."

"So, this one could be proven to be an actual sighting then, not some fake?" Steve asked.

"No comment," Silverton said and took a swig of whiskey.

"I see, and why didn't you dismiss him as a fake? I've met and spoken to him at length, and I thought most of what he said wouldn't have been out of place in a sci-fi movie. Of course, time and context have corrected that assumption, but a man with your background, wouldn't your tolerance levels be set lower?"

"I'm not sure. Maybe he got to me when I was feeling vulnerable in the aftermath of the divorce."

"But this was your fresh start."

"Fresh starts seldom start smoothly, they take time. Besides, some of what he said was compelling."

"In what way?" Steve asked.

"Things were different. Remember that I now had access to hundreds, if not thousands of classified

392

documents detailing UFO sightings from all over the world, in the most intricate of detail. Sandford pinpointed three specific cases and detailed them in ways that no one apart from those who had access to those files could have known. Only those with the highest level of clearance could have accessed those files, and he was certainly not on that list. That was enough to convince me that he was saying these things for real. I mean, I'd read enough about time travel, Michio Kaku and all the rest of them, but to be confronted firsthand with the evidence, well that was different."

"How did it feel? For me, I was just in shock and tried to kick back against what I would later find out was the truth."

"I felt calm. At ease and relieved that after so many years, here was someone who could validate the theories, vindicate all the time I'd spent researching thousands of investigations."

"What were the cases? You have to tell me..."

"I can't tell you."

"Oh, come on! I love this stuff. We're friends now. Surely you can trust me?"

"It's irrelevant to our work. We don't need to discuss them and that's final. I don't want accusatory fingers pointed at me suggesting I leaked classified information. I cannot take the risk. Besides, my value to you and this mission is to ensure I have access to the tools that come with this trade."

"You mean like cleansing crash scenes?"

"Partly. Being in this job affords me certain privileges that make things a lot easier than they might otherwise be, travel, for example, the premises in London, access to information ...do I need to go on?" Silverton shrugged his shoulders.

"No...no, I understand. I'm just fascinated by the whole subject. Maybe it's in my genes, who knows?"

"I know that Kallyuke wanted a small network of people in this time to help smooth things over which is why they approached me via Charley and accepted my recommendation that Roy would be a suitable candidate."

"You recommended Roy?"

"Of course, I did. I don't trust many people, but he is someone who is dependable and can keep a secret."

"He's quite distant isn't he?"

"It's his way. Don't forget that until we met, he was effectively a loner, in a tent."

"So how come the fiasco in Manchester? You know, the time you came knocking on my apartment door?"

"Roy was there as the back-up. We had no idea how you'd react but we needed you out of Manchester and quickly, so Kallyuke and I decided to go with that plan."

"Roy knew all along?"

"He knew what he needed to know at the time he knew it."

"Eh?"

"We didn't want to compromise the plan so Roy had limited information, just enough to carry out his side of the plan if required. The fact that you're here in front of me suggests that despite the efforts of others, it actually went quite well."

"Others...indeed. That was a day I won't forget."

"There will be plenty more days like that; this is far from over."

"Do you think Mark Collins will play ball?" Steve placed his hands on the table.

"This is your idea, so I'd like to think you have some confidence in your own plan," Silverton said.

"Unlike you though, I haven't met him."

"I met him very briefly on the M6 in the aftermath of that incident. He looked like a man who could fall into line easily, with the right incentives."

"I hope you're right," Steve said.

"So do I, believe me," Silverton raised his eyebrows.

"I think we should get to our rooms and get some rest. This room is starting to spin. I don't think a hangover would be a good thing, given tomorrow's task," Steve said.

"That's probably the most sensible thing you've said all night. I'll settle the bill so we can get out of here."

48

Somewhere on Earth.2618.

Terence Armstrong stood aloft a huge sand dune, let out a sigh, and looked across the horizon into the endless desert. In the distance, he could see the gathering storm, its progress marked by swirling clouds of dust and sand. He could just about make out a small dark shape that looked to be his destination, but this was soon to be swamped by wave after wave of dust that traveled relentlessly across the desert floor.

The sun beat down on Armstrong's head and the calmness which had surrounded him only moments earlier was replaced by the early signs of the storm.

Small rodents buried themselves in the dunes, snakes slithered to the nearest bolt hole, and what little vegetation was there started to sway to the rhythmic beat of the wind as the dust storm steadily grew worse. Dirt and sand whistled past Armstrong's head and stung his face. The eye of this particularly vicious storm was hurtling unabated toward him and he needed to find shelter.

His smart leather shoes sank into the loose sand, hindering his progress, and the shot that had grazed his thigh was causing discomfort, though he tried to put it to the back of his mind. His suit offered little in the way of protection; the wind battered his body.

He had little time to find shelter. The sun reduced to a dull, glowing orb, hanging low in the sky; the howling wind pushed and then pulled Armstrong while he frantically searched out his destination.

Armstrong placed a hand up to his head to shield his eyes, offering at least some protection from the onslaught. Buried into the palm of his other hand, CCS offered guidance to the secret location he sought.

Gradually, the images in front of Armstrong's eyes started to turn blue as CCS hooked into his optic nerves and displayed a red directional marker pointing him toward his destination. As if on autopilot, he put one foot in front of the other, using the marker as the guide.

As quickly as it arrived, the eye of the storm passed, dissipating into the dry, desert air. In the distance, Armstrong saw a small, innocuous-looking, dark rectangular shape flapping in the slowing winds. The red directional marker pointed toward it and he picked up the pace, encouraged by the closeness of the location, and his desire to get out of the last entrails of the storm.

Armstrong approached the dark shape, noticing that his vision had returned to normal. CCS had disengaged and removed the guidance assistance. He'd become accustomed to the blue tint and had to blink hard a few times in an attempt to adjust to the natural brightness of the re-emerging sun.

He stood in front of a small, black Bedouin tent in the middle of what was now a perfectly calm desert. He walked around it, probing for an entrance with his outstretched hand. Once inside, he stood in the middle and was scanned by a pencil-thin light that circled him.

The tent sank into the ground until it was completely covered by sand.

The fabric on one side of the tent raised to reveal a metal door surrounded by a concrete wall. Armstrong walked over to it and looked into the small retina scanner on one side of the door. The scan was positive, the door slid open and Armstrong stepped into the small lift in front of him. A bright blue light filled the lift for several seconds, as the light subsided the word CLEAR appeared on a small screen. The lift then descended into the bowels of the desert. Armstrong looked up at his claustrophobic surroundings while the lift descended further into the ground.

After a few moments, the lift came to a halt. Armstrong faced another metal door and looked into the retina scanner. The door slid open to reveal a huge hangar which was a hive of activity. As he exited the lift, a small patch of blood remained on the floor where he had been standing.

Rowena and Mike stood directly in front of him.

"Welcome back Terence." Rowena held out a hand to greet Armstrong.

Rowena was a confident woman in her mid-forties, a scientist of considerable expertise, and someone who had helped in the creation of the initial timeline, she was well aware of Kallyuke and his relentless pursuit of them.

"It's good to be back," Armstrong said and shook her hand.

"Perhaps next time your journey will be a little more straightforward, but for now, we cannot afford to take any risks, we have to protect the integrity of this location," Mike completed the formalities and shook Armstrong's hand.

Mike was a lean man in his fifties, another of the scientists who worked on the timeline, but he was not as involved as Rowena. He was quiet-spoken but of considerable intelligence, someone who would sit back and analyse situations longer than most, but would often provide solutions that others may have overlooked.

Rowena looked down at Armstrong's leg, "You've been shot! We need to get that looked at."

"It's just a graze. It's nothing major," Armstrong replied.

"We can't have you bleeding all over the place, here, wait a moment," Mike said.

And with that Mike walked over to a small cupboard near the lift entrance and grabbed a MediKit.

He produced a small pen and handed it to Armstrong, "Probably better if you do it," he said.

Armstrong grabbed the pen and ran the nib along the small wound through the tear in his trousers.

"That's better," Rowena smiled.

"I'm just glad you managed to track my signal," Armstrong said.

"The improvements to CCS appear to be working. This technology is incredible." Mike smiled. "We were able to track you down. Of course, for us, the issue is about opening timelines."

"Yes. That is something we don't want to do regularly, especially under these circumstances. You know the risks, this is why we have to carry out extensive research before utilising them, so this was a last resort," Rowena said and frowned.

"I understand, and I apologise for the mess I left back there. I wasn't prepared, but I assure you it won't happen again," Armstrong said as he followed them into the bright, open space of the huge underground facility.

"It was only a matter of time before they caught up to you," Rowena said.

"We need to be more careful," Mike added.

The three of them stopped to look around at the busy hangar. "That's a holographic mock-up of the ship – our ticket out of here. It's exactly one-tenth the scale of the finished version we'll use, but this enables us to run certain tests," Mike said, staring at the huge spaceship.

"It's quite something, isn't it?" Armstrong looked in awe at the sight in front of him.

"We have a lot to discuss. The time is approaching fast and we must take steps to secure our future," Rowena said. "We had to restrict what was said via the comms channels as we suspect they are being monitored."

"Or at least they are trying to monitor them," Mike corrected.

"That would make sense," Armstrong said.

"We've been working on procedures to balance the cargo space with the inhabitable space for passengers, plus space for the fuel and supplies needed during the voyage," Mike said as they walked up to the ship. "It's a delicate balancing act, and we have protocols in place, along with relevant contingency plans, ranging from unexpected fuel usage to increased food consumption due to excess travel time. Variables are being factored in and we hope to cover every eventuality. Of course, these things are never perfect, but we are aiming for as close to perfection as can be."

"So, you conduct all the testing here, using this mock-up?" Armstrong looked at the hologram model of the ship.

"It's far more efficient to conduct them here, in a controlled environment. The location where the ship is being built is, shall we say, basic, and bereft of what we need to gain accurate results. And with this being a hologram, it allows us to tweak certain components or designs until we get it right," Mike replied.

"Everything you see is built to scale using a sophisticated piece of software that allows us to model each component to the exact size," Rowena said.

"Where are we going exactly?" Armstrong asked.

"More on that later. We have a lot to discuss. In the meantime, let's walk." Rowena gently encouraged Armstrong to continue walking with them.

They walked slowly past the mock-up ship that was long and sleek with a rounded front. It reminded Armstrong of the spaceships he'd seen in the classic movies of the fifties and sixties. A small cluster of people stood next to one of the two large propulsion rockets near the back of the body. One of them used a small pen to draw in details while another one read notes from a screen on the side of the hologram. Another worker was inside the hologram, inspecting the cargo bays and making adjustments.

"The design of that rocket looks familiar," Armstrong said.

"It's based on the blueprints we obtained from the NASA archives, but with some modifications necessary for stage one of our mission," Mike explained.

"Stage one?" Armstrong questioned.

"Yes," Mike reiterated the statement without elaborating.

"But was it necessary to go to such lengths with all of this?"

Rowena stopped and looked up and down at the ship. "We only have one shot at this, to give us the best chance of success we had to go down this route. Once the final design is tested and approved we will have everything we need in perfect scale to replicate the final version. We are using computer modeling to replicate the actual journey. The data we generate using this ship will hopefully help us avoid any unnecessary issues when we embark on the real journey."

"That final version is being assembled in space from components upscaled using this model, step by step, as each design feature is signed off and then approved," Mike added.

"But for now, let's go to the Relax Room to discuss what developments we've made over the past few months. You must be hungry, and no doubt thirsty," Rowena said.

Armstrong followed Mike and Rowena down a large, brightly lit open corridor that led to a huge recreational area.

"You don't mess around do you?" Armstrong looked around in wonderment.

"We wanted to make our final years on Earth at least slightly bearable. People need space to unwind, living in this facility can be bad enough at times, especially without natural light," Rowena stood and stared at the huge, colourful atrium.

The recreational zone was packed with large green areas, full of plants and trees, places to sit and relax, there were waterfalls and even an ice-skating rink. The overhead lighting gave the illusion of natural sunlight and the soothing sound of normality pervaded the senses.

"We took our styling influences from the bygone era of parks and shopping malls. We wanted to create a space that would allow us to indulge in guilty pleasures and fun before the journey," Mike explained.

"It's essential for the soul," Rowena remarked.

They walked further into the atrium, Armstrong looked down and found himself walking on grass that felt real. The sound of a flowing stream could be heard in the distance, and as they crossed a small bridge over it they were confronted by a towering waterfall. The spray from the waterfall dispersed into the air, and people sat on the water's edge, enjoying the cooling effect of the spray.

"That was my idea," Rowena smiled. "Water has such a soothing effect on the human mind."

They sat at a wooden table in the middle of one of the gardens, and Mike set off to find some refreshments.

"This feels surreal," Armstrong said, brushing his shoes against the grass.

"As I said, we wanted an environment that would help people switch off, also somewhere that was suitable for children to play in." Rowena looked at a group of kids playing football in a nearby area, "After all, we knew we would be here for many years, so why not make the most of it?"

"A city underground though, it's almost mythical," Armstrong looked around to try to take in the scale of the place.

"We have technology at our disposal that made all this relatively easy to develop, but I won't say it didn't come at a price," Rowena looked away as she completed the sentence.

"How many people live here?" Armstrong asked.

Mike rejoined them at the table with a tray full of food and drinks.

"About two thousand," Mike said. "One-thousand- five hundred adults and five-hundred children, the next generation of explorers, and the future of humanity. The main development area you were in earlier is out of bounds unless you are working on it, but other than that we've made it an open space where people can stretch their legs."

"That is apart from the living quarters," Rowena said.

"Of course," Mike said and laughed.

"But this won't sustain life for much longer, which is why we have to leave." Rowena took a drink and a bowl of salad from the tray.

"At the moment, we can grow and develop all that we need, but as this population expands and the pressure on this space increases, we would find these resources severely stretched...and it is not in our make-up to settle for anything other than somewhere we can call home," Mike said.

"And this is definitely not home," Rowena added.

"I understand," Armstrong said and took a large swig from a glass of water.

"We've managed to keep this base off the radar from Kallyuke and his gang, mainly by setting up smaller surface-based facilities that have kept them occupied," Rowena said.

"Earth is dying, let's make no mistake about that. Oh, they can paper over the cracks, create the illusion that there is a future on this planet, but this time it's for real. The planet is dying, it may take a while, but I don't want to see these children growing up to find a planet bereft of life," Mike said.

"Centuries of abuse have taken their toll. Taking too much out and not putting enough back in has created an uncorrectable imbalance that is now irreversible," Rowena explained.

"So where are we going?" Armstrong asked.

"We're going to Mars, or should I say, we're going back to Mars," Mike answered and then took a bite of a sandwich.

"Back? I don't understand," Armstrong said. "Am I missing something?"

"The first manned mission to Mars was top secret and kept well away from the media in case it failed, that was the way they operated back then, in your time," Rowena confirmed.

"When did this happen?" Armstrong asked.

"In the early twenty-first century, the first decade. It was a private mission but NASA kept an arm's length interest in it to see how it went," Mike confirmed.

"Mars has always been the planet of choice. The data gathered during that manned mission, and of course, the data gathered by Curiosity and other surfaced-based vehicles, has always suggested the planet would make an excellent location to build a subterranean base, much like this one, and then develop a ship capable of deep space travel. We would do this, in part, by adapting the existing ship, and then using some of the resources available to us on Mars," Rowena said.

"You're saying Mars is capable of sustaining life?" Armstrong asked.

"For a limited period, yes, but the research suggests it could be used to help top-up supplies prior to launching a deep space mission," Mike said. "That could take one or two generations though. You must understand that whilst not perfect, it is a better option than remaining here and facing almost certain extinction. I know on the face of it we are swapping one version of this existence for another, but on Mars, there's hope, on Earth, there is only the prolonged agony of a slow death."

"A deep space mission to where?" Armstrong asked.

"We don't know yet," Mike said.

"When we managed to power up ISS we gained access to a huge amount of data, but most of it was encrypted, and to a level we've never seen before…even our top people struggled to comprehend the length governments of that time went to secure these files," Rowena said.

"To the point that if you triggered an electronic kill switch by accident, the data was destroyed and lost forever. We found this out by accident. But the information we've unlocked so far is fascinating. I can see why they kept all those files locked behind heavy encryption and stored in space. The technology alone blew our minds when we first encountered it." Mike was excited again.

"So, what do we know?" Armstrong asked.

"We initially thought First Contact was initiated in 2009. This is the established version of events. But NASA took the cameras offline and then put out a series of false flags to take the wind out of any aspiring UFO hunter's sails. But the files onboard ISS that we've managed to unlock suggest that First Contact took place in Peru many years earlier, and I mean many years earlier; problem is, the files are so corrupted and out of date that we've struggled to make sense of the information, so we're having to backtrack through our archives to see if they offer any clues about this new data," Mike said and shook his head.

"This is where it gets strange," Rowena said.

"You mean stranger," Armstrong added.

"The ship you walked past earlier," Rowena continued.

"The mock-up?" Armstrong said.

"Yes," Rowena grew impatient. "Part of the blueprint for the ship we are developing was found on the encrypted data files. So, from this, we concluded that this life form was trying to help us all along by providing us with a means of escape, not hurt us as some believed. But of course, NASA couldn't risk this information getting into the public domain, I mean, why would an alien life form...let's say an extra-terrestrial life form...travel millions of miles to send us the data required to build a ship to escape planet Earth? Can you imagine the questions and the panic that could cause if it got out?"

"And why do it twice?" Mike chipped in.

"Perhaps we simply weren't capable of building anything like that ship when they first arrived? I mean look at it. We probably didn't have the capability or the technology to match their plans…could that be a reason they left?" Armstrong suggested.

"That was our initial thinking, but if you study that era and the texts that support certain theories…" Mike said.

"Let me guess, you're talking Chariots of the Gods, right? The book by Erich von Daniken that theorises the links between ancient civilisations and alien contact. Daniken debates the possibility that the pyramids of Egypt, the NAZCA Lines, and Stonehenge are amongst many ancient constructions that were built to call the aliens back to Earth," Armstrong placed his hands on the table.

"Chariots of the Gods, man, they practically own South America, I mean they taught the Incas everything they know. The Thing. 1982. Directed by John Carpenter." Mike sat back, clasped his hands on his chest, and beamed with pride.

"Well thank you, Mike, for that colourful insight into twentieth-century movie making, I had no idea you were such a fan," Rowena said and then turned back to look at Armstrong. "So how did you know?" Rowena asked.

"Call it a hunch, but a strong one…you get used to searching for this stuff on the fringes of the established texts," Armstrong replied.

"Well yes. Amongst other available texts, that was one we researched. But what we can see from these texts is very clear; there was something substantive to those theories, despite their dismissal by many scientists of the time, and you know what? The data files on the ISS appeared to support them as well," Mike was keen to expand.

"They simply didn't have this evidence in hand to corroborate what the book was telling us," Armstrong replied.

"Exactly!" Mike clicked his fingers.

"But before we get carried away, we must also understand that there are a lot of counter theories that dispute these claims; claims that have an equal amount of theories that do stand-up as well," Rowena turned and smirked at Mike.

"That may be the case, but those theories were posed without knowing the contents of the files on the ISS," Mike replied.

"I understand that, but I don't want to complicate an already complicated situation," Rowena said and tapped the table.

"So, you're suggesting that this life form traveled millions of miles only to leave a blueprint for a ship to help us escape Earth?" Armstrong suggested.

"Yes," Rowena replied.

"Why?" Armstrong asked.

"They must have known that we were flirting dangerously close to an Extinction Level Event," Rowena replied.

"Something instigated by time travel?" Armstrong asked.

Mike nodded, "You could be onto something there but it doesn't tie in with the earlier visit."

"Or do you think they were just being friendly, helpful maybe? But without a motive…" Armstrong persisted in firing back questions.

"Less likely. They traveled millions of miles to impart this information. You wouldn't do that without a motive; irrespective of whether we realised that or not," Rowena said.

"We know of cave paintings that existed ten thousand years ago depicting an as yet unidentified craft; a craft that couldn't possibly have existed in the thought patterns of the indigenous people from that time, so maybe this was a regular thing? Maybe they were waiting for our technology to get to a point where we could utilise their superior knowledge," Mike suggested.

"So, let's just say you're correct, that doesn't answer the question of motive," Armstrong said.

"This is where things take an unusual turn. We discovered something during the development of the DNA tracking weapon." Rowena took another drink

"The one I used in London…" Armstrong said.

"Precisely," Rowena said.

"It got taken off me…" Armstrong looked down.

"Never mind about that we have the blueprints and it'll take them an age to work out how it works. By that time, we should be long gone. However, this is far more important. We think they're kindred!" Mike blurted.

"Excuse me," Armstrong recoiled back and shook his head.

"It's not exact, but the files that helped us create the DNA weapon were an accidental lead to this new revelation. We think they utilised their own DNA to show how the tracking unit would work; whether this was by design or by accident we don't know…you see, these files come with a manual, an explanatory in visual form. They see this as the best way to communicate. This file contained a DNA map of something," Rowena said.

"Something? What something?" Armstrong leaned forward.

"In truth, we don't know if they used their own DNA to demonstrate how the weapon could work," Mike butted in.

"But we would then have to question what DNA they used and where they managed to obtain a DNA sample that was an eighty percent match to human DNA," Rowena said.

"Do you think there's a link to the cave paintings and Chariots of the Gods?" Armstrong placed his hands on the table.

"We're exploring that at the moment, evidence is thin on the ground though, and we can't rule out that some of the files containing that evidence were either destroyed or removed. Plus, we don't have access to those caves anymore, so we're relying on archive data. However, any proof to suggest their DNA is contained within ours would be explosive and throw up many, many questions. Many of which would probably remain unanswered, that is, until we got to meet our friendly ETs," Rowena said and then sat back and folded her arms.

"One other issue we have is that there might be a potential fault line in the DNA on that data file. If this is proven correct, then we think that there could be a connection to the virus. Now that would be interesting if proven correct. I mean, was this a race of beings that were dying? Did they know they were dying? And if so, this was a last-ditch mission to save their species?" Mike raised his eyebrows.

"Are you suggesting that this life form left a virus behind?" Armstrong rubbed his fingers across his lips.

"It's certainly a possibility, whether knowingly or not, but we have no DNA samples from anyone infected with the virus to validate this theory. A facility like this has strict lockdown rules. Even that lift shaft you traveled down contains a high-intensity sterilisation process to protect us," Mike said.

"You mean the blue light?" Armstrong asked.

"Yes," Mike replied.

"So how will you cope on Mars?" Armstrong asked.

"We're taking steps. That is all I can say at the moment. Plans are being put in place and we are looking to see what is needed to make life palatable," Rowena said.

"This is why we cannot transmit any of this information to you via your comms systems. It could be tracked and used against us; like so much is at the moment," Mike said.

"Can they be trusted? I mean, what do we know about this life form? Your thinking is that they may have delivered a virus right to our front door, so what else could they have done?" Armstrong asked.

"I maintain that a species wouldn't travel that distance and leave that amount of data if they weren't to be trusted. And I stand by that statement," Mike replied.

"Maybe it is a trap? Maybe they're the ones looking for a cure," Armstrong suggested.

"I'm not so sure, it just doesn't add up. Of all the motives that could answer the question of why, that seems to be most unlikely," Mike replied.

"Back in London it became clear to me that Kallyuke's operatives are trying to hunt us down, one by one, and stop our attempt to get off this planet," Armstrong said. "My cover is blown, but I think I can still carry out my work, I just need to be more careful. We need to move fast."

"We're almost there, we need a final push and we should have enough supplies to finish the ship and get out of here," Rowena stood up and ushered them out of the vast atrium.

"They knew about China," Armstrong said.

"That's hardly surprising given the scale of the disaster. I imagine the Chinese media were limited in what they could or would dare publish," Mike said.

"Well, whatever they published triggered them to investigate," Armstrong said.

They continued to walk out of the atrium and off to Mike and Rowena's laboratory.

Once there, Rowena stood behind her desk looking out at the messy lab that was full of equipment. Mike sat opposite her and Armstrong sat next to Mike.

"I may have some information that could be of help," Armstrong said.

"Oh really?" Rowena perked up at the thought.

"I have a positive ID on two of their sleeper agents," Armstrong replied.

"How?" Mike sat on the edge of his seat.

"When they sabotaged my offices, they were both walking around me, however, they also insisted I placed my hands behind my back, I engaged CCS and recorded them. It was quite simple really…watch over there," Armstrong pointed to the plain white wall over Rowena's shoulder.

On the wall behind Armstrong replayed the footage he captured via the CCS device. The sound of their voices was muffled and occasionally drowned out by the sound of cars and sirens.

Armstrong paused the footage on a frame that had Steve Garner in the foreground, and Helen just a few steps behind him, but slightly blurred.

"That is Steve Garner?" Rowena asked.

"And Helen Smith," Armstrong replied. "Two of their twenty-six deep cover agents. Garner has a new CCS, but I don't think he understands the power of it yet, if he did, I might not be sitting here right now."

"What shall we do with them next?" Rowena posed the question.

"In my opinion, we do nothing and focus on our mission. We have little time and a lot to achieve. To divert away from that would be a mistake," Mike said.

"And what if we want to halt their counter operations?" Rowena asked.

"Is that a priority?" Armstrong asked. "Given what we know, I would have thought our efforts should be on securing the final components to get off this planet."

"That may be the case, but we have to consider what measures they will take to sabotage our escape," Rowena replied.

"Any attempts to try and locate ISS are being blocked at the moment, but that can only last for so long before they work out how to bypass the jamming tech we're using," Mike said.

"Then I think it's clear. I will try my best to secure what we need as quickly as possible so we can complete the mock-up, carry out the testing and expedite our escape at the earliest opportunity," Armstrong said.

"Once the mock-up is approved, we can complete the final build very quickly," Mike said.

"Complete?" Armstrong asked.

"Yes, what you don't know is that it is about eighty percent complete now. We just need to run some final tests," Rowena said.

"The resources you're sending through are invaluable. They're reducing the construction time by months," Rowena said. "We cannot hope to secure such resources on this barren planet."

"Which is why I think we should focus on that and leave the rest to the side before they cook up some new idea to interfere with our mission," Armstrong said.

"I agree," Rowena tapped the palms of her hands on the table.

"It makes sense all around," Mike nodded.

"Then we must hurry before we lose the ability to choose our future," Armstrong said.

"After your little incident in London, we destroyed the files contained on any of the systems in that office," Mike said.

"As part of our protocol to clean things up," Rowena added. "No doubt they will formulate another cover story...they're good at that."

"I read something about the incident on the M6...who was it..." Armstrong frowned because he was drawing a blank.

"Mark Collins by chance?" Mike jogged his memory.

"Yes. What on earth was he thinking? At first, I was annoyed, but now I just think of him as a minor inconvenience." Armstrong slumped back in his chair, "I mean, who reads that shit and actually believes it?"

"Sometimes the truth is stranger than fiction, which is why certain organisations would prefer that the myth remains the accepted version of events."

"Objectively speaking, he can do us no harm, but now they have a positive ID on you, well, that could change things," Rowena said.

"Unfortunately, we have little choice but to continue the operations as they are. I know you've sustained some losses recently, but I trust your network can sustain this intrusion and is capable of seeing out the mission?" Mike looked into Armstrong's eyes.

"The network will be secure, don't worry about that, it is robust enough to cope. I have no issue where that is concerned. What concerns me is how they managed to trace that office in the first place. Do we have a leak?" Armstrong fired back at Mike and Rowena.

"We've kept access to your operations to a minimum, outside of this room there are only two other people who are aware of your mission, so I would suggest that is unlikely," Rowena replied. "You need to make sure you are less visible during the final stages of your operations, then get out of there. I understand the logic of embedding yourself within the community you are siphoning information from, but this is leaving you exposed and vulnerable to this kind of mishap. After the M6, we had Paris, and now this. Each of these incidents means your cover is being compromised. Of greater concern is that you appear to be getting careless, making mistakes, and taking unnecessary risks...this cannot continue." Rowena folded her arms.

"You want me to execute these extractions so we cause the minimum amount of disruption, I get that, but you're not there. You have no idea how much risk is involved." Armstrong's forehead furrowed, "Look at what happened in China. That mine was supposed to be secure and ready for a full survey when they went in; they had no idea they wouldn't be coming out alive. Then of course there was Paris. Now, if you want to send across people who you think are going to be better suited to do this kind of operation then please, feel free, but until then, check the body count and the people currently sitting in one of Kallyuke's so-called fucking gulags before you make that decision, because I think you'll find that volunteers will be thin on the ground."

"Terence. Terence. Now come on, you know we don't mean to undermine or in any way ridicule your efforts," Mike leaned forward and faintly smiled. "In fact, far from it. But we're this close now and I don't want us to fail at such a late stage," Mike said holding his hands close together.

"The network is secure. As far as I can tell this breach in security happened by chance. They managed to catch me leaving my office, that's all. They had no inside intelligence and we had no internal leak that I'm aware of. But this is only one part of the network; a network that is robust enough to function with me going underground if required," Armstrong said and thumped the desk.

"But how can it function?" Rowena asked.

"This is the early part of the twenty-first century. They're obsessed with faceless communication and anonymous transactions. As far as the people I do business with are concerned, it is an entirely normal way to transact; and one that is easy to augment. You seem to forget all we are doing is skimming the surface for tip-offs, inside information that will help us get what we want. We get the intel, we get in and we get out before anyone notices anything was even there to be missed; simple," Armstrong said. "There are no losers because you cannot miss what you didn't know was there in the first place."

"And what about Paris? How do you explain that?" Mike asked.

"We strayed from the formula. We tried something different. You needed diamonds and that was the simplest solution. We now know that it wasn't.

415

Sometimes it is a learning process, even after all this time," Armstrong replied.

"We lost four people in the aftermath of that so-called learning process!" Rowena spat.

"Sometimes things go wrong, despite what you may think. My part of this operation, unlike yours, is not an exact science."

"So let me get to the next issue we need to solve. We need fuel, and lots of it," Mike declared.

"What do you suggest?" Armstrong asked.

"We want you to explore the possibility of bringing forward nuclear waste," Rowena suggested.

"Won't that be dangerous?" Armstrong tilted his head.

"No. The type of waste we want is stored in highly secure units so the risk would be minimal," Rowena said.

"We've investigated the option of hijacking a container ship that is adapted to carry nuclear waste from a power station. Fuel we can use to power the rockets," Mike said.

"It is the perfect solution because the energy is almost spent, and destined for containment, therefore it won't be missed," Rowena said.

"And due to the potential embarrassment and political sensitivity of any such loss, we think there would be minimal media coverage." Mike smiled.

"No one would want to be held accountable for the disappearance of the waste and the whole incident should simply be brushed under the carpet," Rowena said.

"And we have our fuel source," Mike confirmed.

"So, this could solve the problem then?" Armstrong replied.

"Exactly." Rowena nodded slowly, "We just need to process it into something we can use."

"And you can do that?" Armstrong asked.

"We've carried out some preliminary tests on a cache of waste fuel that was discovered in Paris about three hundred years ago…you know, just to be sure," Mike said.

"Even with such a small sample, we were able to prove the theory in a limited test. If we get enough, I'm confident we can convert this waste into enough fuel to power the rockets," Rowena said.

"What do you need me to do?" Armstrong asked.

"We need to gather information. No extractions at this stage, simply scout out a potential target that can fulfill our mission and report back to us. There are a few variables we need to lock down before we can proceed to the extraction stage. We need you to identify a suitable carrier and examine their shipping routes so we can decide on the best location for extraction. We also need to know what cargo is likely to be present and how accessible this would be. We will then analyse the data and put together a plan to complete the extraction," Mike said.

"Okay, that sounds logical, I'll get onto it," Armstrong tapped the table.

"But time is of the essence," Rowena reiterated.

Armstrong stood up, "I promise that you will have the data, and I promise there will be no more mistakes."

"Good, then we are all on the same page," Mike said.

Rowena stood up to shake Armstrong's hand, "Please try to avoid any more issues. I don't want to spend the rest of my days thinking about what could have been."

49

Manchester.Present-Day.

Steve gingerly walked toward the car only to see that Silverton was already sitting in it, the engine running, cigarette in hand. The hotel car park was emptying and Manchester started to spring into life.

"Someone looks a little fragile this morning," Silverton joked.

Steve opened the door and slumped into the front passenger seat. "Whiskey is the drink of the devil, I'm telling you. The fucking devil." Steve laughed.

They drove off toward the town centre.

"That may be the case, but we need to sharpen up. It seems our friend has been busy again," Silverton said and tossed his phone across to Steve. "Have a look at that."

Steve took a swig from a bottle of water and looked at the smartphone screen; he read the headline: *Paris Crash Latest: Man Held Amid Body Tampering Allegations in Morgue.* Steve fell silent while he read the report.

"How does he know all of this?" Steve quipped, "I mean, that level of detail..."

Silverton glanced over to Steve while he negotiated through the heavy morning traffic. "There must be a source from inside the hospital, maybe someone in the morgue, but whoever it is, they don't want to go on the record because he's written the report in general terms to avoid disclosing their identity; at least I would guess that's the case."

"They know the name of the hospital and that I injected three bodies. Surely, there's only a limited amount of people who would have access to that information?"

"Possibly, but once the rumour mill starts things can get out of hand and wind up in the hands of reporters like Mark." Silverton briefly looked across to Steve.

"You're not keen on journalists, are you?"

"Whatever gave you that idea?"

"Just a hunch."

They continued their journey into the town centre.

"And another thing, he's using phrases like *mounting speculation* and *the allegations also claim* so whoever the source is, I reckon they proofread this report to ensure their anonymity. Who knows, maybe they wrote it and Mark just put his name to it," Silverton added.

"You really don't like journalists," Steve laughed.

"They have their good points, but I'm always guarded about what I say around them, especially given the sensitivity of the work I do. It's too easy to find yourself misquoted, and before you know it, buried knee-deep in official communications from the men in suits upstairs."

Silverton drove down a back street near Deansgate in Manchester town centre. Pulling into the multi-story car park at the end of the street, he found a parking space on the ground floor.

"This is a bit open for you, isn't it? Normally we're driving down into the basement of some elaborate private car park and being rushed into a secret underground office."

Silverton looked across at Steve, "Not everything I do in this line of work is glamorous."

"You're in Manchester, that's glamorous enough for most people."

Silverton was in a hurry and Steve struggled to keep up with him. They walked quickly up a quiet side street just off Deansgate and through the entrance to an old red brick office building that sat proudly on the corner.

The faded red patterned carpet in the foyer was threadbare and had definitely seen better days. A lone security guard sat behind a desk reading a newspaper.

"We're here to see Mark Collins," Silverton produced his badge.

"Second floor, last door at the end of the corridor," the guard said without looking up from his newspaper.

"I see what you mean about this guy." Steve followed Silverton up the dimly lit, rickety old staircase. "If this office block is anything to go by, he's hardly at the top of his profession."

"That was my impression when I saw him on the M6 and it hasn't changed. He's an opportunist." Silverton paused outside the door to Mark's office, looked at the sign which read "M. Collins PR" and leaned against it whilst holding the brass door handle, twisting it slowly.

Silverton opened the door quickly, breezed into Mark's office, and stood directly opposite a smartly dressed man sitting behind a large, wooden desk.

"Who the fuck are you?" Mark stood up and demanded.

Steve shuffled into the office and stood behind Silverton.

"You must be Mark Collins." Silverton pulled out his badge to show Mark who was now leaning over his desk.

"I'll call the fucking police if you don't answer me. I'll ask you again, what's your fucking name?" Mark went to pick up his phone.

"Look at my badge before you do anything too hasty," Silverton calmly replied. "You may get done for wasting time."

"And why would that be?" Mark asked, sarcastically.

In the background, Steve was quietly snooping around the messy office. He made a mental note of the files that were half-open on the shelving unit.

"Hey! You!" Mark pointed at Steve, "Yes you! Just wait will you."

"As you can see, I'm a cop," Silverton replied.

"Whoa! Now just hang on a minute. If you're a cop, where's your warrant? You can't come barging in here flashing a badge!"

"Warrant for what? You doing something wrong here, Mark? You wouldn't be breaking the law, would you? A smart and respectable journalist like yourself wouldn't dare, would you? I mean that is what you do isn't it? Report the news?" Silverton raised his eyebrows.

"Let's not be too hasty, hey guys?" Mark raised and lowered his hands a few times then slowly returned to his seat. Steve stood next to Silverton having finished looking at the files on the shelving unit.

"Who's being hasty? Are you being hasty?" Silverton looked at Steve. "Because I'm not being hasty."

"What can I do for you fine gentlemen?" Mark grabbed a pen off his desk and started to play with it.

"Now isn't that better? I don't know about you Steve, but I'm starting to feel that we're getting somewhere. Now that we all seem to be friends, let us begin with the introductions. My name is Detective Roger Silverton, and this is my assistant, Steve Garner. And you must be Mark Collins."

"Pleased to meet you both, I think," Mark mumbled.

"That's over and done with. Are we okay to take a seat?" Silverton asked.

"Please do." Mark gestured to the pair of them.

Silverton and Steve both sat down opposite Mark.

"You're probably wondering what the hell we are doing here, isn't that right Mark?"

"Now that you mention it, yes. What the fuck are you doing in my office?" Mark placed the pen on the table in front of him and looked up.

"You see Mark, there're a lot of stories going around." Silverton stood up and walked around the small office as he continued, "Stories that, at first, seemed to pose a problem. Stories that appear to have been written by you."

"And what stories would they be?" Mark looked around the office trying to avoid eye contact.

Silverton took his seat again, but Steve stood up, walked over to the shelving unit, picked up a file, and threw it down on the desk. The file was labeled *M6 Paranormal Crash*. "These fucking stories," he said and sat back down.

Silverton grabbed the lever arch file and opened it. Inside there were pages and pages of articles from websites all over the world reporting on the crash.

"I must say you have been a very busy guy," Silverton said as he perused the pages, picking up and looking intently at the content.

"Look, I only reported on this because I was asked to do a favour." Mark's voice quivered.

"Don't give me that. You saw an opportunity to make a fortune and milked it for everything it was worth, isn't that right?" Silverton placed his hand on the pages in the file.

"I promise this is not what you think. I have witnesses. Sources." Mark stood up and threw his hands in the air.

"If that's the case, how come none of your so-called witnesses or sources have gone on the record?" Silverton held up one of the pages from the file in the direction of Mark's face.

"Because they were scared." Mark sat down again.

"Of what? Being sued for spouting a load of bullshit? I don't know how, or why, these people ever trusted you in the first place." Silverton carefully placed the page back in the file.

"Well, for one thing, they were probably scared of people like you turning up at their fucking door unannounced!" Mark was irritated.

"What's wrong with people like us?" Steve asked.

"What's wrong with you? Fucking hell man, first you burst into my office, then you sit there without so much as an invite and you wonder why someone may find that behaviour a bit fucking scary? I should have your fucking badge number and file a complaint!" Mark reached out to grab the file back from Silverton and snapped it shut.

"And what exactly would you base your complaint on?" Silverton leaned across the desk to eyeball Mark.

"Nothing. Now can we go back a few steps and start again?" Mark took a handkerchief from his shirt pocket and wiped his brow.

"Well, that depends," Silverton replied.

"On what?" Mark wrung his hands together.

"You see, I'm a betting man, Mark, and I bet that you got stuck into this by accident, if you excuse the pun, at first." Silverton leaned back in his chair.

"Yes. That's it. By accident, and I can get out of this just as fast." Mark nodded quickly.

"Why would you want to do that? I'm not an unreasonable man. I can understand that this story could make your career and possibly set you up for life, or at least help you afford some new offices with some decent carpets, not to mention some decent security guards. No, what I'm going to propose may seem counterintuitive to what you're expecting. You see, I don't want you to stop writing these reports, but I want you to write them with more facts, you know, so they reflect what's actually going on instead of some fantasy world you have concocted in that little head of yours," Silverton said and leaned forward to look at Mark, tapping the side of his head with his fingers.

"I don't get it." Mark's eyes opened wide and his grip loosened on the file.

"We have a problem," Silverton continued, "and that problem is that people appear to be one step ahead of us, so we want you, through the power of your wonderfully written reports, to help us get back on even footing."

"And what if I don't want to help you? What if I say no? What's in it for me?"

"You're right to ask that question," Steve said.

"I am a journalist, I ask questions. So, what is in it for me?" Mark replied.

"More than you could ever imagine, or probably believe," Steve said with a smirk.

Silverton got up and paced around the office again. "You've been almost correct with most of what you've written, however, in this game, almost isn't good enough. But that got me thinking, what would happen if you had all the facts. What impact would that have, given what you've managed to create?" Silverton stood at the desk, reached across to the file, and shuffled through the pages.

"Nothing can be one-hundred percent correct."

"It can if you have the right witnesses," Silverton said.

"Such as who?" Mark scratched his head.

424

"This man." Silverton gestured toward Steve.

Mark recoiled back and looked at Steve.

"This man is one of your new star witnesses, and between us, we can furnish you with more facts than you could probably cope with. But I guarantee you that your reports will be one hundred percent accurate." Silverton sat down, rested his arms on the desk, and clasped his hands together.

"And what if I say no?"

"That's fine. We simply get up and leave and offer our testimonies to someone who will appreciate the chance to be involved in breaking the biggest news story in the world," Silverton said.

"Let's not be hasty," Mark said and leaned back in his chair.

"There's that word again," Silverton said and looked at Steve. "From that, do I gather you're ready to listen to the voice of reason?"

"What exactly did you have in mind?" Mark put his elbows on the desk, clasped his hands together, and confidently leaned forward to look Silverton square in the eye.

"First, you need to understand a little bit more about the background to all of this. I need you to suspend your disbelief in all that you think you know as this may come as a shock."

"After what I've been told so far that shouldn't be too difficult." Mark smiled at Silverton.

Silverton launched into a long explanation about the incidents on the M6 and in Paris and tried to give Mark as much background information as possible without overplaying the situation. "You see, Steve is from the future, sent back in time to stop someone going by the name of Terence Armstrong from taking things into the future."

"Things? What kind of things?" Mark asked.

"That's not so important right now, but what is important is that you are at the centre of what is possibly the biggest story in the world."

"And where do you fit in?" Mark picked up the pen again.

"Think of me as some sort of guardian angel, here to help Steve carry out his mission."

"So let me get this straight, this man – Steve – is from the future, and he's been sent back to stop this Armstrong chap from smuggling stuff into the future and you're like some sort of good cop vigilante trying to help his cause?" Mark put down the pen and tapped his fingers on the table.

"That's about it I guess," Silverton said and sat back in the chair.

"But like all good stories, the baddies keep trying to steal things they shouldn't and you lot are a bit slow, so you keep getting caught up in incidents like the one on the M6 and the one in Paris."

"It's a simplified version but that's about it, yes," Silverton confirmed.

"And in Paris Steve traveled through time to the exact location where the bodies were stored, but got caught injecting the bodies with some form of compound to deceive the pathologist into thinking the bodies were from this time, and not from the future...am I still on track?" Mark asked.

"Yes, you are, your investigations were quite accurate in some ways," Silverton replied.

"I'm a journalist, my job is to try and be as accurate as I can."

"And given what you knew, you've done a good job so far," Silverton nodded.

"That's it then, this man proves that time travel is possible, and I'm supposed to write reports based on his testimony and put my name to them?" Mark resumed tapping the desk with his fingers.

"That's about the gist of it. You catch on quickly," Silverton nodded.

Mark stood up and held out his hand to shake Silverton's. "Gentlemen, it's been nice meeting you but I'm sure there's someone out there who is better positioned to help you than I am."

"Hang on, why the sudden change of heart? We were doing so well," Silverton said, remaining in his chair.

"Unless I'm very much mistaken, you guys belong in the nearest psychiatric unit." Mark looked at his watch. "As it happens, I have another appointment, so I need to get moving. It's been a pleasure, but as I said, I'm not the right man for you guys."

"Nothing we've said today has contradicted your reports. They have corroborated them, so what's the problem? Are you scared of the truth?" Steve asked.

"I'm not scared of many things. However much of what you've said today is going to be hard, even impossible, to explain without being certified as insane." Mark slumped back into his large, leather chair and took a deep breath.

"What about the earlier reports? How do you account for them, or was it a case of turning a blind eye to the truth because it suited you at the time?" Steve asked.

"I don't know. Maybe I was...oh, shit, who knows?" Mark shook his head and looked down at the open file on his desk.

"I think you saw there was a quick buck to be made," Silverton suggested.

"I'm a journalist, money isn't my primary motive," Mark snapped back.

"Then what was your primary motive?" Steve asked.

"I don't know, I did it because..." Mark ran out of words.

"We're not going to pretend this will be easy...in fact, we know this will be a long and difficult road," Silverton spoke softly.

"You got that right." Mark laughed out loud.

"We won't lead you astray. You'll have access to all the facts, and the chance to break one of the biggest stories of your career. Think of the opportunities that could bring you," Silverton said and watched as Mark continued to read the headline on the page in the file. Silverton continued, "We need to stop these people once and for all, and enhancing the power of the media is just one of the ways we can do this. That's why we want to work with you. And it makes sense because you're halfway there already."

"The pen is mightier than the sword, then?" Mark picked up the pen on his desk. "What makes you think your plan will work?"

"You have to trust me on that one," Silverton said.

Mark pushed the pen along the desk. "You ask a lot."

Silverton took a deep breath. "I know, but any attack on Armstrong via media exposure will help disturb his operations and bring down his network. Without that network he has nothing; no contacts, no inside information and therefore no access to any resources."

"And you think media coverage will do this?" Mark placed the pen back in his desktop organiser.

"Yes. We need to smoke him out. By utilising your skills in conjunction with our own operations we stand a better chance of achieving this. So far, he's managed to stay under the radar, even when things have gone wrong, as in China. But if we can expose his operations in a way that dissuades others from doing business with him, that will slow him down, possibly make him try other untested channels, make him vulnerable and open to making mistakes. That's when we pounce and put a stop to all of this," Silverton said.

"What happened in China?" Mark wanted to know.

"Let's just say that things didn't go to plan," Steve said.

"What things?" Mark persisted. "I think I should know who I'm dealing with here."

"An entire village was destroyed when his operatives went in and tried to access a mine. Giant sinkholes popped up all over the village until it was eventually destroyed," Steve replied.

"I don't recall reading about that, when did it happen?"

"Recently, but due to the sensitive nature of the incident it was, shall we say, smoothed over by official channels," Silverton said.

"To pull off a stunt like that in a country like China takes a lot of muscle. How dangerous is this Armstrong character?" Mark sat bolt upright.

"He has a lot of power but he's too clever to show his hand in public. We think the media is one possible route we can exploit to blow his cover because it will be difficult for him to defend himself against that kind of public onslaught."

"Hang on. With everything that you claim to have at your disposal, you think a few reports will stand a better chance of stopping this guy?" Mark ran his hands through his hair.

"We've tried to deploy other tactics," Silverton said.

"Such as?"

"Let's just say that things didn't go to plan."

Mark turned his chair around to look out of the office window. "And you can promise I'll be the only one who'll have access to this information?"

"I promise you," Silverton replied.

"And you're not going to wipe my memory or something stupid like that after you've finished with me?" Mark asked.

"Why would we do that?" Silverton asked.

"I don't know. I'm just covering all the bases, because so far today, I've met someone who claims to be a time traveler who is hunting a fugitive from the future and a cop who claims to be some sort of guardian angel. You can see how these things kind of escalate from there," Mark replied.

"To be clear, there will be no wiping of memories or anything else for that matter. All we want to do is work together with you to use the media as a way to stop this man and his operations. Once we achieve our goal we will disappear into the background. You won't know we were ever here."

"And you can promise that?" Mark pointed at Silverton.

"Absolutely. Give me one good reason why I would want to fuck this up?" Silverton asked.

"Which reminds me, exactly which police station are you based at?" Mark asked Silverton.

"I'm part of a special unit," Silverton looked down at the desk.

"How special?"

"It's classified," Silverton replied.

"Of course, it is. And let me guess, UFOs is it? Little green men maybe?" Mark smiled.

"Like I said, it's classified." Silverton stood firm. "But you will be well-protected, I can assure you of that."

"Then I guess I would be a fool to turn this opportunity down." Mark looked down at the file and rubbed his hands together.

Steve stood up and walked over to one of the large office windows to look out across the city.

Silverton grabbed the file and started to flick through the pages, looking at all the websites that had covered Mark's story, "Impressive," he said. "You cracked Russia with this shit."

"They know how to spot a well-written report," Mark laughed.

"And India, as well. In fact, looking at these pages," Silverton continued working his way through the file, "there are very few countries that haven't covered this story. I am impressed."

"I like to think I'm good at my job, and that is possibly vindicated by just how much coverage my reports have gained," Mark said and smirked back at Silverton.

"I'll say this, you certainly know how to attract attention to your reports," Silverton said and continued to flick through the pages in the file.

Steve stared at a quiet back road. "Hey guys, I don't wish to break up this love in but we appear to have some company outside."

Outside on the road, four men stood in a row, each was wearing a dark suit, a trilby hat and each held a black briefcase. Steve thought they looked out of place. "What the fuck are they doing?" He muttered to himself.

Steve watched while the four men held their briefcases out in front of them. "This is just too weird. I'm going to check this out."

"Hang on a minute, I'll come with you," Silverton said. He closed the file and stood up but it was too late.

Steve quickly strode out of the office. He descended the tatty staircase, walked swiftly past the security guard, and opened the door leading out to the street.

The men now stood in a circular formation; in the middle of all this, Steve saw his ex-wife Janine. She was writhing in agony, her face contorted with fear, and her body moving erratically. Steve looked on in horror. He was rigid, momentarily transfixed by what he saw. Janine reached out her hand, beckoning for help. It looked to him like she was being given an electric shock.

"Help…me..." Janine somehow managed to say, briefly glaring into Steve's eyes while shaking her head in anguish.

Steve ran toward the circle, he had to get to Janine.

Silverton charged out of the door behind him. "Steve, no—"

Steve reached out to grab Janine, but as he did, her body dissolved into the thin air, pixel by pixel. Steve fell to the ground as the briefcases glowed bright white and connected to form a barrier, trapping Steve inside. The men's faces were cold and expressionless, their features synthetic. Instinct kicked in. Steve tried to stand up but lost his balance; it felt like the ground was moving beneath his feet.

Silverton was on the outside screaming at Steve, but the circle of blinding light was disorientating him as it spun around.

Steve looked up. The birds overhead were motionless. He struggled to take a breath, his lungs felt compressed, the onset of claustrophobia started to take its toll. Darkness edged his vision as he collapsed back to the ground.

50

Somewhere in the late 26th Century.

"Think Steve…think."
"I mean your real past…not this past."
"Think Steve…think."
"I mean your real past…not this past."
"Think…"

The words kept repeating, imprinting themselves into Steve's mind. Steve's heart was thumping so hard he feared it would burst through his chest.

The darkness subsided and Steve was standing alone, a spectator looking on at the unfolding carnage.

Steve was confronted by the sight of a town on fire. He scanned from left to right and noticed that people were sitting on the ground in circles, calm, as if they accepted their fate. The flames raced through the buildings. A thin, translucent shield surrounded the town, preventing the flames from spreading and the people from escaping. This was all too familiar.

Steve was terrified by what he saw, but he could do nothing to prevent death in this place. Seeing Kallyuke and Sayssac in the distance, he let out a scream but no noise came from his mouth. He started to run toward them, each step moving him inexorably closer as he battled the overwhelming heat. He let out another scream but once again no sound came out.

The air cut through his lungs, the burning sensation stopped him in his tracks, his heart was racing, and his vision blurred. Steve doubled over and took huge gasps of air into his lungs. He looked up at Kallyuke and Sayssac. He was compelled to continue advancing toward them but his legs wouldn't carry him further. He slumped to the ground on his knees and threw his arms up in the air in frustration.

Then silence descended.

Steve could just about make out their conversation.

He saw Kallyuke glance across at Sayssac, who stood at a safe distance watching the town burn to the ground. "We had to find a humane way to control the infected. This advanced form of hypoxia is the best way to help them pass on. They feel no pain, only harmony with their surroundings, which is why, as you can see, they don't fight this. There is no struggle, only understanding."

People in biohazard suits ran through the shields that prevented the flames from spreading beyond the quarantine zone and passed Steve as if he wasn't there. Their suits contained a passkey that enabled them to pass through the shields unhindered. They ran around frantically searching. Steve noticed that some walked back from the town holding babies in their arms; the babies were screaming.

"This is murder," Sayssac turned and looked away from the town.

"We have the right to protect our way of life," Kallyuke replied.

"Then you are saying you have the right to murder in the name of that cause," Sayssac reiterated.

"No, we don't…but let us be clear, this is the only way to control the spread of the virus and preserve what is left on the planet for those who have a future, and it is the only way to protect our way of life. There is no other choice." Kallyuke looked on as people collapsed to the ground and became engulfed in the flames.

A single tear ran down Sayssac's cheek as he watched the men in biohazard suits walk past him.

Steve reached out to try and grab one of the men in the suits but his hand wafted through their legs without making any contact.

Kallyuke turned and walked toward the awaiting shuttle, the doors were open and people in biohazard suits were leaving it to go back into the zone.

Steve felt a tingling sensation in his stomach. He reached down to probe his abdomen with his fingers. The sensation continued until he was involuntarily propelled toward the shuttle.

Darkness descended as he approached the shuttle and the next thing he knew he was standing in the middle of the walkway inside the craft.

Kallyuke strode into the shuttle, walked through Steve, and was greeted by one of the men who had now removed the hood of his suit.

"How many?" he shouted to the man.

"Twenty-six…but that will probably be all, the fire has taken control of the zone," the man replied.

"Pull your men out. We leave in three minutes," Kallyuke barked his orders.

Steve felt the tingling sensation return and found himself standing in the middle of a bright, white room, at the front of which was a long, dark desk.

Kallyuke walked in and shook the hand of the man standing behind the desk. "Eldon, I'm trusting you that this plan will work."

Eldon took a step toward Kallyuke. "It will, you have my assurance. We have tracked suitable orphanages that are strategically placed around the world. They are receptive to receiving babies that have no parents. They will put in place all the required paperwork with the authorities to ensure they are placed in good homes. But remember, this is the 1970s, so I've come up with a solution to keep track of their progress that won't arouse any suspicions."

"Oh really? And what's that?" Kallyuke asked.

Eldon pulled something out of a brown case on the desk. "Since we cannot hijack their internet to track them."

"Yes, I'm aware of that."

"We're going to use these tiny RFID tags," Eldon said and held up a tiny black rectangular object between his thumb and index finger. "They are robust, and we can access them throughout the ensuing years because the tracking tech used to monitor them is fairly stable."

"Excellent," Kallyuke clasped his hands together.

"There are going to be risks, though."

"Such as?" Kallyuke asked.

"Well, for example, there are inherent risks for the twenty-six just by living in this time. There is disease for example."

"We've taken care of that."

"What, everything?"

"Everything that we are aware of. We've even taken steps to protect them from diseases that haven't been discovered in their time."

"Well let's just hope they don't have too many ailments that require treatment. I would hate for a medical team from that era to accidentally discover a trace of something we've used to protect them from a disease that doesn't exist yet or track these little tags; that could be very awkward," Eldon looked at the RFID tag.

"That is not something we need to worry about now though, is it?" Kallyuke shook Eldon's hand and left the room.

Eldon sat at his desk staring at the RFID tag. He then placed the tag back in the brown case, grabbed a pen, and started to draw lines onto the white wall behind him. Each line represented a possible outcome in time for a particular conclusion.

One line showed that death at the start would equal failure at the end. Another hypothesised that a paradox halfway through could lead to destruction, and another crossed between the two. Eldon became impatient with himself and scribbled over them all. "I'm being silly," he said to himself.

51

Manchester.Present-Day.

Steve was slumped across his desk, half asleep. A picture of Janine and Tanya stood proudly on the corner of the desk, placed next to the computer screen. His keyboard was partially obscured by his arms which supported his resting head. The open-plan office was only saved by the screens that separated him from the rest of his colleagues; useful for when he wanted a quiet nap.

"Will you get on with some work instead of falling asleep at your desk, please? I need those figures for the audit team in an hour. The head of finance wants to review the balance sheet. I need your costs and expenditure forecasts for the next quarter along with any variables such as consumables. I mean, you've had all day to do this!" Tina shouted at Steve.

"Sorry Tina, of course," Steve said as he stirred from his slumber.

Where the fuck am I? Steve thought to himself as he typed the password into his computer.

He booted up the mail client, opened the search box, and typed the name Charley Sandford...nothing. He tried it again, this time searching files across the computer...still nothing.

Steve rubbed the palm of his hand in a desperate search for evidence of the CCS device; nothing.

"This can't be happening!" Steve smacked the keyboard with both hands.

The phone rang, Steve looked puzzled but picked it up. It was his wife Janine.

"What time are you home tonight?" Janine asked.

"Pardon?" Steve's mind was a blur of memories and questions.

"You heard me, what time are you home? We have an issue with Tanya that we need to discuss," Janine spoke quickly.

"What issue?" Steve tried to sound interested, meanwhile, he opened the spreadsheet on his computer and searched for the balance sheet file.

"She's been caught smoking at school," Janine stated.

"Really?" Steve typed some figures into the balance sheet.

Janine could hear this in the background. "At least sound like you're interested."

"Look I've got to go. This report is due in an hour…" Steve was racing through the spreadsheet.

"That's fine, but we need to talk tonight, I think Tanya is craving a bit more time with you, after all, you are her father," Janine said.

A flock of pigeons swooped past Steve's window. "I know! You don't need to lecture me on parenthood. It's been hectic here recently."

"Just remember that you have a family at home and that work is not everything," Janine said.

"I know, and I will be home as soon as I can, but I've got to go now." Steve kept typing away in the background while he spoke.

"Don't be home late," Janine said and then hung up the phone.

Steve placed the phone back on the receiver and continued typing in the spreadsheet. He pulled a file from one of the plastic trays on the desk and opened it up to review the information on the pages.

"I'm guessing you might need a coffee," Tina said, placing the warm drink on his desk and sitting on the chair next to Steve.

"That's probably the understatement of the day," Steve said, grabbed the coffee, and took a large gulp.

Tina smiled and then pointed at one of the cells on the spreadsheet. "Are you sure this is correct?"

Steve frowned at Tina. "Of course, it is."

"Are you sure?" she continued to question him. "I don't want to suggest that you had a lunchtime drink or anything, but those figures seem to overstate some of the projected miscellaneous expenses we can expect to see from the Paris contract in the coming months."

"Have you been to Paris?" Steve asked.

"Not recently, have you?" Tina replied.

Steve paused for a moment, "I think so," he replied.

"What do you mean you think so? Either you have or you haven't. Let me guess, a spot of lunchtime drinking again, was it?" Tina shook her head slowly and looked down.

"Forget it. Let me get on with these figures so you have them in time," Steve said, quickly tapping on the keyboard.

"Okay, okay! God, someone's a bit touchy aren't they?" Tina held her hands up to calm the situation.

"I need to get on with this, and you're not helping," Steve spat.

"Subtle as a brick, as you always are," Tina rebutted and then pointed to another part of the spreadsheet open on Steve's computer screen. "Can you look at the entries on line 26 by the way? I don't think they're correct."

"What did you just say?" Steve asked.

"Do I have to repeat everything today? I said that line 26 on the spreadsheet doesn't seem to tie up correctly and would you look at it please?"

"Line 26?" Steve repeated.

"Obviously, that lunchtime nap has affected your hearing as well, yes, line 26," Tina said.

"Okay," Steve replied.

" Okay, line 26," she said, still pointing to the screen. "Line 26," she repeated.

Steve reached over to pull Tina's hand away from the screen so he could see what she meant but she tried to resist.

Steve turned to look at her. "What are you doing?" he asked.

"Line 26," she repeated.

"What are you doing?" Steve asked again.

Tina got to her feet, still repeating the words *Line 26*. She slowly walked toward the large office window. She started to slur her words and turned around to look at Steve.

"What's wrong with you?" Steve looked on in horror at Tina's face.

"Line 26," came the reply.

Tina's eyes sank into their sockets and her cheekbones became pronounced. Her skin pulled taut onto them. Her gums receded, exposing the roots of her teeth and her jaw bone began sticking out through the skin. It was as if someone was pulling her skin from the back of her head.

She continued to try and utter the words but it was clear this was becoming harder. The taught skin on her skull restricted any movement. She lifted her arm and touched Steve on the chest with her outstretched index finger. Sparks flew out of her finger and Steve was flung backward, he hit his head against one of the cloth-covered partitions that lined his little space and was knocked unconscious.

***

Steve awoke slowly, rubbing his eyes to focus on what he saw.

"It's your turn, don't be a spoilsport!"

"Yes Stevie, your turn!"

"Come on, play the game, you're it!"

Steve was standing in the safety of the garden of the leafy Mancunian house owned by his parents, John and Susan.

"You've been dead for years," Steve whispered to himself.

"What was that? Oh, come on now, it's your turn so get ready," John placed the blindfold over Steve's eyes and started to spin him around.

"Everybody get ready!" Susan shouted to the other kids. John finished spinning Steve around seeing that he was disorientated enough.

Steve walked around the large garden, while the other kids were shouting at him, confusing him further in his quest for a victim. His outstretched arms made contact with someone, or so he thought…

***

He took off his blindfold.

The classroom was empty, save for Steve and his teacher who stood next to the blackboard, peering over his glasses back at Steve who sat at his desk.

"When I asked you to define Newton's third law of physics, I didn't expect such a detailed and extravagant answer," Mr Thompson said, pointing to the diagram that Steve had drawn on the blackboard.

"When exactly did you study this? We haven't touched on the third law yet, but due to your appetite for science, I thought you may as well give it a go so I could at least correct you in front of the class and help you understand it." Mr Thompson was the lead science teacher at the school and had been for many years.

"I don't know, it just happened," Steve looked wide-eyed at the blackboard.

"Eleven-year-old boys in their first year of secondary school seldom display such knowledge and I won't stand for being ridiculed in front of my own classroom. Do I make myself clear?" Mr Thompson began vigorously wiping the blackboard clean of Steve's diagram. "Next time I ask you to explain something, have the decency to at least ensure you don't come across as a know-it-all. People don't like know-it-alls, Master Garner. Do you understand?"

"Yes sir."

"Now you will do detention for the rest of the week…"

"But sir—"

"No buts, you will do detention for the rest of the week, and you will spend that time doing nothing, and I can assure you that doing nothing for an hour will feel like an eternity. Now, you may go…"

Steve picked up his school bag and left the classroom.

Mr Thompson looked at the smudged-out blackboard just as Valerie, a colleague, entered the classroom and looked at the board. "Has he been causing you problems again?" she asked.

"I don't know what is up with the boy, he is either spending all his time studying, which is not normal or healthy for a child of his age, or he really is that bright," Mr Thompson replied.

"Don't be so hard on him. The school could do with more students like him championing the quality of teaching we provide. We need all the funding we can attract in these hard times and he's a great vindication of your teaching methods. He's a very bright kid," Valerie replied.

"Bright maybe, but this one appears to be a little too bright, the rest of the students can't keep up with him. It's having a demotivating effect on them."

"Then the rest of the students will just have to up their game, won't they?" Valerie looked at the blackboard.

Steve walked down the busy school corridor and bumped into another kid. "IT!" the boy inexplicably shouted at Steve and then ran.

***

Steve found himself standing amongst a small gathering of people all dressed in black suits.

"I'm so sorry for your loss," the man who stood next to Steve said.

Steve looked down at the freshly dug graves of his parents.

"Thank you, Adrian. I still feel numb." They slowly departed the scene for the awaiting funeral cortege.

"What will you do with the house?" Adrian asked.

"I haven't thought about it. I just met this woman, fantastic woman, and was just starting to feel human again after the past few months then this happens," Steve got into the car with his friend, Adrian.

"What was it?" Adrian asked. "What did the doctors conclude about your illness?"

"They thought it was viral. They did so many tests but I don't think they had any idea what was wrong with me. Strange thing is, I felt fine for the last month I was in hospital but they refused to let me out, they just kept doing test after test, it was weird. Then this."

"Such a waste. I hope that other driver rots in hell for what they did."

"That's if they ever find them. I've been told it was a stolen car," Steve said and let out a long sigh.

Their car approached the local pub.

"There's simply no justice anymore; no justice at all," Adrian said.

"Anyway, it's time to put on a brave face and try to get through this, pal. Thanks for coming in the lead car with me," Steve said and shook Adrian's hand.

"You're my friend, and friends stick together, besides, the first round is on you so I wanted to stick close to get my order in," Adrian chuckled.

"Oh, I see!" Steve nodded and smiled.

The pub was full of friends and family, all dressed in black and speaking quietly amongst each other after what had been a very touching service.

Steve reached out to shake the hand of one of his father's greatest friends, Ash Goldsmith. "Thank you for helping out with all the arrangements, I couldn't have done this without you."

"He was like a brother to me, one of the best. I'd do anything for him, and your mother…still can't believe they're gone…look, if you need a friend to talk with, or just want a beer down at the pub, I'm here for you. Ash vigorously shook Steve's hand and they both fought back the tears.

***

Steve was immediately transported to another place. Castlefield, Manchester.

He could hear the voices in the background, kids teasing him, the game of Blind Man's Bluff continued in his mind.

"Are you going to drink that beer or are you just going to watch it get warm?" Adrian asked.

Steve looked around to check his surroundings, they were in a crowded bar near the Castlefield lock. The pair of them stood outside in the sun, beers on the table and the debate raged on about the weekend's football results.

"Anyway, have you got a new woman in your life yet?" Adrian asked.

"Please, give me a chance mate. The ink has barely dried on the divorce papers." Steve tried to gulp down some of his beer.

"Exactly. And that's why you need to be out there, giving it your all. You're a single guy now, don't waste your time thinking about what might have been. You need to look to the future." Adrian finished his beer. "Do you fancy another one?"

"On a school night? No, I'll just feel like shit in the morning," Steve said and slowly sipped his beer.

"Jesus, man, you need to lighten up. You can't go on like this. You're a successful guy, living in the big city, you need to get out there and try a bit," Adrian said and slammed his empty beer glass on the table.

"Look, maybe another night, eh? I need to get home pal, you stay and have another one and I'll catch you soon, okay?" Steve finished his beer and grabbed his briefcase.

"So much for the single life…yeah pal, see you soon, you go easy, okay?" Adrian slowly scratched his head. He sat and watched Steve walk off into the distance on the canal-side footpath.

Steve wasn't drunk, but he felt queasy. He walked along the tight footpath that ran alongside the canal; he passed an elderly woman who noticed he was in discomfort.

"You okay, love?" she turned and said to Steve.

"I'm fine thank you, maybe just a bit tired," he said and stopped to look at her.

Steve looked down to the palm of his hand and began to sway. He then turned around to see that the woman had already disappeared. He looked up at the skyline, it shuddered in front of him, buildings came in and out of focus as they swayed in front of his eyes. He held onto the railings and looked along the path which ran under a bridge to try and regain a sense of balance, but it was no use; he couldn't stop swaying.

His eyes were, once again, strangely attracted to the buildings that shook and then were replaced by the scorching blue sky. He blinked, squeezing his eyelids tightly together, and then re-opened them to see that the buildings had returned. He then fell to the floor.

***

Bang. Bang. Bang.

Steve shook his head to try and regain consciousness. He was in his office again, looking out the window. The glass shattered as the repeated banging sound returned. He could just about make out someone standing in front of him, holding a gun; but his office was on the third floor; how could this be happening?

Live. Die. Extract. DNA. Quarantine. Manchester. Santa Monica. London. Charley. Kallyuke. Silverton. Taxi. Paris. Timeline. CCS. Morgue. Collins. Sayssac. Anton. Helen. FCA. Roy.

Steve's mind was torturing him. Words and images relentlessly bombarded his vision.

"Get out of there! Get out of there!"

Once again, Steve thought he heard the muffled shouting of someone outside the office window. But that wasn't possible because he knew that his office was on the third floor.

Janine. M6. Death. Janine. Tanya. Eiffel Tower. Diamonds. Metro. China. Armstrong. Think. Think. Think. Think. The Shard. Anton. Helen. Bastille. UFO. Diversion. The train. The train. The train.

"Get out of there!"

Bang. Bang. Bang.

The repetition of sound, the dull thudding, suddenly brought Steve out of the clouded world he was being seduced into.

He slowly got to his feet, only to witness sections of the office peeling off into the bright blue sky. The imposing shape of the Hilton Hotel loomed large in his vision. The roof of his office was torn off chunk by chunk and dissolved into a million pixels. The walls, the desks, the floor all followed as they dissolved, swirling into the blue sky and dissipating into the nothingness that now surrounded Steve.

Steve was cold, shaking, and left on the ground in the middle of the quiet road just off Deansgate, Manchester. The quarantine zone was destroyed.

Silverton walked up to Steve and held out a hand to help pull him to his feet, "I thought we'd lost you."

Mark stood in the background, his mouth agape.

"Where was I?" Steve slowly mumbled.

"You don't know?" Silverton asked.

"I was…I was…wait, all of this, none of this…" Steve looked around at the street. "Where have they gone?" Steve pointed to where the men in suits were last standing.

"Gone. They just disappeared into the sky," Silverton replied.

"How long was I in this thing?" Steve asked as he rubbed his eyes.

"Minutes."

"I was in my office…all of this…I was at home…my parents…" a tear appeared in Steve's eye and he looked at Silverton. "What the hell just happened to me?"

"Someone somewhere doesn't want you alive," Silverton said and looked at the sky.

"What do you mean?" Steve grabbed Silverton's arm to stop him from walking toward Mark's office.

"I've never seen one, only heard about them, but that looked like a quarantine zone to me."

"I saw it…Silverton, I saw it…"

448

"You saw what?" Silverton stopped and turned back to look at Steve.

"I saw the future…" Steve looked at his surroundings.

"You've seen the future, many times Steve."

"No, I've seen the future, I know how this happened, all of this," Steve pointed to his surroundings.

"All of what?"

Mark strode up to them both. "I'm sorry, but I'm out. You seem like decent people but whatever the fuck just happened, was not my idea of fun…whatever you guys are caught up in is clearly beyond my humble talents so I suggest…" Mark spoke nervously.

"Have you finished?" Silverton interrupted.

"I'm finished, yeah. I'm not doing this. You need someone with more—"

"Balls?" Silverton butted in. "Is that what you are suggesting? Let me tell you how this is going to roll out, to avoid any unnecessary confusion. You are Mark Collins, and you are our mouthpiece into the world of the written word. You cannot back out, at any point, if you do then I can assure you that there are places I can send you that will take you off the radar for the rest of your life, and without any need for an arrest warrant or a trial. Do I make myself clear?"

Mark took a deep breath. "Perfectly."

"Now stop worrying. I've promised we will protect you, and that is what we shall do. Now we're going to take a trip to the countryside as part of my commitment to honour that promise."

"What's in the countryside?" Mark asked.

"There's a secure facility that I have access to. It will keep us safe from the goon squad," Silverton replied.

"Do I get to come back?" Mark tentatively asked.

"Of course you do, this isn't the mafia," Silverton said while beckoning them to follow him to the car park. "Now let's go before anything else happens."

"I've heard of people like you," Mark said as he kept up with Silverton and Steve.

"People like me?" Silverton asked.

"People who function above the law."

"Well for once, just be grateful that people like me are on your side."

"Ha! That's fine then."

Silverton stopped and turned to Mark. "Just remember, forget anything you know or have read about those so-called people you speak of, we're far worse than them."

"Oh great, why do I get the feeling that this is all a big mistake?"

"Quit whining and let's get to the car. This place is too open for my liking." Silverton took the lead as they made their way to the car park.

The three men jumped in the car and left for the countryside.

52

Cheshire.Present-Day.

"It was so real," Steve spoke quietly as they headed into the Cheshire countryside.

"What did you see?" Silverton asked.

"Life. Then death. Then I saw how this all came about. It was real, too real." Steve turned his head and closed his eyes.

"And you can be sure of that?" Silverton's hands tightened around the steering wheel.

"I don't want to talk about it right now, but yes, it was real," Steve said and slumped back into the seat.

They continued the journey in silence. Silverton turned into the entrance of a nuclear bunker in the leafy Cheshire countryside.

"What are we doing here?" Mark asked. "I mean, this place is decommissioned isn't it?"

Silverton's car drove into the back compound of the bunker and parked in a reserved place next to a nondescript black door that led into the facility.

"Ninety percent of it is very much decommissioned, however, ten percent of it is ready for action and fit for purpose. That part is out of bounds to the public," Silverton said.

"What type of action?" Mark leaned forward in between the two front seats and looked at Silverton.

"It's not really for me to say, but there are certain facilities here that are unique to the area, and rather than build another facility, it was agreed to keep it on standby, should it ever be required," Silverton replied while they all got out of the car.

Silverton used a pass card to open the black door.

"That's a politician's answer," Mark said.

Silverton offered no reply. They walked in silence down three flights of concrete stairs and then along a corridor that led them to a small office.

"Is this part of the ten percent then?" Steve asked.

"Yes. We are completely segregated from the public, and this location is outfitted with all latest comms and intel tech that may be required in the event of an emergency."

"You people don't mess around do you?" Mark looked around the poky room.

"Coffee?" Silverton walked over to the coffee machine; Steve and Mark nodded their approval.

The office had a stale smell, reminiscent of a place that hadn't been used for a long time. It was sparsely equipped with a small desk, plain wooden chairs, and a coffee machine that was on another table set against the wall. The fluorescent lights lit the room adequately, even if they were a tad harsh on the eyes.

"Is this part of your network of facilities or is it military?" Mark asked.

"You ask a lot of questions," Silverton waited for the coffee machine to boil.

"I'm a journalist, wouldn't you expect me to do that?" Mark tilted his head and threw his hands out.

"I guess you're right. Anyway, I have clearance to use the facility, but in the event of an emergency, the military will have priority access." Silverton returned to the small desk with three coffees. "Enough about this place, we need to push on."

"I couldn't agree more," Steve said.

They all took a seat around the desk. Silverton faced both Mark and Steve. The fluorescent light shone off the top of his head. He took out a cigarette, placed it in his mouth, and lit up.

"Do you have to smoke in here? I mean, there are laws." Mark frowned.

"Show me where you see a No Fucking Smoking sign." Silverton wafted the lit cigarette around like a wand and the smoke ebbed and flowed into the room.

"Okay, I get the point." Mark sat back in the chair and crossed his legs.

"So, Mark, you know our motive for bringing you here. We want to help you embellish these reports with facts that will make them far more accurate than they currently are, and also help us to flush out our friend in London, or wherever he may be," Silverton spoke first.

"And you're prepared to confirm these facts?" Mark asked.

"Where I can, yes, but I don't want you going over the top. We still want to control what you send out there, otherwise, we could find ourselves connecting with the wrong people," Silverton said.

"Such as?"

"Well, we don't want fanatical UFO types trying to turn this into something it isn't. We simply want to do our job and then terminate this relationship."

"Terminate sounds like a fairly terminal word, is that me…you're referring to me?" Mark grabbed his coffee and started to tap the cup with his fingers, he quickly glanced over his shoulder. He was in the middle of nowhere and no one would know, or probably care, if he went missing.

"Nothing like that, so don't get any crazy ideas. It was Steve who had the original idea of coming to you. I had mixed feelings about it. But having studied your work to date, I've got an idea that may help us take the sting out of recent events," Silverton said and then paused to drink some coffee.

"You know, as a journalist, I will need to know everything…and I mean everything."

"You already know too much, enough to get both you and us into a lot of heat. We have to be careful about how much we feed you," Steve said and looked Mark up and down.

"Maybe that's the case, but I can't just write this stuff…" Mark replied.

"You appear to have done well so far, and that's without our help," Steve said, glaring at Mark with wide-open eyes.

"We're not here to argue." Silverton placed his elbows on the table. "We're here to achieve a clear goal – nailing Armstrong. But there's one thing we need to do, and with your help, Mark, I think we can achieve it."

"Oh, and how can I do that?" Mark placed his elbows on the table and rested his chin on his hands.

"We need to fake the arrest of Steve, ensure it is publicly known that he was captured and that he's the chief suspect," Silverton said and sat back in the chair, crossing his legs.

"Chief suspect of what exactly?" Mark enquired.

"The main cause of the incidents on the M6 motorway and in Paris."

Mark stood up and stretched his legs. Maybe it was a nervous reaction to the fact that this was happening, that it was unfolding right in front of him and he was actually part of it. He sat back down again.

" So, you want to manufacture this in the media? This arrest you're speaking of?"

"Exactly." Silverton took a drag on his cigarette and placed it in the ashtray on the corner of the table.

"Why do we want to do this?" Steve asked, "And why haven't you discussed this with me?"

"First, Kallyuke is the one I answer to. Second, I've only just thought of it as a solution to an issue that has been bugging me since London," Silverton said to Steve.

"But why an arrest?" Steve asked.

"You have the Gendarme Nationale on your tail, and you are probably on the radar of the very people we are trying to oust from this time. Whereas before, you were completely unknown to them, your cover is most likely blown. After the incident in London, they will undoubtedly be searching for someone that fits your description. They will use all the data they have to find out more about you, so they can track you down. Who knows, maybe they were behind the attempt earlier today," Silverton said and threw his hands in the air.

"Well, if it wasn't them, who else do you think it could be?" Steve asked.

"I don't know. I'm struggling to work out who would have access to that kind of technology unless it was transported back," Silverton said.

"How do you know about these quarantine zones?" Steve drew an imaginary circle with his finger on the table.

"I was informed about them and what they can do. They are tremendously powerful and the fear is that people may try to bring them back to this time to, how can I put it, effect things…it looks like they may have just done exactly that."

"Who told you?" Steve asked.

"Do I need to spell it out…"

"Charley," Steve replied.

Silverton nodded slowly.

"This is all very interesting, but what exactly do you want me to write?" Mark asked.

"First thing I want us to do is take the Gendarme Nationale out of the equation. Claiming you were in their custody, which of course you were, should do the trick because as soon as people realise that you are no longer in their custody, the Nationale will gracefully retreat from the case," Silverton said.

"How can you be so sure?" Steve asked.

Silverton smirked and then drank some more of his coffee. "Because I know that Francois Blanc is part of the investigation team, and once the public is made aware that his chief suspect, how can I put this, is no longer in their custody without a rational explanation to back that up, he will disassociate himself. He won't want the embarrassment hanging over his head."

"And you're confident about that? He didn't strike me as someone who would throw in the towel that quickly," Steve said and shook his head.

"Blanc may be many things, but he isn't stupid."

Silverton took another drag on his cigarette and then extinguished it in the ashtray.

"I have an idea of how we can plot this one using your skills," Silverton said to Mark. "We'll leak certain details into the next report about the incident in Paris. That way Blanc will know this is the real deal and not a fake."

"Like a coded message?" Steve said.

"Precisely. If he sees these reports laced with indisputable facts, he'll know that whoever is behind them must have access to a source within the investigation team or the hospital. I reckon at that point he will want to distance himself from the case because as *we* know…" Silverton chewed his lower lip.

"…the chief suspect is sitting in this office," Steve added.

"What happens if this Blanc character turns his attentions to me?" Mark took another gulp from his coffee and placed the mug back on the table.

"That will happen. I'm almost positive about that, but we'll hit back with the one-two punch of the reports that Steve has been arrested in Manchester. He'll have to back off at that point because there is no way he'll want to be connected to the case. It's too big of a risk for his career," Silverton said. "Especially when it is so public. The reports you wrote with a limited amount of facts gained huge coverage. Imagine the coverage when you release a report with some real facts? The Nationale will not be covered in glory when these start surfacing."

"I like what you're saying. You're a visionary, but there are a lot of assumptions here. Are you sure this is how it will pan out?" Mark asked.

"I can never be one-hundred percent sure of anything, but I know Blanc well enough to guess his thought patterns. He can't issue an arrest warrant to secure his chief suspect's extradition because the first and most important question will be how he slipped out of custody when in Paris. That is going to be far too awkward for him to talk his way out of. He simply won't want to take the risk of a disciplinary, not when that could also mean he risks losing his pension," Silverton said, let out a sigh, and folded his arms.

"I guess I have to trust your judgment then," Mark said and shrugged his shoulders.

"Yes, you do."

Mark looked at the pair of them and smiled, "Okay, so let's do this, eh? I mean reports don't just write themselves."

Silverton paused for a moment. "This next report should be about what happened in Paris. Let's give them a bit more flesh on the bones of what really happened out there. What do you think Steve?"

"If you want to blow this thing wide open, then I guess that is as good a place as any to start with," Steve nodded his approval.

53

Manchester.Present-Day.

"Is this how it's going to be?" Janine and Steve strolled together through a park in the city.

"I'm here, aren't I?" Steve snapped.

"You are, but what about him? Is he going to be in the background everywhere you go?" Janine looked across to Silverton who was sitting in his car, looking out of the window and watching their every move.

"It's not ideal I know, but he's harmless," Steve replied.

"You're damn right it's not ideal!" Janine stopped to square up to Steve. "First, you go missing for days without so much as a word, then when you do turn up, we have him acting like some sort of bodyguard. Can you please tell me what the hell is going on?"

"I can't. I'm sorry," Steve said, his shoulder slumping as if he carried the weight of the world.

"So that's it then, is it? I know we're bloody divorced but I have a right, and so does Tanya, to know where you are in case of an emergency. And while we're on the subject of Tanya have you even bothered to ask about the smoking detention she got? No! Of course not!"

"Can you stop shouting? There are people—"

"I don't care! I really don't care! Hey, you! Haven't you got your own shit to deal with instead of gawking at us?" Janine yelled at a couple who were sitting on a park bench looking over at the two of them. The couple looked down and away.

Janine paused for a moment, took a deep breath, and spoke slowly, "Tanya needs a father figure, I can't do it all, and you know that. This is a difficult time for her. You know what kids are like. She needs the reassurance that you're there when she needs you, surely you can understand that?" Janine turned her back on Steve, let out a long, loud sigh, and then spun around on her heels. "And anyway, what is so important that you have to go missing for days on end?"

"I completely understand, but you have to understand I cannot say anything at the moment," Steve replied.

"Are you in trouble? Are the police harassing you about something? Is it work-related?" Janine shook her head.

"It's nothing to do with work, and I'm not in trouble, I just have to do this. When I can say more, I promise I will."

They walked in silence for a few minutes. The wind whistled through the air and Steve glanced over to see Silverton was still sitting in the car, patiently waiting.

"When are you leaving town again?" Janine asked.

"Excuse me?" Steve replied.

"You heard me, when are you leaving town? I need to know in case of an emergency, and the school will want to know as well. You know you missed parent's evening? Do you know how hard that was for me?" Janine stopped to look Steve square in the eyes.

"I don't know yet. I need to go back to my apartment and get some stuff sorted out. I guess I'll take it from there." They continued to walk through the park.

"Do you know how different you sound from the man I married?" Janine asked.

"You can hardly blame me for that. You're the one that wanted the divorce. What did you expect?" Steve said, throwing his hands out to plead his case.

"Maybe I was, but I've stayed true to the commitment we made to our daughter. What about you?"

"Don't start this shit! I know my responsibilities, but I have to do what I have to do, and that's that," Steve spat.

"That's that? Is that all you can say? Do you know what Tanya told me last week?"

"What?"

"She said the other kids started to tease her about you, saying you were into drugs or something, and that's why you haven't been collecting her from school, as we arranged…in the courts, I might add."

"This is not solving anything and I have to go." Steve looked at his watch.

"When will I hear from you again? And when will you come around to see your daughter?" Janine asked.

"Soon, I promise, but I have to go," Steve looked across to Silverton and raised his hand to signal he was on the way.

"Whatever this is, whatever trouble you're in, remember we're here if you need to talk."

Steve nodded and walked off into the distance.

"That didn't look easy," Silverton said while Steve got in the car.

"It wasn't easy at all," he said, sitting quietly in the front passenger seat of the car. "Just take me to my apartment as I need to get a few things. I'm not staying there, I'll check into a hotel."

"Okay, if you're doing that then make sure you use this ID, that way you don't have to use your real name," Silverton said and passed an envelope of fake IDs to Steve.

"I don't recall you saying I needed these," Steve removed the contents of the envelope and examined them.

"Alan Benson? Who the fuck is he?" Steve examined the ID.

"Well, for the time being, it's you. Treat him with care, he's going to be very useful in the coming months," Silverton said.

"Is this necessary?" Steve placed the fake IDs back into the envelope.

"Absolutely. Standard issue in my line of work. Don't forget, we're having you arrested soon so it won't look good if your name pops up on a hotel register," Silverton said as they drove to Steve's apartment.

"I can walk from here." Steve got out of the car, closed the door, and looked through the window across to Silverton who was lighting a cigarette. "Thanks."

"If you need me, I will be in London. I have some stuff I need to catch up on," Silverton said.

"Okay, I guess I'll be seeing you soon," Steve replied.

"I can guarantee that."

And with that Silverton drove off into the city.

Steve felt relieved at the prospect of having some downtime to himself. He missed those times; times where he would play a few records, feel sorry for himself in direct correlation to the amount of whiskey he had drunk, and times where life was fairly simple.

54

Manchester.Present-Day.

The hotel was clean, simple, and thoroughly lacking in any trace of personality.

Steve drew back the net curtain, opened the bottle of whiskey he bought in the local convenience store, and poured a glass. He sat down at the plain wooden table and stared out the window into the night skyline.

Manchester was alive with the buzz of nighttime activity. Steve looked down onto the bustling streets from his window and watched people going about their business. He missed that but found some solace in the bottom of the glass. He poured another large measure of the warming liquid and sat back in the willfully uncomfortable chair. He knew he shouldn't but felt compelled to try and induce sleep and this was a tried and true method for success.

He looked over to his overnight bag of belongings that were strewn across the bed and ruefully smiled. He hated living out of a suitcase, it reminded him of his divorce.

Steve swiftly approached the halfway point of the bottle of whiskey and the room was starting to twist and turn. He tried to focus his mind on getting some sleep.

His mind drifted again. He even missed his apartment of the future in the Shard. However, that was a distant memory now. He emptied the glass with a single gulp.

The whiskey had done its job; in Steve's mind, he had somehow managed to transform the bed from being a beige-covered lump of sodden foam, into the most desirable place on Earth. Or so he thought.

He clambered into bed, without removing his clothes. He was that exhausted. He hoped that his inebriated brain would allow him to rest.

But it wouldn't.

His mind was bursting with imagery.

People in biohazard suits. Kallyuke striding toward him in Paris and shaking his hand. Busting out of the Paris prison cell. Injecting the bodies in the morgue. Jumping through time to a barren and deserted M6 motorway. Staring at the holographic image of the Tower of London. Armstrong in Park Lane. CCS. The Quarantine Zone. His ex-wife. His daughter. The Catacombs of Paris. Santa Monica. Charley Sandford.

He counted down the minutes while each memory stored in his over-active brain demanded attention. He turned over to check the time on his watch, it was 3:00AM. He reached for his trusty phone on the sideboard and looked for Anton's contact number.

"Would he be back in Paris?" He thought to himself. The phone was ringing.

"Hello?" a croaky voice replied.

"Anton it's Steve," he whispered quickly.

"What do you want, my friend, it's…fuck. It's 4:00AM!" Anton shouted.

"I need to talk with you, I'm coming to Paris to meet you, it's safer that way. I will see you tomorrow," Steve said.

"What do you mean? Where?"

"As before."

"Can't you just fucking talk to me now?" Anton was sounding more awake with every word.

"No. This must be face-to-face. No question about it." Steve paused, "I will contact you when I arrive."

"You have to be careful about traveling here. You know what happened last time. We cannot afford another incident like that," Anton coughed as he finished the sentence.

"I know. And I have a safe route…do not worry…I will be in touch," Steve said.

"Okay, my friend, but—" and with that Steve hung up the phone halfway through Anton's closing sentence.

55

London.Present-Day.

Silverton settled at his desk in London and logged on to his laptop. He was greeted by an e-mail alert displaying the news headline and an extract from Mark Collins 'latest handy work...

Paris Crash Latest: Man Held Amid Body Tampering Allegations in Morgue

Reports alleging that someone broke into the morgue, where four bodies involved in the recent crash in Paris were taken, are beginning to circulate amongst the press in Paris.

The police have refused to rule out the allegations of the break-in or that they are holding anyone in custody for the alleged offense. They continue to maintain that security during this investigation has not been compromised as mounting rumours circulate about the circumstances surrounding the latest event to hamper their inquiries.

The allegations also claim that the person who broke into the morgue injected at least three of the bodies with an unknown chemical which has distorted findings from the subsequent autopsies; these results are due to be released to the public in the coming days.

The crash victims were taken to the Pitié-Salpêtrière Hospital, the world-renowned teaching hospital located in the centre of Paris.

Silverton picked up the phone and dialed.

"Hello?" the voice answered.

"I see you're as good as your word," Silverton spoke quietly.

"Who is this? Your number hasn't come up." Mark rubbed his forehead with the back of his hand.

"You see what happens when you add a couple of well-chosen facts to embellish your report? People start to trust your version of events." Silverton was toying with Mark.

Mark paused for a moment, "Oh, it's you. I would ask how you got my number but that is pointless. Anyway, aren't these calls traceable? I told you, I don't want to be put at risk and I certainly don't want people finding out that that we are talking, at least not at the moment."

Silverton sat back in his chair. "Don't worry, I have access to the system, no one will know this call took place after I've finished, and as for making our connection public..." Silverton tapped on the keyboard to look at how the report was spreading. "All in good time. They will want to verify the source at some stage, but we don't need to worry about that now."

"You kind of people worry me, you know that?"

"For now, focus on how we can manufacture the next report. I want them to think that Garner is out of the equation and in a cell somewhere."

"I know! I know! I'm working on that at the moment, but we need to go slowly with this, we don't want the public to think it's manufactured."

"Let me worry about that, you concern yourself with the next report. You work for me now, so you have nothing to fear...nothing at all."

"Okay...God, you guys are bossy..."

"Oh, and Mark..."

"What?"

"Nice job with the report, you did well," and with that Silverton ended the call without offering Mark the opportunity to reply.

56

Paris.Present-Day.

Anton walked into the crowded cafe in the Bastille region of Paris to meet Steve; the same cafe they had met in previously.

Steve was seated at the back, huddled over a cup of coffee. He looked rough, the lack of sleep, the lack of a shave, and his crumpled attire conspired to give him the appearance of a man on the edge.

"What the fuck are you doing with that?" Anton sat down, he noticed that one of Steve's hands was submerged in a large bowl of water.

"They can listen you know..." Steve stared down at the wet palm of his hand in the bowl. "I'm sure of it," he growled in a low sinister sounding voice, as he looked up, and his tired eyes shifted left and then right.

"Whoa there my friend...paranoia like that can send you to the depths...and anyway what did she say about it?" Anton pointed to the waitress who was busying herself at one of the nearby tables.

"Nothing, I'm British, we're famed for our eccentricities."

"This is true, but this scales new heights of eccentricity..."

"I don't care."

"Why not use a wet towel? I saw that somewhere, I'm sure it worked."

"Don't be facetious, it doesn't suit you."

"So, you took the train?" Anton wanted to move the conversation away from Steve's newly found paranoia.

"I thought it was the safest method of transport."

"What about ID?"

"Covered. I used the fake ID Silverton provided," Steve subtly revealed to Anton the fake IDs in the palm of his other hand.

"Benson? As in George?" Anton said as the noisy coffee machine announced its arrival again with plumes of steam flying into the warm, sweaty cafe.

"As in Alan. I'd like to think I look slightly younger than George Benson."

"You do. I was attempting to be stereotypical and humorous."

"Well, I'm afraid to inform you that you have failed on both counts."

"That figures, anyway, I think we should get out of here, I'm not sure it's secure." Anton looked around

"Who's paranoid now?" Steve looked around at the people in the cafe as he replied.

"Maybe it's contagious. One other thing, I thought I told you to only call in an absolute emergency," Anton snapped.

"This is an emergency…" Steve said.

They got up, squeezed past the other diners in the busy cafe, and walked down one of the many side streets into the anonymity of District 11.

***

Evelyn stepped away from the camera and lighting that shone across the white marble floor. Filming had stopped for the day, the story was in the can, and ready to edit. The Champs Elysees stood proud in the background, as Evelyn walked further down the road and pulled out her mobile phone to make a call.

"Hello," the voice said.

"I don't know where you are getting your facts from, or who your new source is, but you are playing a very dangerous game that could put us both at risk," Evelyn said without interruption.

"Oh, so this is all the thanks I get for showing a bit of initiative and getting on with it..." Mark replied.

"I can cope with initiative, what I cannot cope with is Francis Blanc threatening to close down the station and to prosecute me for jeopardising an ongoing police investigation," Evelyn yelled into the phone.

"Can they do that?" Mark said.

"Don't be so naive! This is the Gendarme Nationale. I've told you before they can do what they want. They will find a reason."

"I didn't realise, okay!" Mark tried to defend himself.

"Next time you get the urge to print something that happens to concern what happened in Paris, have the common decency to contact me before you hit the send button. At least then I can prepare for the inevitable call," Evelyn said as she paced. "Why didn't you wait for my approval? You know how this is supposed to work!"

"I can't say…I just thought…"

"…don't think, and don't play games with me. I thought we were supposed to be a team," Evelyn said.

"I appreciate that, but things change and you know what it's like in this industry," Mark said.

"Is that a nice way of telling me that you are dumping me from your investigation?"

"No, not at all!"

"...you better not be!" Evelyn spat out the words.

"...I wouldn't dare..."

"Keep me in the loop, but for the record, I'm not impressed."

Evelyn ended the call.

"I'm sick of people hanging up on me," Mark said aloud.

***

Steve and Anton meandered through the back streets of District 11. At one point they walked past a small local television repair shop. Steve stopped for a moment to look into the window; seven television screens flickered with interference.

"Watch this," Steve stared at the television sets.

All seven televisions displayed the same image, clouds.

"You just did that?" Anton looked at the TV screens.

"Yes."

"Well, at least you could have fucking come up with something slightly more interesting. Fucking clouds!"

Steve looked down at the palm of his hand that was pointing upwards in the direction of the sky. "And you think I'm being paranoid?"

"Well for sure, I thought that you were...how else do you explain your behaviour? I mean it's hardly normal…anyway, how come you can do this?" Anton's eyes widened.

Steve fell silent. He looked on as the images on the television screens changed back to what they were showing previously. "It's evolving. I don't know how and I don't know why, but whatever Kallyuke implanted in the palm of my hand is starting to connect to my brain."

"And that thing is permanent?"

Steve looked at Anton and shrugged his shoulders.

They continued walking down the back street.

"If I concentrate, I can disconnect it, but it keeps interfering...it's like I've got a demon inside me trying to control my mind."

"Fuck..." Anton drew a deep breath. "Now I can see why you would be paranoid."

"They're watching us, man, I can feel it." Steve looked around, a bunch of kids were playing football in one of the narrow streets, ducking into the side to avoid the cars that ambled past them. Washing that was hung from a clothesline secured between two balconies, swayed in the gentle breeze, while a smartly dressed old man slowly crept past with the aid of a walking stick. The smells of the city permeated the air.

"I've seen something that has made me question much of what we've been told...but this is a culmination of many things I've seen..." Steve sat down at a wooden table outside a small open-front bistro. Anton sat in the other chair.

"You have to tell me what you've seen."

" Too many things. I've seen too many things. It makes me think. Think a lot," Steve said.

"Or are these things you speak of making you rethink?" Anton asked.

"In many ways, yes, they are." Steve paused. "The doubts are starting to creep into what we are doing...who we are...why we are here...there are so many unanswered questions, but no one seems to have the answers. Or at least no one wants to give me the answers. It's like they want to surround us with riddles while we carry out their dirty work."

"But we've had many answers, look at Sandford for example."

"Riddles Anton, riddles and theories, stories to satisfy our immediate curiosity, but no real answers. Boots on the ground, that's all we are to them, that is until we've completed their mission, then who knows what will happen to us."

"But what do you want?" Anton asked.

"The truth," Steve replied.

Anton stood up. "Maybe we should keep moving..." he looked around the narrow street. "Maybe staying in one place is not such a good idea."

"I agree," Steve said.

They got up and continued walking. They turned down a dead-end street and walked into an unused warehouse. The sound of water dripping through holes in the roof and onto the concrete floor echoed around the deserted building.

Steve stood by one of the concrete pillars in the abandoned warehouse. "There's so much that Armstrong said in those few minutes that has made me think."

"Such as?" Anton kicked a tin can on the floor, and the noise reverberated off the walls.

Steve took a small metal hip flask out of his jacket and had a sip of the drink, and then he offered it to Anton who politely declined.

"Drinking like that won't help you," Anton looked at the flask.

"Maybe I'm beyond help." Steve looked at the hip flask in his hand.

"Tell me more."

"He knew about Kallyuke's plans for this Brave New Society shit that he keeps dreaming about, the holograms, he knew about them too."

Steve shuffled around the empty warehouse for a few moments.

"And they've got this thing called a quarantine zone."

"What's that?"

"It's like a fucking doomsday machine."

"Oh, come on, how do you know this?!"

"I was there. I was fucking there man! I've seen it all and you know what? Armstrong was right."

"Right about what exactly?" Anton looked at Steve.

"He made me think, I mean really think, and I saw it...I saw the babies, they were us!"

Steve was shaking like a leaf while he recalled the details of what had happened to him. He kept looking around the abandoned building at the slightest hint of noise.

"Babies? You're not making sense," Anton frowned and shook his head. "Now calm down, put that flask away and try to explain to me what you think you saw."

"I was drawn into one of these quarantine zones, in Manchester while we questioned Mark Collins."

"The reporter? Now, what the hell do you want with that idiot?"

"That isn't important. What is important is that when I was in that zone it triggered some sort of memory sequence that had lain dormant. Somehow, I was able to recall the night they killed our parents and created the group of twenty-six. I saw the men in biohazard suits remove us from the zone, the whole town was on fire, but the people were calm, they had accepted their fate."

Anton recoiled, "You saw us as babies? You're crazy man! Fucking crazy!"

"If I'm crazy, why does someone want me dead? Why do I have this bastard thing in my hand," Steve looked down at the palm of his hand. "You don't understand…"

"No, my friend, it is you that doesn't understand. Why would they do that?"

"They knew we'd be perfect. No families, nothing to trace, and nothing to hide. This is why they activated us now because they knew we wouldn't remember anything. Except I do. Unfortunately for them, the visions triggered by that quarantine zone are telling me that something is wrong; very wrong. I wasn't meant to survive that, Silverton rescued me from it."

"So, you could have died?" Anton asked.

"Yes I could have died in there and then none of this would be out of the bag, have you ever thought of that?"

"Well, no, not until now," Anton replied.

"And if this brave new society on Earth in the future is so perfect, why the fuck are people trying to escape? Have you ever thought of that?"

"Well, no I haven't but we don't—"

"Exactly, we don't. We don't know the full circumstances. We don't know anything about it apart from what we've been told. We don't even know who we are. Everything in 2618 is far too perfect for my liking. It's too controlled, it's like the people of that time have been crushed into submission. But we don't question it because it has little relevance to us. We just do what we're told, just how they like it."

Anton tried to laugh off the suggestion, but Steve's explanation was compelling enough to guarantee his attention. Steve suggested that this was why they were so controlling and that if needed, they could simply "make us vanish without a trace" he said.

"I had a family," Steve closed his eyes. "And it was taken away from me…twice."

"But that didn't change their plans for you did it?"

"You know, they never caught the driver who killed my parents." Steve looked at Anton.

"What are you suggesting? They planned that assassination?"

"What's to say they didn't? And what about you?"

"What about me?" Anton shrugged his shoulders.

"Did you have parents? You've never mentioned anyone."

"I lived in foster homes and care homes all my life. Look, why are we talking about this?" Anton started to chew on his thumbnail.

"Because I think something is terribly wrong with all of this."

"You're wired man, you're on the booze, look at you…you're a wreck, and now this thing is messing with your mind, chewing you up."

"I didn't go home. I'm living lean and portable."

"You mean like a tramp," Anton gestured to Steve's clothes.

"Who cares?"

"It's affecting your judgment, listen to yourself."

Steve drew a breath, "Now let's move on to the incident in Paris."

"Oh, man, give it a rest!" Anton threw his hands in the air and paced around.

"Let's explore your theory that I'm wired. Who decided that the four victims in the Paris crash were criminals deserving of death?"

"Why would I know that?" Anton stopped pacing and tapped his finger on his temple.

"Is Kallyuke playing God?"

"Where's your proof for all of this?"

"Proof? You want proof?" Steve asked.

"Well, without any proof of these accusations, you sound as crazy as any other so-called witness trying to spin a conspiracy theory into a story…"

"This isn't a conspiracy is it?" Steve said.

"Okay, we know it isn't but still…"

"And you think that any other witness would have the burden of proof we have? We know that time travel exists…we've been there, we've seen the future, doesn't that count for something?" Steve kicked some dust up from the ground.

"How do you think people will react if you start talking about this in public? You'd be sectioned. People would think you're insane."

"Maybe that's a risk I'm willing to take, but for now, I'm happy to remain silent."

"Because you're scared that may happen?"

"No. Because I need to get more facts to back up what I think is going on."

"And what happens if you are right? What then?"

"At that point, I will have to decide what is the right thing to do."

"Do you know what that could be?" Anton glared at Steve.

"I have no idea," Steve said and shook his head. "But I know this much, I want to find out why we are here, and I mean the truth, not their version of events. And then I want to find out who we really are, don't you?"

"Maybe." Anton shrugged his shoulders, "Maybe it's better we don't know."

"And live in denial? You want to spend the rest of your life carrying out orders without questioning the motive? You're scared. Don't be scared, we have to embrace whatever truth is out there about us, we have done nothing wrong. We didn't pull that trigger in the Catacombs, we didn't choose those four men…these were orders beyond our comprehension. And we didn't ask to be a part of whatever this is," Steve said.

"But what if they found out we're onto them? Then what? We can hardly run from them."

"Then we get smart. We get covert."

"Covert?"

"Yes. We don't talk on the phone, we don't communicate via CCS, we don't use anything that has been developed by them. We need time to discover what the hell is going on here."

"What about that?" Anton pointed to Steve's palm.

"I'll worry about that. So, will you join me?"

"Join you in what exactly?" Anton asked.

"This. Whatever this is. I need to know what this is before it tears me apart."

"What about Helen? Won't she want to know more, and what about the others? The ones we haven't met?"

"We don't even know if they're activated yet. They may still be completely unaware. As for Helen, let me try to meet her in London face-to-face. I want to see if she's even remotely aware of any of this."

"Why the hesitancy?"

"A hunch."

"Hunch? I don't like hunches. They make me feel uncomfortable."

"Then you better get used to feeling uncomfortable, and fast, because most of what I have is based on a hunch at the moment."

"You don't trust her, do you?"

"I never said that. I just want to be sure," Steve said and leaned up against a concrete pillar.

"And what about me? Do you trust me?"

"I trust you enough."

"That's an interesting response."

"These are interesting times."

"They are."

"I'm going to create a code, a visual code that I will try to make as close to unbreakable as is humanly possible. It will be a three-level code with a moving key that revolves around various triggers. It will be publicly visible using the handle @1of26."

"You want to use a publicly visible platform from the twenty-first century for this code? Won't that be easily spotted? And isn't that handle just a bit too obvious?"

"Too obvious for anyone to take it seriously and by using the comms channels of today it will probably be dismissed as a hoax or a diversion. We're going to play them at their own game."

"So, you've obviously put some thought into it."

Steve pulled the flask of whiskey out of his pocket and took a gulp. "Despite this stuff's best efforts, my brain has been overactive, spinning with ideas on how to solve certain problems."

"Communications being one of them?"

"Yes. I'm going to level with you, this is dangerous, very dangerous. We all know what Kallyuke is capable of, we've seen it firsthand."

"That is if the version of Kallyuke you describe is the man you think he is."

"That is what I want to try to prove to you, you have to trust me on this." Steve nodded at Anton.

"Okay, so if I agree to this plan of yours I have one condition."

"What's that?"

"We still carry out their operations, we cannot allow them to think we are trying to investigate their methods and their motives for all of this."

"I can agree with that."

"Good, otherwise…"

"Otherwise, what? You weren't seriously going to turn away the chance to uncover your past?"

"What if I don't like what I see? What if I like the way things are at the moment?"

"No. I won't have that, if you did like things as they are then I'd know…" Steve bit the inside of his mouth.

"Know what?"

"That you have lost your soul."

"Oh, come on now, let's not get all spiritual about this, eh?"

"We all have a soul. It doesn't matter where or when you were born, and that soul is what carries us, defines us, and makes us challenge our surroundings, our very existence, and it makes us who we are. They won't crush it. I won't let them."

478

57

Germany.Present-Day.

Frankfurt international airport was packed to the rafters.

"Tell me I have a VIP lounge pass," the man asked the woman at the check-in desk.

"It appears you ticked that option online during the booking process so yes, here's your VIP pass Mr Hall," the woman handed a small collection of passes and paperwork back to Colin Hall.

"Thank god for that!" Colin looked to the skies.

"Have a safe flight and thank you for flying British Airways," the woman said with a forced smile.

Colin left for the VIP lounge.

He arrived and soon settled into the hushed luxury of the lounge which overlooked the busy runway. He ordered a green tea from one of the waiters, parked himself on one of the comfortable leather chairs that overlooked the runway, and caught up on his e-mails. Music pumped into the room to add to the air of civility, while waiters busied themselves attending to the other guests.

Colin had earlier set a reminder to research a route for a client who was visiting England from America. The client, one of the top executives in a huge internet firm, wanted to review the corporate facilities in Manchester and Birmingham. That would be followed by a visit to the London headquarters prior to leaving for the Far East.

The client always traveled with a high level of security. Plans would be made in secret, submitted to the internal security department for review and approval or amendment. The method of travel for this particular visit had been decided; by car and via the M6.

This was deemed a low-risk journey due to the location and also public nature of the route, nevertheless, Colin would plan for it in the minutest of detail.

Now was a good time to start the research.

Colin started his initial research into the route. He tapped in some keywords into the search engine about the M6 and locations. These results, along with a risk evaluation would accompany the report he needed to submit for approval; it was a fiddly process that needed signing off at many stages, but Colin wasn't complaining. Business was good in the field of security; it was booming in the light of recent events across the world. Large corporations had an obligation to keep their staff safe and secure while they traveled the world. Colin's business was reaping the rewards of years of hard work building his reputation in providing solutions to deliver the desired level of corporate security.

One particular report caught his eye as it came up time and again on his searches. The report into the M6 Paranormal Crash.

Colin looked closer at the search result. He knew he didn't have the time to become sidetracked, so couldn't look into the reports in more detail, so he bookmarked them for later and carried on working on his report.

"That's one for another day," he muttered to himself, taking another sip of tea.

58

Somewhere in France.
Present-Day.

"This room is fine," Steve said to the owner of the small provincial motel somewhere deep in the French countryside.

Steve held his travel bag and a small plastic carrier bag that contained a bottle.

"We tend not to get many tourists here. You must be our first in…" the owner stood in the doorway to the room scratching his head.

Steve removed his jacket and placed the carrier bag on the quaint white dressing table which set against the wall and had a small oval mirror attached to it.

"Like I said, that'll be fine…I only need the room for a few hours, you know, to get some rest."

"Ah, you have been traveling," the owner played with a bunch of keys in his hands while Steve rolled up his shirt sleeves and walked back to the doorway.

"Yes, now if you don't mind…" Steve said.

"No, of course, I understand," and with that, the owner closed the door and left Steve in peace.

Steve reached down to his jacket that was now on the back of the chair, removed the metal hip flask, and placed it on the table. He sat down on the table in front of the mirror and took a deep breath. He then removed the bottle from the carrier bag; it was acid. He went into the bathroom and returned to the table with a small, white ceramic bowl and a crisp white towel. He sat down and stared into the mirror; his hair was unkempt, his eyes bloodshot. Steve looked exhausted.

481

He unscrewed the lid and then placed the flask to his lips and drank until he could no longer stomach the whiskey. He coughed and shielded his mouth with this hand.

"I either do this now or never," he said to himself.

He poured the acid into the ceramic bowl.

Steve took one last look in the mirror and shed a single tear. He opened the hand that contained the CCS device and stared at it for one last time.

The acid looked completely innocuous, the clear liquid was still and inviting.

Steve took a small penknife out from the jacket and pulled out one of the blades. His breathing was slow and deliberate. He then took a small wooden stick out from the other pocket of his jacket and placed it in his mouth, clenching down on it with all his strength. He gripped the penknife tight and held the shiny blade against the palm of his hand containing the CCS device, slowly cutting it open. His breathing quickened as the pain shot through his arm, the blood seeped out of the wound and started to dribble into the bowl of acid. He took one final look at the blood-covered palm of his hand and then looked in the mirror to register the fear in his eyes; he then plunged the bloodied hand into the awaiting bowl of acid.

Steve bit down on the stick so hard that it broke in his mouth, the bowl of acid was smoldering and bubbling, the liquid reacting with his palm. Sparks flew out of the bowl and it took all of Steve's resolve and strength to keep his hand submerged in the cauldron of pain.

The foul stench of acid and melting flesh filled the room and Steve moaned in agony. The acid was eating away at his flesh. He pulled his bleeding and burnt hand out of the bowl of acid and frantically wrapped it in the white towel. He reached for the flask and took another gulp of the whiskey, this time he knew no limit as the pain took control of his actions.

Steve stood up, staggered back to the bed, and passed out, his bleeding hand still wrapped in the towel.

59

London.2618.

At that moment, the screen in Kallyuke's control room that monitored Steve started to flicker, and then it went blank; Steve had managed to disconnect from the CCS device.

Kallyuke frantically paced back and forth, momentarily pausing to look up at the blank screen.

To be continued…

ABOUT THE AUTHOR

Based in Manchester, ZWT Jameson is a writer whose projects include being part of the creative team behind ARES, a movie in development with Rideback, with a script written by Geneva Robertson-Dworet (Captain Marvel, Tomb Raider, Star Trek). Jameson also recently released an interview with a witness who claims to have been party to a NASA cover up over a first contact event at a Mayan Temple in Guatemala.

Jameson is passionate about music, stating, "Music is an important part of my creative process, helping me escape into the worlds I have created for my upcoming release, 1of26." He likes to listen to artists like John Coltrane, David Axelrod, and bands such as Snapped Ankles and Tame Impala.

Always looking for the story beyond the headlines, as seen in 1of26, where the articles about M6 and the Paris Paranormal Crash have been woven into the narrative, Jameson is careful to preserve the integrity of the original stories that became online folklore.

www.GlobalPublishGroup.com

Printed in Great Britain
by Amazon